Holding

Book 5 in the Moving the Chains Series

Copyright ©2021 by Kata Čuić

Published in the United States of America by

Kata Čuić Books, LLC

All Rights Reserved.

This novel may not be reproduced in whole or in part without express written permission by the author. This includes, but is not limited to, the right to reproduce, distribute, or transmit in any form or by any means. And yes, that includes the internet and social media. Especially those. The only exception is by a reviewer who may quote short excerpts in a review.

Art in any form is created from the blood, sweat, and tears of the artist. In this case, the writer. Please do not engage in piracy or plagiarism. Purchase from valid vendors. Create your own art!

This book is a work of fiction. Names, characters, places, and goings on are the product of the author's ridiculous imagination and/or life experiences and are used fictitiously. Any resemblance to actual events, locales, or persons, living or dead or otherwise, is coincidental. Kind of. Mostly.

Cover artwork by Sarah Kil at Sarah Kil Creative Studio

Editing by Lisa Salvucci

Proofreading by Alison Evans-Maxwell at Red Leaf Proofing

# Prologue
## Lean on Me

### Eva

MIKE MITCHELL IS a knight in tarnished armor.

Turf stains his gray and crimson jersey. Green splotches are all over his bare arms and his legs, too. His brown hair is wild—matted in some places from his helmet, sticking up in others, and all of it is soaked with sweat. None of that matters.

Mike's smile is tentative as fans chant his name from where they refuse to clear out the stands after one of the best games the Wolves have played in years.

Albany has a new hero to worship.

This big teddy bear of a man has no idea what to do with all their adoration.

I stifle a laugh as the first reporter approaches him.

His eyes widen like he can't believe this is his real life, and he gets to live it. In all fairness, statistics say he shouldn't have made it this far. He's come a long way from the twelve-year-old boy who first took me under his wing in our group therapy sessions for abused kids.

He cuts a quick glance at me. I gesture for him to focus. Sadly, I've had way more experience in the football limelight than he has.

Their conversation can barely be heard over the din of the stadium even though I'm only a few feet away, standing on the home team's sideline.

"Mike Mitchell, you rushed for a hundred and fifty-three yards tonight. If that's not an amazing debut, I don't know what is." The blonde with painted pink lips places a hand on his arm in a way that suggests she's interested in more than just an interview.

Ever the gentleman, he shrugs out of her grasp. Gently. "Thank you. It's easy to play my best when I've got a great team around me..."

The Bluetooth earbuds hidden beneath my mop of curls crackle with another update. "Falls is sacked at the forty for a loss of twenty yards. That's the game for Sacramento. After that disappointing display, Rushers fans have to be asking themselves if blowing the salary cap on a single player in the first round of the draft is going to have *any* return on investment this season. It seems football royalty won't be making an appearance any time soon."

Fuck that stupid nickname. And fuck the stupid announcer, too.

Being the masochist that I am though, I don't rip the earbuds out. Nope. I torture myself further by listening to people I don't know tear down a man they don't know at all.

Mike's mom and sisters are waiting for him. I'm here. Who will be on the sideline waiting to comfort Sacramento's new quarterback? I pray, beg, plead that someone—anyone—is waiting for Rob Falls. Even if that someone isn't me.

"What's the score?"

I startle and blink into reality to find Mike staring down at me with a grimace.

"Twenty-eight to three," I blurt, still not quite free of my mental trip to a different sideline a lifetime away.

He arches a single eyebrow and conveys a load of disappointment. "I just asked that last reporter for an update on the Orlando game. She said the final score was thirty-five to fourteen."

Shit. Busted.

He reaches beneath my hair to pull one of the earbuds from its hiding place. "Why are you doing this to yourself?"

The jig's up, so I stuff both the earbuds into my jeans pocket then wrap my arms around Mike's waist and squeeze for all I'm worth. This man—who is more a real brother to me than if he was my own blood—deserves nothing but praise and me being present in this triumphant moment with him. "You played such an amazing game.

I'm so freaking proud of you. You're everything I always knew you could be."

He hugs me back and mumbles into the top of my hair, "I know what you're doing. I'm not going to let you."

I pull away but keep my smile firmly fixed in place. "I called the town car for your mom and sisters just like you asked. They'll be waiting for you at home. Faith and Hope were kind of upset about not getting to stay longer, but your mom put her foot down." My laugh sounds almost like the real thing. "I think she wants them hooking up with your teammates about as much as you do."

Mike's face puckers in an obvious show of disgust. "That is *never* going to happen. Not on my watch. Look what football did to you."

"Me?" I plaster a hand against my chest. My heart thumps wildly beneath my fingers. "I'm fine! I'm happy to be here! Did I mention how freaking proud I am of you? Of all you've overcome to get here? I can't believe I get to tell people I'm friends with *the* Mike Mitchell, starting rookie running back for the Albany Wolves!"

He narrows his eyes and sticks his tongue in his cheek. "While I'm flattered, I call bullshit. You're not fine, and you're not happy to be here."

"Yes, I am!" It's not a total lie. I am happy to be here. I'm also devastated that I can't be somewhere else.

A wolf whistle diverts our attention to one of Mike's teammates standing beside us. His leer makes my skin crawl. "Shit, Mitchell! You tore up the field tonight, *and* you stole the girlfriend of a top draft pick quarterback? Goddamn, man. I'm glad you're on my team."

That same disgust reappears in Mike's expression. "What? No! She's like a sister to me, Templeman! We've known each other since we were kids! We're not *together*."

Templeman puckers his lips like he's kissing the air and leans against the bench. "Wanna come home with me tonight then, baby? You obviously have good taste. One of the finest WAGs in the league should never have been with a loser like Falls anyway. Did you even hear how bad he tanked at his debut game?"

"I am going to rip your eyeballs out of your skull." I lunge at him only to be caught by the waist and hauled back.

"He's not wrong," Mike whispers in my ear as he physically squashes my desire for violence. "Rob Falls is a loser. You need to serve him divorce papers and move on with your life."

"I'll move on with my life when you move on with yours," I hiss as I watch Templeman saunter away laughing. "Have you been on a single date since you moved to Albany?"

Mike waits a few heartbeats more before releasing me from the cage of his much stronger arms. "No, but I've been busy. A guy doesn't play a game like I just did by screwing around all the time."

I roll my eyes. "Excuses, excuses. Just admit you're a hypocrite, and I'll drop it."

"I—"

He doesn't even get out his denial when another teammate approaches us with another sickening leer directed at my chest. "Damn, woman. You're finer in person than in that nude spread I beat off to for a whole month."

"I am going to rip your eyeballs out of your skull," Mike grits out before diving at him.

Thankfully, Templeman is still close enough to help me pull them apart.

"So, as I was saying," I pant. "Just admit you're a hypocrite. That you haven't dated since Chelsie because you're afraid of taking risks, and that's because you're still clinging to the way distant past that has no place in your future."

Mike shakes off Templeman's grasp with a muttered, "I'm good. I'm cool."

"You sure, man?" The lanky guy reminds me of Alex, another friend on another football field miles and miles and heartbreaks away. Templeman wears his charm on his sleeve, but there's an intelligence in his nearly black eyes that can't be hidden by his bright white smile. He glances between us. "I can have security escort her out. Just say the word."

Mike looks absolutely shocked. Whether from a new teammate

stepping up to have his back or that said teammate thinks I'm the problem doesn't matter. He wraps his big, beefy arm around my shoulders. "Like I said, we're practically siblings. She's just looking out for me. Same as I do for her." He squeezes my shoulders for emphasis.

Yeah, yeah. Whatever. The big, overprotective brother thing has worn thin, especially when he won't take his own advice.

I point at Templeman. "Take care of this big guy for me, will you? Drag him out of his house when he's being all mopey and find him a decent woman to date. He only pretends to enjoy his solitude."

Templeman grins and salutes. "Yes, ma'am. I got some prospects lined up. I'll find him a unicorn by the end of the season. You have my word."

"What the fuck?" Mike blurts at his teammate before regaining his composure. "I'll see you later. I'm just gonna finish up here."

Templeman shrugs, winks at me, then walks away, whistling and waving to the fans still in the stands.

Mike turns to me. "I want no part of that guy. He reminds me too much of Alex."

"I know. That's why I like him." I squish Mike's cheeks in my hands, making his face pucker up like the scared little boy who's still hiding under all the grown man's muscular armor. "That's also why I trust him with you."

Mike mumbles around my grasp. "I don't need any help!"

I let go and pat his cheek. "We all need help sometimes, big brother."

"And you say *I'm* the hypocrite?"

# Chapter 1
Over My Head

Tori

I'VE DIED and gone to man-candy heaven. Emphasis on the dying part.

The clank of metal on metal and the grunts of men working assault my ears as I take in this side of the Albany Wolves that I usually have very limited interaction with. No woman alive would be unaffected. As far as the eye can see, male forms in various stages of undress glisten with sweat while their muscles shift beneath the sheaths of their taut skin. Some are blank canvases. Others are works of art in their own right, more ink than anything else. They all have one thing in common—elite athletes at the peak of human physical performance.

I glance down at my skirt, where a hint of a muffin top bulges above my belt. Thankfully, it's mostly hidden by my suit jacket. This isn't a competition anyway. Or at least, not one that I'm part of. Unless I count the whole being a distraction thing. Which I don't. Because it's frankly insulting.

With more than a little effort, I shake off my anxiety and make sure my chin isn't on the floor. There might be more nearly nude, ripped men than I've ever seen in one place at one time, but professionalism is key.

I scan the area for the particular player I seek, but honestly, with so much controlled chaos, it's impossible to tell which mountain of muscle he is. I open my mouth and step toward the first body that approaches me, but he pushes through the door I'm still standing in front of before I can question him, nearly bowling me over as he makes his escape. I gaze over my shoulder longingly. If only I could bail, too.

Squaring my shoulders, I remind myself that the rest of my career might hinge on this assignment. The whole point of invading this sanctum of maleness is to make sure I have the upper hand right out of the gate. Actually, it's so I won't have enough time to talk myself out of it and just start looking for another internship. But he doesn't need to know that.

I clear my throat. "Mike Mitchell?"

All the cacophony present when I first entered silences as every set of eyes studies me with obvious suspicion. I'm clearly an intruder here, and no one is close enough to read the employee pass hanging around my neck.

"Journalists aren't allowed back here," a beefcake announces from his position on some sort of machine that looks like a medieval torture device. "You need to wait in the press room until he's done with his circuit."

"You can wait for me in the locker room," someone from the back calls, resulting in laughter raining down over me.

My cheeks heat. Darn my fair complexion because they're probably the same color as my red hair right now. If blushing head to toe was an actual profession, I'd never have to worry about employment again. "I'm, um…I'm not a journalist?"

*Great, Tori. Way to nail that whole professionalism thing. You're obviously going to ace this assignment. Not.*

The same man who tried to throw me out rises from his perch and swipes a towel from the ground beside his machine-thingy. He approaches me with measured steps and an equally measured gaze while wiping sweat from his hard chest. When he's close enough for me to feel his warm breath on my face, I can't help but stare at the intricate detail of the dragon tattoo on his right pec. It's a great distraction from all the sweaty, half-naked maleness invading my personal space.

I've never been into the whole-body art thing, but I can't deny the artistry is beautiful.

With all the willpower I can muster, I resist the urge to shudder when his fingers graze my breasts as he lifts my employee identification badge to read.

"Mitchell!"

There's no way to prevent jumping with his loud shout.

Another round of snickers follows, which does nothing to cool my hot cheeks or ease the slight trembling of my body. I'm in way over my head—and judging by this guy's once-over—he knows it.

He turns around then mutters, "Aw, hell. He's got his earbuds in. He can't hear a damn thing. Go on back. Third hack squat machine on the left."

Third *what* machine?

When I peer up, he's smirking at me. This is a test. If I fail, I'll be shown the door.

*Vittoria Russo, you can do this.*

The mantra I've been repeating in my head ever since this mission was dumped in my lap propels my feet forward. A smirk of my own creeps across my lips. This isn't so hard.

Mitchell is obviously the only guy continuing his workout rather than staring at me as I cross the room.

He doesn't stop his almost violent leg movements even when I stand in front of him. As Dragon Man pointed out, he's wearing earbuds, obviously not paying attention to anything except his grueling workout. After several moments of a silent staring match, his chest heaves with an irritated grunt.

He pulls the earbuds out of his ears and only now seems to notice everyone watching us. "Is this another one of your stunts, Templeman?"

The guy beside him practically vibrates with laughter. His words come out panted. "I have nothing to do with this. I swear."

Even with his face twisting in a weird mixture of what I'm guessing is contempt, fury, then finally resignation, Mike Mitchell is a darn fine specimen of the male species. He's apple pie, bonfires on a cool fall night, and the epitome of what most women imagine when they hear the words "football player." In short, he's an all-American stud whose good looks almost overshadow his annoyed expression. His full lips form an upside-down horseshoe. With that kind of expressive control, he's probably a fantastic kisser.

He drags a hand through sweat-soaked hair that's a much lighter shade of brown when it isn't wet. From what I've seen of his team photos, he keeps it neat and doesn't go overboard with products or style like the kind of guys who probably spend more time on their hair in the morning than I do.

Like Ben does. Or maybe he doesn't anymore. I wouldn't know because he made it perfectly clear that we needed a break to find ourselves. Whatever that means.

I snap out of my daze when Mitchell speaks.

"I don't need it, guys. Really."

A bark of laughter redirects my attention to the doorway. The same man who tested me stands at the entrance of the room like some sort of guard dog, his arms crossed over his chest. "Oh, we think you do."

Mike throws his arms in the air, clearly frustrated. "Why? My numbers are solid. I'm pulling my weight—"

A round of boisterous laughter cuts him off. Another player shouts, "Yeah, because this is the *weight* room!"

He rolls his eyes at that admittedly horrible joke. "Butt out of my personal life, will you?"

"I knew it!" someone else calls. "He's got butt problems!"

"Oh my God," Mitchell mutters, rubbing his forehead. Then louder, "I'm not gay! Give it a rest already!"

"If you're not gay, then explain your lover's spat with Fossoway last week."

My ears perk up because that name is precisely why I'm here. I open my mouth, but I don't get a chance to speak.

"Gay or not, you need to get laid, man!"

"How long's it been? *Years*?"

"Are you a Boy Scout?"

"Relax and live a little! You're in the big leagues now! Enjoy it!"

With each additional piece of life advice, Mike's face gets redder and redder. I'm not sure whether it's from anger or embarrassment. Both of which I totally empathize with. He finally explodes, leaping off his bench like his butt might actually have problems. In that it's on fire. He stands so close to me; I can actually see the split second of hesitation in his eyes.

In the next heartbeat, my theory is proven right. So right.

If only it wasn't so wrong.

That thought is impossible to maintain when strong, capable hands grip my hips and knead until I'm nearly purring. A decidedly inelegant squeak escapes my throat as I'm hauled against six feet of solid muscle. The instinct to let my hands explore every plane and deep ridge forces me to fist his damp shirt to stave off my baser instincts. Firm lips and a warm, soft tongue obliterate any other attempt at sensibility. If I've ever been kissed like this, I don't remember it. I'm not sure I'll remember my own name after even one more minute of this exquisite torture.

Thankfully, he pulls away before I can completely lose myself.

All my hopes for salvation go up in flames as his mouth migrates to the sensitive spot just below my ear, his lips tickling my prickly skin as he speaks. "Follow my lead."

I'm not sure I could walk a straight line right now, much less follow him anywhere.

Seeming to sense my knees are close to buckling, he drags me away as laughter and more comments pelt me from all sides. The cacophony is barely enough to stop my mind from spinning.

"Give it to her good!"

"Don't come back here until you're a man again!"

"Can I watch?"

Heck, *I* want to watch what Mike Mitchell is undoubtedly capable of, and pornography is not something I've ever engaged in.

Once we're safely in the much quieter hallway, he releases me from his surprisingly gentle grip then rounds on me. "I'm sorry, but

I'm not interested. I'll pay for your wasted time though, unless whoever hired you paid up front."

The conversation and events that went over my head in the weight room catch up to me with his offer. "You think I'm a *prostitute*?"

He grimaces, avoids eye contact, and stuffs his hands in the pockets of his athletic shorts. The stance enhances every bulging muscle in his arms. "I'm not judging. I don't know your life story, just like you don't know mine. But I can vouch from personal experience that sex doesn't solve everything. If you're looking for a way out of this life, I'll do whatever I can to help. I'm sorry for the kiss, I—Well…it was the fastest and safest way to get you out of there."

I open and close my mouth no less than ten times, but nothing escapes. No words form. Of all the ways I imagined our initial meeting, being mistaken for a sex worker was never a consideration. Neither was experiencing the sort of kiss I've only seen in movies. Or hearing the man who gave it to me say he's sorry for it.

The problem is…he's not entirely wrong. I am being paid to be at his service. Management didn't expressly say if he requested sex that I should acquiesce, but they didn't exactly convince me they wouldn't be down for that method either.

I might be young, inexperienced, and naïve in this world of professional sports, but I am *no one's* call girl.

With that reinforcing thought in place, I take a deep breath to prepare my spiel. "I'm afraid you've misunderstood—"

"No. You've misunderstood." His angry gaze snaps up to meet mine directly. "I don't care what they told you, what they promised you, or who hired you. I don't care if you're in this for the money, for fifteen seconds of internet fame, or for the chance to sleep with any professional football player without caring who he is. I don't need to get laid. I need to do my job. Nowhere in my job description does it say I'm required to fuck a hooker just to get my teammates off my back and prove to the whole world I'm not gay."

Wow. I thought I had it rough. This went from bad to worst-case scenario in a hurry. If this is what his teammates have been putting him through since he signed on with the Wolves; if this is what he's used to dealing with as an NFL player; if this is how little he thinks of me from only our first meeting, I'm not sure I can fulfill my role as his assigned babysitter, much less use this opportunity to hone my social media expertise to turn around his career before it tanks completely.

I tilt my head to the side to study him for a moment, carefully thinking about my words before I lose my temper, which is dangerously close to boiling over. "That's funny because my job description clearly states I'm required to help you even if you don't want me to."

He throws his arms up in the air, much in the same way he did in the weight room. "I'm not going to fuck you!"

A moment of clarity calms my frazzled nerves. He doesn't know. No one has said anything to him yet beyond his teammates teasing him about last week's post-game gaffe. He has no idea he's already screwed. In more ways than one.

# Chapter 2
## Thanks for the Memories

### Mike

I'VE NEVER SEEN a hooker in a business suit before.

In my time during college ball, I thought I'd seen it all. I guess this is the big leagues though, and I'm bound to experience some new things. I've gotta give it to Templeman, he isn't giving up easily. The dumbass probably thinks I'm harboring some secret naughty librarian fantasy, so he prepped her on exactly how to play the part. The skirt and matching jacket this woman's wearing look about two sizes too small for all the curves they're hugging in just the right places. If she moves too much, those buttons are bound to pop open. I'm honestly surprised she didn't go all out with some fake glasses.

Some guys are really into the whole nerdy thing, and the women I'm used to turning away know how to market to their clientele. Too bad she doesn't know a thing about me. My teammates are just taking stabs in the dark to see what I'll respond to at this point.

The woman frowns. She must be new at this and doesn't know how to handle a difficult customer. Then again, most of the jersey chasers I've ever met—paid or not—aren't usually this timid. I've definitely never seen any of them blush the way this one does.

And what a blush it is. If I was into casual sex with someone who might have already slept with my entire team, she might be able to persuade me. There's something about her that's just...light and happy. Peach colored hair, peach colored cheeks—she even smells like peaches—and I can't help but notice...a great rack. She's a little on the softer side than most of the jersey chasers and call girls who hang around. A lot less makeup, a little less confidence, and maybe a hint of a temper? I don't know. It kind of freaks me out that I *want* to know if that color staining her cheeks is from anger or embarrassment.

There has got to be something wrong with my head. All these pranks are getting to me.

As the minutes tick by in silence while she continues to stare at me, a hint of guilt creeps over my already exhausted muscles. I don't usually lose my temper like I just did. Staying calm, cool, and level-headed is important, especially in the worst circumstances. Emotions in the heat of the moment usually end in disaster. I guess it doesn't matter though. Lately, no matter what I do, my life off the field is nothing but chaos.

Chaos breeds tragedy.

Careful, controlled order saves lives. In more ways than one.

Stuffing away all the weird emotions I usually keep locked away, I shake off the missed play and try a different route. "I'm sorry. That wasn't fair. You're just trying to do your job, and you don't deserve—"

"Oh!" she interrupts, a hint of light breaking over her admittedly beautiful face. "That's okay! I get it. You're a man of action, not words. I can sympathize with that. Maybe it would be better if I *show* you..."

She fishes her phone out of her jacket pocket.

I wince, expecting a thousand-dollar bill for less than twenty minutes of her time to be shoved under my nose. These stupid pranks are seriously cutting into my budget for sending money home to my mom to help pay off her four times over refinanced mortgage and for making my sisters' college tuition payments.

Instead of an invoice with a bright red button I can tap to pay off another debt, a familiar video plays that I've rewatched way too many times in the past week. That's time I could have spent studying videos of the next opponent.

I've wanted to strangle Alex Fossoway a million times since I met his cocky ass in sixth grade through our hometown's rec football league, but these days? I am literally forcing myself to use training as a distraction from flying to Florida to commit homicide.

Been there, done that, don't need a repeat.

The sight of us arguing on the field after the last game between Albany and Orlando makes me grit my teeth to keep my muscles from trembling with the rage that threatens to escape my mental cage.

It doesn't matter that most people don't understand the years of shared history that brought us to the point of me literally dragging him away from the Wolves' sideline. Hell, even I can't deny it looks like the kind of argument only people who are intimately acquainted would have.

Alex Fossoway and I are intimately acquainted all right. Blood brothers for all the wrong reasons. And through the one person I wish we didn't share a *very* intimate history with.

"So, you see?" the redhead begins again with a gentle tone of voice. "That's why I'm here."

My stomach twists in knots, and that old urge to commit physical violence returns with a vengeance. "If you're looking for a threesome, I hate to break it to you, but he plays for a different team in a different state. We don't see each other unless it's for a matchup between our teams."

Maybe never again off the field.

That thought makes me sadder than it should. What the hell is wrong with me these days?

Fire incinerates her previous calm. "Oh my God! I'm not a prostitute! I'm not angling for a threesome! I'm only here because you completely embarrassed your team in a very public venue, and *our* bosses think you need some help!"

Help isn't something I've had since around the time I met the guy who apparently started all this. She's got my attention. I'll give her that. "Who are you again?"

She crosses her arms over her chest in a way that suggests her breasts are actually off-limits, but she's ready to get down to business anyway. "My name is Tori Russo. I'm your new PR manager."

Cancel all the promises I've made myself to never commit physical violence again.

I'm going to kill Alex Fossoway.

Maybe twice. Just for fun.

# Chapter 3
## Bite My Tongue

### Tori

THE WHISPERS ARE TOO low to make out, but their unmistakable stares raise the hair on the back of my neck. It's the exact same scene I just barely escaped unscathed, but I'm not sure I'll be as lucky for round two even though this is a much more familiar environment than the weight room.

Why did I have to lie and tell him I'm his new PR manager? There's self-preservation and achieving a desired outcome, then there's being overly ambitious. If any of these actual marketing reps find out what I've done, I'm well...done for.

The usual suspects stand around the proverbial water cooler, undoubtedly placing bets on my success...or much more likely failure. It shouldn't please me as much as it does at the prospect of informing them it was a wash. Actually, I don't know that for sure. Mitchell never gave any indication he was agreeable to our forced partnership. He simply stormed away without a word when I told him who I was and why I sought him out. It's not even like my little white lie helped the situation.

"So?" The ringleader, Kaylie, steps away from the pack, her eyes bright and her perfectly painted lips poised in a hopeful smile. "How did it go?"

They're going to find out anyway. No sense lying about it. "They thought—*he* thought—I was a prostitute."

Kaylie cackles. Everyone else has the decency to at least try to hide their smiles behind their coffee mugs. The effect of which is completely spoiled by one person in the group handing a twenty over to Kaylie's waiting rose-gold, talon-tipped clutches.

The only loser who didn't bet against me stands in front of me with a frown, studying me from head to toe. "I really thought I chose the perfect outfit to dissuade them from that belief."

"Wait a minute." My cheeks heat for the umpteenth time. They may never be cool again as long as I'm stuck in this horrid assignment. "You all knew they would think I was a hired sex worker?"

"Of course. They've been pulling that same prank on Mitchell since the game when this all blew up." Kaylie raises a well-manicured eyebrow in clear challenge. "You didn't know?"

The entirety of the PR department waits with bated breath for my de facto admission of ignorance. It's no secret they resent me for being handed this job. Why shouldn't they? I'm the lowest woman on the totem pole as an intern, and any of them would kill for this opportunity to work one-on-one with an up and coming player on the Wolves' roster. It doesn't matter that I've been ordered to be a glorified babysitter.

"I didn't know," I confess on a whisper.

"It was the shoes." David, one of my only co-workers who I'm pretty sure isn't out for my blood, clucks his tongue like a mother hen. "I shouldn't have put you in stilettos for this initial meeting. Never mind the nude color, they still scream sex on a stick."

Kaylie laughs. "Nudity and sex are definitely two things they were expecting."

"I thought the whole reason the team keeps pranking Mitchell is because he never has sex?" another co-worker, Mason, pipes up. "His nickname in the locker room is Monk for a reason."

His nickname in the locker room is Monk? Really? No wonder he's so salty.

David turns a severe expression toward the group still huddled around the department Keurig. "You all know his nickname, but you didn't know for sure whether he's finally accepted his teammates' offerings?"

I almost want to laugh at the way they all cower before our

department lead. David Helms runs the PR sector of the Albany Wolves with an iron fist because he has the skills to do so. While upper management constantly comes up with new, fresh ideas for how to make the team seem better in the public eye, David is the one who makes the magic happen behind the scenes—whether that's organizing charity functions that run smoother than a submarine deployment or simply making fans feel appreciated during team events like training camp. He does it all, and he does it better than anyone else ever could. His creativity is only slightly eclipsed by his work ethic, attention to detail, and organizational skills.

I could learn so much from him.

Except how to boss people around. Pretty sure I'm never going to hone that skill set.

Right on cue, he barks out orders. "Kaylie, pull all public footage of Mitchell's and Fossoway's interactions. Leave no stone unturned. Go all the way back to when they first played together in their hometown's recreation league. Mason, you're on SO duty. Give me all the details you can find about Mitchell's love life. No, I don't care how you get that dirt. I want concrete proof there's no one warming his bed lately. If you can track down his ex and get the real story of why they split, even better. We all know Fossoway's a player both on and off the field. Caitlin and Zoe, you two are on jersey chaser duty. Find me the most recent women Fossoway has slept with. If Mitchell's back story provides nothing, then we'll have Fossoway's womanizing ways as a back-up plan to defend Mitchell's reputation."

They scatter like leaves on the wind, eager to do our collective master's bidding. Everyone has a lot riding on this assignment being a success after all. Even if they enjoy watching me fumble at it.

David turns back to me and immediately rolls his eyes. "Don't give me that look."

I trail after him as he strides quickly to his desk to begin his own research for the day. It's probably beyond stupid on my part, but this feels wrong. "I know it's not my place, but...despite their argument last week, Fossoway and Mitchell are friends. They played together in college and in high school! If you go after Alex like this and run him through the mud, that's not going to make Mike want to play nice with us."

David sits at his desk and wakes up his computer, immediately opening several websites that I'm not at all familiar with. They look like trashy gossip rags, but for sports. "You're right. It is not an intern's place to question the methods of her boss. You're getting a pass because you're so eager to learn, and I admire that about you. It is as important to know our client as it is to know our enemy. For now, and under these circumstances, Fossoway must be treated as the enemy."

"But that's my point. He *isn't* the enemy. This is the wrong play for this situation. Couldn't we just—I don't know—play up on the fact they're old friends, and friends sometimes argue?"

David stares at me with a deadpan expression that screams, *Shut up and let me do the heavy lifting, darling.*

Yes, he calls everyone darling. And yes, I'm well aware my co-workers think I'm too inexperienced to handle this delicate situation. Let's not even mention the fact that I know virtually nothing about football and am only well-versed at online stalking my favorite band rather than ripped professional athletes.

Honestly, I'm not even sure how my dad got me this internship that most college grads in my position would be thanking their lucky stars to land.

David rests his elbows on his desktop then steeples his fingers. It's a sure sign he's about to put me in my place, which he never hesitates to do in equal measure as taking me under his wing. "You researched enough to know our client, Mike Mitchell, is old friends with enemy number one, Alex Fossoway. And yet you never questioned why I felt the need to carefully choose your attire for today's meet-cute, in spite of needing to use our lunch hour to shop for your clothing. You either didn't notice or chose to remain willfully ignorant of the bets being placed in the department about whether the team would mistake you for a hooker. And you have yet to tell me how receptive Mr. Mitchell is to your new role in his life. So, please. Explain to me why I should heed your suggestion about the best way to proceed with righting this media nightmare."

"As a gay man, you should be more supportive of one of our players having his sexuality questioned after a stupid fight that probably had nothing to do with sex at all!" I slap my hands over my mouth to stop any actual vomit that might escape after all the verbal diarrhea I just released on probably the worst possible target in the department. Surely, he's going to eviscerate me for that completely honest yet horribly abrasive statement.

Surprisingly, he smiles. It's not even evil like Kaylie's usual grins. "Tori, you're cute. I like you. But you have a lot to learn if you want to succeed in *any* career in public relations. As a gay man, I know first-hand how questions about sexuality can impact a professional male athlete."

Oh, now I just feel like dirt.

He gestures with his finger for me to lean down, presumably to keep our conversation more private. Like I should have.

His gaze gentles as his eyes roam over my face that's—once again —probably the same color as my hair. "You've just been given the kind of assignment no one in this industry will ever bestow upon me even though I have a proven track record of doing a damn good job. Management doesn't trust me to be professional, and neither do the players. In a world where sex sells, they don't want to buy what they believe I might try to peddle. Do you understand?"

I don't actually. "If most professional athletes are heterosexual, then shouldn't working with a member of the opposite sex be even more frowned upon? I might not know him personally, but Mike Mitchell seems like a genuinely good guy. I'm sure he'd be happy for the best possible PR person the Wolves have on staff to represent him. He wouldn't care you're gay."

David shakes his head. "Oh, darling."

*There it is.*

"You're so naïve." He pats my hand that's resting on his desk. "No worries though. We'll fix you right up and send you on your way, ready to tackle whichever industry you land in."

And there it is again. I may be young, but I'm not as stupid as they think I am.

# Chapter 4
Natural

## Mike

*Pick up. Pick up. Please, pick up.*

Just as I'm about to end the call, she answers. "What?"

"You sound like shit. What's wrong?"

"I've been throwing up all day." A crackly sigh filters through the speakers. "I don't think I'm done yet, so make it quick."

On instinct, I hop out of my cushy leather recliner and search for my keys. By the time I'm slipping my sneakers on at the front door, I realize...I can't do a damn thing. "Why did you have to move to New York City?"

"Because this is where I got a job."

"You could've gotten a job in Albany just as easily! If you weren't almost three hours away, I could take care of you!" I toe off my shoes and retreat back to my living room where SportsCenter is still on the TV that I never bothered to turn off in my rush.

I brace for the expected *I don't need anyone to take care of me.*

"Why did you call, Mike?" She doesn't even argue, so she must be feeling really shitty.

I hate to burden her with my problems when she's so sick, but there's no one else who has the perfect mix of insider knowledge to help me sort out this mess. "The team assigned me a PR rep, and I don't know what to do."

"Um, listen to him and do whatever he says?"

"It's a she. And I can't do that."

Evie cackles then coughs. "Oh, that's hilarious. A woman is about to own you. I actually do wish I lived closer to witness this for myself."

"Hey! I get along just fine with women!"

"Sure," she drags out. "Whatever you say, Mikey."

"You're my best friend, and you're a woman. What does that tell you?"

"It tells me I'm stupidly loyal. A fact you love throwing in my face when it suits you."

I click the remote to turn off the TV when a clip of Rob's latest game plays. "I deserve your loyalty. Unlike some people who you still haven't served divorce papers."

"Right." Her voice is tight like she might actually be swallowing back the puke she warned me about. "Good talk. Bye."

"Wait!" I listen for a beat to make sure she hasn't hung up on me yet. I'm willing to hold while she throws up if it means nipping this problem in the bud now. "How am I supposed to keep this PR chick from poking into things I don't want the whole world to know?"

Another deep sigh carries across the line. "Shit. I do empathize with that."

"I know you do," I choke out around the ball lodged in my throat. "And you're one of the only people who knows what sort of skeletons are hiding in my closet. These scavengers find things that we think are buried. It's their job. And I can't..." I breathe through the vise grip around my chest. "I can't let that happen. Not again. I couldn't protect you. Help me at least protect them."

Evie blows out a breath that cuts straight to my heart. "Use me as bait. All my skeletons are already exposed, but it still might be a good enough distraction to keep her from digging any further into the past."

"What? No way! You've been through enough!"

There's a clattering sound followed by unmistakable retching. After a toilet flushes, her voice is hoarse and monotone. "Apparently not."

"Evie..." I hate to kick her when she's down, but maybe if she would just listen to me, she wouldn't be down so low. "Are you even taking your meds anymore?"

"Yeah. They're just not working anymore. We're not talking about me tonight. You called to talk about your problems for once. I'm trying to help you, so why don't you just accept it?"

"And you call me a hypocrite?" I'd laugh if this conversation wasn't so fucking sad. "I'm not going to use you as a distraction. There's gotta be another option. We just haven't thought of it yet."

"Well...play nice. Don't get into any more fights with people who used to be your friends. That's the most obvious option."

I stare at the blank television screen, trying to imagine how that would play out. History tells me it won't be so easy. "That won't work. It's too simple."

"Sometimes the most brilliant solutions are the simplest."

"Yeah? Then divorce Rob already."

She hangs up on me.

Great. I'm so screwed.

# Chapter 5
## Tightrope

### Tori

THE SOUND COMPETES with the reality show on my television, instantly springing goosebumps across my skin. No one ever knocks on my door. I glance at the clock. A little after eight, so not too late to automatically mean trouble. Not early enough to be a neighbor seeking a cup of sugar either. Do people even do that anymore?

I grab the baseball bat my brother gave me from its resting spot by the door before checking the peephole, then I tighten my grip around the Louisville slugger. I might be needing it after all.

Still, it's my job, so I swing the door open to reveal a very irritated-looking Mike Mitchell.

For some reason, the sight of me guarding the entrance to my tiny kingdom makes him crack a smile. He raises his hands in defense. "I definitely can't mistake you for a hooker now."

I glance down at my SpongeBob SquarePants pajamas that were a gift from Ben. Because he knows how much I love cartoons. Another furious blush heats my cheeks as I lower my weapon. "I..." I cough to force my voice into something resembling professional. "My apologies. I wasn't expecting visitors."

Mike stuffs his hands in the pockets of his worn, faded jeans. He stares at his sneakers. "I wasn't expecting to be handed a PR person, but here we are."

"Here we are..." I trail off, unsure why this up-and-coming celebrity is even standing in the dingy hallway of my apartment building after he stormed off from our first meeting.

With his eyes still firmly fixed on the ground, he clears his throat before speaking with more confidence than his appearance suggests. "I'm sorry to bother you after work hours, but I wanted to...apologize." He winces then takes a deep breath. "We got off on the wrong foot, but I wanted to take the opportunity to set the record straight. I swear I'm not a spoiled asshole football player who thinks he's above the rules. I understand my poor behavior caused all this, and I'm ready to make amends. I asked my coach for your address, so I could offer you my total cooperation."

Huh. This is completely unexpected. I can't afford not to run with the golden opportunity he's laying at my feet. Or, maybe...his feet. Which he still won't quit staring at.

"Thank you for the olive branch. Apology accepted. Would you like to come in? We can get started right away if that's what you want." I totally don't have a plan for this, but marketing is nothing if not pivoting direction when the situation warrants. It actually *is* my job to keep him as occupied as possible when he's not under the direct supervision of his coaches.

"Sure. Thank you."

Several beats of silence pass by as he remains frozen outside my front door, avoiding eye contact.

"Is everything all right?"

He makes this weird sort of choking sound and gestures with his hand toward vaguely where I'm standing. "I don't want to offend you again, but could you maybe, uh...cover up a little? I'm cool to wait here if you want to change."

I know SpongeBob isn't a business suit, but geez. What's this guy's problem? He's the one who showed up on my doorstep after all. He could've just called or texted.

"Excuse me?"

"Side boob," he coughs out, almost barely audible.

I glance down again, and sure enough. I am dangerously close to giving him a reason to think I'm a sex worker. My tank top is twisted so far to one side that I'm in a full-on wardrobe malfunction with a nip slip. "Oh my God! Please, come in! I'll be right back!" I fling the front door open wide before hightailing it down the hallway to my bedroom. I call to him as I yank a hoodie from my closet, "I'm so sorry, Mr. Mitchell!"

"Please don't call me Mr. Mitchell," he yells back with a strained voice.

By the time I'm covered enough and already sweating in leggings and my old university hoodie, he's sitting on my couch, one of my throw pillows strategically on his lap.

His eyes are squeezed tightly shut, and he swallows thickly. "We good?"

"I'm so sorry, Monk." Every part of me feels as red as my hair. For so many reasons. The heat further short-circuits my brain. "I mean, Mr. Mitchell. I mean, Mike. If it makes you feel any better, the other day in the weight room was like live porn to me. It's been years since I've had sex either."

I'm going to throw up. Seriously. How bad can I possibly screw myself over? Why on earth did I think I could salvage this horrid assignment into a professionally beneficial launching pad?

His chest rumbles with a strange mix of sound that's somewhere between a groan and a whimper. He thumps his head back against my couch. "You know about that stupid nickname?"

I cringe. "Yeah. I have it on my list of things to help you improve upon."

He trains a suddenly sharp gaze on me. His gorgeous brown eyes are all business. "What else do you know about me?"

I gesture to the bean bag situated in the corner of my little living room—a relic from college I can neither afford nor bear to part with. I mouth silently, *I'm just going to sit over here.* Quickly, I turn off the TV before he can judge me for my choice of programming. Not that he shouldn't be judging me. There's plenty to judge tonight.

He nods but doesn't break his forceful eye contact, obviously waiting on my answer.

I pull my laptop from the coffee table as I collapse into the soft, pink cushion. My file on him is already front and center on the screen. "Um, just the basics. Your position and number on the roster.

Stats so far this season. Where you went to college and high school, and how you performed there. When you were selected in the draft. Since we're already in the habit of not holding anything back..." My self-deprecating laugh does nothing to relieve my anxiety. Or his, by the looks of it. "It's not a ton to work with, honestly."

Honesty must be the best policy when dealing with Mike Mitchell because he finally relaxes, and the expression on his face turns into a bright smile. "Great! That's why I'm here! To give you something to work with!"

He wouldn't be so excited if he knew the Albany marketing team already has plenty of dirt to work with. This is just another chance to prove myself. To the team and to him. Then again, maybe he already knows I'm just his babysitter, and he wants to use that to his full advantage. A good marketing agent always runs an A/B test on any theory. I glance at the pillow still covering his crotch.

He follows my gaze then snaps me a wide-eyed stare. "I did not mean it that way."

I have too much to lose to get smothered by this blanket of awkward sexual tension. He might be scorchingly hot, but he's off limits. Our abysmal sex lives have no place in this relationship. We're co-workers. He's my client. Sort of. That kiss between us that I keep replaying? The one that was Oscar-worthy even though it was built on total miscommunication? I hit my mental delete button.

With a few cleansing breaths and a renewed vow to be a true professional, I square my shoulders. "You know what? Let's start over. I'm Tori Russo, and I've been assigned as your PR manager. I'm at your service."

The thing about marketing is that you have to be good at bending the truth. Not blatantly lying because most people can see through that in a heartbeat. Spinning the truth for the purposes of accomplishing a goal is fair game though. If I had told Mike the Wolves assigned me to be his handler, he would never have shown up at my door to offer his cooperation. My little white lie benefits him as much as it does me. He gets to save face, and I get more experience.

Mike nods. His chest heaves with a deep sigh. "I'm Mike Mitchell.

And…apparently, I'm in trouble. I would appreciate your help with turning around my image very much."

"I can definitely do that." I flash him a smile that hopefully conveys we're starting with a clean slate.

"So…" He blows out a forceful breath then places the throw pillow in its original position in the corner of the couch. "Where should we start?"

I can't help but sneak a peek at his crotch. It seems his issue is completely under control now, which means we're finally on the same page. "You said you came here to offer me your total cooperation. I admitted I don't have much information to market you with. How about if we start there? How would you like me to present you to the world?"

His relaxed posture doesn't match his heated words. That's a skill we can use to our advantage if he can be taught to use it all the time. His body language has been all over the place so far tonight. "I'd rather you not market me at all. I want to prove myself on the field by working hard, but my coaches flat-out told me if I don't play nice with you, they'll bench me."

I wince because I empathize with his situation more than he knows.

No one made me aware of how much is on the line for Mike in this arrangement. As far as I know, I'm just supposed to keep him out of trouble by being a glorified babysitter while feeding intel to the actual marketing department. The words "look pretty and be a good distraction" might have been used. Which I have no intention of doing. Mike's just given me a very good reason to add to my list for not doing exactly what I've been told.

"I want to make this as easy as possible on you, so let's start at the beginning." I have my own ideas, but it's time to run another test. "Tell me what the fight between you and Alex Fossoway was about."

"I would rather not," he states flatly. "It was personal. Our argument had nothing to do with football."

So, when he told me he was here to offer his full cooperation, he lied. That makes me feel a little bit better about my ruse. "Because you're old friends, and friends sometimes fight?"

Darn it. I wasn't supposed to lead him in any way.

"Yep." He nods. "You've got it. Wow. You're really good at this whole marketing thing. Case closed. Guess we're done here."

I watch in confusion as he hops up from his seat on my couch and wipes his hands down the front of his jeans that cling to his muscular thighs. "Mr. Mitchell? I mean…Mike? We're not nearly done here. Remember the whole threat about getting benched thing?"

He offers me a completely fake smile before plopping back down. "Oh, right. Well, can't blame a guy for hoping."

I sigh. This is going to be more difficult than I thought. My career ambitions have always been corporate marketing, not personal. If I'm going to make lemonade out of lemons, I have to hone in on my primary target market—Mike Mitchell. I need to sell myself to him before I can promote him to the masses. "I'm going to go out on a limb and guess you don't really know how to market yourself, and the very idea of it makes you really uncomfortable. Can I suggest a quick exercise to give you a feel for how I can help you?"

He nods again, but he also visibly swallows like I've just shoved a horse pill in his mouth.

For his powerful size, I suddenly feel like I'm dealing with a skittish animal. With more than a little bumbling effort, I rise from my bean bag with my laptop in hand and oh, so slowly, approach to sit at his side. "This is going to be painless for you, I promise." I thrust my computer toward him. "We're going to use me for an example instead of working on you tonight, okay? Google my name."

As hoped, this is an easy enough task for him to complete. He does so with more than expected eagerness. "All right. You have every social media account known to man. Now what?"

I grin at his compliment. I've been building curated content for years while working toward my degree. "Now, click a link. Any link."

At least he chuckles at my stupid game hostess impersonation. "Am I supposed to be looking for something specific?"

"Nope. Just tell me what you think of when you look at my profile, timeline, and social interactions."

Instead of immediately firing off his initial impressions, he takes his time scrolling through one social media site then clicking the next link in the search results and doing the same. Another and another and another until he's exhausted all easy possibilities.

Already knowing he's a man of action rather than words, I wait silently as he drinks his fill. I'm not even a celebrity, but the longer he reads the internet version of *all about me*, the more I squirm in my seat. This is good practice though. I can't market him as effectively if I never get a chance to walk a mile in his shoes.

He glances at me with a strange expression on his face. "I feel like I know you without really knowing you. Is this all fake? Or is this the real you?"

"That's the whole point," I tell him gently. "I think—and please, feel free to correct me if I'm wrong—you're the type of guy who values his privacy even though you're in the limelight all of a sudden. I can help make fans feel like they know you and can relate to you, all without violating a shred of the privacy you hold so dear."

He drapes his arm over the back of my couch—an invisible touch against my shoulders. "Tori Russo…I have no idea who you really are, but I think this partnership could work after all."

That's music to my ears.

# Chapter 6
Crush

## Mike

I HATE AWAY GAMES. There's something about being in a strange bed in a strange city with some dude who I'm not sure I want to be friends with snoring in the bed next to me that doesn't make it easy to sleep.

Templeman rolls over and starts talking in his sleep—mumbling about unicorns.

Great. At least after years of sharing hotel rooms with Rob and Alex through high school and college, I knew what to expect even if it wasn't always pretty. Or at least...I thought I knew those guys who were like my brothers. I also thought there were no secrets between us. I couldn't have been more wrong.

I hate being wrong. Being wrong leads to nothing good. Trust is the absolute foundation for any relationship, and I'm running seriously low on that. My temples throb.

I've had a constant headache all week. Another fucking fight with Alex turned my life upside down in just a few minutes. My pisshead teammates have been sending hookers my way all week. And then... the straw that's breaking this camel's back.

Tori Russo. Vittoria is her full name. Saying it out loud gives my tongue a workout. Not that I've been practicing saying it out loud. At home. Alone.

She reminds me of peaches with her orange hair, pink blushes, and pale skin. Peaches and cream. Cream I want to lap up like a starving cat.

Cat. Pussy. Cream.

I'm so fucked.

Even my internal monologue is horny. This is all Evie's fault with her insistence I date again, and my stupid teammates' fault because of all their prostitute pranks. I was fine being in a committed relationship with my hand. Really.

So, there's a natural explanation for why I can't stop fantasizing about bending Peaches over my kitchen table and…

But I will not, *cannot*, let myself act on those fantasies. I haven't jerked off once while thinking about her.

Which honestly might be making my blue balls worse at this point. I'm not sure.

I give up on sleep and roll on my side to grab my phone from the nightstand. A little green dot indicates she's online.

Not that I care.

Okay, fine. I care a little. But only because I can still make this situation work to my advantage by using her the way she asked me to. She's at my service as she said. Multiple times.

> Mike: Can't sleep either? It's after midnight.
> Tori: That is correct. Is something wrong?
> You need to rest before game day.

SOMETHING IS DEFINITELY WRONG. I reach under the blankets and adjust my stiff dick in my shorts. I haven't been faced with this much temptation since college. I can't put my finger on why she's getting under my skin more than any of the women Templeman has thrown my way. It's annoying me to no end. I don't have time for a distraction like her. I need these stupid hard-ons to stop, and the only way that might happen is if I get her out of my system. There has to be some flaw I can latch onto…

> Mike: Is your first name really Vittoria?
> Tori: It is.
> Just like your first name is really Michael even though you go by Mike.
> Is my name what's keeping you awake?

ONLY A LITTLE. That was just a warm up question.

> Mike: What if I tell you I also like SpongeBob?
> Are you going to use that against me?
> Tori: Against you? No. For you? Yes. But only if you want me to.

SO MANY THINGS I'd like her to do for me, which is a huge problem.

> Mike: That doesn't seem like something that would make me more relatable to football fans.
> Tori: Touché. It probably wouldn't.

I STARE with way too much anticipation as those three little dots blink on my screen. She's going to send me something big. Or else she's typing, deleting, then trying again. I would know. Every word I text feels like a loaded gun, and I'm playing Russian roulette.

> Tori: I didn't want to overwhelm you last night, and I definitely don't want to keep you awake now, but I'd like you to think about five simple things that define who you are as a person. We'll use those

things to build curated content on your social media profiles to create a better image of you for the fans. For example, my five pillars of being are: SpongeBob, the beach, music, food allergy awareness, and family. You can make it as personal or as generic as you want, but it still has to be true to you.

I REREAD her five things at least five times. So many questions pound on my poor brain, but it's the last one that really sticks with me.

> Mike: You have five brothers, so I guess family is a big one for you. Your dad was in the Navy, and you don't have a mom? That's what I got from your social media. Doesn't it feel weird I know that about you when you've never told me yourself?
> Tori: Not really because that's my life, and I'm used to it. Is that something that makes you curious to find out more about me?

YEP. And that's another problem. If it was just lust, I might have given up and jerked off until my dick was raw by now.

> Mike: I don't want my family in the media. I chose to be a professional football player. They didn't. Fame isn't always a good thing.
> Tori: I agree with you, and I respect your decision to protect your family. We don't have to use anything you're uncomfortable with. The idea is just to give fans a glimpse of who you really are in a way that will make them want to know more about you.
> Mike: That's not gonna work for me. If they don't want to know me for my skills on the field, then that's not my problem.
> Tori: I didn't mean to upset you. You really need to get some sleep.

SHIT. This isn't moving the chains forward at all. I'd actually like to play the rest of the season instead of riding the bench, and she's being nicer than ever.

> Mike: Can we use your things for me?
> Tori: We could, but it won't be authentic. That will make it more difficult for fans to really relate to you for the rest of the season.

So, she's saying we only have to lie for the rest of the season? Score. We're already five weeks in. I can fake it 'til I make it for a while longer.

> Mike: Sounds good. Let's do it.
> Tori: Okay, if that's what you really want. I have tons of SpongeBob memes saved. I'll still need something to replace family with since you don't want to use that. When you get back from your game, I'll need a list of your favorite bands, any charity or cause you want to bring awareness to since you don't have any food allergies, and pics of you at the beach.

SHIT. I'm from Ohio, and I eat, breathe, and dream football. Mostly. I've never been to the beach.

# Chapter 7
## I Knew You Were Trouble

### Tori

"Do you understand what I'm saying, Miss Russo?"

The actual freaking CEO of the Albany Wolves is in my cubicle, staring at me as he waits for my response. His laser focus incinerates any hope I had for a relatively quiet escape now that the season's over. He didn't send his assistant. He didn't even send his assistant's secretary for this task.

With David acting as the moderator between our two worlds of lowly intern and powerful administrator, I have no choice but to accept the team's offer.

"I understand, Mr. Gallo. Thank you so much for this opportunity and for your generosity. I won't let you down."

He winks. The dude actually winks at me before his gaze slides down my body. "I know you won't, sweetheart. Keep up the good work and make our boy shine."

I don't like the implication in his undertone nor in his slimy eyes, but I'm not about to question his proposal of paying for my master's degree if I'll only sign on for another year of indentured servitude.

As if he senses I'm all out of gushing—albeit fake—excitement, David chimes in, "We're going to make Mike Mitchell the MVP of this team. Not just on the field, but off of it. Your star player is in good hands, Mr. Gallo."

The CEO barely hides his sneer in David's direction. "He's off to a good start. The goal for the upcoming season is to elevate him to the next level. We want him to be competitive in the wide market with the other products of his draft like Fossoway and Falls. Underwear ads are out; personal touches are in. Make it happen."

David and I watch as Mr. Gallo intercepts Mike in the bowels of the marketing department. If David has miracle hearing to decipher their conversation beyond the obligatory handshake and overly-bright smiles, he doesn't let on.

"You did too good of a job," he mutters.

"I only wanted to help!"

"You've helped yourself to another season of this nonsense." David continues to stare at the impromptu meeting between Mike and our CEO. "You're in the big leagues now, kid. Whether you agree with our marketing tactics is irrelevant. Your cute, simple social media campaigns aren't going to be enough to achieve the goal Mr. Gallo has given you."

"I know." The sad thing is I didn't do anything special. Mike wouldn't let me market him organically, so his social media campaign didn't get as much attention from the wider fan base as hoped, even if it was enough to put him back onto the good sort of radar. The rest of the PR department hates me for taking matters into my own hands because they were ready and waiting to run a smear campaign on Alex Fossoway that ended up not being necessary after all.

As for my so-called client? Judging by the lightness in his step and the smile on his face, he's more pleased with this new development than expected. "It looks like we're partners for another season."

David raises an eyebrow at Mike. "What instrument does Squid-ward Tentacles play?"

Mike's face scrunches in confusion. "Who?"

I wince when David turns his displeasure in my direction.

"This will not stand, darling. It is officially the off-season, so we have a little time. We need to plan carefully for how to rectify this mess you've gotten us all into. Mr. Mitchell, we'll schedule a meeting for next week to go over your full media plans."

Mike glances back and forth between me and David. "Why? Tori's done a great job. Mr. Gallo just told me so. Besides, I won't be here next week. I have to attend a wedding in my hometown, then I'm gonna spend some time with my family. I won't be back in Albany until the end of the month."

David rolls his eyes to the ceiling like he's praying for deliverance from all the non-believers around him. "Will Mr. Fossoway also be in Ironville during your stay?"

Mike shrugs. "Yeah. He's in the wedding party, too."

"You want to help, do you, Miss Russo? Pack your bags," David commands. "You're taking a little trip to Ohio."

The sound of my forehead hitting my desk echoes around the marketing department. What have I gotten myself into?

~

"That's where I played in high school." Mike gestures to the stadium that we pass by at a cool fifty miles per hour in a rental car, thank God.

The flight from Albany to Cleveland was bad enough with him talking my ear off, but at least I didn't have to make an eight-hour road trip with chatty Cathy over here.

"And that's the old rec center field. Where it all started." He aims a tight smile my way. "Shouldn't you be taking pictures? You're always telling me we need personal photos to post."

Since we're both wearing sunglasses, my glare goes unnoticed. "How am I supposed to take pictures when we're just driving by all these places?"

"With your phone?" He says it like I'm stupid.

Which I'm not. I bite my tongue—literally—to keep from lashing out at my client. I am well aware that venting all my frustration out on him would be as beneficial as my phony social media campaigns have been.

I'll just dig myself deeper into a hole it feels less and less like I can climb out of without help.

Steady posting to his accounts hasn't been a failure, per se. It's just much more likely that Mike keeping his nose clean and playing well for the rest of the season helped his image more than my stupid SpongeBob memes. Which is exactly why Mr. Gallo's offer makes me so nervous. Surely, the bigwigs in the front office realize I'm not worth what they're promising to pay me.

This feels like a trap. A setup. A ruse.

If David knows the real deal, he's not sharing. Instead, he's pushing me further into this mess by insisting I actually be the babysitter I was supposed to be during this trip. Honestly, this feels like a punishment.

"Do I...make you uncomfortable?" Mike's hesitant question snaps my attention to the bulky man in the driver's seat.

This is the perfect opportunity to come clean about everything. To assuage my client's fears by telling him the truth. The only problem is that a professional wouldn't burden their client's much more capable, muscular shoulders with any amount of baggage. Our job is to shoulder the load on our own, so the client never knows any extra weight is even hanging around.

"No," I say as brightly as possible. "You don't make me uncomfortable, Mr. Mitchell."

He swallows like we're in a convertible instead of an inconspicuous sedan, and he's just inadvertently choked down a bug. "You're back to calling me Mr. Mitchell, so I'm gonna go out on a limb and say I *do* actually make you uncomfortable. You've barely said a word since we met at the airport in Albany."

"It's just this whole situation." I think on my feet as best as I can under the circumstances. David certainly didn't give me detailed guidelines before we boarded our flight other than to prevent Mike and Alex from creating more bad press. "I'm about to meet your family, your hometown friends, your old teammates. I have no idea how you want to play this. If you introduce me as your PR manager, but Falls and Fossoway don't have theirs in tow, that will seem weird. It'll be obvious to people who have known you forever that I'm not an actual friend of yours. I just..." I swallow and part with the small bit of honesty I'm willing to reveal. "I don't know the best way to play me being here with you."

An expression of unmistakable shock crawls across Mike's face from forehead to chin in slow motion, almost like the setting of the sun. "I hadn't even thought about that."

His admission rattles something inside me. This might be the most authenticity he's shown in the entire past season I've sort of known him. I don't take it lightly. "I know you're sick of hearing it, but I'm at your service, Mike. However you want to spin this to all these people is what we'll do. You only need to tell me what you want."

"I...I don't know." The words seem to come from a deep place in his chest that he doesn't mean to expose.

It's my job to recognize and work with anything he gives me, and he's sure as heck just given me more than in the entire past season of working together. "That's okay. You obviously understand the main reason I'm here is to prevent you from coming to blows with Fossoway like what happened last season. You said that argument wasn't related to football, and I don't want to pry. Even though you're a private person, and you won't be as much in the public eye in Ironville, there are smartphones everywhere. Just think of me like the little angel on your shoulder, reminding you to behave no matter what you're faced with while you're home."

"I'm about to be faced with my best friend being in a wedding party with her secret, not-so-ex-husband who's blackmailing her into getting treatment for a chronic health condition in exchange for getting his shit together. I don't know whether to be more worried about that shit show or about Alex. Sometime during our senior year of college, he became the other guy who sees an opportunity to try to get Evie into bed next. That's what started all this. That's what we were fighting about on the field. You don't need to worry about me making bad press for football so much as Falls and Fossoway."

If I thought Mike was being authentic before, he absolutely looks like he's going to puke all over the steering wheel from his blurted honesty now.

Holy crap. This is way above my pay grade. I knew I was walking into a lion's den with this trip, but not like this. David would never have sent me otherwise. "Mr. Mitchell, I don't want to seem like a fangirl who's dying to know every little tidbit of sordid information about your life, but I need way more of an explanation than that if I'm going to keep your career in the fast lane."

# Chapter 8
Wicked Game

## Mike

GODDAMN. I didn't know vomit could smell so much like the same thing it went down the hatch as. I'm not a big drinker anyway, but I will never, ever drink gin after tonight. I might not be able to even stand the scent of the stuff ever again.

"Okay," Tori sighs then swipes her arm across her mouth. "I'm done."

Yeah, I highly doubt that. "I think we should stay here just in case."

She blows a raspberry that reeks of alcohol and shakes her head a little too wildly as she laughs. "Oh, no. I'm gonna puke some more. I meant I'm done. With this job. You're gonna go back to Albany at the end of the month, tell Mr. Gallo you had to hold my hair back while I barfed my intestines up, and then I'll be fired."

I sit on the tile floor beside her, so the boobs that are practically hanging out of her dress won't be in my direct line of sight anymore. "I'm not going to tell Mr. Gallo about this."

"You should actually," she slurs. "Maybe he'll write me a decent letter of recommendation at the least." She gestures with her hands in front of her like she's showing off a billboard. "Willing to do anything to get the job done. And I do mean *anything*. Client is about to get into a fistfight at a wedding reception? Tori Russo will drink herself stupid to distract him. This woman does what it takes. She cares more about the client than her own liver."

I can't believe my ears. "You got this drunk, *on purpose?*"

"Yep." She pops the P. "Things were getting a little too tense back there. I didn't know what else to do to prevent another media nightmare." She cradles her head in her hands. "I'm so bad at this, but you won't be stuck with me for much longer. I'm sorry."

I feel like an absolute ass. "No, I'm sorry. You shouldn't have to be in the middle of this. We fight a lot, but they're still my friends, and it's...it's complicated."

"I know," she mumbles through her fingers. "You actually told me something for once. I'm not heartless even though I hate that they've put *you* in the middle of this. I can understand why they did because you're a natural problem solver, but I still don't think it's fair to you. I care about what she went through. What they went through. What you all went through. But you're my responsibility, not them. I get you've all got big problems. That's why I resorted to drastic measures to get you out of there." She laughs, but it sounds more like a sob. "Nothing but my finest for you, Mr. Mitchell."

"Thank you," I tell her with as much honesty as I can show with just my voice. I'm absolutely floored she's gone to bat for me like she has. We barely know each other. "I'm, uh...I'm so used to fixing everyone else's problems that it's kind of nice for someone to have my back for a change."

She thumps her head against the wall, more laughing tears making streaks of black down her cheeks. "Well, I'm glad. I'm glad me completely embarrassing myself for a man who is the hands-down best kisser in the entire universe feels kind of nice for you."

Wait. What, now?

"You think I'm the best kisser in the universe?"

She scoffs, points a thumb at herself and then, weirdly, also her thumb at me. "I can admit that to you now. Not because I'm drunk, but because I'm never going to see you again after tonight!" She cackles. The sort of crazy sound actually bounces off all the tile surrounding us. "Fuck you for giving me the best kiss I've ever had in my entire life! Fuck you, Mike Mitchell! I'm twenty-three years old, was in a committed relationship with the same guy for all of high school and college who I thought I was going to marry and have babies with, and he never kissed me like that! It almost makes me think he was right to break things off with me when he went to grad school at NYU, and I got my internship with the Wolves! I think he might have been right! All because you kissed me when you thought I was a prostitute! Fuck you very much!"

Holy shit. I've noticed Tori never swears, and I'm not going to lie. Part of my obsession with her is wondering what it would take to make her swear. I never imagined it would be me. At least…not like this.

She makes some angry grunting noise then hoists herself upright.

All I can do is stare. What am I supposed to say to that? Thank you seems inadequate. I was with the same woman all through high school and not nearly all of college, but she certainly never accused me of being the best kisser in the universe. Of course, she also didn't tell me to go fuck myself because of it. She just told me without words to go fuck myself in general.

Tori slides one strap of her dress over a shoulder and then the other until it pools on the floor at her feet. She's wearing a matching black lace bra and panty set that makes me forget I saw her puking just a few minutes ago.

My brain goes offline. All the pent-up lust I've been fighting barrels into me. She's way more gorgeous than in my imagination. Milky white, pale skin. Curvy hips I could sink my fingers into, and a body that doesn't look like I'd break it if I enjoyed it to the fullest.

She practically tears off her bra with a sound that might be frustration.

My mouth goes dry. I have seen a lot of tits in my time as a football player, but these are hands-down the finest in the entire universe. Full, naturally round, topped with peachy pink nipples that would probably be the best thing I ever put in my mouth with whipped cream.

She slides her panties down next.

Oh my God, she's a natural redhead.

"Peaches?"

She narrows her eyes. "Peaches? Did you just call my boobs

peaches? These weigh at least as much as cantaloupes, I'll have you know."

Jesus Christ, I said that out loud.

I should look away, but I absolutely can't. Instead, I rush to explain, "I use mnemonics to remember people. You have peachy hair and peachy blushes all the time, and you smell like peaches. It's been a lot of new faces and names ever since I signed with the Wolves, and I have a hard time keeping them all straight."

She tips her head to the side in thought. "That's actually kind of brilliant. I'll allow it."

She's allowing a lot of things that I still can't stop staring at.

"You do realize I'm still in this bathroom with you, right?"

"Yep." She pops the P again.

"So, what are you doing?" Best kisser in the universe or not, this seems wildly...wild.

She gapes at me like *I'm* the crazy one. "I have puke in my hair, a trail of it through my cleavage, and I smell like a freaking bar! What does it look like I'm doing?"

It looks like she's doing the weirdest, most erotic striptease I've ever seen.

Or, maybe I really have been single longer than is healthy for a guy my age.

"I'm taking a shower," she announces flatly after waiting for my answer that never comes.

"Are you sure that's a good idea? You're really drunk. What if you fall and get hurt?"

She's already turning on the water and stepping into the bathtub. Sort of. She basically holds herself up by aimlessly clinging to the tile walls. The shower door slides closed, not doing anything to hide her mesmerizing body from my view.

I clear my throat. I might be hornier than I swear I've ever been in my entire life right now, but I'm not going to be an ass any more tonight. I glance away. "I'm going to uh, stay here just in case. Okay?"

"Sure," she draws out over the sound of running water. "It's fine.

This is fine. I'm fine. This will all be a bad memory by the end of the week anyway."

It's a memory all right. One I'm pretty sure I'll still be able to recall in old age.

A thump echoes through the room, so I bolt to my feet, practically ripping the door apart to get to Tori on her back under the spray, laughing.

"Are you all right?"

"I'm great, Mr. Mitchell!" She laughs harder.

This is the hardest test I've ever been put through, but I strip down anyway and climb into the bathtub with her. "Let me help you before you kill yourself."

Her laugh turns to a husky chuckle that makes my cock really strain with the effort of keeping it together. "Oh, yes. Please help me, Mr. Mitchell. Right there. Just like that."

My hands freeze in her hair that I'm trying to wash the puke out of while earning my place among the saints for good behavior. "Are you mocking me or being serious?"

"No, seriously," she moans. "Right there. My head is pounding already. That feels so good."

My throbbing dick is sandwiched between my stomach and her back. She doesn't seem to notice, but if she keeps it up, I might get off just from the sounds she's making.

Thank Christ, she quiets down and lets me finish my work in silence. After what she put on the line for me tonight, cleaning her up and tucking her in bed is the least I can do. Even if it just might kill me.

"Do you need anything?"

She hums something that sounds like nope right before smashing her face into the pillow and rolling onto her stomach.

I clench my hands into fists.

If I don't do something with them, I might actually grab two handfuls of the finest ass I've ever seen—plump, heart-shaped, attached to long legs I've imagined wrapped around me way too many times.

There's only so much a man can withstand. I'm human, too. Since there's no way I can leave her alone in this hotel room tonight, I head back to the shower to take the edge off.

A full-on ice bath isn't all that unusual after game day, but this cold shower isn't doing shit for me. I glance down at my dick—rock-hard and ready to go.

I switch the temperature over to as hot as I can stand, forcing my tense muscles to relax. It's no good.

I'm going to break, so I might as well make it worth my while.

The fantasies come on as hard and fast as ever. There's plenty of real-life hotness still fresh in my mind to work with. Minus the puking, but that doesn't even matter anymore. Not after having her firm tits in my hands as I washed them.

*I grab onto that round ass and haul her to the edge of the bed. A single swipe of my finger up her seam confirms what I already know. She's wet and ready for me.*

*I slide the head of my cock as slow as I can stand towards her entrance.* It's a piss-poor imitation, but I squeeze my fist around the top of my dick.

*Her wet, hot pussy feels like heaven.* I pull down to the base of my cock, letting the hot water mimic my imagination.

*She writhes and moans, begs me to get inside her. That's all I've been waiting for...*

My groan echoes off the tile walls as my release washes down the drain. I haven't come that hard in so long, but I haven't exactly withheld from myself like this before either.

A choking noise outside the shower stall snaps me out of my haze of bliss. Shit. She must be puking again.

I open my eyes to see Tori staring at me, wide-eyed. She's sitting on the toilet.

This shower glass is not frosted.

She has a crystal-clear view of me still holding my dick, and I can plain-as-day see a wad of toilet paper being similarly strangled in her hand.

"I can explain. It's not what it looks like. Well, it's exactly what it looks like, but I have a good reason."

"I couldn't hold it! I figured I could sneak in and out before you'd notice!"

It's a tie.

We're both caught red-handed with our pants down. Neither of us can break our silent staring match of epic mortification. Her face is redder than I've ever seen it. If I let go of my dick, she's going to get the Full Monty.

Not that we both aren't already acutely aware of exactly what's going on.

I clear my throat. "I'm going, to, uh…turn around and let you finish."

She nods, her eyes still wide as the full moon. "Full disclosure. This is one of those never-to-be-shared, never-to-be-used-against you things. I'll never speak a word of this again—not even between us—if you won't."

That orgasm fried my brain after going so long without. "How could you possibly use this against me?"

It's not like she has video proof.

She licks her lips. "You have the biggest dick I've ever seen. That is definitely marketable material, Mitchell."

I should be pissed. I should have her fired. She knows way too much. More than I ever intended to tell—or show—her.

But this woman thinks I'm the best kisser in the universe and that I also have the biggest dick she's ever seen.

I'm definitely going to keep her around.

I'm only human after all.

# Chapter 9
## Don't Hurt Like It Used To

### Tori

"I don't think I can do this after all."

Mike smiles behind the wheel of his truck. Easy. Affable. Like nothing is weird between us now. "Trust me. I'm a natural problem solver, remember? This will be good for you."

"I'm supposed to be solving your problems, not the other way around," I grumble as the city looms in the distance. My insides coil like springs the closer we get to our destination. I'm eventually going to snap, and I don't want Mike to see that. He's already seen more than enough of me in less than my finest state. He's seen me in my *whole* state.

"Hey, you took one for the team by going to that wedding with me and puking for half the night to keep me out of trouble. This is the least I can do to repay you."

"Technically, I got paid by the team to do that." *No one* could pay me enough to ever drink a gin martini again.

"True," Mike concedes. Right before his lips spread into a devious grin. "But you're going to repay me for holding your hair back and seeing you pee by going through with this."

"You promised never to speak of it!" I shriek. I have to cling to the indignity of it all, so I won't think about…other things.

"I promised never to speak of it *publicly*," he emphasizes.

My cheeks flame, but I can't argue. The morning of the worst hangover I've ever had in my life, I woke up bleary-eyed, cotton-mouthed, and naked under the blankets in a hotel room to find Mike sleeping on the floor—fully clothed—beside the bed.

Throughout rounds of dry heaving that had nothing to do with potential alcohol poisoning and everything to do with dire embarrassment, he reassured me that everything would be fine. That not only was he not going to have me fired, but that he wanted me to continue working for him.

He even changed the subject when I started hyperventilating by asking me about Ben and convincing me to make this trip to get some closure over our breakup that completely blindsided me.

So, here we are. Almost to New York City. Burying the elephant between us in favor of him helping me make the sort of clean break he wishes his friend would make, and me getting the opportunity to snap some completely clothed shots of him enjoying the sights in his new home state for his media campaign.

"The way I see it, today should be easy for you. You're already over Ben." There's an actual grin in his voice. "Because you're stuck on me."

My embarrassment burns away, replaced by something much stronger. Dignity. "I'm not one of those women who's willing to sleep her way to the top. I apologize for my behavior, my lack of filter and better planning that night to keep you out of more bad press, but I'm a professional. I respect your personal privacy, and I will never use anything against you. I would appreciate the same respect from you."

His brow flattens. "I respect you, Tori. And I trust you. I wouldn't have told you all the shit going on between my friends if I thought you'd blast it all over social media just to make me look better. You proved yourself when you weren't willing to do that to Alex last season even though it would've been much easier than what I gave you to work with."

"It would have," I agree, straightening my shoulders. "Don't think this little trip to New York City is getting you out of holding up your side of the marketing bargain either. Just because you're trying to distract me with this whole closure thing with Ben doesn't mean I'm going to forget you also promised me some actual shots of you in the Big Apple today."

"Damn," he mumbles, but there's a smile on his face. "You figured out my evil plan."

"You're darn right I have."

Mike laughs. "That's another thing I've learned about you that I didn't find out from your social media. You never curse unless you're seriously drunk. Why is that?"

I latch onto the fact that he cares more about my sober vocabulary than what I look like stark naked. "My Dad was a captain in the Navy—something you did learn about me through social media. He forbade cursing as long as we were under his roof. Said it was an unimaginative way of showing displeasure, and he expected better of us."

Mike glances at me with a raised eyebrow. His gaze never strays south of my eyes. "There are plenty of studies that suggest otherwise. People who curse frequently are generally more intelligent and quick-witted."

"I'm not going to argue either perspective. My dad put food in my stomach and kept a roof over my head. He raised six kids all on his own and gave us all the love in the world even if he was stricter than most of my friends' parents. I did what I was told, and it just kind of...stuck."

"Kind of like you did as you were told by doing whatever you had to do at the wedding reception to keep me out of trouble?"

My cheeks flame. Not in embarrassment but anger. Mostly at myself. "It's my job to keep you out of trouble because you have a bad habit of getting yourself into it. The methods might need some work, but they get the job done."

David's similar words echo in my mind. He's poised and waiting in Albany with a marketing campaign of his own to elevate Mike to the status the team is paying us to accomplish.

Mike pulls into a parking garage on the Jersey side of the river that he's apparently familiar with from visiting Evie's apartment nearby. Even though he makes millions every year, he still prefers not to overpay for parking in the city. The very idea makes me chuckle, but I appreciate the knowledge that his substantial pay raise hasn't changed who he is at all. At least not yet.

I guess I'll know for sure if he ever decides to hold my sins against me.

He shuts off the engine but doesn't unbuckle or make any move to exit the vehicle, instead staring out the windshield that's facing a dilapidated building across the street. "I appreciate you being willing to get your hands dirty in the interests of keeping mine clean. That's why I'm never going to say a word to anyone about what happened in the hotel room that night. I'm sorry I put you, myself, and the team in this position at all. I need this job. I love this job, and I'm not going to do anything else to jeopardize it. I've been stuck on this rollercoaster with Rob, Evie, and Alex since senior year of high school, and it's..." He blows out a breath. "It's fucking hard. I'm supposed to be the stable one, the problem solver, the man with all the answers, but the fact is I'm struggling as much as anyone. I've never been very good with change, and it's been a hell of a lot of change over the past year or so. New city, new faces and names, new plays to learn, new...everything."

I'm so shocked by this level of sharing while we're both sober that I can't form a single word even when he pauses.

"I have a hard time making friends because I don't trust anyone. I learned that lesson a long time ago. Ever since confessing to you all the shit that's been going on with my friends and our crazy night together, I feel a lot lighter. I didn't even realize how much carrying their secrets was weighing me down. How much I needed a friend. We might both be embarrassed as hell about that night, but...it's weird. It actually makes me feel like I can trust you more now. So, thank you. I know it's not really a part of your job description to embarrass yourself for me, or to be my unpaid therapist, but you kind of are because I've learned you won't use this shit against me. Just like I won't use anything against you. I'm ready to do whatever hard work you have in store for me to turn my image around for real this season. There are too many people depending on me to fail now."

Any indignation building in my veins during this drive has fled the scene. I always thought marketing would be a rewarding job, but I never imagined it like this. Nothing I might say feels sincere enough to convey what it means to hear him admit these things to me. *Especially* after that night.

Mike's phone rings, taking the opportunity to apologize away from me again. He grimaces when he looks at the screen. "Shit. It's Rob. Hang on."

I wait in silence as he lifts the phone to his ear, obviously listening to a voicemail.

"Fuck," he breathes then glances around the cab of the truck with building panic in his eyes. "Fuck! I gotta go!"

"What?" So much for our moment of honesty. "Go where? What's happening?"

"Evie's stalker tracked her down. I gotta go." He pulls his keys out of the ignition then pauses with his hand on the door. "Shit. Peaches..."

Maybe we do know each other better in good ways after that wild night because I hear all the things he leaves unsaid.

*I'm sorry. I'll be back for you. Please understand.*

"Go!" I yell at him as I shove him toward the door. "The photoshoot doesn't matter! Go!"

～

FADING rays of sunlight filter in through small windows at either end of the dim hallway, creating a golden glow that makes the worn beige carpet seem pretty instead of dirty. My feet ache with every step toward relief. They mimic the unsettled feeling in my chest which grows as another hour ticks by without any word from Mike.

I'm not even here to complete his little challenge anymore. I just need to get off my feet for a while. Ben promised we'd always be friends, and it's time to put that to the test. I knock on the cracked wood door, then do it again. My hands shake with exhaustion and worry. The last train to Albany doesn't depart for hours, but I don't want to leave Mike to fend for himself after what's surely going to be an emotionally draining day. I cannot possibly consume another cup of coffee while waiting though.

"Can I help you?"

I glance up at the unfamiliar female voice. Her expression looks as confused as I feel.

"Oh, I'm so sorry. I must have the wrong apartment." I offer her a sheepish grin and chuckle to ease her obvious distrust. "I've been walking around window shopping for hours, and I'm just dead on my feet at this point. I apologize for interrupting your evening."

She leans forward with a conspiratorial sparkle in her pretty hazel eyes. "Honestly, window shopping is so much more exhausting than actual shopping. Fantasizing about all those beautiful purses I can't remotely afford? I'd rather run a marathon, and that's saying something because the only reasons I run are for coffee if I'm out or if someone is chasing me."

This woman is a complete stranger, but in another life, we could be fast friends. "Oh, I agree. If only real life was more like the movies, I'd have no problem blowing half my rent money on a pair of Louboutins. I'm convinced I could rock the black patent leather stilettos look for every day wear if only I had a rich man buying me La Perla lingerie to wear beneath my Target business attire."

She shakes her head in mock disappointment. "Every woman's fantasy, for sure. But why stop there? It's the modern era. We should have billionaires falling at our feet and spoiling us silly while they ravish us in the bedroom with alpha dominance and also cook gourmet, Keto-friendly meals, so we can keep our slender feminine figures even as we pop out as many heirs to their fortunes as they desire."

I can't help but laugh. There's a kernel of truth to her ridiculous suggestion, and we both know it. What's so wrong with wanting it all?

"Ah, fantasy." Her cheeks are tinted with a hint of embarrassment, but she winks at me. "Between you and me, I don't consider it settling to find a man who works hard, loves me completely, and offers me the promise of a less than perfect future, so long as it's together."

I couldn't agree more. "There's a time and place for everything, but yes. Reality is where we must all exist."

"Speaking of reality…" Her smile is warm and inviting. All traces of skepticism from when she first answered her door are gone. "Who are you looking for?"

"Oh." I wave my hand like a completely exhausted idiot who's lost all sense of decorum. As if having this conversation about female fantasies isn't enough. Then again, fantasies aren't far from my mind these days. "It's the Big Apple. I don't expect you to know all your neighbors. We're modern women after all. Can't be too careful."

She nods in agreement even as she shrugs. "True, but New York is friendlier than most people think. We're not the stereotypical hardened city people who mind our own business to the detriment of leaving helpless victims to fend for themselves. Try me."

Why not? She seems nice; she's entertained me for a few minutes and provided a far better distraction than window shopping ever could. There's little chance she'll actually know him. "Ben Sharp is a dear friend of mine. We don't get to catch up nearly as often as we'd like, but since I was already in the city, I thought I'd drop by."

She's not able to quite mask the suspicion that returns to her gaze, even if it's muddled with curiosity. She opens the door wider. "Any dear friend of Ben's is a friend of mine. Come on in."

"That's okay." Awkwardness electrifies the air between us, and I'm not quite sure why. Only that I want to be rid of it. I have enough anxiety pecking at my brain lately. I was looking for refuge, not another layer of imprisonment over things I can't control. "I'll just move over and knock on the right door this time."

"You knocked on the right door the first time," she insists. "Ben isn't here just now. He's at a study group. He texted to say he'd be back within the hour, so you're welcome to come in and wait for him."

Much like earlier, I replay the past few moments over in my mind to be sure I understand correctly. "This is Ben's apartment?"

"One and the same." The woman holds out her hand with a formality that didn't exist between us seconds ago. "I'm Bethany. And you are...?"

Her question stifles the air between us, far sharper than the awkwardness before.

"Tori." I clear my throat to be sure she can hear me this time, strangely wishing I could channel Mike's quiet confidence in the face of anything life throws his way. "I'm Tori Russo. I take it you haven't heard my name before if you didn't recognize me."

Her eyebrows pop up into her stylishly sharp bangs. "I take it you've never heard of me before either if you seem surprised to find me here. Please. Come in."

Unlike when I shoved Mike out the door of his own truck, I hesitate. "I really shouldn't. I don't want to impose."

"I insist." She gestures again for me to step inside.

Not knowing what the next few hours may hold, my options are limited unless I want to wait at another cafe.

The moment she closes the door behind me, I find myself in a new and untraversed territory. Ben's apartment in college was the quintessential workaholic bachelor pad—sparse furniture, the bare minimum in home décor, and an empty fridge that only contained a nearly empty six-pack of craft beer and a few condiments left over from takeout.

I have a feeling if I was to open that door now, I'd find the healthiest, freshest produce lining the shelves of his refrigerator. Much like the plants flourishing on the few windowsills and the framed art gracing the walls. And the art books on the coffee table. He has a coffee table now! Not just old milk crates holding up lamps in the far corners of the room. Those have been replaced by stylish end tables made from repurposed old library card catalogues. On top of the one nearest me is a photo of the smiling couple, their arms wrapped around each other in an intimate embrace as they stand in front of the Statue of Liberty. She's holding out her hand. So, everyone who sees this picture can't help but notice the shiny rock on her ring finger.

They're engaged. He's been exploring his options all right. So much for being friends.

"Can I offer you something to drink?" she calls from the kitchen as the sounds of her rooting through cupboards float to my cotton-filled ears.

"No," I barely manage to cough out through my shock. "No, thank you. I really can't stay long. I'm meeting a friend soon on the other side of the river. It's the whole reason I was even in the city today in the first place."

Using the word friend to describe Mike tastes so unfamiliar on my tongue, unlike the photographic image of the man who was my first...everything.

His fiancée stands beside me, smiling as she gazes at the picture I can't stop stupidly staring at. "That was months ago, but you're the first friend I've met of Ben's who isn't mutual between us."

I have no idea what to say to that. In spite of—or maybe *because* of—the leading tone of her unasked questions.

*Who are you to Ben?*
*How far do you go back?*
*Why do you seem so upset?*

I'm upset, but not for the reasons she obviously thinks. Honestly, I'm surprised at how little this hurts. Shouldn't it feel like a knife stabbing me in the chest?

Still, uncertainty rolls off her in waves, and I feel genuinely bad about that. I didn't come here to wreck another woman's happiness. "I've known him since high school. We went to college together and broke up shortly after finishing our degrees at U of M, but we remained friends."

I wince when she gasps. That might have been a little *too much* honesty. I'm great at that lately.

Her gaze burns the side of my face, but there isn't any venom in her tone. Neither pity. "Not that good of friends if he didn't even share the exciting news of his engagement with you."

"No. I guess not."

She faces me fully. "Be straight with me—woman to woman. Should this raise red flags for me? You were obviously together for a long time. I've never heard of you, and you've never heard of me."

I study her expression. She's not gunning for my imminent death as she would be completely justified to. There's an underlying tension in the current between us, but also an openness that can't be denied. "Do you have doubts? About how much he loves you?"

"I don't know," she confesses, splaying her hands wide. "It all happened in the blink of an eye. We joked in the hallway about fantasies, but it was exactly that. A whirlwind romance that happened so fast, I didn't have time to second-guess myself until just now. I'm suddenly terrified I know nothing about him. Not really. Should I have doubts?"

She poses a genuine question, so I pause to give a thoughtful answer. Nothing sticks out in my mind to warn her about. Ben was good to me. I can't deny that. He never promised marriage, white picket fences, or a happily-ever-after. When he wasn't feeling it anymore, he broke it off rather than string me along. "No. He wouldn't have asked you to marry him if he didn't mean it. Ben is nothing if not a man of his word. Of honor."

"Are you okay?" She places a hesitant hand on my shoulder.

I want to hate her so much, but I can't.

Because I am okay. She said it in not so many words. For some reason, they just clicked. He offered her everything, and she felt confident enough in that moment to grab his promise with both hands.

We should all be so lucky.

I don't get a chance to answer because my phone dings with an incoming text.

Mike Mitchell: Where are you?

"I need to go," I tell Bethany. "Please tell Ben I said hello. And…don't doubt the love between you because of me. But, if at any time, you feel like you're not getting his one hundred and ten percent then be a modern woman. Don't settle for less than everything. We can have it all now, right?"

"Right." She nods, but it's more sad than resolute. Woman to woman. I like her more than ever. She leads me to the door she welcomed me through in spite of her misgivings. We both know it will be the only time we'll ever meet. Some open doors lead to closed ones and all that crap.

"I wish you the best," I tell her with sincerity.

"I hope you meet a billionaire who buys you La Perla. And who's an animal in the bedroom."

"Ben prefers vanilla missionary." I hate myself so much in this moment.

The sparkle in her eyes speaks volumes. "Not with me."

She closes the door, and I walk away. Down the stairwell, out into the suddenly damp New York City air. I gulp in lungfuls of it. There's something inherently cleansing about knowing for sure where I stand in the world. Soon, the rain will come.

> Tori Russo: Just left Ben's. I can meet you wherever you are.
> Mike Mitchell: I'll come to you. Text me your GPS location.

"Tori!" Even on a crowded sidewalk with my back turned after years apart, he still recognizes me. Just as I know his voice above the constant din of the city.

I turn around, and he's there. The finest droplets of a light mist sparkle in the air between us like the most poetic montage of first love. His memory will always make me smile.

"Goodbye, Ben," I whisper then turn around and make my way forward through the throngs of people.

"Tori, wait!"

I don't. I have my closure.

# Chapter 10
## Bad Day

### Mike

It's pouring. I never knew monsoons were a thing in New York City until today, but by the time I find Tori sitting in a window seat at a crowded cafe in Manhattan, my clothes are soaked through.

There's no way I can go in there. I'll only make a scene dripping water all over the shop, and I need to stay out of sight as much as possible. I knock on the window.

She startles, and her phone clatters to the tabletop. The second she locks eyes with me, she jumps up and collects her things then hightails it out of there to meet me on the sidewalk.

"What the fuck happened to your face?" she shouts over the noise of the downpour and car horns blaring through stalled traffic.

"Got in a fight with a frying pan and lost." I shrug and add another item on my mental list about what will make Peaches swear.

She reaches out to touch the claw marks that are plain as day across my cheek then thinks better of it and lets her hand fall to her side. "Frying pans don't leave marks like that."

"It looked a lot worse hours ago before all the rain washed away the rest of the Mace." I shake my head when she opens her mouth and cut her off at the pass instead. "How'd it go with Ben?"

"He's engaged."

I guess we've both had a shitty day. "Staring at each other while we get soaked to the bone is a little too dramatic for my taste. Can we get out of here?"

She frowns but nods. Then, she throws her arms around my waist and nuzzles her face against my chest.

She hasn't been able to look directly at me since that night in the hotel room, but now she's hugging me in the pouring rain in the middle of the busiest city in the world. Like no amount of embarrassment could hold her back.

I can't remember the last time someone put my needs above their own so plainly, and I want to give her the same in return. I wrap my arms around her, squeeze back, and bury my nose in her wet hair. She smells like her nickname—peaches and sunshine. I never knew happiness had a scent before.

It's not enough to shake off this shitty day, but it's a hell of a start.

She pulls back and gazes at me with a furrowed brow. "Where are you parked?"

We wind our way through throngs of other rain-soaked people. She follows where I lead without a word, linking her arm through mine when the crowds threaten to separate us. She silently holds her hand out for the keys. I oblige. My head is pounding. With the concussion the ER doctor diagnosed me with, I'm in no shape to drive.

If the team docs find out I refused to be admitted for overnight observation...hell, if they find out about the concussion at all, I might be benched from off-season training activities.

Tori doesn't press me for any more information. She's got her hands full with heavy traffic, heavier rain, and my giant truck that was the only thing I bought for myself with my signing bonus.

It's not until we're on the highway headed north that she finally breaks. "Where's Evie?"

I tell her the run-down of today's events.

Tori chews her lip and blinks at the windshield a few times. "I want to hate her for what she's put you through. For what she obviously did to you today, but I...can't. I just can't. I'm a woman, too. Never in my worst nightmares can I truly, really imagine living through what she's been through." She takes a deep breath. "Don't be mad at me, but after the little you revealed at the wedding, I had to dig deeper and do my own research to fully know what you're up against with that situation. I'm not about to pretend I understand what you and your friends have been through or to give you even free therapist type of advice about how to cope. What I will promise is to do my best to keep this out of the press. I will call in whatever reinforcements I need to make that happen, okay?"

The only thing stopping me from reaching across the cab of my truck to hold her hand is the horrible driving conditions. She needs to concentrate, and I need to man up instead of using her for comfort she's probably not comfortable with. "Rob's taking care of it, actually. The only thing I'm going to need your help with is laying low until my face heals."

"Done."

We drive the rest of the way to Albany in silence.

# Chapter 11
Lie to Me

## Tori

"You're sure this color matches my skin tone? I'm warm, and you're cool."

I smother the urge to laugh. Not that it's not funny. But when a six foot, two-hundred-twenty-pound professional football running back asks for the hundredth time if my concealer is the right shade for his face, I know he's genuinely concerned about wearing makeup for the first time in his life.

"I can't even tell you have anything on," I assure him. "We didn't need to come out in public tonight. Not that I'm unappreciative of your offer to take me to dinner, but you could've thanked me for all the work I've done in the privacy of your home without anyone else seeing us."

He leans back on his side of the booth, finally seeming to relax about his appearance. "I needed to get out of there for a while. I'm a jock. I know practice makes perfect. I've gotta get back to team activities eventually, so I'm going to have to get used to either wearing makeup all the time or lying about a cat I don't actually own."

"I could *actually* adopt a cat for you, so you won't have to lie," I offer.

He doesn't laugh, so I try another route. "The scratches are healing nicely. I don't think the scars will be permanent. It's just going to take a little more time than we expected for the marks to fade to normal."

He barks out a laugh then glances around before leaning across the table to whisper, "It sounds sick, but part of me wishes they wouldn't fade at all. I've been riding Evie's ass for years about how to deal with the way worse scars she still has, and this is the closest I've ever been to getting a taste of my own medicine. I get it now more than I ever did before. And hell. It's not even nearly the same thing. My best friend attacked me in a terrified moment of mistaken identity. As soon as she realized what she'd done, she couldn't stop crying and apologizing. A fucking sicko attacked her in a much worse way and almost killed her, and now he's out of prison. It's not fair. Fuck, it's so unfair."

"It is an absolute privilege to know you, Michael Mitchell." I stare at him in awe. As handsome as I thought he was at first sight, as much as he's gained my respect for the way he's reacted to my drunken antics, he looks absolutely brilliant in the dim light of this elegant restaurant. His glowing appearance has nothing to do with the fact that he's footing the bill for this very expensive meal. He's gone from all-American stud to knight in shining armor in my opinion. "My job aside, I am so honored to be sitting here with you right now."

He scoffs. "Why would you say a thing like that? I literally just admitted to you I've been a terrible friend for years to someone who means the world to me."

I swirl the wine in my glass and think about how to say what I want to tell him in a way that won't send him recoiling. I'm all too aware Mike isn't comfortable being in the spotlight even though he's one of the most deserving players—on and off the field—of accolades. I probably wouldn't be this honest with him at all if not for the fact that he's already seen me at my worst. "Here's the thing. I conducted research about Evie, so I could be aware enough to manage any potential bad press that could happen as fallout from the situation you're caught up in, but it's impossible for me to research your relationship with her beyond what you tell me. What you've *shown* me by your actions is your deep love for her. My brothers love me, but they would never, ever admit to someone else that they haven't always necessarily done right by me. I don't even think they're as aware as you are that they haven't given me what I've needed over the years."

Mike smiles tightly as the server delivers our dinners, nodding instead of answering with words that everything looks to our liking. He waits until the guy's well out of earshot before continuing our conversation. "What have you needed over the years that they haven't given you?"

"Are you asking because you're curious to learn more about me or because you need some free therapy to figure out how to move forward with Evie?"

He tries to hide his smile behind a mouthful of steak. It's adorable and unsettling. He already knows way more about me than he should. "Both."

Well, then. My answer better be doubly worth his time and attention. "I appreciate any love that someone gives me. Don't get me wrong. God knows there are all sorts of horrible stories out there, and I'm not comparing myself to those. I guess...I want their support more than them trying to do everything for me. I want to know they trust me enough to let me stand on my own two feet and make my own mistakes. *How can I help* goes much further than *I told you so.* Does that make sense?"

Mike swallows thickly. "It's about trust?"

I didn't pare it down quite that simply, but..."It is. Love without trust is just affection. Affection isn't a bad thing, but real, selfless love? That requires a heck of a lot of trust."

"Shit." Mike leans back and wipes his mouth with his napkin. "That's why she's still clinging to Rob." He shakes his head and stares at his lap. "All I saw were his failures—the way he stepped out on their marriage when she asked him to—but I guess she saw it as proving he could be trusted to do what she needed instead of what he wanted. I've never done that. Not with her, not with my sisters, not with anyone."

"I don't think that's true. You certainly proved to me you understand trust very well." My cheeks flame. "I did not at all mean to imply you love me just because you haven't blabbed about the horrid hotel incident."

"Maybe you love me because you haven't said a word about it either."

We stare at each other.

He glances between his empty plate and my untouched one. "Do you not like your dinner? I can send it back if you want something else."

Thank God he's giving us another out. I honestly had no idea where to carry this conversation from there. "I, um, didn't want to talk with my mouth full."

"And I inhaled my food while yours went cold." He chuckles. "Please eat. Enough about me anyway. I don't want to be the kind of guy who only takes and doesn't give anymore. I can't change the past, but I can do better going forward. Just like on the field."

"With an attitude like that," I point my fork at him and stick to a safer topic, "you won't even need me this season. You're going to be the best player for the Albany Wolves all by yourself."

"I need you, Tori," he insists. "I have no idea what's going to happen this season, but I have this bad feeling things are going to get way worse before they get better."

I have to force myself to concentrate on our conversation because this steak cuts like butter and is without a doubt the best thing I've ever put in my mouth. "What do you mean? Things seem settled. Everyone appears to be behaving themselves in the public eye."

He pushes his plate away and leans closer across the table, lowering his voice to a harsh whisper. "Yeah. For now. What happens if Rob and Evie's secret marriage gets out? I'm one of only two other people who know about it. I'm not a rocket scientist, but I'm not stupid either. The press will figure out the timeline, and then they'll hound me and Alex about it. Alex is a wild card as it is. My teammates already got the wrong idea about Evie attending some of my games last season. What are they going to think if she's not here this year? I'm about to start training camp. I can't afford that kind of gossip interfering with my sophomore season. I promise to behave myself, but I can't control anyone else."

"Hmm." Those are all valid points. Considering the gossip sites David often uses to research his marketing plans, professional players are judged by way more than just their stats on gameday. These potential scenarios could all very well end up being the wrong kind of publicity to elevate Mike to the level the team wants him to be in this year. "We need some sort of distraction in case any of this stuff pops up. Something that will make the press and fans focus on *you* instead of the people close to you."

"If you think adopting a cat will do the trick, then let's do it." Mike gazes at me evenly. "I *trust* you, Peaches."

Suddenly, there's a lot more resting on my shoulders. I can't afford to make mistakes that won't only affect me. Like that last time.

# Chapter 12
## Beautiful Distraction

### Mike

"So, I have good news and bad news. Which do you want first?"

Uh-oh. Peaches doesn't usually interrupt me while I'm working, so this must be big. I lower the leg press back into position slowly. "What's up?"

"You got some news for me, too, baby?" Templeman leers at Tori from the machine beside me.

The guy has turned out to be all right in spite of acting like an ass sometimes. He's one of the few teammates I sort of consider a friend after an entire year of getting to know the other Wolves, but my prediction has come true. He's like dealing with another Alex. If Templeman isn't talking about football, then he's blabbing about his latest conquest. I have no idea how he has the energy to perform at a professional level with all the energy he's expending between the sheets. Or in the back of an Uber. Or in the champagne room at the exclusive strip club my teammates are always trying to drag me to.

"Shut up and finish your reps," I snap at him. "You know damn well she's one of the people who make us look good in the media, so she's off-limits. She deserves a little respect unless you want her to leak a story about your secret love for unicorns."

Templeman shakes his head. "No shame in my game. Just because I haven't found the perfect unicorn yet don't mean I'm gonna quit trying."

"Why can't I just have normal friends?" I mutter.

He grins.

Tori clears her throat to get my attention. Her face is redder than her hair, which I didn't think was possible. "Mr. Mitchell, follow me, please."

She turns on the ball of her foot and storms out of the weight room, not even waiting for me to follow.

Templeman whistles. "Shit, man. She must have really bad news. I've never seen her look that mad."

I have. The morning after she got shit-faced in a hotel room and stripped for me. She wasn't mad at me so much as herself. I guess that's changed.

"Text me if you need help," Templeman says in all seriousness. "I got your back, bro."

I might take him up on that depending on what the good news is. Already, worst-case scenarios of my hotel room being bugged with a nanny cam are popping up in my mind.

The hallway is empty when I exit the weight room, so on a wild guess, I find the nearest conference room.

Sure enough, Tori's waiting for me, tapping her foot against the linoleum with her arms crossed over her chest while she does her best to glare a hole through me.

"What's wrong?"

"Remember that little conversation we had about being supportive instead of trying to fix everything?"

Fuck. I called it. "Someone has a video of the hotel room incident, don't they?"

"What?" She cocks her head back in obvious confusion. "No! I mean back there with Templeman! You should have let *me* handle it."

I can breathe again. This is not a problem at all. "I can't let him talk to you that way."

Her eyes narrow. "Every member of this organization had to earn their right to be here, whether on the field or behind the scenes. Just because I have breasts and a vagina does not mean I get an exception. If they can tease you by sending you prostitutes and nicknaming you Monk, then I can take a little heat, too."

I hear the words coming out of her mouth. I do. They just don't make any sense, and they're getting blurred by the mental image of her naked body. "Um, *no*."

"Um, *yes*," she insists. Right before she all but collapses into the nearest chair and lays her head on the desk. Her voice comes out muffled. "Fuck. It doesn't matter anyway. This is never going to work."

Double shit. She cursed. This is worse than I thought. I close the door behind me to give us a little privacy. If she's here to tell me I'm about to ride the bench for the upcoming season, then I'm going to need some time to regroup before facing my teammates again.

"Peaches." I take a deep breath then sink into the chair closest to her. "Give it to me straight. Bad news first."

She raises her head. There are actual tears glistening in her eyes. "*I'm* your distraction for the rest of the season."

Yeah, she is. It's a problem, sure, but I'm handling it. We keep things professional between us, even as friends. "I asked for the bad news first."

"That is the bad news!" she shrieks.

I still don't understand why she's so upset. "Is this because I saw you pee?"

She narrows her eyes then pushes a folder toward me that I hadn't even noticed her carrying before. I've gotten a lot better at reigning in my dick with the practice of having her around all the time, but I'm not blind enough not to be sidetracked by the dress she's wearing that hugs all her curves. The problem is that I know exactly what's under her clothes, and it's becoming a huge distraction from focusing on my job.

I open the folder only to stare at a picture of myself. With Tori. At dinner over a week ago before my face had healed enough for me to show up for conditioning without makeup on.

There are more.

Photos of Tori coming and going from my home when she brought me groceries and all sorts of weird creams to help my face heal faster during the two weeks I laid as low as possible. Tori and I staring at each other in the pouring rain in New York City. My arms wrapped around Tori when I gave in and accepted her comfort.

I can't believe my eyes even as I say a silent prayer of thanks that there are no photos of us leaving the hotel in Ironville together. "People have been following me? Taking pictures of us when we didn't know? Or give permission?"

"You really don't understand how this whole celebrity thing works, do you?"

I glance up at her sullen voice only to find her not looking at me. She's rubbing her forehead with her eyes closed like she's rocking the sort of headache I had after being whacked with a frying pan that thankfully wasn't cast iron.

"I'm not a celebrity. I'm a football player."

It's a definite sign how annoyed she is by the amount of glare she manages with only one eye cracked open. "You're a *professional* football player who made a name for himself by being one of the best rookies the Wolves have ever signed to the roster. Your hard work is paying off on the field, which means you're now a celebrity off of it."

Holy hell. I'd never admit it to them, but I've spent many years being a little jealous of Rob and Alex. No matter how hard I worked or what my stats looked like, they were always the stars of the show. Quarterbacks are like the lead singers on a football team. They get all the attention anyway, but Rob also comes from a famous football family. He didn't necessarily enjoy the limelight, but Alex sure as shit still lives for it. His personality is as big as the numbers he puts up on his record in any given season, and the ladies love him because he loves them right back. He's always been the fan favorite—both in high school and in college.

But me? I'm just the guy who busted my ass to get where I am today. I don't come from football stock. I don't sleep around. I play the game I love, and I'm sure as hell grateful for the obscene paycheck that allows me to provide for my family.

I can't screw up this chance before my body gives out, but I don't want to give up my freedom and privacy either.

"Do you, uh... Am I supposed to make a statement about these shots to clear up any misunderstandings?"

"No," Tori answers, her gaze downcast and her shoulders slumped. "We're going to run with them."

Maybe I should confess my concussion diagnosis to the team docs because nothing this woman says to me today makes any sense. "I don't understand. We're running with what, exactly?"

"I'm your distraction against any bad press for this season," she repeats slowly. "There aren't too many of these photos floating around the internet, but management wants to blow on these embers until they're flames elevating you to the next level of celebrity status."

Oh, hell no.

I let myself whack off to fantasies of Tori's naked body exactly once a week, and that's it. I've given in enough. There's no way I can afford to have her temptation shoved in my face for the entire season. I'll never make it.

"Absolutely not." I put the pictures back in their folder, crushing them a bit for good measure. "If you're telling me we're supposed to fake a relationship just to give the fans something to talk about that isn't related to my stats, then no way. I watched football slowly crush my best friend for years. I won't let my sisters anywhere near my teammates. I'm never going to willingly sign you up for this shit."

Tori nods slowly, but she still won't meet my gaze. "You have every right to tell management you don't want me to be your fake girlfriend."

"Okay." I stand up so fast the chair goes rolling back into the wall behind me. "Who do I need to talk to?"

She sticks her tongue in her cheek and finally makes direct eye contact. "The CEO of the Albany Wolves."

# Chapter 13
## In the End

### Tori

"I'M GOING to miss you so much, sweetie," Kaylie croons as she watches me shut down my computer for the last time. Adding insult to injury, she's been assigned to escort me from the building after ensuring I don't steal any confidential team documents.

"No, you're not."

She scoffs. "Honestly, Tori. You were an intern. It's not like you've ever been a permanent part of the team. You weren't even happy about being signed onto another season, and you're always going on and on about how you can't wait to get started on your master's degree. Well, now you can! I'm happy for you that you finally get to move on with your life and do whatever you want!"

She's not wrong. Except that I'm going to have to find another job until I can apply for a program *next* year. All the spots are already full for the upcoming academic calendar. Basically getting fired from this internship means I can't use it on my resume. No one here would give me a glowing recommendation either. I'm back to square one. The past year has been a waste after all. I cringe just thinking about my brothers saying *I told you so* when I return home with my tail tucked between my legs.

I take a deep breath and continue shoving the few personal mementos from my desk into a small cardboard box. At least I can leave with my head held high. I am *not* sleeping my way to the top, no sir.

I am going to miss my friend though. If I had any doubts about the nature of our relationship, Mike's insistence he would not put me through anything he wouldn't want for Evie or his sisters erased them.

A horrible, awful thought slinks into my brain. One I should have considered earlier in spite of being too shell shocked to absorb anything other than the impossible directive assigned to me.

"Who's taking over Mike's PR now?"

Kaylie grins.

My stomach drops.

"You have to be careful with him," I warn her. "He doesn't want his family involved, and you need to respect that. He values his privacy and that of his friends. If you don't prove to him that he can trust you, you're not going to get anywhere, no matter what top-tier media campaign David has planned. He's sensitive, Kaylie. He's a good man. Don't think of him like a big, bad professional football player. He's more like…like…a teddy bear!"

She rolls her eyes. "If he wants to take his place at the top of the league, then he's going to have to learn how to do what he's told."

"You're not going to be his fake girlfriend, right?" My words speed up as panic freezes my veins. "Because that's a horrible idea! If his fans think he's in a relationship with me, then moving on to you is only going to be the wrong kind of press we want for him, right? Right? I mean, it's not like David has a list of women waiting for him to run through like the kind of player we *don't* want to market him as. We want him to make the team and the league look good, not bad. We don't want him to seem like…like…well, like Alex Fossoway!"

Kaylie gapes at me like she's dealing with a raving lunatic. "You're really putting a lot of thought into this considering you never wanted this assignment."

David appears at Kaylie's side. "You put so much thought into last season's assignment that you won another, and yet now you are giving up without a fight. Explain that to me, darling."

"David!" I latch onto the lapels of his jacket. "Oh, thank God you're here! You have to talk to Mr. Gallo. This is the wrong way to go with Mike's career, and he wants no parts of it. Kaylie can't be his fake girlfriend!"

David disengages my hands from his likely expensive jacket the way one would pick up a dead bug to dispose of. "Unlike you and Mr. Mitchell, the rest of us realize we do what the front offices demand if we want to be paid. However much I agree with your sentiments, I do not question Mr. Gallo's direct orders."

So, no one in this department actually cares what Mike wants. "He'll never agree to it."

David tsks. "He will. He doesn't strike me as the careless type of player who would risk jeopardizing his contract or his playing time. It might be uncomfortable at first, but he'll get used to the act. It only has to be public enough to generate some interesting publicity."

I can't believe my ears. I always thought football players were treated like gods who could do whatever they wanted. Isn't that why they tend to generate bad publicity? According to David, they're more like slaves.

"What's going on?"

I jump at the low voice behind me.

"Mr. Mitchell." David smiles, but it's full of pity. "We were just discussing you."

"You're leaving?"

I turn toward the accusation in Mike's voice with my shoulders hitched up to my ears from guilt that's only getting worse by the second. "Um…"

"Mike," Kaylie croons, stepping up beside me with her hand extended. "I'm going to take over as your new PR rep. And…we have plenty to talk about."

Mike's gaze darts between me, Kaylie, David, and my empty desk with the single box on top. His eyes return to my face, a frown pulling down his mouth. "You're being fired."

David steps up, his voice soothing and meant to deescalate. "Miss Russo has elected to give a more senior member of our staff the chance to represent you the way you deserve."

One of Mike's big hands wraps around my waist, then he drags me toward him, leaning down so he's staring directly into my eyes with a focus that sends shivers down my spine. "Peaches," he whispers on a rumble. "Do you want this job?"

At first? No. Now? I can't just throw him to the wolves, even though that's the name of the team that's forcing us to make this stupid choice. "Yes."

The kiss that I never thought I'd experience again has nothing on this one.

# Chapter 14
Whatever It Takes

## Mike

"You're mad."

"I'm not mad! I'm thinking!"

Sure. That's why she hasn't said a word to me in hours. The last time she was this silent for this long, she was nursing a severe hangover and clinging to a shit ton of morning-after embarrassment.

We've been sitting across from each other in my living room ever since I dragged her away from her office, so we could huddle over these new developments.

She's on the couch. I'm in my favorite chair.

This living room is huge.

"Are you mad because I over-helped instead of supported, or are you mad because I kissed you?"

She glares at me. "So help me God, if you apologize for another kiss, I will actually let them have their way with you."

I smother the grin threatening to erupt on my face. Thanks to her night of drunken blabbing, I already know exactly how she feels about the first kiss. It wasn't too much of a gamble to assume she wouldn't hate a second. I would never have done it otherwise.

A drunk woman's striptease is a sober woman's thoughts and all that.

"Okay, okay..." She rubs her forehead. She's been doing that a lot today. "Tell me again what Mr. Gallo said when you refused the fake relationship thing."

Alex tried to warn me about this before we got into our public blowout that brought Tori into my life. He flat-out told me our teams own us, and we have to lick whatever they tell us to if we want to stay in the game. I didn't believe him.

Now? I almost want to call him up and apologize for being wrong. And thank him. Tori might be a beautiful distraction I can't afford, but I can't imagine my life without her either.

"Mr. Gallo said he understood my reservations, but he didn't see the harm in me having a little fun and enjoying my down time in a way that would make me seem more interesting than a sack of potatoes."

Tori narrows her eyes. "I can't believe he said that to you!"

"I can't believe you were almost fired for refusing to sleep your way to the top."

That's the other reason I rolled the dice and kissed her in front of her co-workers. She would rather lose a job she deserves than have it for the wrong reasons. I can't just sit by and let that happen.

She finally opens her eyes to me even though her shoulders slump. That's another pattern from today I hate to see. "Just because you point-blank told them you won't work with anyone but me doesn't mean Mr. Gallo is going to give me my job back. We'll have to wait and see if David's able to smooth things over."

"He will. Mr. Gallo wants this to happen. Even though they're willing to go against what *I* want, he's not going to rock the boat any more than he has to. He also wants me to cooperate, not be a sack of potatoes."

Finally, a smile breaks free on her face. I even get a little laugh out of her. "For the record, I don't think you're a sack of potatoes."

"I know." Her smile lets my own free. "You think I'm a stud who kisses better than any man in the universe."

She falls back against the couch, all laughter evaporating. Her voice is a whisper against my skin. "I honestly figured after that horrible display, that was the main reason you didn't want me to be your fake girlfriend. And heck...I couldn't blame you. I still don't understand why you're going to bat for me like this. Kaylie would be much better at this job than I am."

She's not wrong, but for all the wrong reasons. "That's what you've spent hours thinking about over there? Trying to figure out my *motives*?"

She nods.

"Are you worried I only want to keep you around to get you into bed? Because I've already seen you naked?"

She shakes her head so rapidly, her hair flies around like a whip to her face. A burst of peach darkens her cheeks.

I lean forward, resting my elbows on my knees. Apparently, I need to be even more crystal clear. "I already told you, and I wasn't lying. That night actually made me trust you more, not less. What if that had been Kaylie assigned to accompany me to the wedding, huh? How do you think that would have played out if she had caught me with my dick in my hand?"

I wouldn't have been beating off to fantasies of Tori's co-worker, but that's not the point.

Tori flattens her brow and does her best to glare at me, but she can't quite pull it off. "Kaylie would never have gotten stupidly drunk to keep you out of trouble. She would have used…other methods."

"Yeah, and it wouldn't have worked," I admit. "So, I probably would have gotten into a fight anyway, and then she would have used my *definitely marketable material* against me."

I'm between a rock and a rapidly hardening place. I can't trust anyone as much as Tori, but no one else would be this dangerous to my focus on my job either.

Tori's lips twitch with a smile she tries so hard to hold back. She cuts a quick glance to my crotch before her cheeks really flame. "If she didn't get as drunk as I did, then she wouldn't have been in the same hotel room with you to…see you…anyway."

"You just said she would have used other methods," I argue. I can guess pretty easily what those other methods would be.

"You just said those other methods wouldn't have worked." Tori raises her eyebrows.

Well, shit. We're at an impasse.

"Fine." I lean back in my chair. "I did. That doesn't mean I still don't think you're the best woman for this job. I don't want to work with Kaylie. I don't want to have to refuse her methods. We're actually friends, and you've already done great work for me. I don't see why we can't keep this going as long as we need to—for both our jobs."

Tori sighs. "Whether I actually sleep my way to the top or not, it's going to look like it to the media. As soon as I found out they were planning to run with the fake relationship thing with or without me, I intended to find you and warn you. I don't want to tarnish my career, but I can't let them steer yours in a direction you don't want either."

This is exactly why I meant what I said when I told David I wouldn't work with anyone but Tori. Sure, she knows some of my secrets, but after today, I'm willing to bet the rest of the PR department knows everything about six degrees of Mike Mitchell, too. If they know the worst of it, there's no one I trust more than Tori not to use all my skeletons against me.

"Anyone in marketing is going to understand the situation you've been put in. You don't have to worry about me overstepping your bounds, so just keep doing the great job you've been doing all along."

I'm patting myself on the back for not letting my dick override my brain, but Tori winces.

"I have to...confess something to you."

Every muscle in my body snaps to attention. Dick? What dick? She's about to castrate me like she could have that night if I'd confessed I was jerking off over fantasies of her.

"There's a very good chance Mr. Gallo won't rehire me because... I'm just an intern."

I breathe a sigh of relief.

"I lied to you when we first met, and I introduced myself as your assigned PR manager. I only have a bachelor's degree in marketing and business. I wanted to take a year off before pursuing my master's to gain some real-world experience. My father landed me this position, and I honestly have no idea how. I never even watched football before I got hired by the Wolves." She takes a deep breath then expels it in a rush I feel all the way across the room. "After your fight with Alex, I was assigned to be your handler. I was told to look pretty and be a good distraction to keep you out of any more trouble." She shakes her head and casts her gaze to her lap. "I wasn't willing to sell myself for a position I didn't even really want, and I let my ego get the better of me when I tried to take matters into my own hands by running the sort of media campaign you wanted last season instead of the smear campaign against Alex that the rest of the department was ready and waiting with. I did just barely good enough passing off my curated content as yours to convince Mr. Gallo that I was worth offering to pay for my master's degree in exchange for me signing on for another season."

"So, you're still in the same position you didn't want to be in." Damn. And I thought I had it bad.

She lifts her eyes, which are full of tears. "Out of everything I just confessed to you, that's what you're zeroing in on? Trust is everything to you, and I lied! To your face!"

I don't want to make her feel worse, but I kind of figured out most of her confession on my own. I might not be the same sort of star player as Rob and Alex, but I've been around my fair share of media specialists. Tori's methods have never been as devious and complicated. Like the one we're caught up in now anyway.

I abandon my comfy spot and cross the room to sit beside her, taking her hand in mine to show her I'm serious. If she wants an easy out, then I'll give her one. Maybe she can save us both. "If you want to move on and get your master's, then I'm behind you one hundred percent. If you want to do that while getting your real-world experience, then I'll just hire you privately as my PR manager on the side. Most players do. It's kind of weird that the team assigned me one, in-house. I might not be the kind of celebrity the team expects me to be, but I do know that much. It was my own stupid behavior that caused all this in the first place. We'll do whatever you want to do, Peaches."

There's a fire burning in her warm brown eyes I've only seen hints of until now. "I want to prove them wrong. All of them. About both of us. You are going to be a bigger football celebrity than even Alex without giving up a single thing you hold dear. And I'm going to get you there. I'm not selling out; I'm doing *my job*."

My dick really hates being referred to as a job. My brain says this won't end well.

# Chapter 15
## Faking It

### Tori

"Stop acting so awkward," I hiss.

"I can't help it," he mumbles back.

"If this doesn't look as organic as it did in those photos, this new plan is going to go over as well as my SpongeBob memes that I posted to your accounts."

Not only that, but Mr. Gallo is only giving me a month to see if we have the chemistry to pull this off. If he decides he doesn't like what he sees, then Kaylie takes over.

Mike's hand hovers over my back instead of actually making contact with any part of my body. It's a wonder he's as expert of a kisser as he is. "We weren't on a date in any of those photos."

"We're not really on a date now," I whisper then smile as I spy a smartphone pointed in our direction while we wait in the lobby for our reserved table at Albany's newest restaurant that's already garnering five-star ratings. "People are watching, darling."

His face puckers. "Are they listening, too?"

"I don't know. Maybe. Why?"

He sucks in a breath through his teeth as he tries—and fails spectacularly—to smile. "Darling sounds so...wrong."

I agree, but at least I'm trying. "You call me Peaches. Most couples who are in love have pet names for each other. I'm just trying to make it feel as authentic as possible for you, so you'll loosen up."

The fake smile slides off his face. "We're supposed to be in love? I thought Mr. Gallo just wanted me to act like I'm having fun instead of staying in my house when I'm not at work."

I stifle the urge to roll my eyes. Between the two of us, the fans who are here spying on their favorite Wolf are going to think we're arguing, not out on a date. "Again, I'm trying to tailor this to meet your specific needs and personality. You're not the kind of guy who has commitment issues and only serial dates for the benefit of hookups. That's not how you want to appear in the public eye, right?"

He raises an eyebrow. "Maybe I do have commitment issues, and that's why I never date at all."

I lean in to study his face in the dim lighting, but his expression gives nothing away. "You were with your ex-girlfriend for like, four years. You don't have commitment issues."

Frankly, my bet is on her having commitment issues. How could she just throw away a man who kisses like Mike does and is packing the sort of...package...Mike has?

"Maybe I have them now *because* of the ex-girlfriend I was with for four years who cheated on me for unknown reasons."

That's a fair point, and information worth knowing in case she ever pops back up now that her ex is a millionaire celebrity. "Do you want me to do some digging to see if I can find an actual reason for her cheating on you? Or at least to make sure she isn't a threat now?"

"No." He cracks a small smile. "Leave the past in the past where it belongs."

I'm definitely going to check up on her anyway. "Will do...Mikey?"

"I don't hate it, but Evie calls me that. And we have never kissed. Ever." He shudders.

"You really do think of her like a sister, don't you?" My brothers always swore to me guys and girls could never be just friends.

"I really do. She's one of the few people who knows everything there is to know about me. She actually knows me better than my real sisters."

The way he says it makes me wonder what secrets she keeps for him the way he's kept quiet for her. Their bond is obviously stronger than anyone knows after everything they've weathered together. Mike bears absolutely no ill will about the fact that she attacked him.

He suddenly perks up and does a double-take as a server barrels past us, loaded down with trays of food. "Hey, Peaches?"

"Yes, honey?"

He shakes his head. That one isn't going to work either. "How severe is your seafood allergy?"

"Severe enough that I carry an epi-pen with me everywhere. I should probably teach you how to use it, just in case."

He finally grabs onto me, but it's not romantic at all. His large hand circles my elbow in a vice grip before he pulls me toward the door. "We can't eat here."

No matter how much I dig my heels into the modern, chic cement floor, I'm not strong enough to withstand his manhandling. "Mike," I hiss. "Stop! You're creating a scene. We can't just leave! It's good publicity for you to be at a new, raved-about restaurant in town."

He glances down at me with a pointed expression. "It would be bad publicity if you die while we're on a fake date. A waiter just went past us with all kinds of seafood on his tray. What if you inhaled some of it?"

"My allergy isn't that severe. I wasn't going to order seafood. I'm not trying to make you look bad by doing anything that's going to cause *a scene*," I re-emphasize.

"How do you know the table next to us won't order seafood, and traces of it won't get onto your plate?"

"It's a five-star restaurant, not a dingy diner. I'm sure it'll be fine."

He holds the door open for me. "That's like asking a team to play a Superbowl-winning game during the preseason. The staff hasn't gelled yet; they haven't had enough practice. Give it a month or two, then maybe we'll come back after we call ahead to make sure all necessary precautions are in place."

"Mr. Mitchell!" A balding man who looks to be in his mid-fifties races toward us, an expression of panic etched into his face before he screeches to a stop nearly an inch from where Mike has suddenly positioned himself between us. "My apologies for the wait! Don't leave yet! We're getting your table ready right now! Your meal is on the house!"

Mike wraps a protective, beefy arm around my shoulders. "Oh, no worries. It's not about the wait, and we're perfectly willing to pay like any other customers. I'm just not feeling very well, so we thought we'd head out. We'll be back though. You can count on it."

The man who's obviously the owner sweeps his gaze up and down Mike's large body with suspicion.

Knowing very well how to read a tough opposition, Mike clamps his other hand over his stomach and leans more heavily against me. "Do you mind driving, babe? I might need to puke out the window."

Why does *babe* sound so natural coming out of his mouth in the middle of a hefty lie?

I'm always telling Mike I'm at his service, so I hold my hand out for the keys to help him sell this ruse to the manager who's taken a healthy step away from us.

"You will have a table ready and waiting anytime you want to return!" The man says before turning and dashing away.

Mike leads me out to the parking lot like he's quite happy with himself.

"That wasn't necessarily good press for you either." I open the passenger side door for him in case anyone is still watching. "Instead of embarrassing yourself to anyone within earshot, you could have just told him you were concerned for my allergy. That might have even given him enough motivation to make a safe space for others with food allergies in Albany."

Mike leans against the door of his truck, that same smug smile still firmly entrenched on his award-worthy lips. "Like I said, this success is all still so new for him and the entire staff. You saw how busy they are in there tonight. Even if he *wants* to do the right thing, he's not *capable* of it just now. Give it some time, then we'll use your food allergy awareness platform to effect some changes in the Albany area."

I'm a little too enchanted by how much Mike just proved he genuinely cares for my welfare in spite of being on a fake date. He didn't even use me as his excuse for bailing. He simply took the load onto himself without question or hesitation.

I've known since our first meeting that he's an absolute gem of a man. If I'm not careful, I'll be blinded by his brilliance and lose myself to the charade that it's my job to sell to the public. It's time for a dose of professionalism.

"Is that why the Sing Out foundation doesn't get more publicity from you, Alex, and Rob? Because you think the general public is aware of the problem, but not ready or willing to take action to solve it yet?"

My question erases the smile from his face. His voice exudes a deep sadness. "That foundation should never have been created in the first place."

"Why not? It's a truly noble cause—one you're all organically invested in. If the three of you put a little effort into making it your main charitable platform, you might be surprised at how many people would support ending sexual violence."

Mike leans down into my personal space. "None of what Evie went through— what we *all* went through on the sidelines—should ever have been made public. The only reason it was is because fans can't seem to draw the line between professional and private anymore. You should understand exactly how that feels since you're caught up in this mess. We're out on a date even though you never wanted to sleep your way to the top. You were willing to put your life on the line to make me look good just in the local press tonight. It's only a hop, skip, and a jump to having your deepest, darkest nightmares splayed out for the world to judge." He straightens and heaves a deep sigh. "Sometimes, I think football isn't worth it. Having my life—the lives of the people I care about—on full display isn't worth the money. But when I feel like quitting, I remind myself that my mom and sisters are counting on me. I owe them whatever I can give. I don't have the brains to be a rocket scientist, but I work damn hard to be good at football. I'm *capable* of that. So, I'm going to keep doing it until I can't anymore. That doesn't mean I'm going to share the people I love with the rest of the world, so I can get to the next level of celebrity and land a bigger underwear deal than Alex."

After such impassioned words, his heartbeat is surprisingly steady when I place my hand on his chest to hopefully soothe his warranted fears. "I'm willing to put my life on the line for you because I understand—and can manage—my own risks. In my opinion, you are worth every ounce of energy I can give, just like you believe your family and friends are worth your protection and effort."

He runs a gentle hand down my cheek that feels anything but fake. The backs of his rough fingers say more in silence than any pet name ever could. "I am not so selfish that I would ever ask *anyone* to give up *anything* for me. I'll do what I can without expecting anything in return. Now...since we have to be on this fake date for both our jobs, how about we find a restaurant that won't potentially kill you?"

I chuckle and step back from the illusion of his caress. "It's not surf and turf, but how do you feel about pizza? Hold the anchovies."

He stares at me with a deadpan expression. "Peaches, I'm a professional running back. So long as we're not putting pineapples on our pizza, I'm down for anything I can eat to keep up the energy required to do my job."

I round the bed of the truck then hoist myself up into the driver's seat as Mike buckles his seatbelt. "I still feel bad about you giving up a five-star meal in favor of fast food. How do you know so much about food allergies if you don't have one, anyway?"

He glances over at me as the engine turns over. "Rob is deathly allergic to coconut. Evie hasn't eaten any in years because of it. To this day, I don't think he has any idea it used to be her favorite flavor."

"So, technically, not only does Evie know more about you than your own sisters, but you also know more about her than even her husband."

Mike nods. "Yep."

"Does she know why you don't like pineapples on pizza?"

He laughs. "That doesn't take over a decade and a flood under the bridge to figure out. Pineapple on pizza is disgusting. If that's what you're into, I'm not sure I want to even date you for show."

As we pull out of the parking lot, it occurs to me that for as much as I've learned about Mike Mitchell in the past year, I have no idea what would make him fake break up with me. Except fake cheating, of course.

# Chapter 16
## Smile Like You Mean It

### Mike

"Peaches! Hey!"

I'm not excited to see her. I'm *pretending* to be excited after two weeks of my Tori-less existence because there are a ton of cameras floating around the field.

*Keep lying to yourself, Mikey.* Strangely, the voice in my head sounds a hell of a lot like Evie.

My fake girlfriend's forehead feels warm beneath my lips. I take a quick hit of the peaches and cream scent of her hair before pulling back. Just enough affection for show, but not enough to get lost in it. "I didn't expect to see you here this weekend."

"Oh, well, you know…" Her cheeks pink up, and it's not because of the blazing sun on the field. "I figured it would look bad if I wasn't around while you hang out with a bunch of women for a few days. Can't have people thinking I don't care."

"So, you're here to play the part of the jealous girlfriend?" Normally, that kind of behavior makes me cringe. With Peaches? I'm already entertained by the way she fakes a glare at the chick who's watching our interaction with a dirty look of her own. At least we're having fun with this mess.

Tori leans in and whispers, "Do you like her rack better than mine? Do you call her Apples?"

Another question that would ordinarily feel like a trap only makes me laugh. "I've been enough of a problem child for you. I would never do anything that would get me slapped with a sexual harassment lawsuit."

Tori glances between me and my most devoted trainee. "I'm glad to hear that because I wouldn't want you to do anything to embarrass yourself in front of your family."

What the what? "My family isn't here…"

The women's training camp that closes out the team's training camp is one of the few off-season team activities that would be totally safe for my mom and sisters to attend. I invited them, but between my sisters taking summer courses at college, and my mom working like she still needs her paycheck, they declined.

Except when I follow Tori's gaze over her shoulder, there they are, waving at me from the sideline.

My mom is wearing a Wolves t-shirt that has…glitter on it. Maybe diamonds? The team logo sparkles in the sunlight, threatening to blind me more than the glare I'm used to from the field. She actually has so much Albany gear on that it looks like the fan shop threw up all over her. My sisters both have sunglasses on, so I can't tell if they're actually happy to be here, or if they just got dragged into this mess.

"Why are they here?" It's not that I don't miss them, but this time, all their excuses not to visit actually worked in my favor. I can explain away the photos on the internet of me and Tori over the phone, but it's going to be a hell of a lot harder to lie to their faces.

Tori's blush deepens. Her shoulders creep up toward her ears. "David thought it would be more good publicity for the team's star player to have his family involved in Wolves events, especially since this is a female-centered activity. He called your mom and worked his magic."

Great. Just great. More like David knew this would be the ultimate test, and he's using it to press his advantage to see if Tori and I can hack this act.

I've got bad news for him. I want my starting position, and I will do whatever I have to do in order to keep it. "Peaches, this has to be Oscar-worthy. We can slide past my mom because she doesn't like to think about my love life too much, but my sisters are an entirely different story. If we don't make them believe it, they will call us out. They're relentless when they sink their teeth into something. They will absolutely take their suspicions about this whole situation to the internet."

Tori's shoulders fall. "I can't lie to your mother, Mike! The woman gave birth to you! I would never try to lie about this to my family!"

Why the hell did Tori's dad pull whatever strings he pulled to get her this internship? She's not nearly cutthroat enough for the business of football.

I tap her forehead. "You're not thinking like a winner. You said you wanted this opportunity, and you want to prove everyone wrong about both of us. For now, this is part of the game plan. Don't think of it as lying. Think of it as helping me provide for them. If I stay in the starting lineup and gain more ground with the fans, then I can land more side contracts that will help me pay for my sisters' tuition, so they don't start their adult lives underwater in debt. I can finally pay off the mortgage to my mom's house, and maybe convince her to take an early retirement that she absolutely deserves. And hey, if they think we're together, then they won't be on my case about settling down all the time, so it's like a triple crown."

"Settling down?" Tori's lips twist into a deep frown. "You're only twenty-three!"

"I want them to be happy. They want me to be happy. That's family, right? So, let's just all...be happy." That sounds just as great out loud as it did in my head. I totally understand marketing.

Tori doesn't look convinced. "I drove them here from the airport. I introduced myself as your PR manager. I didn't think you'd want me to lie to them, too!"

Oh, this just keeps getting better. We're going to have to make up some lost yards. "Faith and Hope didn't interrogate you the whole drive? They keep very close tabs on me even though I tell them not to, so I know they've already seen the pictures on the internet. They're just waiting to grill me in person about them."

"They point-blank asked me if we're sleeping together!" she hisses, her face turning from red to green. "In front of your mother!"

That sounds about right. "What did you say?"

"Nothing! I changed the subject!"

"Perfect. They'll think you were just maintaining plausible deniability to save face in front of Mom." Her shoulders are actually trembling when I wrap my arm around them. "Come on. Let's get this over with."

She tries so hard to drag her feet against the turf. "I can't do this. I can't, Mike! Fake dating for fans to post pictures of us together on the internet is one thing, but this is your family! I don't have to sleep my way to the top to sell this lie to strangers! Your mom and sisters will see right through us, just like you said!"

"That's why we have to put on our game faces." I turn her toward me and kiss her for everything I'm worth.

I already know she likes the way I kiss her, and I'd be lying if I said her drunken confession wasn't a huge boost to my ego. A tiny part of my brain feels guilty for playing on her weakness, but since it's both our jobs on the line, I tell that guilt to take a hike. I'm getting the best of both worlds, and it's actually good for both of us for me to take it.

Her hair feels like silk beneath my rough fingers and her soft lips like pillows against my sunburnt chapped ones. I haven't gone this long without Peaches since before I realized how much I need her. The grueling conditions of training camp are enough to wear down the most dedicated football players, but hell. After over two weeks of giving everything I have to give for my team, I'm hungry for a taste of Tori's sweetness.

She sways on her feet a bit when we finally break apart for air. "Do that one more time, and I'll be good to go for saying or doing anything you want."

This sober confession feels a hell of a lot more valuable than her drunk one.

"So, you're saying if I kiss you one more time, you'll be cool with me dropping to one knee and putting a fat rock on your finger for the cameras?"

She laughs. Just like that, we know where we stand. Lines are drawn, and our relationship—the real and the fake parts—all fit into nice, neat little boxes.

"We don't have a believable backstory," she mumbles as we approach three of my favorite smiling women.

"Sure, we do. Stick to the truth as much as possible. We met at work, became friends, and the rest is history."

"Speaking of history, what's my favorite color?"

I...have no idea. "We're screwed."

She cuts me a look that says *I told you so* before plastering a smile on her face. "Sorry to keep you waiting!"

There are two things to know about my mom. For one, she doesn't do or say anything overtly, but she never tries to hide the way she feels either. Any thought she ever has rolling around her brain can be read clear as day in her expression even if she'd die before saying the words out loud. The other thing is that no matter how she feels, she never, ever withholds love.

In spite of the raised eyebrows of disappointment, she wraps me in a big hug.

I cover up my wince of pain like a pro. "I thought you couldn't make it."

My sisters take turns with their greetings, but they're much more careful with my sore post-training camp muscles.

Faith rats out Mom first. "We weren't given a choice."

Hope nods. "Either show up or face sanctions for the rest of the year."

I ruffle her hair because I know she hates being treated like anything but an adult. Too bad she'll always be my kid sister to me. "I would've still made your tuition payments. I'd never blackmail you to come visit. If Mom cuts you off, you can always ask me for spending money."

Mom scoffs. "Honestly, Michael. Just because you make more money than I do does not automatically make you the parent."

Faith rolls her eyes. "Honestly, Mom. It's not about the money."

This has all the makings of a classic family fight, and while it might make for a great distraction from the Tori situation, this is not the time or place.

"Well, I'm glad you're all here! How long are you planning to stay? This is the last day of the women's training camp, so I'll be able to go home with you tonight." I can't wait to take the hottest shower imaginable in my own bathroom then pass out in my own bed.

Mom pats my cheek. "Why didn't you tell me you volunteered for this? We would have come for the whole weekend if we'd known."

Now is also not the time to remind her that I *did* tell her, especially because she's making googly eyes at Tori. Mom's obviously trying to get in Tori's good graces, and we definitely need her on our side to pull this off. "I know how busy you all are, so I didn't want to push the issue. I'm always happy when you come visit for any reason, and I'm happy to get to introduce you all to Tori in person."

I tug her beside me with more effort than it should take. "Mom, Faith, Hope, this is Tori Russo. My girlfriend."

The attraction I feel for Tori that I refuse to give in to makes faking it a hell of a lot easier than it would be otherwise. Introducing her as my girlfriend rolls of my tongue so easily because if things were different...

"That's not what you said when you picked us up at the airport," Hope accuses.

Tori tenses beside me, so I squeeze her. I've got this. "That's because she knew I wanted to tell you myself, and she was probably nervous about spilling the beans before you got here."

Mom beams. She totally buys it. The twins, however, study every place my body touches Tori's with laser-like focus. Their identical narrowed eyes do not believe my words. At all.

I'm not giving us away. Tori's tense posture is.

I squeeze her hip again. "Babe, did you already get them registered?"

She smiles up at me. Her lips look like they're seconds from cracking under the pressure. "David took care of it. They're registered for the rest of the day's activities."

Why am I not surprised? Mom would barely accept a jersey from me, but I'm guessing she scooped up all of David's obvious Wolves gear gifts gratefully.

"All right, then. Mom, you're with Tori. She'll take you to the field house where dinner and the women's health presentations are being held in a few hours. Girls, you're with me on the field."

They whine simultaneously.

I grin. This is easy and familiar. If I play my cards right, I can buy Peaches a few more hours to regroup. "Hey, you know I love giving you a taste of my life whenever I can."

Hope points at me. "False. You won't let us anywhere near your teammates because you're afraid they'll corrupt us."

She's not wrong, but a brilliant plan forms in my mind to shock her into submission.

I yell, "Templeman! Add my sister to your practice squad for the rest of the day!"

"You got it!" he calls back from somewhere behind me.

"What position does Templeman play?" she asks.

"Offensive line."

Hope shakes her head and takes a step backward. "I'm good staying with you."

That's what I thought. I don't tell them there's no actual tackling allowed at this camp. And frankly, I could use their help keeping my top fan with the grabby hands at bay. "Awesome. We'll all meet up again at the field house in a few hours. Sound good?"

Mom has this almost creepy glaze to her eyes when she smiles at Tori. She's imagining grandkids. I just know it. "Sounds wonderful."

Tori's entire body goes ramrod straight at my side.

I lean down and whisper in her ear under the guise of another kiss. "Trust me. You're getting the lesser of two evils. Mom is a walk in the park compared to the twins."

# Chapter 17
Close

## Tori

"THIS IS NOT the lesser of two evils!"

Mike leans against his closed bedroom door. "You did great today. Calm down."

Oh, no he didn't.

"Calm down? *Calm down?* Mike! Your mom and sisters are under the impression I am sleeping in here with you tonight! How am I supposed to calm down?"

His firm hands on my shoulders actually *do* make me feel a little calmer, but that is beside the point.

"They assume you're sleeping here tonight because they bought it, Peaches. David wanted to test us, and believe me when I say, there is no bigger test than the twins. If they think we're really together, then we've got this in the bag. Your job is safe. I'm going to be on the starting lineup again this year, and it's smooth sailing for the rest of the season for both of us."

I am well aware from the reports I've been following like it's my job—because it is—that Mike has gone above and beyond with his performance during training camp. He's still putting his nose to the grind and making a name for himself where it counts—on the field.

I glance around at the sparse furnishings and the empty walls that are a serene shade of blue-gray. The king-size bed that's the focal point of the room has a deep gray comforter and sheets that are already turned down. It looks like a beautifully comfortable place to pass out after this exhausting day, but this is definitely not the field. Neither of us wanted to do business this way, but here we are.

"I don't understand why you wouldn't let me play the respect card with your mom here. It's not like we're engaged to be married. It's rude of me to sleep with you while she's under your roof! My dad would never stand for something like this."

His hands knead into the tense muscles of my shoulders and upper back, even as he holds me at arms' length. "Yeah, it's a weird combination of past and present ideals. Mom thinks she understands the pressures I'm under as a pro football player, so she just kind of ignores the parts she doesn't agree with because she wants me to be successful. I get that. Because the twins are modern women, and they expect us to sleep together after a few weeks apart. I one-hundred-percent do not want to think about them sleeping with anyone. This is all actually kind of my fault for keeping them out of the reality of football. I just let them assume whatever they want without giving them too many of the facts."

His eyes are droopy, and his words are a bit slurred. I can sort of follow his logic, but he also seems to be all over the place with his explanations. I should let him go to sleep, but...I'm too tantalized by the carrot he's dangling in front of my face. I'm in over my head with this act. I need all the help I can get. "What are the facts I need to know? You're the only person currently in this house who realizes I have no idea what it's like to date a professional football player."

"Fact number one." He yawns and squeezes my shoulders one more time before letting go and stumbling toward his bed, which he collapses onto face-first. "Do not touch us after training camp. I'm so sore, my skin hurts. All the press you see about players being...players? That's only after a big win when the adrenaline takes a while to wear off. For a few hours, we feel invincible, but most of the time? We feel like we've been in a car accident."

That's information I never learned from even the likes of David. "What do you need?"

He mumbles something incoherent into the mattress then turns his head to the side, so I can actually hear him. "I'm so tempted to take the easy out and ask you to call Evie for advice, but she's a pro at this. There's not a snowball's chance in hell we'll fool her. For tonight? I have extra toothbrushes and shit in the bathroom from away-game swag packs. Plenty of t-shirts in the drawers. Just make yourself as comfortable as possible. It's a big bed, and I'm not gonna move for at least twelve hours. If you wanna sneak out before everyone wakes up in the morning, I'll come up with a believable excuse."

I've known Mike for over a year, but this is our first training camp together. I had no idea it would look anything like this. "Do you want a massage?"

"No!" He actually picks his head up from the bed to fix me with a look of absolute horror. "That's lesson number two. If you don't know what you're doing, you can actually hurt us more. Leave the massages to the pros. Seriously. I'm going to pass out soon. I won't do anything to make you uncomfortable. Just...stick to the game plan, Peaches."

All of five seconds passes before he's snoring. The sounds of his family making themselves at home floats through his closed bedroom door. If I'm going to be trapped in here, the least I can do is a little reconnaissance since I've been given carte blanche to make myself comfortable.

The problem is...there's nothing in here to gain better knowledge of the most intimate workings into what makes Mike Mitchell tick. There are no photos—not even of the people I already know he's closest to. His bedroom honestly resembles a hotel room. Richly appointed, but no personal touches. On one hand, I suppose that's to be expected from a bachelor who gives all his time and energy to his chosen profession. On the other? It makes me sad that this is where he sleeps every night.

With nothing better to do, I wander into the adjoining bathroom to shower off the sweat and anxiety of this exhausting day. As promised, there's an extra toothbrush and plenty of sample toiletries hiding beneath his massive vanity. They're all masculine scented. Very good branding. If David would actually let me speak with Mike's agent, I could maybe get him a contract marketing one of these spicy-scented body washes. The kind that promise to hydrate a man's skin, while still stroking his masculine ego by also swearing to have extra-tough exfoliants for the rough parts.

Mike definitely has rough skin. His fingertips alone send goose-bumps racing across my entire body. My sensitive skin already itches with imagined hives from using any of these cleansing options, so I forego them for what's in the massive shower stall that's separate from the jacuzzi tub.

I shouldn't be surprised about what I find in here because this is the Mike I know. Simple, inexpensive scentless bar soap and shampoo greet me from the built-in shelves in the shower.

The waterfall showerhead does wonders for my tense muscles, but nothing for the throbbing between my legs. Mike's kiss from the field still lingers on my lips. Try as I might to erase the memories, I can't help but imagine a similar scenario of him in his own shower as the one I witnessed for myself in a hotel room. The whole problem with this forced scenario is that it would be all too easy to let my baser instincts take over my mind. He's the kind of man any woman would fight to keep—thoughtful, loyal, in control of himself, and with goals he works hard to attain.

The sort of bathroom only the wealthiest in society can afford is just a fringe benefit.

If I'm going to get any sleep tonight and be fresh-faced and ready with more lies in the morning, then Mike's right. I have to relax. With shame clouding my every movement, I jill off with my own fingers. But I absolutely—one hundred and ten percent—do not imagine Mike doing the same thing for himself when he's in this steamy space.

Okay. Maybe I do. Just a little.

Then, I do penance. Right after I don one of his t-shirts that's big enough to swallow me whole.

"Mike," I whisper as I oh-so-gently rub his back. "Come on. Move up onto the pillows. Let's get you comfortable."

He mumbles at me, but he cracks open his eyes. "Babe, you coming to bed yet?"

Tingles from my self-inflicted orgasm compete with the memory of his kiss on my lips. "No, teddy bear. I didn't work as hard as you for the past two weeks. I'm not tired yet. I'll come to bed later. Okay?"

He smacks his lips together a few times, sits up then whips off his shirt, and finally crawls high up enough on the bed so that tucking him in beneath the silky soft sheets is at least possible.

His skin is smooth and cool when I run my hand across his forehead. "Do you want anything? A glass of water for the nightstand? Some ibuprofen for your soreness?"

He smiles even as his eyes slide closed again. "A peach."

Thank God he's still aware enough to crack a joke. His sculpted chest and arms are on full display. He's left plenty of space on one side of the bed for me to climb in with his arm extended over like a silent invitation. I was *this close* to kissing him goodnight, and there's not a soul around to perform for.

Silence blankets the massive house, so I crack the bedroom door open to listen. His family must have gone to sleep. As quietly as possible, I creep downstairs for the glass of water and pain relievers. If I can't behave myself, then I can at least be useful.

The house is dark and quiet. A clock ticks somewhere on an unknown wall. Shadows cast long lines across the expanse of the open floor plan between the living room and kitchen. This isn't the first time I've been in Mike's house, but it still feels like I'm an intruder lurking around. I don't belong here in the intimacy of the middle of the night.

The grocery order I placed before we even left the stadium complex fills the fridge. I consider a quick snack for myself but think better of it. I'm a guest here, so I don't want to make myself too at home. I grab a bottle of water for Mike, close the fridge, then turn around.

The plastic bottle hits the ground with a dull thud, but it's enough force to break it open and splash cold liquid all the way up my calves. I slap a hand over my mouth to stifle my scream.

Sitting in Mike's favorite armchair, one leg crossed over the other, arms spread like a queen on her throne, a woman stares at me silently in the dark.

My shoulders impossibly tense further, and I brace myself for the interrogation that's been brewing all day. Without Mike as a referee, I'm about to get what's coming to me.

Except the longer we stare at each other, the more I realize her presence is unlike Mike's mom or either of his sisters. She seems to fill the entire vast room with a judgmental silence, yes, but there's also an inexplicable attraction that draws me closer like a moth to the flame.

"Eva Falls." Her name falling from my lips cuts like a flashlight through the darkness.

"Tori Russo," she returns evenly.

"What are you doing here?" It's a rude question, made even ruder by my harsh tone. She has more right to be in this house than I do. A fact I'm acutely aware of, clothed only in one of Mike's t-shirts. I should have asked how she knows me, or why she seems so unfazed to find me here in the middle of the night.

She barely moves except for a slight tilt of her head as she studies me with an unnerving focus. "Mike's mom let me in when I arrived an hour ago. I didn't realize they were visiting this weekend, or I would have rescheduled my flight."

"Let me rephrase," I grind out. "*Why* are you here?"

I feel bad for what this woman's been through, sure, but if she thinks she's getting another crack at Mike's poor head or face, then she's got another thing coming. I'll claw her eyes out first. Then, maybe give her a hug when I'm satisfied she's no longer a threat.

Movement outside the sliding glass door that leads to the pool area catches my eye. A different sort of threat prompts me to point and open my mouth to squeak out an unintelligible warning.

Eva simply lets out an irritated sigh and raises a single hand in the air before flicking her fingers in a dismissive motion.

"Who-who is that? Who's out there?" Maybe I should wake up Mike...

"My annoying bodyguard," Eva mutters.

"You have a bodyguard?" It's amazing—and slightly disappointing—how quickly I've gone from protective to curious.

"Yes, and he follows my husband's orders, not mine." She rubs her forehead. "Please, sit down. He'll just keep pacing out there unless he sees us being civil."

I sit on the edge of the couch, but there's no way I'm going to relax under these circumstances. "Why does he think we wouldn't be civil?"

A slow smile spreads across her face. "Probably because you look like you're ready to claw my eyes out."

Wow. She's good.

"Which means I like you." She thumbs behind her toward the man standing guard just outside, dressed all in black so that he nearly blends in with the darkness. "Him? Not so much."

"It's kind of hard not to feel like I'm in defense mode when there's a stranger outside in the dark, and you've been sitting here staring at me silently for God knows how long." I square my shoulders. "I understand how close you and Mike are, but *you* need to understand I'm not going to let you anywhere near him this close to the beginning of the season."

Like a scale that finally collapses beneath too much weight, her smile climaxes then falls away. "Just doing your job, Miss Russo?"

I don't like the implication in her tone. "Yes. Just like your bodyguard views me as a threat to you, I view you as a threat to Mike. Everything you've been through together withstanding, I won't let you hurt him again. He has too much on the line, and he works too hard not to be given every chance to succeed. I actually care about my job, Mrs. Falls. You'd better believe I will do anything to make sure nothing—and no one—interferes with Mike's ability to do his."

Her gaze slides up and down my bare legs. "I see. Good. I've been keeping tabs on you, and I'd hoped you'd say that."

This is...completely unexpected. Mike's always telling me what a pro Eva is at navigating the world of football, but to know she's been watching my every move from a distance is both intimidating and somewhat validating. She obviously likes what she's seen from me so far. "Why are you here?"

Her sigh is so long and heavy, it seems to stretch out over the expanse of the house. "I'm here to give Mike some long overdue closure he won't admit he needs. I'm going to need you to be ready to pick up the pieces when I'm gone."

Oh, I don't like the sounds of that at all.

# Chapter 18
## Only the Lonely Survive

### Mike

"What are you saying?"

She's already said it a million times in a million different ways, but she might as well be saying it in Chinese while writing calculus proofs on a chalkboard.

I don't understand any of it.

Evie takes a deep breath. She's been strangely calm for the past few hours—almost zombie-like—even with Tori pacing just inside the door, watching our conversation like a spy zeroed in on a target.

The only thing I know for sure is that I'm not her mark. Evie is.

Tori blatantly glares at her for a split second through the sliding glass door before she continues trying her best to wear a hole in the living room carpet. At least Mom and the girls already left. I'm so fucking glad they aren't here.

"Did you already tell Tori everything you've said to me? Is that why she refuses to leave? Am I the *last* to know?"

"No." Evie shakes her head slowly, her voice low and sad. "She has no idea what we're discussing. There are also plenty of other people who were there that night that will likely never know what happened."

"But, why?" The strongest urge to actually tear my hair out forces me to sit on my hands. My muscles twitch with the barest restraint. "Why would you—of all people—keep silent about this for so long?"

She casts her gaze to her lap. "I'm sorry."

More foreign words without a translator in sight.

She's *sorry*. Sorry doesn't nearly cut it.

"You said they blackmailed the girlfriends into staying quiet. That they watched you all to make sure you'd keep your mouths shut. Chelsie barely spoke to me again after that night, but what about all the nights you slept in the same bed as Rob after what happened, huh? They weren't watching you then. All you had to do was tell him the truth, so he could've huddled with the rest of us. We could've made a plan. We could've fixed it."

"You couldn't have fixed it," she whispers. "You were at their mercy. None of us had any power in that situation."

Jesus fucking Christ. I vividly remember me, Rob, Alex, and all the other rookies talking about that night multiple times. We knew something bad had happened. We just had no idea *how* bad.

All I wanted was to know *why*.

Why she cheated. Why Chelsie threw me away like trash without ever saying a word. Why I wasn't good enough for her.

Well. Now, I know.

My ex-girlfriend was forced to watch me come down another woman's throat while I was drugged out of my mind by the upperclassmen players who cared more about hazing us every chance they got rather than being our mentors.

They were supposed to show us the ropes, to help us get to the next level of play, to teach us how to adapt to a new brotherhood on a new team.

They taught us some shit all right. Lessons I carry with me even in a new locker room with new teammates in a new city.

"You never liked Chelsie," I spit. "None of you did. You didn't keep quiet about this to protect us. You kept quiet because you were happy to see her go."

Evie lifts her gaze. "That's not true. She cried on my shoulder, Mike. I held her while you…while…"

She swallows like she's going to throw up.

That makes two of us.

"You're not putting this on me." I jump out of my chair and pace, just like Tori's still doing. "No way am I going to be the bad guy here because Rob was the only one who held out!"

Evie's expression crumbles. In this moment, her pain doesn't even faze me. "Rob didn't hold out either. TJ was the only rookie who did."

"Son of a bitch!" I yell. Right before picking up my chair and throwing it into the pool. It lands on the surface of the water with an unsatisfying splash.

"You divorce him now!" I roar. "Right the fuck now! I'm done playing around!"

"I'm not going to do that," she replies, her tone devoid of any of the emotion that's spilling over my usually careful control. "It wasn't cheating. It was rape. He wasn't to blame, and you aren't either. I'm sorry the other girlfriends didn't see it for what it was."

"You do not get to fucking come into my house, confess all this shit to me *years* after the fact, then act like a goddamn martyr!"

"That's not what I'm trying to do." Her voice comes out soft, the exact opposite of mine. "I will have to live with my silence and my regrets for the rest of my life. I love you too much to burden you with regrets, too."

"What the fuck is that supposed to mean? You literally just said it wasn't my fault!"

Evie rises from her chair, as steady as I'm not. "It's not. It's not your fault. I'm not here to drag you down or hurt you. I'm telling you this because you have been stuck in a spin cycle for years, and I don't want to see you waste another single day of the rest of your life by clinging to the past. You have never moved on from Chelsie. You haven't even tried. Because—deep down—you thought you did something wrong." She places a hand on my heaving chest. "You didn't. You did *nothing* to cause her to cheat on you. You are a wonderful, loyal, talented, hard-working man who deserves everything you give to everyone else but keep none of for yourself. You're always telling me to let go, big brother. Now, it's your turn. You know the facts. You know you're not to blame. Now…let it—let *her*—go."

"Why now?" I have no shame left, so begging isn't out of the question. "Why not after Jamal and his henchman graduated? Why not after *we* graduated? Hell, why not stay silent for the rest of your life?"

Evie glances to where Tori's practically plastered against the window, watching our every move. "Because if I didn't speak up now and give you a damn good reason to move on, then you might just throw away the best thing to happen to you since getting drafted."

"I already told you the truth," I bite out. "Unlike you, I'm not trying to hide anything. She's my PR manager. The photos you've seen online are just a media stunt."

Evie steps back and tsks. "Maybe to fans who don't know the real you. I do. Even in pictures online, I see the way you look at her. I also know you're not letting yourself go for it because you're convinced you'll fuck it all up somehow."

"Get out." After everything she's revealed to me today, the last thing I want to hear is that she knows me better than I know myself. I'm hanging on by a very slim thread. If we don't get some distance between us, I'm going to do and say things I can never take back. "Go back to Sacramento. We're done here."

She nods and rolls her lips in between her teeth as tears fill her eyes. "Please forgive me. I've made a lot of mistakes in the past, but I'm trying to do and be better. I hope you will, too."

# Chapter 19
## Pressure

### Tori

OH, no. No, no, no, no, no. My worst nightmare is playing out in front of my eyes at the worst possible time and in the worst possible place.

I race toward the mob surrounding Mike on the sideline. I knew I shouldn't have given them family passes even though it's only a pre-season game. Never mind that I'm not high up enough on the totem pole to be given tickets for a regular season game.

I push my way through the tight knit bodies to plaster myself against Mike. "Leave him alone! You guys *cannot* do this!"

The ringleader smiles. It's devious, evil, conniving. His teeth look extra sharp today. "We weren't doing anything."

His second in command mumbles, "Much."

Mike leans down and whispers in my ear, "I think they're planning my murder."

It's the most he's said to me in two weeks, and I don't think he's joking.

"This is my *job*," I hiss to my brothers. All five of them. "You can't behave like this here."

They don't budge an inch.

"Lay off," a gruff voice commands.

The throng parts like the Red Sea to let my dad through.

He eyes Mike—still strategically behind me—with clear disapproval, but he's too set in his ways not to extend his hand anyway. "Mr. Mitchell. I trust you're treating my daughter well."

Mike reaches around me to shake my dad's hand.

"He's treating me just fine," I interject before Mike's sour mood lately can make a bad situation worse.

Do I think I can pull off a lie this big to my family? No. Am I going to try? I don't know. Mike hasn't exactly been giving off warm, fuzzy vibes these past few weeks. Maybe he just doesn't have it in him to pretend anymore. I empathize with that. If it wasn't for his bad mood, I would say his distant behavior has been a nice break from my constant internal battle.

"Mr. Russo. It's an honor to meet you, sir. You must be very proud of the fine daughter you've raised." Mike finally manages to pull his hand away with a wince that doesn't go unnoticed by me.

Dad perks up a bit at Mike's proper address. Or, it could be that he's pleased to have crushed Mike's very valuable hand.

My oldest brother, Theo, cackles. "We already know you think she's fine. You're the one dating her. Pro football players aren't exactly known for sleeping with dogs."

Mike's voice seems even, but there's an undercurrent of warning in his tone. "That is disrespectful not only to your sister, but to all women—including *my* sisters and mother."

Dad purses his lips. His eyes narrow infinitesimally. He's not sure whether to be impressed with Mike or insulted on his oldest son's behalf.

Since I have no idea what to expect out of anyone, my best hope is a sure distraction. "Are you guys ready to head out? A co-worker told me about this amazing Mexican restaurant last week that I'm dying to take you to. My treat!"

They all seem eager enough.

Unfortunately—but perhaps not unexpectedly after the past few weeks of the silent treatment—it's Mike who rains on my parade. "Which Mexican restaurant?"

"El Patrón."

He shakes his head, the same frown that's been tattooed to his lips still firmly in place. "You can't go there. Most of the menu is seafood."

The scales seem to be tipping in favor of respect, judging by Dad's expression. He hasn't fully made up his mind though. There's more testing to be done. "Where do you suggest we go for dinner, Mike? From the pictures the boys have shown me on the internet, you've taken Tori to the nicest, safest restaurants in Albany."

Mike's response is immediate. He doesn't even blink at the subtle dig from my dad. "We've vetted 677 Prime. The staff knows about Tori's allergy, and they're extremely careful with food prep for her plate."

My smile becomes achingly brittle. "Darling," I mutter through gritted teeth. "Half that menu is seafood, too."

One hundred percent of that menu is out of my price range. I don't have a professional football player's salary. It will be difficult to afford six grown men's appetites as it is, but I'm determined to show my family I'm doing well on my own.

"Yeah." Mike shrugs off my imperceptible headshake. "But we've been there. We know it's safe."

"It's settled then." Dad's tone is final. "How much longer will you be?"

This is my chance. "Oh, he'll be hours longer. He's still got some interviews to do, post-game with the coaching staff and his teammates, showering and cleaning up in the locker room. I don't want you guys to wait. You must be starving. Besides, 677 Prime requires reservations sometimes weeks in advance. We wouldn't be able to get a table for this many people at the last minute anyway. I'll take you out to dinner while he finishes up here!"

Mike squints at me like he can't possibly understand why I'm being difficult. "Just call and give them my name. They'll open a table for us."

Dad's expression curdles. He obviously isn't impressed with Mike dropping his name anywhere for anything.

"I won't be long." Mike continues to thwart me at every turn. "It's pre-season, so there's not as much post-game stuff to get through. Call and ask for the table. I'll meet you there in half an hour."

He walks away without another word.

I turn to face my family who's watching me like I'm in the crosshairs.

Theo speaks up first. "Wow, Tor. You sure know how to pick 'em. No kiss? No hug? Nothing but bossing you around?"

Owen picks up the trail, shaking his head. "This is why you should never mix business with pleasure."

Dad levels them with a glare. "I do not want to hear the words pleasure in the same sentence with Tori for the rest of the night. Are we clear?"

"Crystal, sir." Theo's response is born from years of careful conditioning.

So are the side-eyes, snickers, and smirks from my other brothers. They'll follow orders all right. They'll use every word except *pleasure* to exact their torture.

Oh, this night smells like disaster already. I still haven't recovered from the last disaster. I can't pick up Mike's broken pieces if I still don't know what shattered him in the first place.

# Chapter 20
## Not a Bad Thing

### Mike

TORI POUNCES on me the second I step into the restaurant.

"Just go," she hisses, literally trying her best to shove me back out the door. "Send me a text telling me you got caught up with the coaches as proof. They're all at the table. They'll never know you were here."

I haven't exactly been a pleasure to be around since Evie dropped her bombshell on me, but Tori's behavior seems a bit extreme. "A deal's a deal, Peaches. You wanted to prove to everyone you can hack this job. If you want them to believe we're really together, then I can't bail on you after making dinner plans with your family. Since it's the first time I'm meeting them, it only seems fair to take them to a nice place."

"I can't afford this place!" she whisper-shrieks.

"I can."

My offer only makes her angrier. "I hate to kick you when you're down, but remember that little conversation we had about being supportive instead of solving everyone's problems for them?"

I am down. She hasn't so much as nudged me with her toe, let alone begged me to tell her why I've been in a funk. Tori has been nothing but quietly supportive of me for the past two weeks while I try to work out what to do with the information I've been given. It's only fair to pony up to my end of the arrangement. Besides, our jobs are on the line. It's just good business.

"If you want to pay for everyone's dinner, then go ahead. I'll pay you back later."

She releases her hold on me only to rub her forehead. That's a sure sign of trouble. "Mike. You've barely spoken to me for weeks. There's no way my family is going to buy that we're in a relationship. Let's just cut our losses on this one."

"You look beautiful." I lean down to kiss her cheek. Just that barest contact makes me sigh in relief after two weeks of feeling like I can't breathe at all.

"Thank you," she responds automatically before literally shaking her head. "Seriously though. Just go. I'll handle it."

Oh. I get what this is about. "You don't want them to think you're sleeping your way to the top."

Her shoulders slump. She raises her gaze to mine. "I do not. I want them to believe in me. To see I can be successful on my own. It's bad enough my dad pulled strings to get me this internship. They're all expecting me to fail. Even if I keep my job and get an endowment from the team to pay for my master's, they're going to think I basically cheated to win. For me, it's a no-win situation."

"So, let's tell them the truth." Evie's words about the most brilliant solution being the simplest ring in my ears. A lot of Evie's words are still ringing in my ears.

"I can't ask you to take on that much risk." Tori lowers her gaze to the floor. "Just because I don't think they'll say anything online doesn't mean it's worth jeopardizing your starting position if the truth somehow gets out. All it would take is one of my brothers getting drunk at the bar and saying something to a friend for this house of cards to crumble."

If she doesn't trust her brothers completely, then I can't either. "Do you trust *me*?"

Her deep brown eyes are full of sadness. "To worry about my welfare? Yes. Even though you've gone right back to being a closed door to me, you still care enough to make sure I won't die by taking my family to the wrong place to eat. If you don't trust me enough to tell me what Evie said that's upset you so much, then…"

I know exactly what she leaves unsaid. She's already told me before. It's not just about supporting someone instead of solving their problems for them. Relationships are about trust. It's a two-way street and a hotter commodity than a spot in Sports Illustrated.

Emotion I'm still fighting against clogs my throat. I clear it away. "Thank you for giving me the time to absorb what she said that night. I really appreciate that you haven't pushed. I swear, nothing she told me is going to affect my ability to do my job. It's not that I don't want to tell you. I don't want to burden you with it."

She nods slowly.

"Hey! Are we gonna eat, or are you two gonna make out over there all night?"

Tori winces.

I turn toward her oldest brother who's watching us from near the hostess station. The dude's kind of a douche in my opinion. I'm already sick of her family shitting all over her, but maybe I can still turn around this losing game. "We'll be right there. Go ahead and order."

He grins. "We already did."

I hold out my elbow for Tori to take. She does, but even that slight movement screams defeat. We follow her oldest brother to a private table, separated from the other patrons. It's not because I'm a local celebrity. The staff here is honestly great about accommodating customers with food allergies. Since it's nearly impossible to avoid seafood in restaurants in the Capital Region, an additional bonus to the more expensive places is that they cater to even the most sensitive clientele.

All eyes zero in on me as I help Tori into her seat.

One of the brothers smirks. "What a gentleman."

He does not say it like he means it.

I take the empty chair on Tori's right. "My mom didn't raise me to be a rude jock." I wink at their salty expressions. "Just a dumb one."

Tori whips her wide-eyed gaze to me so fast, she's probably going to have neck problems for a week.

I pick up my menu and pretend not to notice she's basically

screaming at me to behave. Without words. "So? Did everyone order the most expensive thing on the menu? Tori said dinner is her treat, and I'm starving. The wagyu is worth every penny. I'm thinking at least sixteen ounces."

Tori chokes on her water.

That prime cut of beef is priced at twenty-five bucks for a measly two ounces. It's good, but it's not *that* good.

"I really hope someone ordered the Tomahawk. There's a reason it's the priciest item on the menu."

Tori kicks me under the table.

Honestly, this is the most fun I've had in weeks.

I lower my menu and smile at Mr. Russo, who looks like he's ten seconds from being overdone. "Did you order a drink, sir? This is the finest bar in all of Albany. They even have table service if you don't want to drink from an opened bottle."

"Been doing a little wining and dining, Mitchell?"

I think it's the youngest brother who asks, but I'm not sure. They all look like male versions of Tori with red hair, pale skin, and brown eyes. I feel a little bad for them because they do not pull off the ginger look as well as their sister. Maybe that's why they have such bad attitudes. They're not convinced she'll fail at life; they're jealous she'll outshine them.

She already does.

Her smile is warm and genuine when the server who's usually assigned to us approaches our table. "Julian! It's so good to see you! Did Amber say yes?"

Julian rattles off the results of the proposal plans he gushed to us about a few weeks ago. He and Tori go back and forth, excitement bubbling between them.

Stuff like this is why Tori has a chance to make it in marketing and public relations. She's great at the public relations part, even if her marketing style isn't what people expect at this level of business. She genuinely cares about others and is an expert at making strangers feel like old friends.

As I glance around at the various expressions at our table, it's obvious her family doesn't appreciate her for the amazing woman she is.

Mr. Russo clears his throat. Loudly.

Julian immediately stops his conversation with Tori. "My apologies. May I take your order, Miss Russo?"

She offers him a sympathetic half smile. "My usual, please."

"Do you want gin or vodka this evening for your martini?"

A silent sigh heaves Tori's chest. "Gin, please. Thank you."

Uh-oh. Tori hasn't touched gin since the hotel incident. She must really be feeling the pressure. Maybe I should ease up a little.

Mr. Russo raises a disapproving eyebrow. "You don't need a drink."

"Yes, sir. I'll have a sparkling water instead, Julian."

He nods and waits for my order, but food is suddenly the last thing on my mind. Every male member of Tori's family has a rocks glass of something or other in front of them. They're all apparently allowed to have drinks.

As ballsy as Tori's always been since I've known her, she balances hunger for success with being a professional. I've never seen this submissive side of her. I don't like it. I don't think she does either. Her face is redder than ever, her eyes cast down to her empty place setting.

"I'll have my usual, too. And Miss Russo will have whatever she wants."

Julian's green eyes laugh, but his face gives nothing away. "Yes, Mr. Mitchell."

He flees the scene before a full argument can break out.

Surprisingly, it doesn't come. Mr. Russo's tone is flat. "That young man isn't professional enough to work in a classy place like this. Discussing his personal life with patrons? Shameful."

Tori calmly spreads her napkin across her lap. "That young man is responsible for making sure I don't die while eating in this fine establishment, and he takes his job very seriously. He treats Mike the same as any other customer and has never once asked for a photo, an autograph, or any other favors. He's extremely professional, and he's our *friend*."

Now, this sounds more like the Tori I know and—

Aw, shit. Evie's right.

No time to dig into that though. I've got a bigger problem in front of me.

I take a sip of my water. It's always a good idea to hydrate before playing a tough opponent. "Speaking of professional...To answer your question—Owen, right? Yes. I've been wining and dining your sister for months now, but she won't give in. She insists our relationship stay business, only." I shrug. "The media spins it the way they want. Tori's so devoted to her job, she indulges my crush because she knows her market well. Fans want to see football players in committed relationships more than they want to hear another TMZ story about the latest domestic assault in the off-season. She makes me look good, and I get to spend time with her. It's a win-win."

Mr. Russo seems equal parts relieved and horrified. "This is all an act? A media stunt to make you look better?"

I rest my arm against the back of Tori's chair. "Well, it's all an act on her part. I'm not acting."

*I'm not acting.*

Julian arrives with Tori's drink.

The second he places the martini glass in front of her, she snatches it up and downs the cloudy liquid in three long swallows. She doesn't even bother with the olives that are usually her favorite part. "Gonna need another of these, thanks."

Julian's worried eyes meet my steady gaze, but he pivots back to the bar without a word.

Tori's oldest brother looks ready to breathe fire. "Do you need us to teach him a lesson about how to be a real gentleman, Tor? Because we can take him out back and do that right now if he's forcing you into anything you're uncomfortable with."

That's the first thing any of these guys have said tonight that I actually respect.

Tori just laughs. Snorts. Then, laughs harder.

This play was a gamble, but at least I haven't pissed off the most important person sitting at this table.

I straighten in my seat and give her brothers and father the reassurance they deserve. Shit, I wouldn't have asked permission before beating the ass of any guy who talked like that about my sisters. "I'd never do anything to hurt Tori. Honestly. I respect her decision to keep things professional between us. Spoiling her with nice dinners and nights out on the town are my ways of thanking her for all she's done for my career so far. Would I like more? Yes. Would I ever force her into anything? Absolutely not." I make sure my gaze is trained solely on her. "I respect the hell out of this woman."

She won't look at me, but a slight smile tips the corner of her lips. "It's fine, you guys. Really. Mike and I both work very hard at our jobs. We've become friends since last season. It's nice to have someone to blow off some steam with once in a while."

"Blowing off some steam, huh?" The oldest brother leans back in his seat and crosses his arms over his chest. "Sounds like friends with benefits to me."

Mr. Russo growls, "What did I tell you?"

He straightens immediately. "I did not use the word 'pleasure,' sir."

Every time I think Tori can't possibly blush any harder, she surprises me.

# Chapter 21
Fix You

## Tori

"Focus, Peaches."

The low rumble of his voice goes straight to my lady bits. My fingers have gotten more of a workout in the past week than they did during finals my senior year of college when I stayed up for nights on end, typing away furiously on my laptop to finish my assignments on time.

I'm losing sleep for an entirely different reason now. I blame it on my stupid brother and his stupid misinformed idea about friends with benefits. And Mike's Oscar-worthy act in front of my family.

He sighs then rolls his neck, which makes a gross cracking noise. "I think we need a break."

Yep. A break sounds like a fantastic idea. All this forced proximity with one of the most handsome, loyal, and caring men I've ever met is frying my brain. Short-circuiting my better business sense. Threatening to make me give in to urges that I would normally stomp out like embers from a bonfire before they can spread into something unmanageable.

I pull my laptop away from him. "You know what? I can finish this up. You've been more than generous with your time, and this is your last week of freedom before the season starts. I have enough of an idea about what you want your social media feeds to look like. I'll round out the rest and run it by you for approval. How does that sound?"

He relaxes his large body against the couch, sprawling out his limbs. His very, very muscular limbs. Which are attached to such a glorious set of chiseled chest and abs that the definition is unmistakable even beneath a super soft-looking Wolves tee. My gaze travels down to sweatpants that define something else entirely. Something I fantasize about way too often to be good for my mental health.

I'm drooling. If I don't get out of here, he's bound to notice.

I shove my laptop into my messenger bag and hop up from my seat on the other end of the couch. "So, I'm just gonna get out of your hair now. Enjoy the rest of your evening, Mr. Mitchell."

Even though it's resting against the back of the couch, he somehow manages to cock his head back and squint at me like I've lost my mind. It certainly feels that way. "Did I do something to offend you? Are you mad about what I told your family? I thought I split the difference between what you wanted and what's good for our careers pretty well, considering we didn't have a lot of time to prepare."

"Oh, no. It's not that," I squeak out. Very convincing. "You did great. I appreciate you putting yourself out there for me so much. Thank you. So much."

He slowly rises from his seat, advancing for every step I retreat.

Predator and prey analogies race through my mind. This is exactly my problem. I am increasingly willing to be the object of his focus, time, and attention. All because I can't separate acting from reality.

He said what he said to my family to help me, to support me and my decisions. That's all. I'm the only one overcomplicating things when this situation is actually very simple.

My back hits the wall.

Nothing feels simple when he cages me in with his muscular arms, his face hovering so near to mine that I can feel his breath dust my lips. "Why are you calling me Mr. Mitchell again?"

His eyes practically dare me to lie to him.

"Because you're my client, and I'm your PR manager," I manage to whisper. It's not a lie. It's the absolute truth.

He nods slowly then rolls his lips in between his teeth as his gaze roves over every millimeter of my face like he's trying to see deeper truths that have no place between us. "Why are you leaving?"

"Because I have a job to do!" I yelp. "The season's about to start, and I have no idea how to be the public girlfriend of a pro football player. I need to go home and do some research, maybe update my wardrobe to something more appropriate, learn how to actually apply makeup, probably get a manicure…"

His arms fall away, then he scrubs his face with his hands. "Peaches. If there's one thing I want from you in this mess, it's this." He levels me with a very serious expression. "Don't change who you are just to be with me on the sidelines. Be yourself."

Myself is about to ruin this. For both of us. "That's not part of my job description, Mike."

∽

THE MASCARA WAND jabs my eyeball when a knock on my front door interrupts my latest attempt to follow a basic makeup tutorial.

This is it. I'm blind. I always thought I'd lose my eyesight from staring at a computer screen too long. Who knew mascara could do so much more damage?

"Hang on! I'm coming," I call as I stumble my way toward the front door, bumping into furniture with only half of my usual depth perception in working order.

I don't bother with the peephole. I can barely see anyway.

The flowers thrust out toward me the moment I throw open the door are kind of hard to miss though. "Mike! What are you doing here? What are these for?"

He leans down until his worried expression enters my half-field of vision. "I guess they can double as a get-well gift. What the hell happened to your face?"

I probably have black streaks running down my cheeks from involuntary tears. I definitely botched the contouring part of the tutorial. "I told you I have makeup research to do!"

He nods, still at an awkward angle as he stares up at me. "I thought you were just trying to get away from me."

If I was that obvious about needing a little space, then he probably knows exactly why. My cheeks flame. "You didn't offend me in any way. Thank you for the flowers, but there's no apology necessary. I really do have a lot of work to do to get ready for the season. Shouldn't you be…I dunno…bonding with your teammates this week?"

He mumbles something unintelligible before nudging me inside then closing the door behind him. "You only have to do all this stuff because of me, so…as long as you promise to never breathe a word of this…I can help you."

That's an intriguing offer. One I shouldn't even be entertaining. "Help me how?"

He stuffs his hands in his pockets and rocks on his feet. "I sort of… know how to do makeup."

Oh. That's much more decent than the sort of help I'm perversely thinking about. I guess his offer isn't so surprising. "Because you grew up surrounded by women?"

"Yep." With a gentle hand on my elbow, he guides me down the hallway to my little bathroom. "Wash all this off and flush the mascara out of your eye with plenty of water, then we'll start over."

I follow orders. It takes me longer than it should to return to a blank canvas. Mostly because I can't stop thinking that he's skirting the truth somehow. His response was a little too rushed, a lot too curt, and followed up by a quick distraction.

It's the same behavior my brothers use when they know they're toeing the line with my dad.

Mike's sitting on the bench in front of my vanity, sorting through the various tubes, brushes, and compacts scattered all over the place. He looks hilarious with his large body threatening to break the tiny pink stool, but the funniest part is that he's choosing items deliberately. He forms a pile of makeup products on one side of the dresser then picks out coordinating brushes and even a sponge that weirdly resembles a sex toy.

I shake that thought right out of my skull and sit on the floor between his spread legs when he gestures for me to do so.

I can't win no matter what I do. Thank God he's at least not wearing sweatpants today, which would only accentuate the package that's now at my eye-level.

"Wait a minute." I suddenly realize why this situation feels like such a lie. "If you know how to do makeup, then why did you let me paint your face with concealer to hide the scratch marks Evie left behind?"

He frowns. "I kind of had a lot of shit on my mind at that point. I didn't want to add more to the pile by blowing open another secret."

That's fair enough.

"Oh my God!" I blurt, desperate for a distraction from the sight directly in front of me. "That's why you were so concerned with the color not matching! I just thought you were uncomfortable wearing makeup."

"I was." He pops his eyebrows. "Never thought I'd be the one who needed concealer. It was a mindfuck to be on the other side of that fence for a change."

Without any more of an explanation, he lifts my chin then gently turns my face in all different directions. He studies all my flaws with a focused gaze. His voice is a soft hum. "You don't need me to prep you at all."

"Excuse me?" *Get your mind out of the gutter, Vittoria.*

The corner of his mouth lifts in a weird half smile, half grimace. "You have perfect skin. You don't really need any primer. You probably don't even need foundation, but we'll use it anyway. Maybe it'll help cover your blushes on the sidelines, so the press won't think you're embarrassed to be seen with me."

"I'm not embarrassed to be seen with you!" I'm such a jerk. I'm worried about not crossing any imaginary lines, and he's thinking that I don't want to be around him for totally different reasons. "I'm sorry I made you think that."

His smile is more genuine as he dabs foundation all over my face with his finger. "I'm messing with you."

"You shouldn't. I am now in possession of very juicy information about you that I could accidentally leak to the press." I close my eyes when the sponge gets a little too close as he blends the makeup over my face, expecting—hoping—he'll tell me he's going to make me look like a deranged clown in retaliation.

"I'm not worried. You won't."

I open my eyes when all sensation leaves my face. Mike's holding a tube of concealer, studying his canvas again.

"I thought you said I have perfect skin? Is the foundation not enough to cover the evidence of my lack of sleep?" I never had to worry about dark under-eyes before. I only have concealer because he needed it.

Mike blinks like he lost his train of thought. "No, I—" He throws the tube down on the vanity with a little too much force. "Habit. You don't need it. It's fine."

I don't believe that for a second. He's withholding again. I can feel it. "Really?"

"Really," he reassures me with a more confident smile before turning to check my pile of makeup again. "You do need setting powder though. I can't find it."

"I didn't buy any powder. I didn't know I needed to."

He raises an eyebrow. "All right, then. We'll put it on the list to buy before game day."

This might be the sweetest, weirdly most heart-melting interaction I've ever had with a guy, but we still have a problem. "Um, okay, but...you're not going to be able to do my makeup before game day. You're going to be kind of busy with more important things."

His smile softens as he tickles my cheeks with a blush brush. "If you like this look, then I'll teach you how to do it for yourself."

I take a stab in the dark about his cryptic explanations. "Just like you taught your sisters because your mom was busy being a single parent?"

"You've never fished so obviously before." Mike's smile turns sad as he rests his arm against his knee, still clutching the blush brush in his capable, big hand. He blows out a breath. "You believe me without question when I say I can do makeup, and there's a hell of a lot of trust involved in actually letting me do it. I guess it's time for me to make this more of a two-way street, huh?"

I can't fathom where he's going to go with this, but I scoot closer anyway. I'm all ears. "That's what friends do, yeah. They trust *each other*. You know by now I'll never use anything you tell me in confidence against you."

He switches out brushes—eyeshadow replaces blush. A tap with his finger against my nose, followed by a murmured, "Close your eyes."

As he feathers the gentlest caresses against the most sensitive parts of my face, he weaves further instructions between horrific stories of hazing and abuse from college.

"Look up....it all started with rookie training camp...close your eyes again...circle jerking for the cameras...look down...we were, uh, apparently drugged out of our minds...open your mouth a little...so, that's it. That's what Evie finally told me when she came to visit."

I work in PR for football, so I'm aware being a professional athlete isn't all sunshine and roses. The nastier parts of marketing are what brought me into Mike's life to begin with. But never, ever, ever in my wildest dreams could I imagine the utter horrors of what he's just told me.

"I...I have no idea what to say other than I'm sorry." I gaze up at his face that's completely devoid of any emotion at all. "That doesn't seem like nearly enough. Is there anything I can do for you?"

He swallows thickly then glances away. "Evie told me all that because she thinks I need closure I've never gotten." He returns an even gaze to my own. "I don't necessarily agree, but I do want to make sure Chelsie is all right. The only problem is I can't seem to track her down. I have no way to know where she is now or how she's doing. I've moved on with my life, and I guess I just need reassurance that she has, too. That what she went through because of me didn't fuck her up too bad."

I rise from my seat on the floor with shaky legs. "Don't be mad at me..."

Mike actually barks out a short laugh. "Famous last words."

I truly hope not.

I cross my bedroom and retrieve a file folder from my nightstand drawer before returning to Mike and dropping it in his lap. "I did a little digging. Just to make sure she wouldn't be a threat to your career now."

He doesn't open the folder, just glances up at me with apprehension in his eyes. "This *is* part of your job description?"

"Yeah."

After a deep, bracing breath, he reads the information I've found —complete with current address. "I don't think I should do this alone. She would be completely justified to slap me in the face if I show up on her doorstep. Would you, uh…would you maybe come with me?"

I don't hesitate a second to jump over the line of professionalism. I shove the folder to the floor then climb onto his lap, wrapping my arms and legs around him like I can possibly hug all the hurt out of him. I nuzzle my face into the warm, smooth, delicious-smelling skin at his neck. "She would *not* be justified to slap you in the face. I don't know if it's a good idea for me to go with you. I might just cause more bad publicity. Because I'm going to punch that cunty bitch right in her stupid face for even thinking for a second that you cheated on her first."

His laughter rumbles through me. "It's so wrong, but I love it when you get mad enough to swear, Peaches."

I lift my head, only to be horrified at the yellowish-brown stain I've left on his otherwise pristine, white tee. "Oh my God, I'm so sorry!"

He glances down to where I'm gaping then chuckles. "This is why we need to get you the setting powder."

# Chapter 22
All These Things That I've Done

## Mike

"Why does she live in Jersey now? We're from Ohio."

It's a stupid question, and it doesn't matter. I'm standing on my ex-girlfriend's front porch like a freaking creeper while my fake girlfriend shrugs beside me.

"I don't know the whys or hows. I only dug up the whats." Tori's voice softens. "Stop stalling and ring the doorbell."

It's not a rocket science deduction that I'm absolutely stalling. I have no idea what to say. No clue what to ask. This could all blow up in my face. Frankly, that's exactly what I'm expecting, but I can't live with myself until I've paid my dues.

Tori's hand on my shoulder doesn't even calm me down. "Tell you what? I'm going to take a walk around the block. Maybe having an audience is making this harder for you. If you need me for any reason, I'm just a text away."

That's a horrible idea. "You can't just go walking around in a strange neighborhood! There could be...creeps! Lurking!"

Her smile is soft, and just like Tori—genuine. "Just because something bad happened to Evie doesn't mean it's going to happen to me." She gestures at the tree-lined street in what appears to be a quaint little neighborhood filled with small but well-kept houses. So much like my hometown. "There are plenty of other people out for a stroll, so I won't be alone. I have my phone. I'll be fine."

"But, but, but..." I would be more embarrassed about stuttering like an idiot if my heart wasn't racing at the same pace.

She reaches up on her tiptoes to plant a gentle kiss on my cheek that finally, finally warms all the cold places inside me. "I have the utmost faith in you, Michael Mitchell. You're gonna be just fine."

I call out to her as she turns tail and bounds down the stairs. "You're really afraid you're going to punch her, aren't you?"

"Yep!" she yells back as she flees down the sidewalk at a brisk pace.

I blow out a breath and push the doorbell since the clock is officially running down now. I sure as hell hope Chelsie's husband isn't a Newark fan. This is going to be awkward enough as it is.

The door slowly swings open. A face I barely recognize stares back at me. Her blond hair that felt like silk in my greedy teenage hands is frizzy and crazy. The blue eyes that could build me up or cut me down with a single look seem tired and ringed with dark circles. It makes me feel like an asshole to notice, but the body I once knew so well has, well…changed.

"Mike?" She obviously recognizes me still.

"Hi." *Solid opening, Mitchell.*

She opens the door wider then pushes past me to glance up and down the street like she's expecting cameras to announce she's being punked. Satisfied that nothing looks out of the ordinary, she steps back inside. "What are you doing here?"

"I, uh, was in the neighborhood…" Wow. I never knew I was the shittiest liar in the world until now.

She chuckles, shakes her head, then glances down at her feet before returning a slightly amused gaze to me. "I thought you got drafted to Albany?"

I thought she hated my guts. So, how does she know what team I got drafted to?

"I did. I am. I live in Albany, I mean. I play for the Wolves still." *Man up, Mitchell.* "I'm sorry to show up here and probably annoy the hell out of you, but…uh…can we talk?"

She swings the door open wide and gestures for me to come in.

The hallway is littered with clumps of dog hair and toys—both for kids and pets. A few pairs of small shoes and women's shoes are not-so-neatly stacked by the doorway. No men's shoes.

"Is this a good time?"

She crosses her arms and raises a skeptical eyebrow at me. "You obviously drove here all the way from Albany. The regular season is starting soon. I'm guessing this is as good a time as you're going to have for a while."

She's not wrong, but...hell. I don't even know where to begin.

"Where's the dog?" That's not the best place to start.

She snorts. "I don't have visitation this week. Since when are you afraid of dogs?"

"I'm not. I was just expecting one." Awesome. This just keeps getting better. I might as well tell her to sweep the fucking floors because her house is filthy.

Wait a minute..."Visitation?"

"Ah, yes." She nods and purses her lips. "The soon-to-be ex-husband doesn't give a shit whether he sees his kid on the weekends, but the dog is apparently non-negotiable."

That's why her body looks different. She has a kid now. That wasn't part of the information Tori dug up.

"Soon-to-be ex?" I recognized Chelsie's last name had changed, but again...missing information.

She calls to me as she strides down the hallway. "Come on. If we're going to talk about this, I need an afternoon delight."

Holy shit. Is she offering me rebound sex?

She disappears around a corner. "We have exactly forty-five minutes until Charlie wakes up from his nap, so get a move on, Mitchell. I know you're faster than this."

I don't feel fast at all. I feel like I'm bogged down in quicksand up to my ears while a coach screams at me to push harder. Drills next week are going to be a cakewalk compared to this.

She's uncorking a bottle of wine when I make my way into the kitchen. A wry grin twists her lips. "I hope you like cheap red and sob stories because I'm all out of pretending everything's fine for today."

"Chels..." That old nickname doesn't taste right on my tongue. "What the hell happened?"

For the next God knows how long, she pours out her sob story to me—a husband who cheated while she was pregnant with their first child, fighting to keep the house they bought together and planned to raise a whole family in, having to see his mistress every day in the halls of the same interior design firm they work at, being a single working mother while trying to raise her young son.

That last part hits a little too close to home.

"Why don't you sell this house for a profit and go home?" Shit. I think I slurred that question. I didn't want to be rude by refusing her offer of a completely non-sexual afternoon delight, but I don't drink anymore. My job demands that my body be firing on all cylinders at all times. "Isn't your family still in Ironville? You could start up your own interior design company there and have help with Charlie."

She scoffs at my suggestion. "You know how Ironville is. If I crawl back with my tail tucked between my legs, I'll never hear the end of it." Her blue eyes soften into something that resembles a memory. "I was supposed to be the wife of a professional football player, not a single mother divorcee of an IT grunt."

I reach across the kitchen island to grasp her hand. "I am so fucking sorry, Chelsie."

She swipes at the tears streaking down her cheeks with her free hand. "Sorry for what? You didn't cheat on me while I was pregnant."

"I did." My brain is wine-fuzzy, but I came here with a plan, and she's given me the perfect opening. "You weren't pregnant. At least not that you told me, but I recently found out about what happened that night during the rookie hazing at State. I had no idea you cheated on me because I cheated on you first. If I had known then what I know now, I would have fought for you. I would have tried harder. Instead, I just let you go, thinking that's what you wanted. I'm so fucking sorry."

She wrests her hand free from my grip.

I brace for the expected slap.

Instead, she gently knocks on my temple. "Did you take too many hits during the preseason? You didn't cheat on me! You were drugged!"

Wait. What? "I'm sorry, but...what?"

She chuckles then pours out the rest of the wine into her glass. After finishing off the bottle, she sighs. "Mike. I didn't cheat on you as a way to get even. I was young and stupid, and I was eager to see what—who—else was out there. Who marries their high school sweetheart these days? I'm sorry you found out the way you did. I kept meaning to have a talk with you once we got to campus, but you were always so busy with practices, or team activities, or..." She tips her empty glass toward me. "Getting blowjobs from women who weren't me."

I can't believe my ears. Is she doubling back on her absolution of my sins? Thank Christ Tori isn't here. This would not end well.

Chelsie's smile is half-hearted at best. "I honestly figured since you enjoyed it that I didn't need to face the music. You were ready to move on, and I already had."

Wait...what? "How long had you been cheating on me?"

She winces. "The first time was the same afternoon as the hazing, but I thought I had more time to talk to you about it and break it to you gently!"

Well, shit. All the guilt that's been eating away at me for nearly a month evaporates. It was always going to come to this. I just didn't know it at the time.

"Still." I hold my open palm out to her. She was my first...everything. For that alone, she deserves my forgiveness and respect. She took a chance on me at a time when I believed no one ever could. Or should. "Evie told me everything. I'm sorry for what you went through as my girlfriend. Even if you already had a foot out the door."

Chelsie laughs and shakes her head. "You know, I always hated Evie in high school. I couldn't stand how much of your time and attention she took up that I truly believed belonged to me. She was really there for me that night. She held me up when I was bawling my eyes out about what was happening. How's she doing, anyway? I saw that nude spread she did our senior year of college, and honest to God, it made me feel so guilty for ever thinking poorly of her at all."

I don't know if it's the wine or all the revelations from different perspectives than I ever had before, but I shake my head to try to physically make all these vectors merge into a single straight line. "She's, uh…she's good. Some high school sweethearts actually do get married."

"To Falls?" she guesses.

I wince. If I wasn't drunk, I wouldn't have let that slip.

Chelsie laughs. "I hope Rob has a better season than the last one. I couldn't even believe that was the same guy I used to know."

That makes two of us. "It was a rough transition, but I think you'll recognize the guy on the field this season."

She takes my glass and hers to the sink to wash them. "What's the secret to your better transition?" She shoots me a wink. "Were you still in the honeymoon phase with your new girlfriend? Trying to impress…Tori? That's her name, right?"

Suddenly, the nameless, faceless fans who see photos online of me and Tori aren't so ambiguous. Shame creeps up my neck. I didn't come here to rub anything in Chelsie's face, especially not after what she's told me about her shitty situation.

"Nah." I wave off her assumptions. "I never have to impress her. She likes me for me."

Chelsie's smile is the most genuine it's seemed all this time. "I'm glad. You're a good man, Mike Mitchell." She wags her finger in my direction. "She'd better be deserving of you."

"She is."

Damn. That's the surest I've been about anything since I arrived in Chelsie's new hometown. An invisible weight has been lifted from my chest. I'm gonna have to call Evie and apologize for basically throwing her out of my house when I had a temper tantrum like a fucking toddler.

A different toddler's babble carries through on a speaker that's sitting on the kitchen island.

Chelsie's eyebrows pop. "Time's up. You need to go. Charlie's only two, but he's smart. He knows what his daddy looks like even though he doesn't see him much anymore. You do not fit that description. Anytime someone asks me why I'm not dating again, I simply tell them I'm not ready to have that conversation with my gifted toddler."

I rise from my stool. "No apologies necessary. Time to get back to the mom gig. I get it. It's a way more important job than mine."

She escorts me to the door and gestures vaguely in my direction. "I hate that all this misplaced guilt brought you here, but it was good to see you. I'm glad we finally got the chance to set the record straight between us."

I give her a hug that oddly feels like letting go. "If you ever need anything, don't let what happened between us keep you from calling. Even if it's only for a free babysitter when you decide you're ready to date again."

She laughs as she opens the door. "I might take you up on that, buddy."

"Please do."

Chelsie peers past me to my big truck parked at her curb then slaps me hard enough on the arm that it's probably going to leave a mark. "You left her out here all this time? What in the hell is wrong with you? She's gonna think you were in here cheating on her!"

Sure enough, Tori's sitting in my truck. She seems content, playing on her phone and bobbing her head to a beat I can't hear. The truck engine is running. Her hair moves slightly from the breeze of the AC. She must have gotten overheated on her walk. Pale skin like hers burns easily, and I didn't see her apply any sunscreen before our road trip.

"She kept me company on the drive, but she wanted to give us some privacy. She trusts me." That sounds a hell of a lot better than admitting Tori didn't trust herself not to commit physical violence.

Chelsie clicks her tongue against her teeth. "Wife that one up, Mitchell. Trust is worth its weight in gold these days."

"I hope you find someone you can trust again, too."

She winks before she closes the door. "He's upstairs, calling for his mommy."

I didn't admit to Chelsie that I never pictured her as my wife—not even in the distant future. I was holding onto something that I never really had in the first place. It wasn't about love; it was about failure.

Staring at Tori as she sings along to whatever she's listening to, I don't have the willpower to keep lying to myself. I want her. I'm pretty sure she wants me, too. My career can't afford the sort of distraction she has the potential to be, and she doesn't want to sleep her way to the top. I need to find a way to obliterate this friend zone while giving us both what we want.

# Chapter 23
Truth or Dare

## Tori

"I can't believe I let you talk me into this," Mike mutters behind a glass of expensive scotch that he's not actually drinking.

"Hey, not only did I rock doing my own makeup, including false eyelashes, but I also think I did a great job after the game today playing a totally supportive, loving girlfriend for the cameras."

It wasn't all that difficult of an act to pull off. The Wolves—and Mike—had another amazing season opener, and I'll admit I got caught up in the excitement on the sideline. Kissing Mike isn't exactly a hardship.

He tips his untouched glass toward me in a half-hearted toast. "That's an argument for why you deserve a reward, not for dragging me here."

"It's called leverage, Mitchell. You agree I deserve a reward for all my hard work. My reward is getting you to attend your team's post-game celebration. Two birds, one stone."

He raises a skeptical eyebrow at me, shakes his head and sighs, then takes a tiny sip of his drink.

I understand now more than ever why Mike isn't tight with his teammates; why he never seems to let his guard down around them, and why there's almost no social media proof of him bonding with them. The press is starting to paint him as being a loner among the Wolves. A player who thinks he's too good to rub elbows with his co-workers who don't necessarily perform at his level. That's not just bad publicity. It's fodder for his teammates to resent him, which could lead to problems in the locker room that I can't mitigate. What the general public doesn't know is that Mike has every reason to not only distrust his teammates, but quite frankly, to be terrified of the guys he shares a locker room with. It's my job to make his job easier—on and off the field.

"Part of your media profile is bonding with your teammates. You need to be seen out and about, having a good time with them."

"Peaches." He levels me with a stern expression. "I might be a professional football player, but I have never considered going to a strip club a good time."

"Night club," I correct him.

He rolls his eyes then gestures vaguely to the stage. "And I suppose your PR brain would label her an exotic dancer instead of a stripper."

Just to prove my point, I glance over my shoulder at the nearly naked, oiled-up woman on the stage who obviously gets full-body waxes because there is no way that two-piece could hide even a single stray pubic hair. "That is correct. She is an entertainer. A dancer who is performing a routine for paying customers."

"Mmhmm." Mike sticks his tongue in his cheek. "So, from a marketing perspective, Templeman up there—stuffing Benjamins into her G-string—is tipping generously for excellent services rendered like a good customer should?"

"Yep." I manage not to squeak. "There are plenty of videos circulating on the internet about teams celebrating a big win in exactly this way. It's...expected."

"Sure," he drags out. "I just didn't think strip club patron was the image of me you wanted to present to the public."

"That's why I'm with you." I smile my brightest to lessen his justifiable anxiety. "You're hanging out with your teammates in their favorite party spot, but you're still wholesome enough to bring your girlfriend."

"There is nothing wholesome about half the team being in champagne rooms right now."

"I thought professional football players don't drink much during the season?"

Mike's body rumbles all around me as his face turns a weird shade of purple from obviously trying not to laugh in my face. After a few deep breaths, he manages a stuttered, "Nope. I can't be the one to take away your innocence."

I haven't been a virgin in a very long time, but Mike's words send a jolt of anticipation through my tense muscles. A literal shudder rolls through me with the effort of holding myself together. In hindsight, sitting on his lap to act as a human security blanket for him wasn't my brightest idea.

"You cold?" His tone is genuinely concerned.

I take a healthy sip of my martini. "Nope. I'm fine, thanks for asking."

His expression shows he doesn't believe me for a second, but his attention is diverted by a large body plopping into the cushy leather seat beside us. "Finally run out of cash?"

Templeman shakes his head with a frown. "Nah. I got plenty left, but she ain't the unicorn for me."

Mike chuckles, releasing a wave of way-too-pleasurable vibrations beneath me. "I keep telling you that you're looking in all the wrong places, man. You won't listen to me."

A decidedly evil grin lights up Templeman's face. He leans closer. "How you doin' tonight, baby? Enjoying yourself?"

"No," Mike commands in no uncertain terms. He places his glass down on the end table between the chairs then wraps his solid arms around my waist, pulling me closer against his chest.

Torture, thy name is Mike Mitchell.

"Tori is not your unicorn either."

"Right. Because she's yours." Templeman visibly pouts. "How is the front office gonna assign you a dick-gracer and not me? This shit ain't fair."

Mike punches Templeman in the arm.

"Ow!" He yelps then rubs the spot. "You have any idea how bruised I am from blocking for you today, motherfucker?"

Mike grins. "Yep."

Templeman punches him back.

Mike glowers. "You do that again, and I swear to God, you won't be able to play next week."

Even though I understand Templeman is one of the few Wolves who Mike has somewhat of a relationship with, this situation has the potential to turn into a PR nightmare if they keep up this pissing contest.

"Elliot?" My gamble pays off. Using his first name gets Templeman's attention faster than throwing my drink in his face to cool him off. "Why are you so obsessed with unicorns?"

Mike laughs again, his body a delicious—torturous—shuddering all around me. He picks up his glass and gestures toward Templeman. "I couldn't bring myself to explain champagne rooms. I'm not going to even try to explain your definition of a unicorn. Mostly because it's stupid."

My arousal evaporates. I suddenly feel like the butt of a joke instead of a mediator. Templeman's usually happy expression changes into something resembling anger.

He leans over, his gaze a laser on Mike. "Number one, it's not stupid. Number two, how you gonna bring a sweet woman like Tori here if she don't even know what a damn champagne room is? That ain't right, Mitchell. I thought you were better than that."

"This was not my idea," he grumbles back even as his expression shows obvious shame. "I didn't want to bring her here at all."

I snap my fingers between their almost touching faces. My temper is running dangerously hot. "I am right here, so please stop talking about me in the third person. There are plenty of other players' wives and girlfriends at the club tonight. It's not like I'm the only woman. One of you better tell me right now what a champagne room is because I don't like feeling stupid."

Templeman straightens in his seat and turns a pitying gaze to me, which doesn't make me feel better in the slightest. "Baby girl, these other women understand exactly what they're getting into. The whole team knows you're Mike's PR. No one expects you to have a jersey chaser mindset. You're about the business of football, and that's all right." He clears his throat as he glances around at the chaos then gestures with his chin toward the quarterback, whose wife is also sitting on his lap. "Derek over there? In about an hour, he's gonna tell his old faithful she should head home for the night to check on the kids, and that he'll follow once he makes sure the team ain't gonna get into any trouble without him. Soon as she leaves, he'll be back in one of the champagne rooms."

A sinking sensation takes root in my stomach, but I don't dare interrupt. Templeman is giving me a behind-the-scenes play-by-play that no one in the front office would ever trust me with.

"Castle? You know him?" He goes on without waiting for me to nod. Obviously, part of my job is knowing everyone on the team. "That ain't his girlfriend. She's still in Georgia, and she knows damn well he's got a woman in multiple cities. She's hanging on, thinking she's gonna wait out his wild side. I almost feel bad for this new chick. She don't know the score yet. She thinks she's winning because he'll take her back to a champagne room later. He sure as hell wouldn't take her to his home though."

Mike nods and follows another sip of his drink with a hard swallow.

"The fellas who don't have a guaranteed spot on the roster are in the champagne rooms right now, blowin' damn near all the money they're making in a single night. Living it up like kings with women who worship money. They're enjoying themselves past what's smart because they know if we don't win next week—if they don't play their best—" Templeman snaps his fingers. "This'll all be gone in a heartbeat. They'll be beggars who can't be choosers overnight."

I don't need to hear anymore. I place my empty martini glass on the side table and wave to a waitress who blatantly ignores me.

Mike's warm lips brush against my ear. "If you want another, I'll get it for you. But, Peaches…it's a good idea to keep your wits in situations like this. You never know what's gonna happen when everyone else has had too much."

Of course. This is the full innocence Mike didn't want to steal from me even after he confessed the horrors he's already lived through. I nestle my head into the crook of his neck, wanting to give comfort enough for the both of us.

"Can you get me a water, please?" I whisper.

He kisses my forehead in response.

Templeman relaxes fully into his chair with a deep sigh. "Do you understand what champagne rooms are now?"

I nod, a deep sense of dejection weighing me down. How am I supposed to fix any of this for Mike? "I'm not sure I want to know about unicorns anymore."

Weirdly, Mike chuckles.

Templeman's eyes light up. "We ain't all bad, sweet thing. Some of us just wanna play the game we love and find the right woman to enjoy the ride with us. She gotta be perfect for this crazy life—understanding, loyal, beautiful, confident, got her own goals to attain, not willing to take any shit from us or from anyone else."

This concept is way more confusing than what a champagne room actually is. "You do realize most of those qualities seem contradictory, right?"

Templeman cackles. "That's why she's a unicorn! A woman like that is a myth!"

"I told you it was stupid," Mike mumbles into my hair. "And that coming here was a bad idea."

Templeman scoffs. "It ain't a bad idea. Ya girl just needs to know what she's dealing with, that's all. She ain't gonna be able to work effectively for you if she don't know the rules of the game." He gestures to me with his glass. "Now you know."

I know Mike is protecting me with his big arms as much as he's clinging to me for help to get through this. I know Templeman doesn't have to sit here and teach me some of the ropes, but he is.

"You're right, Elliot. You're not all bad. The bad ones just get more press. So, help me out some more. Tell me about the good guys."

He grins. "On this team? Girl, you're sitting with the only good guys."

"That's not true." At least for their sake, I hope it isn't.

He laughs. "All right, all right. It's not completely true. A football team is like any other group of people. Bad ones, good ones, everything in between. So long as we work together to play good ball on the field, we deal with the rest."

"We've been playing some damn good ball," Mike concedes.

Templeman nods. "So, we get to celebrate a little and to hell with the rest of it." He flags down a waitress who immediately responds with a wide smile. "We'll have three shots of tequila, three Dos Equis, and three waters."

"Sure thing, Mr. Templeman."

Mike barks out a laugh that jostles me. "Hearing someone call you *mister* Templeman is so weird."

Templeman grins. The kind that just screams trouble. "Do you call him *mister* Mitchell when there aren't any cameras around?"

I do sometimes. He absolutely hates it.

"You're going to get punched again," Mike warns.

Not on my watch. "Tell me more about your unicorn search, Elliot."

This smile is entirely different. There's a sparkle in his nearly black eyes that can't be contained. Over tequila shots, gross beer chasers, and laughter, Elliot Templeman weaves a tale of his desperate search for his one true unicorn to share the ups and downs of life with.

I'm a quivering mess of romantic hope by the time he finishes.

"I want to find my unicorn, too." My sigh is full of girlish wistfulness. It's not even the tequila talking. Mostly. I had dreams of a big wedding once. I could still have that. Someday. With *my* unicorn.

Templeman drains the rest of his beer. "You can't find what you're not looking for."

"I can't look. Not as long as the front office wants me to play pretend. I can't even casually date." I wince as soon as the brutally honest words leave my mouth. Rude doesn't even come close to saying that out loud to one of his teammates while I'm sitting on Mike's lap, basically curled up into a sleepy ball.

Instead of being justifiably offended, the backs of Mike's fingers sweep up and down my arm in a soothing motion. "I think it's time to get out of here. You slurred that last part."

I peel myself away from the solid warmth of his chest, meeting his gorgeous brown eyes directly. "I'm sorry. I didn't mean that how it sounded."

He smiles in return. This one also offers an entirely different world of trouble. "No offense taken."

Templeman clears his throat. "I'm gonna, uh...head out, too. Night, y'all."

Mike barely even acknowledges his teammate's departure.

And me? I'm trapped in his focused gaze—my tongue heavy in my mouth, my heartbeat racing faster than the tempo of the club sauce blaring over the speakers.

He's so deliciously handsome, made even more so by the warm, genuine person he is behind the scenes.

Mike drags the rough pad of his thumb across my bottom lip. If my carefully applied lipstick doesn't hold up, red will be smeared across my cheek, following the path of his touch.

Something about that mental image sends curls of pin-prick awareness rushing through me.

He's putting on a good show in the public eye. That's all this is.

He leans closer, his breath a ghost against my lips. "How real do you want this to be, Peaches?"

"It's not real," I whisper. Crumbling. Oh, so slowly giving in to the attraction to him that's only grown stronger since we first met. "It's all for show."

He licks his lips. "It doesn't have to be. You could date me for show and have something real behind closed doors."

"Like a champagne room?" That doesn't sound real at all.

He studies me carefully. Like he knows I'm so very close to giving in, and a single breath from him will send me careening over the cliff. "If that's something you want, I'll make it happen. Just say the word."

"Word."

# Chapter 24
Crash Into Me

## Mike

I CAN'T GET her clothes off fast enough. My elbow hits the door frame with a jarring thump, but I barely even register the pain. At least I closed and locked it before pulling her shirt off.

"Are you okay?" She laughs then soothes my elbow with her lips and tongue.

My elbow.

Sweet baby Jesus, I want this woman to lick me from head to toe.

I *need* her.

I'm only getting this opportunity because she gave me a very clear route, so this can't be all about what I need.

I press her body against the door with my own, effectively cutting off her ability to make me lose my mind. Hauling up one of her legs to wrap around my waist, I slide my hand up the smooth expanse of her thigh. My fingers curl around the edge of what definitely feels like the same kind of lace panties I've seen before. I murmur in her ear between kissing her neck until her head lolls back to give me better access, "You're so much softer than I imagined."

"You were imagining me?" she asks, breathless.

"You stripped for me, Peaches," I admit between pulls of her tongue. "Who did you think I was jerking off for?"

"Oh," she chuckles, the vibrations shared between our mouths. "I shouldn't have done that. I'm so sorry."

I pull back to meet her eyes. We can't go any further until some things are crystal clear, with no room for error. "I'm not sorry. If you still want this, I will work harder than I ever have to make it worth your time. But if you have any doubts, you need to tell me now. We can forget any of this happened. Just like last time."

Those words taste like shit on my tongue that I'd much rather drown in Tori's flavor. My muscles tremble with restraint. If she shuts this down, no amount of jerking off for the rest of the season is going to be enough to satisfy me.

She bites her lip and studies me with obvious hesitation in her eyes. "You don't want this, too?"

A sigh of relief pushes my chest more firmly against hers. If that's all she's worried about, then game on. "You have no idea how much I want this."

So, I show her. I prove it.

Peaches admits she loves the way I kiss her. I pour everything I have into owning her mouth, her lips, her tongue—nipping her full bottom lip that's the sweetest thing I've ever sunk my teeth into, trying my damnedest to suck all the happiness she brings me into my chest.

She grinds herself against me shamelessly. Riding me in the open foyer of my house with our pants still on while she's balancing on one leg because I'm still holding the other hostage around my waist.

Her nails dig into my ass with enough pressure to startle me even through my jeans.

My cough of laughter spooks her.

She pulls her hands away, curling them into her chest like a barrier between our bodies that I instantly hate. "I—I'm sorry."

"Ssh," I soothe her swollen bottom lip with my tongue then drop her leg, so I can put her hands back exactly where she had them. "No apologies between us. Take what you need from me, babe. I promise I'll enjoy every second of the ride."

Her breath ghosts out in a rush that presses her lace-covered tits against my bare chest. That bra is going to be the next thing to go. "I haven't done this in a long time, but I don't want to be selfish. If this isn't going to be an even exchange of goods, then maybe we should stop."

Hell no.

This mix of confident and submissive Tori only makes me want to see how far she'll go in either direction even more. Just like the first time we met, I'm eager to peel back all her layers to see who she really is at her core. To see what we could be together. I haul her up with my hands on the ass I've been dying to grab onto for weeks, situating her center right where she'll get the most out of what I have to offer.

"I haven't done this in a long time either," I confess, pressing her into the door with enough weight to make my dick really angry with the hint of more. "I don't know how long I'll last once I get inside you so, *please*. Take what you need before I can disappoint you."

The vibrations of her husky chuckle have me *this close* to coming in my pants, which only reinforces my admission.

She slides her hands from my cheeks, down the sides of my neck, to rest on my shoulders. "I love how honest you are, Mike Mitchell."

All my brain hears is that she loves any part of me at all. "Then, I'm honestly telling you—get off now because when I take you upstairs to fuck you? I'm not going to be able to hold back."

A shudder rolls through her right before she clamps her hands in a vice hold at the back of my neck and crashes her mouth against mine in a way that's going to brand me for all time.

Her movements are frantic as she tightens her legs around my waist and grinds her heat against me so hard, I'm already close to seeing stars.

I press her harder against the door, pistoning my hips in a matching tempo, kissing her until my lungs scream for air, kneading her ass until my hands tingle.

She rips her mouth away only to let out a gasp then a long, low moan.

"Fuck, yes, Peaches." I roll my hips around with slow, even pressure to draw out her pleasure, studying every flutter of her eyelids, the open gape of her mouth, the way her pulse throbs in her neck. I inhale it all like a starving man. "Give it to me."

Her head rests against the door, her body lax in my arms as she blinks her eyes open. "I gave it all. Your turn."

"Do you still want to take it all?" I double-check as I take the stairs to my bedroom two at a time with her still in my arms.

"If you don't show me what you can do with that dick I've been fantasizing about since the first time I saw it, I...I'll..."

I laugh as I lay her in the middle of my bed. "You can't even come up with anything."

"I'm all comed out," she admits, her eyes falling closed with a deep sigh as her body relaxes against the comforter. "Get in here, so we can enjoy the relaxation together."

As I take in her red hair fanned out on my bland, gray blankets, her milky white skin a sharp contrast to the lifelessness of my bed, I'm anything but relaxed.

This is going to be the shortest game of my life. There's no way around it.

She opens her eyes to find me staring at her. A frown pulls at her swollen lips. "I'm on the pill if you're worried about getting trapped into anything."

Of course, she'd think that's what I'm worried about.

I crawl over her then reach beneath her to fumble with the clasp of her bra until she takes pity on me and sheds it herself. I talk with my mouth full of the sweetest peaches, "I trust you. I've seen your pill case in the bathroom."

I take my time licking, sucking, nipping at every millimeter of her round, firm flesh.

She threads her hands through my hair, holding me to her as I suck her nipples into hardened peaks.

"Delay of game, Mitchell," she murmurs through her moans.

I chuckle against her warm skin. "If you're calling penalties now, just wait until I jump the snap."

"Huh?" She raises her eyebrows in complete confusion as she lifts her hips to help me peel her jeans and panties off.

"I'm trying to cool down a bit before I completely embarrass myself," I admit. Not that running my nose along the inside of her thigh before taking a taste of her sweet center accomplishes that.

"Oh, sure. But you'll let me completely embarrass myself against your front door." She tugs my head away by my hair then offers me a soft glance to soothe the sting. "I won't judge. It's been a lot longer for you than it has for me."

"Almost four years," I admit then immediately wince. Honestly isn't always the best policy.

Judging by her expression, Tori's already doing the math in her head, and those numbers don't add up. She doesn't call me out. "You've already seen my strip show. It's only fair to show me yours."

I stand up by the foot of the bed. My hands shake as I slowly unbutton, unzip, then pull down my jeans. Not because I'm embarrassed of the body I work so hard to keep in top shape, but because none of the roadblocks I'm throwing up are slowing me down at all tonight. Unless she calls the game, I'm going to cross this line. Hell, I'm going to jump over it.

She lazily circles a finger in my direction. "Keep going."

I slide my boxer briefs down inch by inch, not bothering to keep the cocky grin off my face. I already know she likes this part, too.

Tori licks her lips. "Do I need to admit to you how many times I've fantasized about that being inside me since I first saw it? Would that make you speed things up just a little?"

"It would not." Call me an egomaniac, but I'm absolutely basking in the glow of her heavy gaze.

Coming from a woman other than Peaches, the obvious want in her expression wouldn't faze me at all. Another lesson learned the hard way.

"I saw condoms in one of your away game swag-packs," she blurts. "Don't take this the wrong way, but I still have to protect you. Even from me," she murmurs the last part.

I lower myself on top of her, the glide of bare skin on bare skin enough to send my eyes rolling into my skull. Nothing my mind has cooked up over the past year could ever come close to this. Her lips are soft beneath mine.

"I know you do. I'll protect you, too," I promise. "Be right back."

Not even the snug condom is enough to dull the sensation of finally, finally pushing inside her tight heat.

I collapse my full weight on top of her, trying to breathe through the pure pleasure incinerating my mind. After seconds that feel like an eternity, I lift my upper body, shifting my weight onto my arms and thrusting forward until she swallows me whole.

She throws her head back, exposing her long throat to me. Her hands claw for purchase at my back, her legs tightening around my hips as I piston in and out, faster, faster, chasing a rush that's already engulfing me in flames.

"Oh, God! Oh, God!" she cries, her legs spasming around me.

I can't last. No matter how satisfying it is to see Peaches flying apart around me.

I jerk into her, my orgasm barreling through me so hard, all I can do is grunt through my release that feels never-ending.

"So good," I breathe into the skin at her neck, completely spent.

"Ruined me," she whispers through what sounds like choking tears.

Her body still trembles beneath me, squeezing my sensitive cock almost to the point of pain as her chest stutters with struggled pants.

Fuck. I went too fast and hard. It's been a long time for her, too.

I peel myself away and slide out slowly, ready to apologize and tend to the body I just ravaged like a fucking animal. "God, Peaches. I'm sorry. Did I hurt you?"

She opens and closes her mouth several times, her naked tits heaving with deep breaths. Her voice comes out panted. "Feels like…like…I'm still coming. Can't stop. Ruined."

I derail the grin threatening to make me look like a complete asshole by brushing my lips against hers. "If you're only stroking my ego because you feel like that's also part of your job description, then this arrangement isn't going to work out for me."

She closes her eyes on another deep sigh then swings her head wildly back and forth. "No. Never been like that before. Never. So good. Mmmm. Multiples aren't a myth."

Nope. Can't fight it anymore. A stupid smile feels like it's cracking my face in half. I kiss her again. Just because I can. "Does that make me your unicorn?"

Her eyes pop open. "No."

"No?" Even the bliss still humming through my veins isn't enough to keep my stomach from dropping. Just like giving in and jerking off to thoughts of her wasn't nearly enough to satisfy me, having her once won't be either.

Maybe I'm the only one assuming this isn't a one-time thing though.

"This is just a rebound, bridge, fling…thing," she trips over her words, but she gazes up at me with familiar determination shining in her eyes. "For both of us, right? We got closure from our pasts, but we're both focused on our careers and the future. We're moving on with our lives as consenting adults with needs. This is just…a convenient way to scratch an itch."

I roll off her onto my side of the bed.

She's giving me an out I would have grabbed with both hands last season. Why does it feel so shitty now? Tori's right. Nothing has changed. My job comes first. I should be happy she's thinking clearly enough for the both of us. With this new level to our relationship, she's not a distraction to my focus anymore. I'm getting to have my cake and eat it, too, without having to worry about cleaning up the mess left behind in the kitchen.

"Mike?"

I turn my head to the side to find her watching me with a wary gaze.

"That's all this is, right?" She swallows thickly. "Friends with benefits?"

"Yeah, Peaches." I hold my hand out for her to take. "That's all this is."

# Chapter 25
## We Are Never Ever Getting Back Together

### Tori

I SMOTHER the laughter building in my chest as I covertly read Mike's texts, glancing around my cubicle to make sure no one's watching. I'm supposed to be building a proposal of content for his upcoming social media announcements, not enjoying him ratting out his teammate.

> Mike: He asked our flight attendant if she wants season tickets and if she'd consider moving to Albany. He's convinced she's the one.
> Tori: Leave Elliot alone! Maybe she is his unicorn!
> Mike: Sure. And maybe I was right. Maybe I'm yours.

I DON'T NECESSARILY THINK he's wrong, but I can't admit that to him either. He has definite unicorn potential.

I squirm in my standard-issue office chair and rub my thighs together, where the ghost of Mike remains between my legs even when it's been days since he's been there last. The man is ravenous after going so long without. He does things to my body that I am one-hundred-percent certain no other man could—or ever will—be able to replicate.

I hope I satisfy him even a fraction as much as he does for me, but I'm not stupid. His focus is on football, not love. I admire him for his tenacity and ten-year plan. I have my own goals to achieve. Our worlds do not collide past this season, but I don't regret giving in to my attraction. Much. I'm happy to be a comfort to him for as long as we're in this forced mess together. God knows Mike deserves a little good in his life for a change.

Tori: You don't have to convince me to come over tonight, you know. I'll be ready and waiting. Let me know when you land at the airport.

A THROAT CLEARING JUST over my shoulder sends my phone jumping out of my hands as I fumble for recovery with my heart beating out of my chest. I place the evidence of my guilt face-down on my desktop before spinning in my chair.

"Ben?"

Of all the faces I expected to be frowning at me, his wasn't even a remote consideration.

He shrugs. "Hey. Did I, uh...catch you at a bad time?"

"No! Not at all!" I clear my throat to make my voice sound normal. I'm not actually the one who has any explaining to do. "What are you doing here?"

He thumbs over his shoulder to where David is watching us like a hawk as he leans against the fake wall of his own cubicle. "I didn't actually think anyone was going to let me in, but I was lucky enough to run into your boss in the lobby. He must have recognized me somehow because he believed me when I told him we're old friends."

More like this is another of David's tests. My eyes cut to the empty space on my desk where a picture of Ben and I used to reside. That old photo hasn't been on display in quite a while.

"So...what are you doing here?"

His expression turns sheepish. He shoves his hands into the pockets of his khakis. "Owen called me and said you were in a bind.

He asked me to drive up here and check on you every once in a while."

I fight the urge to roll my eyes. My brothers have no idea that Ben is the last person who should be checking up on me. They only know his New York City address is slightly closer than where they live in Virginia. "I'm sorry you wasted a whole day making this trip, but as you can see..." I splay my hands wide. "I'm just fine."

He tilts his head to the side and sticks his tongue in his cheek. "Really? Because from those texts I couldn't help but see, I'm guessing you got forced into a less than fake part of your social media stunt."

A simmering rage spreads through my limbs, warming me from stomach to fingertips. This is exactly why I warned Mike about giving my family too much of the truth.

I grind out, "I haven't been forced into anything."

What I really want to say is *Mike Mitchell is a better lover than you could ever hope to be.*

That would just be cruel. Also—according to Ben's fiancée—a lie.

He nods, but he doesn't look like he actually believes a word I'm saying. "Well, I'm already here. The trip doesn't have to be a waste. Let me at least take you out to dinner. It's almost quitting time anyway."

He's not wrong, and I have no good excuse to refuse his generous offer. The least I can do is make sure he's fed before he gets back in his car for the three-hour drive.

"Can I choose the restaurant?" Okay, so maybe a tiny bit of me is petty enough to make him pay for keeping me out of the loop about his life.

～

"This is..." Ben blows out a breath as he studies the menu at 677 Prime. "Not gonna lie, Tor. Way above my pay grade."

"Oh." I wave off his embarrassment like I don't know exactly how he feels. "No worries. You drove all the way up here to check on me, so dinner is my treat. Order whatever you want. Really."

If he can afford a fat rock for Bethany's finger while he's getting his master's degree, then I can surely afford dinner for two on my internship salary. Besides, coming here means he's on my turf. Apparently, he needs proof that I'm doing well.

"Hey, Julian!"

My favorite server eyes the man sitting across from me with suspicion. "Miss Russo. How are you this evening?"

I'm starting to feel like no one is on my side tonight. Gone is the friendly banter I've shared with Julian in the past. Maybe I was wrong about him not treating Mike differently.

"I'm well, thank you for asking. Can I get a vodka martini with extra olives to start?"

He nods then waits on Ben's order.

"A sparkling water, please and thank you."

Julian barely raises an eyebrow at our decidedly different choices before turning toward the bar.

"So." Ben sighs then closes his menu. "Tell me what's been going on with you."

"Nothing much." I relax into the cushy leather chair. "Working."

He nods then takes a prim sip of his flat water. "Owen told me. I thought your internship was only for a year? What happened to getting your master's?"

I wasn't going to brag, but if he insists... "I did so well the first season that the team offered me a second year *and* a scholarship if I agreed to their terms."

He doesn't look impressed. "Owen told me about that, too. Your brothers are concerned about the team's, um, terms."

I snort, much in the same way I did when my brothers threatened to take Mike out to the parking lot to teach him a lesson on gentlemanly behavior. As if all of them combined could even land a single punch on a guy packing that much muscle. "Their concerns have been noted and duly dismissed. You're all caught up on what's going on with me. Tell me about you now. How's grad school? How's Bethany?"

His shoulders fall, and he at least has the decency to appear contrite. "I figured you'd met when I saw you on the sidewalk outside our apartment building."

I nod and smile at Julian as he delivers our drinks. Perfect timing, as usual.

"May we have a few more moments?" Ben returns his full attention to me, his dismissal of our server assumed. He reaches across the table to grasp my hand in his own.

Any spark that was between us has well and truly been snuffed out. I don't feel anything except discomfort when he swipes his thumb along my skin.

"I'm sorry you found out that way. I should have at least called and told you about Bethany, but…I didn't want to hurt you unnecessarily. Surely, you've moved on as well. And not in the way the media would have everyone believe."

I squeeze his hand then pull free of his grasp. "Apology accepted. I'm truly happy for you both. She's a lovely woman."

Ben sighs and fiddles with the napkin in his lap, not quite meeting my gaze. "She is. Unfortunately, she broke off our engagement. Said she thought we were moving too fast."

"I'm so sorry." Not entirely surprised though. She blatantly asked me if she should doubt the speed at which their relationship had progressed. I guess my reassurances weren't enough. "I hope me showing up at your door didn't cause her to question things between you two."

"It did exactly that." He raises his deep blue gaze to mine. "She accused me of using her to get over you." He takes a deep breath. "She's not wrong."

A shameful laugh threatens to spill from my lips, but luckily for me, Julian reappears to take our orders.

Long after he's left for the kitchen, we stare at each other across the table in strained silence.

Ben clears his throat. "It's true that Owen called and asked me to check up on you, but that's not why I'm really here."

I swirl the martini in my glass, chew on an olive, and wait for him to get on with it.

Sensing I'm not waiting with bated breath, he continues with an outstretched open palm in the middle of the table. "Could you find it in your heart to give me another chance, Vittoria? I was stupid to throw away what we spent years building together. I shouldn't have jumped ship at the first sign of hardship."

I chew another olive and consider my options.

Before I can even form a coherent response, Mike practically jogs up to our table.

He's still wearing the required suit for team travel, and he smells like stale, recycled plane air when he bends down to place a tender kiss at the corner of my mouth. He murmurs, "Hey, babe. Missed you."

"Ben Sharp." I point my sadly empty toothpick across the table then at Mike, who pulls over a chair from a nearby table. "Mike Mitchell."

Ben rises from his seat and extends a hand to Mike. "It's a pleasure to meet you."

"Likewise." Mike accepts the handshake gracefully then sits down beside me.

I stare at him in silence.

He finally gestures for me to glance under the table, where he's holding his cell phone up for me to see the screen. A picture of Ben holding my hand singes my eyeballs, followed by several texts.

Julian: WTF? Who's the bro making a move on your woman?
Julian: I'm delaying their dinners, but there's only so much I can do.
Julian: You better get here! He's going in for the kill!

THE LAUGH I've been keeping locked away in the innermost recesses of my chest breaks free.

"Something you want to share with everyone?" Ben looks like a justifiable combination of fury, embarrassment, and regret.

"No, no." I force myself to calm down. "Just a funny meme. It's kind of our thing."

The only emotion left on Ben's face is disappointment. "It's true, then? You're really together?"

Mike's eyebrows pop into the shock of hair falling over his forehead before he whips his gaze to me, silently asking, *Is this guy for real?*

I nod.

"*Please*, let me punch him," Mike begs on a muttered whisper.

Ben looks horrified that it might actually happen. He scoots his chair back from the table. Just a little. "I apologize. I didn't know. Her brother told me it was all for show, so I thought I could ask for a second chance. She's clearly all yours. I didn't mean any harm."

"You didn't mean any harm?" Mike narrows his eyes at the suddenly pale-faced man on the opposite side of the table.

I gesture with my empty glass to Julian, who's watching the circus from a safe distance at the bar. If he's going to cause shit shows, the least he can do is refill my drink. He'd also better delete those photos before they end up on the internet to ruin everything Mike and I have been working to build.

"No bad publicity, Mitchell," I remind him.

He's already leaning over the table, but the expression on his face isn't menacing at all. His gaze on Ben is full of pity. "Even if she wasn't mine, you sure as hell don't deserve her."

For some reason, those words are enough to make Ben regrow his spine. He scoffs. "And you do?"

Mike shakes his head slowly. "You are missing the point entirely, my man. Tori isn't a toy to be put on a shelf when you get tired of her, only to play with her again when you're feeling it. If you really wanted her back, you sure as shit didn't prove it just now by caving to the competition."

"You're not really competition," Ben hedges.

Mike straightens in his seat before turning his attention to me. "What do you want to do, Peaches?"

"Can we get out of here?" I'm beyond done with this entire situation. This feels more and more like a pissing contest for bragging rights instead of any kind of prize.

"Julian!" Mike calls. "We'll take our dinners to go, please."

Ben rises when we do and has the actual nerve to grab my elbow. "What are you doing, Tori? You're too smart to sleep your way to the top. This is a bad idea, and you know it."

I do know it, but at least I'm making my own decisions for a change.

Mike crosses his considerably large arms over his chest. "I know if you don't take your hand off her, I'm not going to ask permission a second time to punch you."

I shake off Ben's grip and address Mike. "Let's go home."

I walk away with my head held high, my arm through Mike's elbow. Ben is my past. My future is just beginning.

By the time we're lying face to face on our respective sides of his bed, Mike's eyes are half-lidded. "Did I overstep instead of supporting again?"

That gets a smile out of me. "You didn't. Thank you. Even though I didn't need rescuing, it means a lot that you came straight from the airport to support me. And after such a close game, too."

The moment I place my hand on his shoulder to show my earnest gratitude, he winces. I pull away.

He catches my hand in his own and kisses my palm before flattening it against a spot on his chest that must not be as sore.

"I'm a little sad that we're just going to sleep tonight," I confess, hoping to make him laugh after the disappointment of a loss. "Seems a shame to bring me here and not use me for your pleasure."

"Who says that's not what I'm doing?"

I give him a skeptical raised eyebrow, but his eyes are already closed, his breathing evening out.

"Good night, babe," he mumbles.

I gently rub my fingertips against his warm, bare skin.

He hums in response, a small smile etched on his face even as sleep pulls him under.

"Good night, teddy bear," I whisper.

The more I think about it, the more it's a perfect nickname. He'll never be my unicorn, not when our goals are so different. That doesn't mean he's not warm, comforting, and all softie under his big muscles. I'd never tell him that out loud when he's awake though.

# Chapter 26
Honest

## Mike

THE SENSATION of her hand caressing my face wakes me. My body is sore but warm beneath the blankets. She's learned not to touch me much after a rough game, but her feet are entangled with mine. Even if I'm not up to giving her more proof that multiple orgasms aren't a myth, I still like some part of me to be touching some part of her while we sleep.

Maybe to prove to myself she's not a dream.

"Good morning," I rasp.

She smiles in return. It looks like she just woke up, too.

Her red hair is a mess of tangles, but the sunlight coming in through a crack in the curtains catches on the strands, making them seem to glow. Her eyes aren't quite alert yet—not like when she's pecking away at her phone, coming up with the latest and greatest content for my social media feeds. There are pillow lines on her chest, running down her arm. That milky white skin can't hide a thing. Especially not the red patches I leave behind on her neck, breasts, and between her legs if I haven't just shaved. But it's her fingertips—light as a feather as they dance across my face—that are really distracting me this morning.

"What are you doing?"

I know what I'd like to be doing. My dick is already hard. If she keeps it up, I might be late getting to the team facilities for our traditional post-loss ass chewing from the coaches later this morning.

"Thinking," she admits on a murmur.

That single word brings my dick down a few notches. Being stuck in your own head never leads to anything good. I would know.

"About last night? Your dinner with Ben?"

She shakes her head against the pillow. "Wondering why you still have all your teeth."

Just to make sure I'm not hallucinating this conversation, I run my tongue across my teeth. Yep. Still all there.

"Ahhh, you're thinking of hockey players. They lose teeth a lot. Football players, not so much."

"Hmm." Her fingers slide over my lips. "Why is that?"

"Mouthguards and different types of helmets, mostly."

"Interesting. What are the most common injuries for football players, then?"

Wow. Now I know what it feels like to be on the receiving end of distraction techniques. Or maybe I just haven't been this invested about what's really going through someone else's mind in a long time.

That makes me feel even shittier.

"We can talk about it, you know. We might be in bed together, but we're friends, too."

Her husky chuckle brings my dick back to full mast. "I suppose I have myself to thank for that."

"That's true," I admit. "If you hadn't said you wanted more, I never would have made the first move."

The lips I haven't kissed yet today pull down in a frown. "I meant the part about teaching you that friends talk to each other and trust each other."

"So, trust me. Talk to me." I have never wanted to have an honest conversation so much in my goddamn life. If she's considering her second chance with the guy she always imagined marrying, then I sure as shit want to know about it.

"Like you talk to me?" She raises an eyebrow. "How did Evie's surgery go? I overhear your conversations with her and Rob, but you never say a word about them to me. I learn more about their lives from SportsCenter clips than I do from you—the guy who's supposedly a very close friend of theirs. You never talk about or to Alex when I'm around. For all I know, you two still haven't buried the hatchet about your fight last season."

My defenses go on red alert, and my dick goes into lockdown mode. "I wasn't aware you broke your golden rule to be in my bed just to get closer to my friends."

She doesn't try to hide the obvious hurt in her expression as she pulls her hand away, curling it into her chest like a barrier between us. "I wasn't aware you had suspicions about the reasons why I'm in your bed."

"I didn't until just now."

She rolls away from me then sits up at the edge of the bed, her bare back a crisscross of angry looking lines from my sheets. "If knowing my ulterior motives will make you *trust* me again, I'm only asking because I don't have any friends left. They all faded away because I spent so much of my time with Ben. I understand why it's going to take you a long time to trust your Wolves teammates, but I don't want to see the same thing happen to you with people you already consider friends because you spend your precious free time with me."

That doesn't make me feel better at all. "What about your co-workers in the marketing department?"

She laughs, but it's not the kind that goes straight to my dick. "They view me as the enemy. I'm the lowly intern who stole the kind of experimental assignment they'd be all too willing to bet their much higher salaries on. Not to mention, I'm a good decade younger than most of them. We have nothing in common outside of work."

That sounds…lonely.

"So, you really *are* considering Ben's offer."

"No." The word lands like a grenade between us.

She rises from the mattress then immediately pulls the first shirt she finds on the floor over her head. She's obviously trying to make a point, so it's one of her shirts instead of one of mine. The fitted kind that doesn't nearly cover her bare ass even though I know damn well she's trying to hide herself from me. Again, to make a point.

This morning is starting off on the wrong foot, riding on the wave of a shitty last night, clinging to the coattails of an even shittier loss on Sunday. I dig in to the misery because...old habits die hard, I guess. "I get it. It makes sense. He's familiar, easy. You could have a life outside of work again. You flat-out told me at Jeremy and Alyssa's wedding that you always imagined marrying him, popping out two-point-five kids, adopting a puppy, and living out the American dream. Go for it."

She rounds on me, her face red, her eyebrows practically up to her hairline. "Oh, since you're giving me your blessing, I'll just get right on that."

She storms out of the bedroom, still naked from the waist down.

Since this is my house, and I have nothing to hide—fuck, I'm a shitty liar even to myself—I follow. Completely naked.

I find her in the kitchen, popping a K-cup into the coffee maker she brought from her apartment when she basically moved in here without either of us ever having a conversation about it.

"You're forgetting one very important thing. You can't go back to him. You wouldn't do anything to create bad press for me or to jeopardize your scholarship."

Her shoulders shake with silent laughter, but she doesn't turn around. "Oh, Mr. Mitchell. I can promise you that if I dumped you and went back to Ben, you would gain so much sympathy from your followers. I'd be the villain, and there would be women lining up to comfort you. That might actually be one of the most brilliant marketing ploys I've ever heard. We absolutely should go for it."

Fuck that. "You can't call me Mr. Mitchell when you're standing in my kitchen without any panties on!"

She glances at me over her shoulder, a single eyebrow raised. Then, she slaps her own bare ass hard enough to leave a handprint behind.

It's red, and I'm already mad as a bull. I rush her, spinning her to face me before I hoist her up onto the edge of the countertop to get us at eye-level. Cock to pussy level, but whatever. "Call me Mr. Mitchell one more time. I dare you."

"Do it, Mr. Mitchell," she fires back, her eyes sharp, her cheeks flaming. "I dare *you*."

"Not trying to trap me into anything, huh?" I practically spit the words into her mouth. "I don't have a condom on."

"I'm still on the pill." Tori digs her nails into my shoulders, not trying in the least to be careful where she can see obvious bruises from Sunday's game. She wraps her legs around my waist, pulling me closer. "So, no. Your move, big boy."

If she thinks she's going to call my bluff, then I've got news for her. I shove into her in one hard push. Her pussy is tighter than it's ever been, strangling my dick past the point of reason.

I fuck her. Hard. Right on the kitchen counter.

She pierces my skin. Her grunts echo off the cabinets in time with my pounding thrusts. Somewhere in the back of my mind—cutting through the pure bliss slicing down my spine—I'm aware I'm bareback in a woman for the first time in my twenty-four years, but that's not enough to make me slow down and savor the moment.

I come into her so hard, *I'm* going to be feeling it for days. Weeks. Months. Forever.

Peaches is relaxed all around me, her muscles limp in the circle of my arms, her foot trailing a lazy path up and down the back of my thigh.

I pant against the sweet-smelling skin at the curve of her neck. Guilt pecks at my back, but I'm too exhausted to answer the call.

Tori strokes her fingers through my damp hair, murmuring at my ear, "You could have just admitted you're jealous, and that you don't want to lose me."

She's right. I don't. Marking her as my territory like a fucking caveman isn't going to save me from the inevitable though.

Tori physically lifts my head with a hand on either of my cheeks. Her gaze bounces between my eyes before she enunciates her words clearly enough for me to hear over the blood still rushing through my veins. "You want to convince me that you're my unicorn, but you can't even give me this."

I can't. Not yet. Not until she has all the information to make her choice.

"Yeah." I nod and step back, transfixed by the sight of my release seeping out from between her legs. Right onto the cabinet below the countertop. "My mistake. You didn't have an orgasm this time, so I'm not holding up my end of the bargain."

That's a shitty way for me to give her one last chance to spare me the confession swirling in my gut that's begging to be freed. I recognize I'm being an asshole to give her a push, but that awareness isn't enough to make me stop.

She hops off the counter and walks away without a look back. She does, however, slap her red ass again. "Get ready, Mitchell. It's time to go to work."

I guess that's my answer to the question I'm too afraid to ask. She's not leaving, so it's time to cough up all my guilt.

# Chapter 27
If I Lose Myself

## Tori

"No."

In all fairness, I don't like that one either. I click over to the next slide.

He barely glances at it. "Pass."

We repeat this process twenty more times until I'm all out of options.

"I don't know what to tell you." I slam my laptop closed. "We have until next weekend. Since you don't like any of my ideas, maybe you can ask David to design the posts. There's still enough time for him to create something from scratch."

Mike leans back against the couch in his living room, stretching his arm behind me. He's had a full week of grueling practices, and he looks absolutely exhausted. A fresh bruise blooms on his left bicep.

"Look." I curl up at the opposite end of the couch, well out of accidental striking range. "If it was up to me alone, I wouldn't even be bothering you with this crap at all. The team just suffered their first loss of the season, and you have more important things to worry about. It completely defeats the purpose of PR to concern you with stuff that should be smooth sailing behind the scenes."

"This is my life," Mike murmurs, his gaze still focused on the abandoned laptop that rests on the coffee table. "So, you need my approval for something this big."

"I do," I confirm.

He lifts his brown eyes to mine. "What about your approval? This is your life, too."

I thought so, but even the only choice I felt I was making for myself seems to have slipped through my fingers. In the past week, I haven't felt Mike's lips on mine a single time. He hasn't called. I haven't slept in his bed. We run into each other occasionally in the halls at the training facility. We appear in public for our weekly dinner reservation, but that's it.

I probably wouldn't even be in his house right now at all if it wasn't for the sort of private conversation we need to have about this next play.

"This is my *job*," I emphasize. "We agreed to the terms at the beginning of the season. It's too late to change my mind now."

Mike might be able to renegotiate with Mr. Gallo though. There's not a chance in hell the Wolves will bench one of their star players. Not when he's proving himself so reliable during what should be his sophomore jinx season.

"None of those felt real. Aren't you always saying this stuff needs to seem organic?" Mike gestures toward my computer. "Were any of those posts remotely close to the kind of official relationship announcement you made when you and Ben got together?"

I snort in spite of my bad mood. "I was fourteen and a freshman in high school when Ben asked me to be his girlfriend. The extent of my social media prowess was overuse of emojis to convey excitement."

The corner of Mike's mouth tips up. Just barely. Almost unnoticeable. It's gone just as quickly. "Maybe because you knew him, so you had a good reason to be excited. You don't really know me."

The first words perched on my tongue are something witty about the biblical definition of knowing a person, but I swallow them down. Mike isn't wrong. He might be able to play my body like a master fiddler, but he's also content not to learn any new techniques.

He settles himself against the opposite side of the couch, resting his head on the arm and stretching his legs toward me. He opens his arms. "Come here."

"Aren't you sore?"

He raises his eyebrows subtly then gestures with his hands again for me to climb on top of him.

I do. Very, very tentatively.

"Get comfortable," he murmurs against the top of my head. "Don't just pretend to be."

Oh. I see where he's going with this. He thinks he can do better than my posts. Okay, fine. I'll play along. For organic marketing's sake.

I slide my arms around his sides, burrowing them a little between his body and the couch. Next, I wrap one leg over his muscular thigh and wedge the other between his legs. He's my human body pillow. Finally, I wriggle on top of him until all his hard planes and deep ridges align perfectly with my softer spots.

"Since we've apparently scratched all our itches, don't even think about popping a boner, pal."

"Sex has nothing to do with intimacy." His lips brush against my hair as he speaks. He holds his phone at his considerable arm's length and takes a few shots of us cuddled together. "Now, shut up for a minute and let me think."

"Wow." I bark out a laugh. "You could teach a master's class on intimacy."

He holds his phone above me, slowly tapping at the screen.

I glance over my shoulder, but he moves out of my line of sight.

"No peeking. You'll just try to make suggestions before I'm even done."

Still not wrong. I relax against him again, honestly curious as to what he'll come up with. He's never been so invested in his posts before.

He places the phone face down on the coffee table then wraps both his arms securely around me.

"Couldn't come up with anything, huh? Ready for me to take a crack at it?"

"No. I'm ready to tell you some things, and I need you to listen. When I'm done, you can decide whether I post that picture. Or not."

Oh. This setup was two-fold. I get the distinct impression he can't look me in the eyes right now.

His chest heaves beneath me with a deep breath. "I had a one-night stand in college."

*That's* what he's so afraid to tell me? People have one-night stands all the time. "I, um, kind of figured that out when you told me it had been almost four years since you last had sex. I knew those numbers didn't add up. Your stupid ex broke up with you six years ago."

He jerks his arms around me a little. "Hey. You're supposed to be listening, remember?"

"Just trying to make it easier on you," I mumble into his soft t-shirt. "I'm not judging you for that, Mike."

His chest moves beneath my cheek again with a sigh. "Peaches, I'm trying here, but you've gotta help me, help us. I can't get all this out if you keep interrupting."

I'm honestly a little worried now, but I'm more impressed he's not using me as an excuse to give up. "Sorry. I promise I'll stay quiet until you tell me I can talk again. Go on."

A few moments of silence pass between us, but I keep my trap shut.

"You sure?" he asks.

I nod against him.

"Okay. Um…So, the one-night stand. She taught me a really important lesson, and I honestly earned my nickname in the Wolves locker room because of her. It was junior year. I was well over Chelsie by that point. Alex kept dragging me to parties, trying to get me back on the horse, and I was finally ready to do it. So, I did."

Still not seeing the point of this confession other than learning he's never thought of his nickname as a bad thing.

Mike's muscles tense all around me. "The problem was we were both drunk. That was a stupid rookie mistake. Consent isn't possible if both people aren't sober. Anyway, we did the deed, passed out for about an hour in one of the rooms at the frat house. When we woke up and the lights came on, she was pissed as hell."

I am practically bursting with the effort of keeping quiet. His dramatic pauses are not helping my cause at all.

"She thought she'd slept with Rob." Mike barks out a laugh that jolts me against his chest. "She must have felt really special to be the woman who finally broke his loyalty to Evie. When she found out she wasn't, she actually threw a shoe at me as I was walking out the door. Missed my head by only an inch."

I peel myself away from his chest, murder undoubtedly written all over my face.

He laughs again. "You can't track her down and punch her, Peaches. I don't remember her name. I couldn't even tell you what color her hair was."

I'm going to explode from all this pent-up pressure. My face must be absolutely crimson.

He rolls his eyes. "Go ahead. Permission to speak."

"What a bitch!"

He chuckles then cups my hands with his cheeks to pull me down for a quick kiss. "God, I—" He stops short then situates me in the pocket between his chin and chest again. "Thanks for the laugh. I'll try to hang onto that for the rest of it."

"There's more?"

He taps my back with his fingers. "You're on silent mode again. Got it?"

I nod. All the anxiety I let fly with my anger reappears like a heavy blanket.

"I was way more ashamed of myself than I was mad at her. She must've been a hell of a lot drunker than I was because Rob had left the party hours before that chick dragged me upstairs. Evie was drunk as fuck, and he took her home. I headed to their apartment to check on her and took out all my frustration on Rob, who sure as hell didn't deserve it." Another deep sigh rolls like a wave beneath my face. "He wasn't fucking some drunk random at a frat party. He was taking care of his girlfriend. She was..." Mike blows out a breath. "She was in bad shape. I, uh...saw for myself that night the...um..."

He swallows so thickly, I feel his throat working against my temple. "The scars. That she has. On her breasts. From that attack."

I pat his shoulder with my hand to let him know I'm actively listening. What I'm really doing is actively holding back tears. I've seen the evidence online of what his best friend went through. What she still bears. While I know all the facts and how much Mike cares for this woman, this is just another thing he's never talked *to me* about. I don't dare interrupt as he tries to pull himself together to continue.

"I, uh...I really lit into Rob after seeing that. Poked and prodded and made goddamn sure he was up for the job he seemed to want so fucking much. The next year when their relationship blew up, and he ended up cheating on her even though they were already married...I was done. I was so fucking done. I was never going to let myself get so completely gutted by someone the way they eviscerated each other, let alone ever fuck another woman who didn't even know my name."

I press a kiss to his chest and let my tears spill over. How could I have known that Mike has already given me more trust and intimacy than he promised himself he ever would again?

He runs his hand down the back of my hair, squeezing me tighter. "Peaches, I'm gonna warn you right now. That was actually the warm-up. My lack of faith in relationships goes back way further and way deeper. Evie is both the reason I ever tried one in the first place and the reason I gave up on them again."

I nod, absolutely terrified of how deep this rabbit hole goes.

"Only three people on the entire Earth know what I'm about to tell you, and one of them recently passed away. The cop who responded to the 911 call that night, my mom, and...Evie."

I'm starting to understand why their bond is so strong. Why they will always be part of each other's lives, no matter what.

"Evie and I went to school together since kindergarten, but we didn't really know each other until we were both placed in the same therapy group for abused kids when we were in fifth grade. Her alcoholic dad lost his shit one time and ended up putting her in the hospital, and me? I never had a finger laid on me."

That doesn't make any sense.

"All the other kids there were abused way worse. They had the mental problems to show for it. Most of them were angry and violent themselves because that's what they'd always been exposed to. One of them really picked on Evie. She was so small and so scared and just so...fucking awkward." My head jostles with another unexpected laugh. "You'd never know it to see her college WAG pictures, but she had the biggest glasses, the frizziest hair, and the skinniest arms and legs. She was an easy target, and those kids knew it."

His laughter dries up.

"I offered to teach her how to stand up for herself, but I gave her all the information to make her choice that I'm about to give you."

I don't think he's pausing for dramatic effect now.

"You're lying in the arms of a murderer."

I don't move. I quit breathing. My heart ceases to beat.

"I killed my own father to save my mother."

My blood pumps harder than it ever has through my veins. I'm going to hyperventilate. Pain shoots through my chest.

"He beat her senseless all the time. I don't know why he never came after us kids, but he just...didn't. My sisters were only six. I worked so hard to hide it from them, but fuck. I heard it. I saw it. I begged her to leave, but she didn't think she could make it on her own with three kids. Then one night, he made the choice for her. For us. He was going to kill her. Said as much. Was literally strangling her to death right in front of me. He must not have even known I was in the room because there is no way in hell I could've got the drop on him otherwise."

Mike takes another deep breath.

"I hit him over the head with a cast iron frying pan. Literally bashed his skull in. Once I got started, I couldn't stop. I rained down hit after hit, giving him back everything he'd ever done to my mom over the years. She couldn't even pull me off him. The twins were at a slumber party that night, so thank God they weren't around to see what I'm capable of. Mom must have called 911. It was the cop who finally dragged me away from Dad's body, but I think I was just out of steam by that point anyway."

I'm a sobbing mess in his arms, but Mike forges on.

"He had to file a report obviously, but they flubbed it. My mom killed my dad in self-defense. She had all the injuries to support the story. I had none. Not physical anyway. Apparently, everyone in town knew what a piece of shit my dad was, and they already guessed what was going on at home, so no one ever questioned his death. I think they sort of looked at my mom as a badass for finally doing what had to be done and protecting her kids. All the neighbors rallied around us. My mom didn't have to cook for a solid month, thanks to all the casseroles people kept dropping off. The local dentist offered her a job as a receptionist, and she still works there to this day. My sisters never went to daycare when they weren't in half-day kindergarten because the old lady next door became their nanny—for free. And me? Officer Manning drove me to that damn therapy group three times a week because he didn't want me to become just another violent offender on his caseload. He volunteered as a youth football coach in his free time, and he insisted I find a more constructive outlet for my aggression. So, I did."

I can't believe what I'm hearing, but...I can. So many pieces of the puzzle that's Mike Mitchell fall into place—his devoted loyalty to Evie, his drive to provide for his mom and sisters, his lack of trust in others. It's a wonder I'm lying in his arms at all. Or that he ever gave Templeman a chance to be his friend.

"I want you to know I don't regret it," he murmurs, swiping his hand down my hair in a soothing, rhythmic motion. "Not for a second. If I was transported back in time to that exact moment, I'd do it all again."

I retract my claws when I realize I'm actually digging into his skin in an effort to cling to him as tightly as possible.

He coughs out a bitter laugh. "It's still fucking hysterical to me that Evie whacked me over the head with a frying pan. Damn if she didn't learn everything I ever taught her."

After all he's said to me, I have no idea why this is the thing that makes me break. I pop up from my place on his chest, horror blooming in my brain at the thought of never getting to live this moment. "She could have killed you!"

The corner of his mouth tips up. His eyes are tired, but there's a hint of sparkle in them. "Nah. It was a cheap old thing. The handle actually broke off when she hit me with it."

"You weren't mad at her because you're *proud* of her."

He nods, his expression growing serious. "I am. Hell, she's teaching *me* a thing or two these days."

Something about the way he says it—the way he looks at me—sends shivers of anticipation down my spine.

"What is she teaching you?"

He chews on his lip then reaches for his phone on the coffee table.

I stare at the photo he took of us lying together on the couch. There's nothing fancy or staged about it. My hair's a mess; he clearly looks exhausted.

The caption reads:

It's been 547 days since she came into my life, and I can't imagine another single day without her.
Love you, Peaches.

TEARS SPRING INTO MY EYES. I glance up from the phone screen to find him watching me carefully.

"I, uh..." He clears his throat. "I figured that first season if I kept you at a safe enough distance that this thing I feel for you would just fade away. That it was just lust, you know? That didn't work. And then the whole hotel thing..."

A laugh that sounds a touch hysterical sneaks out of my chest. "Seeing me pee made you fall in love with me?"

A full, glorious smile spreads across his face. "Yeah," he admits, sounding surprised himself. "Maybe a little. It didn't barrel into me all at once, but it picked up in speed and intensity until I couldn't lie to myself anymore."

My emotional pendulum swings the other way. A sob catches in my chest. "But, but, but...you said you would never have made the first move!"

Oh my God, I thought he gave in. I thought he just wanted sex. He hasn't been scratching an itch at all. He didn't offer himself up to me until he was already in too deep to do anything else.

"No. I wouldn't have. That wouldn't be fair to you. Being with me isn't easy, Peaches. I know that. My life, my job, my fucked-up past... those aren't small hurdles." He wipes my damp cheek with his big hand. "Just because you're my unicorn doesn't mean I'm yours."

I cannot possibly abuse everything he's given me tonight by lying to his face. "I...I'm not there, Mike. I can't tell you what you're telling me."

"I know." His eyes are soft and his touch even softer. "That's partly my fault. How could you possibly fall in love with me when I haven't even shown you who I really am?"

I shake my head and bite my lips. I'm so tempted to say he's already shown me who he really is time and time again, but I won't do it. Not tonight.

He pulls the cell phone from my grip and places it on the coffee table again before folding my hands in his own. He stares at where we meet. "You have some decisions to make, Tori. And I...I can't make them for you. All I can do is give you the full picture, so you can make the best choice for you."

"And hope?"

He glances up at me with confusion clouding his eyes.

"You can give me all the information I need and hope I'll choose you?" I clarify.

His smile is small and tinged with sadness. "I'm not the hoping kind. I'm the hard work type."

Another entirely different sort of shudder rolls down my spine.

"After all the hard work you've put in so far tonight, I'm a little worried about what else you might have in store for me."

His smile turns predatory. "There are a few things I haven't tried yet."

If he intends to make good on that offer tonight, the front door bursting open definitely kills the already tenuous mood. Like he's afraid we might be riddled in a burst of gunfire, Mike pulls me down to his chest so fast and hard that my teeth snap together. He rolls me beneath him like he's practiced this move a million times.

Maybe he has.

"Who is it?" I can't see a thing beneath my human shield.

"Alex? What the fuck are you doing here?"

# Chapter 28
Glimmer

## Mike

"You gonna tell me why you're really here, or am I just gonna watch you drink yourself stupid for the rest of the night?"

He didn't want to talk in front of Tori, and I wasn't about to push. Not when I have no idea why he's sitting at my kitchen island. Peaches isn't willing to leave me alone with the guy, so she's upstairs, getting ready for bed. He doesn't have any excuses now.

Alex raises his already bloodshot eyes to mine. "Jesus, Mike. What's with the interrogation? It's my bye week. I can't drop in on an old friend?"

"Unannounced? No." I'm just thankful Tori wasn't naked on top of me in the living room when he arrived. We've christened most of the house already. I never had to worry about unexpected visitors before.

He rolls his eyes then lifts his third beer to his lips. "I told you I was coming. It's not my fault you never read your texts."

He clams up when Tori comes into the kitchen, wearing nothing but one of my t-shirts. She glares at him the entire time. He winks and checks out her bare legs.

"You really do have a death wish tonight, don't you?"

He smiles at my threat. "Maybe."

Tori grabs a bottle of water from the fridge then slams the door shut. She stops at the edge of the island, staring Alex down.

She's too beautiful to ever look threatening, and Alex is too stupid to consider cowering—even if only for show.

He smiles his trademark grin at her but weirdly says nothing.

She points at him, points at me, shakes her finger in the air, then finally slides it across her throat.

He outright cackles at her silent threat.

I have to bite my tongue to hold in my own laughter. I hold out an open palm for her. "I'm dying to hear how many curse words he can pull out of you. You can talk again."

"Ooh. Silence games." Alex winks. "Kinky. Didn't think you had it in you, Mitchell."

Surprisingly, Tori doesn't lunge at him. She places her hand in my own and squeezes tight.

That simple gesture erases all my fears—over what she thinks of me now, why Alex is really here, all of it.

She lets me pull her into my side and wrap my arm around her waist.

I drop a kiss onto her shoulder. "We're good, babe. Don't worry. You can go to sleep if you want."

Alex showing up might actually be the perfect reason for her to take some time and really think things over. I dropped a hell of a bombshell on her, and I don't want her automatically reacting with pity. It's obvious she isn't afraid. She didn't run away screaming after all. I want her to be able to look at the guy sleeping next to her in bed and feel like she can trust him—even knowing all the reasons why she shouldn't.

Peaches slides her hand down the back of my head in a way that would make me purr if Alex wasn't watching us like a hawk. She leans down to press a kiss at my temple. "I'll be upstairs if you need anything."

Such simple words, no innuendo, but full of promise anyway. I can't fight the automatic smile on my face. I don't even try. I don't want to.

She ascends the stairs like she does almost every night.

"She looks good on you, Mike." His tone is genuine. He's not talking about the compromising position he caught us in when he barreled through the front door. "Been a long time coming. I'm happy for you, bro."

I'm not out of the woods yet, but I don't think Alex is popping the top off a fresh bottle to hear all about my problems.

"You get a call from Rob?" I guess.

He nods and stares at the marble surface of the island. "I've already lost her, haven't I?"

"Yeah." I don't know how much Rob told him about his second marriage proposal plans, but Alex doesn't need me to lie to him either way.

He raises his gaze to mine. There's a little bit of his old fire—the real one—burning in his deep blue eyes. "What the hell did he give her that I couldn't?"

Alex and I don't have conversations like this. Never have. Suddenly, I understand what brought him here. He genuinely wants to know what he did wrong, and he knows I'm the only person who isn't too biased to tell him the truth.

"You didn't give her everything."

"Bullshit," Alex spits. "She needed a shoulder to cry on? I was there. She needed someone not to treat her like a fucking toddler the way you two do? I was that man. She needed loyalty and someone she could trust?" He leans across the island and hisses, "I haven't had sex in two years, Mitchell! Two fucking years! And I've had plenty of opportunity!"

I almost feel bad for him. Almost. My mind worked exactly like his a few years ago. I thought I'd given Chelsie everything, so I was just as angry as him when she called it quits without even bothering to tell me.

If Alex hadn't inadvertently brought Tori into my life, maybe I'd still be the same way. For that alone, he deserves the tough love I'm about to dish out to him.

"You didn't give her everything," I repeat slowly. "All that shit you just said? That's called being a decent fucking friend. Anyone can do that. Did you ever once call her up to cry on her shoulder after a shit game? Did you ever confide in her your deepest fears? Your darkest secrets? Did you trust her enough to shoulder your burdens and make your relationship a two-way street?"

He rolls his eyes. "She's been through enough. She needs someone she can count on, not someone who's going to take more from her."

"I thought so, too," I admit. "But you know what? Evie is stronger than all of us combined. Hell, she's proven it so many times, it's a fucking tragedy it's taken me this long to realize it. She wants to *give* love just as much as she wants to receive it. She's a grown woman who's capable of making her own choices. She's choosing Rob because he doesn't always play the fucking white knight in her life. He laid out every one of his goddamn flaws for her to judge, and she judged him worthy of her love."

What am I going to do if Peaches doesn't judge me worthy? There's nothing left for me to lay bare. I've given it all.

Alex scoffs then downs the rest of his beer. "He wasted her love on another woman. You don't honestly believe half the shit that just came out of your mouth. You were there that night. If I hadn't decked him first, you would have."

"I was wrong." Fuck, that's still hard to admit. "He gave her what she needed. Not what he wanted. We've been so busy accusing him of being selfish that we didn't realize what he did was *selfless*."

I always thought love was the most selfish thing a person could experience. We like the way it makes *us* feel. Most people throw in the towel when that feeling goes away. That's something Rob and Evie taught me, even though I wasn't necessarily the fastest learner. Loving each other made them fucking miserable. I judged the shit out of them for not walking away from all that pain. I thought they were only digging in their heels to spite all the people who kept trying to tell them what to do with their lives.

It took the prospect of losing Tori to teach me the rest. I would never have been able to say all these things to Alex if I hadn't lived them for myself for a change, instead of being on the outside looking in.

That's the kind of perspective he still doesn't have.

"Evie's not your unicorn, Alex. If she was, you wouldn't know how long it's been since you last had sex."

Even putting it in terms I think he might be able to understand isn't enough.

He cocks his head back and stares at me like I'm insane. "What the fuck are you talking about unicorns for?"

"One of my teammates," I try to explain. "He's constantly looking for his unicorn. The perfect woman…"

Evie always tells me I'm clinging to the past. I've never felt it so much as in these moments when I recount to an old teammate the exploits of a new one. Accepting the changing of the guard for the position Alex used to hold in my life.

Whether we acknowledge it or not, time pushes on. The pain we're capable of experiencing in a single moment might define our lives, but it doesn't last forever. We build scars strong enough to withstand the next round of agony. We adapt for better or worse. Sometimes we can choose how we react; sometimes not.

I've made my choices, both good and bad.

All I can do now is wait for Tori's choice.

# Chapter 29
## You and I

### Tori

"Post likes are down, engagement is down, and don't even get me started on views." David's expression looks like he just ate an entire package of Sour Patch Kids as he stares at the projected image of the Albany Wolves' social media insights on the wall.

The entirety of the PR department hangs their heads in shame. Some of them are pecking away on their phones beneath the conference table. Either trying to boost the current numbers with new posts or chronicling the indentured servitude nature of working for an NFL team on their personal feeds.

"We have just secured a playoff run, people!" David claps his hands to regain their attention.

His exclamation only further serves as proof of how far behind we've fallen. The Wolves have not made the playoffs in five years. We should be rolling in fan engagement, but we're not.

"No one thinks we'll make it past the first round," Kaylie admits. Her shiny lip gloss looks a little dull beneath her lowered lash extensions. "The expectation on all the fantasy sites is that we'll choke in the second round. Real football fans know we don't have the depth chart to go the distance. One major injury on the starting lineup will kill this drive."

I've seen those same message boards, but the mood in the upstate makes absolutely no sense to me. I'm not even a football fan, but I'm excited for all this potential.

No one else seems to be willing to offer any suggestions to an increasingly frustrated David, so I raise my hand.

He puts his hands on his hips and glares at me. "Miss Russo, this is not the third grade. If you have something to say, then say it."

"If the fans don't have any faith in us, then we could actually capitalize on that. Everyone loves a good underdog story."

A few snickers and eye rolls go around the table. I'm just the intern who's supposed to look pretty and be a good distraction after all.

Fuck. That.

"Look at what happened last year during the Superbowl between Scranton and Boston. Not even the bookies in Las Vegas predicted that upset, and with a back-up quarterback to boot."

Now I've got their attention. It's honestly sad no one else has thought of the obvious comparisons.

"We could run in-depth coverage of our second string. Give the guys on the practice squad a few shout outs. Prove to the fans that we actually *do* have the depth to see this thing through."

A few murmurs of agreement go up from my co-workers, but David looks as skeptical as ever. "Miss Russo, we cannot outright *lie* to the fans. They will see through that in a heartbeat."

His subtle dig hits its mark. Fans didn't respond well to Mike's and my staged official status. The posts went live with barely any notice. I couldn't go through with sharing the organic one Mike created.

That was too personal. Too honest. Too real to be served up for judgment by the uninformed masses.

That's mine to keep. Or to discard.

It's been weeks, but I still haven't made up my mind. Every dinner reservation we appear for, every smile when I know a smartphone is aimed our direction, every time I accept pleasure from him that I didn't believe existed…I still don't feel like any of it is real. In spite of his intimate confessions, even though he's been inside my body with nothing between us…there's something still missing.

I don't know what that is. Maybe because he's only my second serious relationship. How could I possibly know what true love feels like? In this, I admit I am actually naïve. I only know I've learned not to settle for second best.

I can't shake off the feeling that I'm still the lesser of two evils in Mike's life—be completely alone, or begrudgingly open himself to me to avoid that very same thing.

David dismisses the meeting after a consensus is reached to hold a holiday charity ball. We'll all dress up on a Friday night, command the players to appear and smile for the cameras, and auction off luxury prizes for hefty donations.

In my opinion, that still doesn't make the team accessible to the average fan who can't afford a thousand-dollar dinner plate, but my opinion doesn't matter. Average fans don't believe in the team enough according to the latest data, so we're apparently going to stick to marketing to the season ticket holders who have money to burn.

My phone rings as soon as I'm in the hallway.

"Hey, Daddy."

"Hi, Princess." His tone carries the usual gruffness, but I hear the undercurrent of love most people miss. "I haven't heard from you in a few days. Haven't seen any new pictures online either. Is everything okay? Mitchell still being good to you?"

"Well..." I want him to trust me to be independent, but I sure could use a trusted ear, too. "I'm busy. Mike's busy. The Wolves have secured a playoff spot, but fan engagement is down. I actually just got out of a meeting about that."

"Is your scholarship in jeopardy?"

That's my dad. Short, sweet, and straight to the point. You can retire the Captain from the Navy, but you can't erase the bureaucratic efficiency from the man. I'm pretty sure that's how he was able to raise six kids all on his own, actually.

"No." At least not that I know of. "I don't think I'm going to be able to make it home for Christmas though."

"We'll come to you." His word is his bond, and his tone leaves no room for argument.

I cough out my shock. "Dad. I have a one-bedroom apartment. We can't have Christmas at my place!"

So much for seeming successfully independent.

"We'll make it work. What else is on your mind? I can tell you're holding back."

This. This is why I will jump through hoops for this man. Even from hundreds of miles away, I can't put anything past him. He cares enough to dig deeper, even if it's uncomfortable for him.

I sit down in my cubicle, gathering my things for the day. No one else is going to eavesdrop on my conversation when they're all so eager to flee, too. "How did you know Mom was the one?"

He makes a humming noise that carries clear as day over the line, like I'm sitting with him in the living room, watching his expression turn serious. "This about Mitchell?"

"Yes." There's no point beating around the bush.

"You have doubts?"

"So many, Daddy."

"I see." He pauses for a few moments, but I don't consider that the call has dropped. My dad is the type to always think before he speaks when it's important. "Was your meeting today good or bad?

"Bad. No one cares what I think. Since I'm just the intern, no amount of research I do matters. They walk right over me, even though they don't have any better ideas."

He hums again. "And who did you want to talk to about it? Don't think. Tell me your immediate gut reaction."

"No one." My answer is honest. "If you hadn't called just now, I probably wouldn't even have mentioned it to you."

"That's a problem, baby girl. I knew your mom was the one because she was the first person I wanted to share every joy and every heartbreak with."

"What about now?" I press. I've lived my whole life without my mother. Who's been the person my dad runs to all this time?

"She might not be here physically, but I still talk to your mom first about everything. She's probably mad as hell that I've raised you to be so independent that you feel like you can't count on anyone to be there for you."

I snort in spite of myself. Dad hasn't raised me to be independent at all. The problem is that I *can* count on him—to do everything for me.

"I'm serious, princess. Everyone thinks relationships are about give and take, and they are. The mistake is thinking you only have to give your best. If you can't show someone your worst and expect they're going to love you anyway, then that's not a relationship at all. That's friends with benefits, as Theo would say." He practically pukes out the last part.

I am absolutely alone in this room, but my cheeks fire to life anyway. My dad didn't even have the birds and bees talk with me. He signed a form to give the high school health teacher permission to do it. There are just some things fathers and daughters don't ever need to share.

"It's a little more complicated than that." I am all for changing the subject. "He's a professional football player. The season is tough on these guys both physically and mentally. They're about to enter the playoffs, and they're already exhausted. Mike doesn't need to hear about my bad day."

"Maybe not, but what concerns me is that you don't seem to even *want* to share it."

My dad's words flatten me to my chair.

I accused Mike of holding back, of not confiding in me, but…I've been doing the same thing all along.

I can't hide behind the temporary label anymore. He might not have said the words out loud, but Mike's told me he loves me. He's absolutely not the kind of man to admit that flippantly. Certainly not if he thinks this thing is over before it begins.

I'm not giving *myself* the chance to fall in love with him.

"Tori?" My dad's voice is softer than I've ever heard it. "You're worrying me, baby girl. A scholarship isn't worth your suffering. Maybe it's time to come home."

A laugh drowns out my threatening tears. Same old Dad.

"No can do, sir. I have a job to do. I'll see you for Christmas."

"I'll work out a schedule with your brothers, then I'll call you with our itinerary."

Long after we've ended the call, I sit at my desk with my head in my hands.

"Bad day?"

My scream echoes off the walls. I press my hand against my chest, sure I'm having a heart attack at the ripe old age of twenty-four. "Mike! God, you scared the crap out of me! What are you doing here?"

His grin is a little sheepish. He shrugs and stuffs his hands into the pockets of his sweatpants. How does this man make embarrassment and athletic wear look so darn good?

"I always drop in here after I'm done for the evening. It's usually empty."

"We had a late meeting," I explain then pause, rewind, and replay the words Mike spoke. "You...stop in here every night on your way home?"

"Yeah," he admits. For once, I'm not the one blushing.

"Why?"

He shrugs again, toes the carpet with his sneaker, and doesn't quite meet my gaze. It's so odd—so heartwarming—to see a man this powerful act anything less than completely confident. "Maybe you'll still be here. Like tonight."

*Why* am I not giving myself the chance to fall in love with him?

I hoist my messenger bag over my shoulder then rise from my seat. He towers over me when I stand in front of him. The muscles in his arms bulge and flex with his stance, but I could never be afraid of Mike Mitchell. Especially not after what he's confided in me.

I wrap my arms around his waist, plaster my face to his chest, and let myself feel totally and utterly protected when he wraps his arms around me in return.

"I need your help with something," I mumble into his shirt.

His answer is immediate. "Absolutely. What do you need?"

"What are your plans for Christmas?" It's not totally baring myself, but it's a good start.

He combs his fingers through my hair. "We don't have a game, so they're giving us the day off. My mom and sisters are actually flying in. Why? Did you want me to do some other charity event?"

I feel awful that his first guess is something PR related instead of assuming I wanted to make plans for us. This isn't really a romantic idea, but I don't retreat. "My dad and brothers are driving up, too. They'll stay in a hotel, but my apartment is too small to host them there. Would you mind sharing your place for Christmas dinner?"

He wraps his hand around my hair like a human ponytail holder, then he tugs on it, bringing my chin up until our gazes meet. His eyebrows are raised.

"It doesn't have to be dinner," I backtrack. "It could be breakfast, or brunch, or lunch, or...or, even just dessert! It doesn't have to be Christmas day either! It can be any day that's convenient for you!"

A slow grin spreads across his mouth until all his straight, white teeth are visible. "We can host Christmas together for both our families. I'd like that."

"You would?"

He brushes his lips against mine. "I would. We already crossed the line of a pretend relationship a long time ago. Why not go all out and spend the holidays together?"

"You've met my brothers, right?" I remind him.

He laughs against my mouth. "I have. Honestly, we're kind of similar. I probably treat my sisters the same way your brothers treat you."

It's my turn to raise my eyebrows. "Doubtful. You're not that big of a jerk."

"It's just because they have chips on their shoulders that you're the most attractive sibling."

"What?" I laugh out.

"It's true," he insists. "I think they act the way they do because they're jealous."

"That's absurd." I glance down only to be faced with the big yellow spot I've left on his shirt. Again.

He follows my gaze and just laughs. "Forgot to use the setting powder, huh?"

Oh my God. In hindsight, I had no idea how much that moment meant at the time. "You didn't learn how to do makeup by teaching your sisters, did you?"

"No," he confirms, swiping his finger down my cheek. "My mom taught them how to do that."

He helped her cover up the bruises she was too beat-up to deal with. There's something to be said for sharing hardship, but I'm still a big believer in building other people up. "Lucky girls. I bet she even had the sex talk with them."

His face puckers. "Yeah. Unfortunately, she also tried to have it with me."

"Really? My dad didn't. He left that up to my high school health teacher."

Mike wraps his arm around my shoulder and steers us toward the exit. "I weirdly learned way more sex ed from the quarterback of my high school team."

"Rob?"

"No." He laughs like that's the funniest thing I've ever said. "God, no. His name was Jeff Black. He was a senior when I was a sophomore."

This seems like a much happier memory. "I'd love to hear more about this story when we get home."

We stop at my car, where Mike waits for me to unlock it and shove my bag into the backseat.

"Speaking of home...why do you stop in the marketing department every night before you leave if I'm just going to inevitably see you at your place in a bit anyway?"

"The same reason I'm all for hosting Christmas together." He bends down to dust my lips with a kiss when I'm seated behind the steering wheel. "If I only get to have a little time with you, then I'm not going to waste a second."

I stare at him as he strides to his truck after closing my door. So, he does believe this thing between us is finite. He told me he loves me and bared his soul to me anyway. That's a gift I haven't fully appreciated until just now.

I want to give him a gift in return. I'm going to make sure he has the best Christmas ever.

# Chapter 30
## I Knew You When

### Mike

"This is a disaster."

I couldn't agree more. At least I don't have to worry about beating the shit out of Tori's brothers. If even one more lewd joke is shared, I'm pretty sure Hope is going to castrate all five of them.

That would normally make me proud as hell, but the tears in Tori's voice carry more weight.

"Everyone's hangry and mad the rents won't let us open our gifts on Christmas Eve. That's all." I can't believe I'm excusing anyone's bad behavior, but honestly? My mom and Tori's dad are in the kitchen, arguing about the best glaze for a baked ham. Even the adults aren't setting a good example.

"We could never get married." She sighs. "Our families would kill each other. This is like the Capulets and Montagues."

I'm pretty sure that's a Romeo and Juliet reference, but all I'm paying attention to is Tori considering marriage. To me.

I'm kind of disappointed now that I didn't buy her diamonds for Christmas. I didn't want to scare her off more than I probably already have by going too far in the other direction to prove I'm a worthy contender for her heart.

"We could always elope." It's a joke. A test. A stupid thing out of my mouth.

She nods like it's an entirely plausible suggestion.

Suddenly, I'm having the best Christmas ever even though I am absolutely beat up from our last game.

"I wanted you to have the best Christmas ever, and this is turning out to be the worst." She actually sniffles back a sob, not realizing she's just given me the gift of a lifetime.

I could go into the living room and scream and yell at our siblings to behave themselves. That's not going to improve anyone's mood, and I'm too tired to strongarm everyone into doing what they should be anyway.

"Well..." This has the potential to either backfire spectacularly or be the best idea I've ever had. "You're the lady of the house. Take charge."

Her laughter rains over my skin like a thousand invisible kisses that make all my bruises feel better.

"Seriously." If I'm going to do this, I might as well go all the way. I have this feeling I've only seen glimpses of what Peaches is capable of. I hate that her family snuffs out all her potential. "This is *our* house. They have to learn how to respect that. Lead the way, and I'll *support* you."

She raises her eyebrows, hopefully impressed that she's taught me anything. "Since this is going to be a team effort, I'm open to suggestions of how to accomplish holiday goodwill between opposing sides."

"I read a story in history once about soldiers in World War I who called a cease-fire on Christmas Eve and sang Silent Night to each other..." I might not have been able to run with the Romeo and Juliet reference, but I don't want her to think I'm a complete idiot either.

"I don't think our families are really the sing-along types."

Damn. Foiled again. "Okay, fine. I vote for putting on National Lampoon's Christmas Vacation and making them play the hat game."

Tori gapes at me like I am an idiot. "What's the hat game?"

I can't believe she's even asking, but I also can. Her family has sheltered her to the point of gross innocence—the total opposite of what I learned from a very young age. "It's pretty simple. You put a Santa hat on the corner of the TV. Every time someone on the screen looks like they're wearing it, you drink."

She narrows her eyes, obviously trying to work out how this

would play out. "You want to get our siblings drunk on Christmas Eve?"

I'm all out of better ideas at this point. "Yep."

She sighs then places her hands on her hips. "Mitchell, I like what you're bringing to the table, but I have a few concerns."

I hope she likes what I bring to the table. More than the other guy anyway. "I'm all ears. Go on."

"Number one, if we get them drunk, they might just be more belligerent. Number two, you don't keep alcohol in your home, so even if your suggestion is brilliant, it's a moot point."

Oh, shit. She's right. I didn't think this plan through. "It's early. I'm sure liquor stores are still open. I can run out and get enough booze to sedate ten people. Do you have a better idea?"

I bite back a smile because she's obviously ready and waiting with a counter-offer.

"I vote for guilt-tripping them into shoveling your insanely long driveway since you're so sore from work." She grins.

It's evil, devious, and nothing I associate with Peaches, but I love it instantly anyway.

I'm not about to bring up the fact I can call a service to plow the driveway. "Rock, paper, scissors to decide?"

She immediately cocks her arm back, geared for battle. "Two out of three?"

"Come at me, Peaches." I *want* that. I want it so much.

It's a Christmas miracle that I win. I'm not firing on all cylinders, but I honestly want to give her this opportunity to make her voice heard.

"Okay." I pretend I'm disappointed. "Guess I'm heading out in all the snow and ice to fetch the booze. On Christmas Eve."

I might pretend a little *too* well.

She frowns. "Maybe I should go. If you show up at the liquor store, buying out all the stock, that could make for bad press."

I flip up the hood of my Wolves sweatshirt. "I have sunglasses in my truck. I'll go incognito. Besides, I'm from Ohio. You're from

Virginia. I have way more experience driving in the snow than you do."

She squints her eyes at me.

"If all else fails, and someone recognizes me, I'll tell the truth—that we're in the middle of holiday, blended-family chaos. That's relatable, right? Fans would probably eat that shit up right about now."

She puffs out a breath of defeat. "It absolutely is relatable. You're learning, Mitchell."

I hope that's not all I'm learning. I plant a kiss on her lips. "Good luck, future Mrs. Mitchell. I'll be back in about an hour."

She glances around at the mayhem, not looking the least bit confident—either in me pushing the envelope or her abilities. "I wouldn't blame you if you made it three hours."

"I never want to be away from you that long."

Like baby Jesus himself is against me landing this deal, it actually takes me over two hours to fight through the shitty road conditions, weirdly heavy traffic, and to find a liquor store still open on Christmas Eve.

When I pull into my driveway though, it's clear of the fresh five inches of powder. Several bodies are engaged in a fierce snowball fight on the lawn. I wouldn't be surprised if they're hiding rocks in the middle of the white stuff.

"Are you trying to kill each other for real?" I yell as I pull boxes from the back seat.

"Yep!" Faith shouts back. "Tori was right! This is totally therapeutic!"

That pulls a laugh out of me. I've come to really appreciate Tori's off-the-wall ways of accomplishing anything.

I don't want to pull our siblings away from their wholesome therapy, so I haul the boxes inside myself. The glass bottles clank against each other. It's a different sort of jingle than the traditional sleigh bells, but hopefully it'll help everyone be jolly.

The sight that meets me in the house stops me dead in my tracks.

Tori's in the kitchen alone, stirring something in a pot on the stovetop. I've seen her in this kitchen a million times, wearing a lot less clothing. There's something about watching her prep dinner on Christmas Eve wearing an ugly holiday sweater—a tradition in her family—that really makes my heart thump in my chest though. Next year might be totally different. More peaceful, sure, but also more empty.

I really can't imagine my life without her in it anymore.

I'd love to pretend she's in the middle of a phone call with anyone other than who I know damn well is on the other end of the line though.

"I'm fine," she hisses into the cell she has propped between her cheek and shoulder. "Stop trying to make this out to be something it's not just because it's suddenly convenient for you."

My heart goes from thumping to still in way less time than it takes me to run a fifty-yard dash.

At face value, her words make it seem like she's been seeing him behind my back, even though I know that's not possible. We're both way too busy near the end of the season for her to have any free time that she isn't already spending with me.

"Look, Ben." She sighs. "It's Christmas. I don't want to fight, okay? More importantly, I don't want to look back on all the time we spent together and have it seem ugly because of the way you're acting in the present. Let's just leave those memories where they belong—in the past. I'm so very sorry that your engagement ended. But...this needs to be the last time you call me."

Damn. And I thought I had it rough with my ex.

"No." She straightens her spine and actually slams the spoon she's holding down on the countertop. "Listen very carefully to my words. I need you to hear them. We are never getting back together. It has nothing to do with my relationship with Mike. You and I are done. Finished. Over." Her shoulders slump and her voice softens. "Merry Christmas."

I'm not about to fist pump the air even though she can't see me.

This doesn't mean I've won. She said it herself—permanently ending things with her ex has nothing to do with me.

She startles when she turns around to find me watching her.

Even though this is my house, I feel like shit for eavesdropping. Especially when trust is the foundation Tori and I have built our entire relationship on.

"I'm sorry he ruined your Christmas."

She shrugs. "He didn't ruin mine. He ruined his own."

We stare at each other in silence for a few minutes. Our families are at each other's throats, but it feels like battle lines are being drawn between us, too. I can't figure out *why*.

I've given my all. She's obviously not afraid to sleep with a guy who's capable of murder, so my sins aren't what's holding her back. There's nothing more I can do, even with Ben out of the picture.

I pat the cardboard boxes on the kitchen island. "I got rum for the eggnog, whiskey for hot toddies, and some boxes of pre-made shots for the hat game. We can still turn this thing around, Peaches."

I'm not talking about Christmas with our families at all.

Maybe she knows it because she walks steadily toward me and throws her arms around my waist then burrows her face against my chest. It's a gesture so familiar, my response is automatic.

I wrap my arms around her back. One of my hands plays with her hair like it can't help but do anything else. I have no control over the way I love her. It's a fucking miracle I denied it as long as I did.

I was so convinced she'd be the worst kind of distraction, but the truth is…fighting this thing between us was way harder than giving in.

"I knew you could handle this madness, but I'm dying to hear how you got our parents out of the kitchen."

She chuckles against me. "I told them they deserved to relax for a change and that their adult kids could take care of everything else."

I can't believe that worked. It's too simple, too easy. "Where are they now?"

She lifts her face away from me with a grin. "In the hot tub, enjoying the snow while staying warm."

If anyone ever doubts Tori's PR prowess, this day alone should be the biggest selling point on her resume. "Are we...trying to fix up our parents?"

The smile slides off her face to be replaced with an expression of horror like I've just suggested they're in our bed, banging. "God, no! My dad will always be hopelessly in love with my mom! He still talks to her first about everything even though she isn't physically here!"

I can't relate. Not even a little bit. My mom never dated again, thanks to a hefty helping of PTSD where men are concerned. Maybe Mr. Russo's devotion to his dead wife makes him a safer bet for a friend in my mom's eyes.

"Should I fix some drinks and serve them?"

Tori gives me the smile I've learned means she's honestly happy and not faking it. "That would be really nice, Mike. I genuinely do think they've earned having a relaxing holiday. We should all do whatever we can to give them that."

That's how she got everyone to do her bidding. She was just... herself. Honest almost to a fault, but one of the most genuinely caring people I've ever met.

So, for the rest of the night, I'm at her service. She gives orders, and I carry them out. No miraculous peace treaties are signed between our siblings, but the booze does its job. They all pass out in heaps of bodies in front of the television. A silent night after all.

Long after Tori's gone to bed, our parents are back out in the hot tub for round number two. She's convinced nothing will ever happen between them, but I'm not so sure.

Snow still steadily falls from a moonless sky. The silence doesn't muffle their conversation the second I step out of the sliding glass door, but at least I'm not hearing moans.

"I hope I'm not being too forward, but...how did your wife die?"

Of course, Mom doesn't want to be too forward. She's learned the hard way how to mitigate anger.

Tori's dad sighs. It's not the pleasurable kind, thank God. "Cancer."

"I'm so sorry," my mom murmurs. "That must have been just as hard on the kids as it was on you."

"It was a nightmare," he admits. "Kelly raised the kids mostly on her own while I was deployed. Suddenly, I had a two-month old baby girl and five older boys whose attitudes were in the toilet because they were too young to understand why their mom just gave up."

"I don't understand," Mom says.

That makes two of us.

"She was diagnosed when she was five months pregnant with Tori. We just thought her symptoms were from a difficult pregnancy. By the time the doctors realized what was going on, the cancer had already spread. She had to choose—fight the fight of her life or forfeit Tori's life."

My mom gasps.

I suddenly feel like I've been catapulted back in time to when I read all about Tori on the internet. If I thought then that it was like finding out about her life without her ever telling me, hearing this now makes me feel like a freaking chump.

I poured out things very few people know to her, trying to bare myself. All so she would finally trust me. She can't even tell me this? I had to find out by eavesdropping on another conversation that wasn't meant for me to hear? Did I spill my guts for nothing?

I let myself back into the house as quietly as possible and creep up the stairs to my bedroom.

Tori's sound asleep on her stomach as usual. Her red hair and pale skin are noticeable against the gray sheets even in the dark. The thing is...I still want her here. Still can't imagine going back to an empty bed.

I've tried everything I can think of. I have nothing left in my playbook. As much as I hate admitting it, I need advice.

There's only one man I think might be able to give it to me.

I scroll through my contacts as I walk down the hall to the home office.

He picks up on the fourth ring, just as I'm preparing to leave a lame voice mail, wishing him a happy holiday.

"Hey, buddy. Merry Christmas." His voice is raspy.

I pull the phone away from my ear to double check the time. It's only eight in Sacramento.

"Same to you. Did I wake you?"

"Yeah," he croaks. "We had a rough day with YiaYia, so we're all exhausted."

Evie's family was always my family, too, thanks to the whole adopted siblings thing. I'm kind of ashamed this is the first I'm hearing about her grandmother having trouble. Maybe if I wasn't so caught up in my own life, I'd still know everything about my friends' lives.

"What's going on with YiaYia?"

"She's ninety-six, Mike," Rob whispers. "Honestly, we're all kind of surprised she's hung on this long without Papou. It's way worse around the holidays though."

"They really are your family now, aren't they?"

"Yeah?" He says it like he can't understand the question.

After the family feud I refereed all day, I'm jealous of Rob for something other than football.

"I'm sorry I gave you shit at Papou's funeral." It feels weirdly good to get that off my chest. "I'm sorry I gave you shit about a lot of things."

This isn't why I called, but maybe I need to secure my own Christmas Eve truce before I get down to business.

"Who is it?" Even in the background, it's obvious Evie woke up, too.

"It's Mike." Rob's voice is muffled like he's covering the phone with his hand. "He wanted to say Merry Christmas." More rustling in the background. The sound of him kissing her, sheets rustling. "Go back to sleep, baby." His voice sounds clear again. "Hang on. Let me go down to the kitchen, so I don't wake everybody else up."

I've been in Rob's townhouse in Sacramento. He doesn't have to go down to a kitchen. Everything's on the same level.

"Where are you?"

"Ironville." He yawns. The distinct, familiar sound of stairs creaking filters through the line. "We flew in this morning. I've gotta head back tomorrow afternoon, but Evie's going to stay until Sunday morning."

Another punch of jealousy hits me square in the chest. He talks about their joined lives like it's no big deal that they juggle cross-country travel in between grueling season schedules.

I close my eyes and picture him walking down the stairs of the old Papageorgiou house, into the outdated kitchen, sitting at the worn table I sat at many times. He belongs there now. I don't.

I don't feel like I belong in Albany in this giant house that's empty most of the time either.

"Are we gonna breathe at each other for half the night, or are you gonna tell me why you really called?"

I bark out a short laugh. "I said the same thing to Alex when he showed up here a few weeks ago. Swap out drinking for breathing. He was the only one getting shit-faced."

Damn. I miss *my friends*. I miss the break I had for a few years when life was a hell of a lot simpler, and I knew exactly where my place was in the world.

Rob chuckles like the same regrets are rolling through his mind. "He didn't exactly seem eager to bury the hatchet with me at dinner, but he said he wouldn't hold a grudge. Do you think he'll really show up?"

"Yeah." I don't even hesitate. "For her? He will."

"Yeah." Rob sighs.

"How the hell did we get here?"

"It's Christmas Eve, and I still don't know why you called." Rob chuckles, but this one sounds more relaxed. "So, do you want the long answer or the short version?"

I already know the facts. I'm looking for something...deeper. Time to cut the shit. "How did you do it?"

"Do what? Fuck up my whole life in just a few seconds? Multiple times? Well, it all started when I saw the most beautiful girl in the world for the very first time..."

I used to think that whole idea of love at first sight—of Templeman's unicorn—was such bullshit. Now? I'm not so sure. The goal is clear, but for the first time in my life, hard work on my part isn't enough to reach it.

"What's going on, Mike? Trouble in paradise that online pictures aren't showing?"

Damn, he's good. Then again, that's why he's an elite quarterback. The man can read shit most of us don't even see.

"Wait a minute. How do you know about me and Tori being more than meets the eye?"

Rob laughs. "Are you kidding me? Evie's been gushing about you two like a full-fledged fangirl ever since those first pictures were leaked. She's convinced you finally found the one. I should thank you, honestly. It's kind of a nice break between all the shit we usually deal with."

Great. No pressure or anything.

"I, uh..." I cough away my hesitation. No point making this call if I'm not going to actually do anything with it. "I can't get there, Rob. She won't let me. I've tried everything. I've told her shit only Evie knows, so she'll believe I'm really in this, but...She's a blocked route. Over and over again."

I know damn well he can't call an effective play if he doesn't know the opposition like the back of his hand. So, for the first time in my life, I tell someone who doesn't *need* to know...everything.

By the time I'm done, silence stretches between us for so long that I pull my phone away from my ear and check the screen to see if the call dropped.

"Jesus Christ, Mike," he finally says.

Embarrassment and shame threaten to strangle me, but I've pushed through tougher setbacks before. "I bet you're really pissed about all those times I acted better than you, huh?"

"No," Rob rushes. "I'm not judging you. If anything, I'm happy you and Evie had each other all this time. I'm grateful as fuck you're in her corner. Hell, I'll breathe easier tonight knowing you're the man who will have her back if anything ever happens to me."

Yeah, I will. Forever.

That's not the point I'm trying to make here though. "I need to know how you did it. Me and Evie? We have walls for reasons. How did you break through hers even after all the shit you two went through? No matter what I do, Peaches won't let me in."

"Peaches?"

I can almost hear the lightbulb turn on in his mind.

"Oh! Tori! You call her Peaches?" He laughs. "Holy shit, that's adorable." Then he mutters, "Oh my God, I sound like my wife."

"That's not a bad thing." *Focus, Falls. Tell me how to get there.*

It takes him a few more beats to control himself. He's still chuckling when he says, "You're a professional football player, so act like one. Work as hard as you have to. Push through the pain. Achieve the goal."

My cell is going to crack from the pressure of me squeezing it since I can't strangle him through the phone. "Aren't you listening? I can't! I need a better play! So, be my fucking quarterback again and call one!"

Rob's hysterical laughter only makes me angrier. "I accept your proposal. I'll be your quarterback until the end of time."

"You know what? I'm sorry I wasted *both* our Christmas Eves by calling you."

"Wait!" He wheezes through laughter. "Wait! Don't hang up! Come on, you gotta give me this! Call it a Christmas gift! You admitted you acted better than me for years. You never come to me for advice, so you obviously really need it."

Fine. It's true. I would probably be gloating, too.

He sighs, all traces of laughter gone. "There is no secret play, man. Only a goal nothing can change. Football is a game, but this is real life. When your time on the field is done, who do you imagine beside you? Who do you want to be there? If you can picture an empty rocking chair, then let it run its course."

Fuck. This really has been a waste. "That's not my problem! I can't imagine my life without her in it, but just because I imagine her there doesn't mean she imagines me."

"No. You're right about that." Rob's voice is more serious than it's been so far. "Even if she doesn't imagine you in a rocking chair beside her, you have to believe without a shadow of doubt that you'd be the happiest man in the world just to lay at her feet on the floor while she holds hands with someone else in that other rocking chair."

"I'm already there." I blow out a breath of frustration. "So, what? You're telling me I just have to be happy with whatever scraps she's willing to give me?"

That's not brilliant advice. It's just a fact.

"Yeah," he says, his voice full of annoying pity. "I'm sorry I can't give you more, but it's the truth. There's no magic play for winning a woman because love isn't a game. Her heart isn't a prize. It's a gift."

"Great," I grumble. "So, I'm fucked."

"I'm about to give you some of the tough love you've been all too willing to dole out for years," Rob says.

I brace for a heavy dose of karma.

"Have you ever stopped to think that maybe you're being selfish? Because from what you're telling me, you expect her to open up to you just because you already have. You want her to do, be, and feel all the same things as you. She's not you, Mike. She's her. With her own baggage, her own experiences, and her own way of doing things. It's not a competition. If you really want to be in it for the long haul, then you have to learn how to appreciate all the things that are different between you instead of trying to mold her into what you need her to be so you can stay in love with her."

Shit. He's right. I've said all along that love is the most selfish thing a person can experience. I fell into that trap and didn't even realize it.

"Bottom line is I need to back off and let her come to me in her own time?"

"Pretty much." Rob's words come out all garbled in between the annoying sound of crunching.

"What are you doing?"

"Eating all the special Christmas cookies Evie made earlier."

Aww, hell. She didn't mail any to me. "I hate you sometimes."

Rob laughs then nearly chokes on a cookie. Good for him. "You already accepted me as your quarterback for life. No takebacks."

I hang up, knowing Rob and Evie will *both* always be in my life. Will Peaches?

# Chapter 31
Love Me Now

## Tori

"Hey, babe. How'd the meeting go?"

There is no reason Mike should sound so cheery after such a tough loss in the second round of the playoffs. Except painkillers. Lots and lots of painkillers.

He's lying on the couch in the living room, an ice pack on one knee that's elevated with a throw pillow. A heating pad beneath his right elbow. He switches them out every twenty minutes, following trainer's orders to the letter even though he needs my help for almost everything else.

I haven't been here even though this is where I'm most needed. For the past four hours, I've been stuck in PR department meetings to figure out how to spin the end of the season in the best possible way for the franchise and key players.

The verdict isn't pretty.

At least we have a few weeks to prepare. Even David agrees there's no point trying to run a media campaign while football fans are engaged with the other teams still on the hunt for a trip to the Super Bowl.

Our players deserve a break—to rest, recuperate, and for our unlucky backup quarterback, to find a new team.

I blink the tears from my eyes as I perch on the edge of the couch.

Even though his gaze is glassy, Mike takes one look at me and knows I'm the bearer of bad news. "Are they taking away your scholarship? We did everything they wanted! It's not your fault the team couldn't seal the deal in that last game! We've been the picture-perfect couple for the media!"

"They're not taking away my scholarship," I soothe.

His heart races beneath my palm on his chest even though his expression is disturbingly blank.

"When did you take your last pain pill?" His answer could make this difficult conversation either much easier or much harder.

"Uh..." He glances at the fancy watch that's monitoring all his other vital signs and reporting them directly back to the trainers. "About a half hour ago. Right on time. It's definitely kicking in. I'm not hurting, but my brain is like mashed potatoes. You could ask me anything you want, and I won't have any filter." He winces the moment the words leave his mouth. "Should not have admitted that."

Taking advantage of my favorite teddy bear seems like a much more fun way to spend the afternoon instead of discussing the next phase of our media campaign. I do have pity for him though, so I start off easy. "Who has the best rack you've ever seen?"

His eyes impossibly glaze over more. A sort of dopey smile spreads across his face. He's looking right at me, but also through me. "There was this stripper..."

On second thought, this is a horrible idea.

"...my teammates hired to tempt me because they're a bunch of assholes. She was so temptacious."

That's not even a word, and I hate this story, but I laugh anyway.

"Best rack I've ever seen, even with clothes on. Full, round—definitely real." He tries so hard to wiggle his eyebrows, but it just looks like he has a tic. "Turns out she wasn't a stripper at all. Still got to see the goods though. She stripped for me when she was drunk, and she ended up being my unicorn, and yeah. Best rack ever. I even get to play with them sometimes."

I almost, *almost* slap him for messing with me. As in, my hand is a centimeter from his arm before I remember the whole reason he's being so funny and loose-lipped. "Okay. You got me good. I have the best rack you've ever seen."

He grins. "They're the best peaches I've ever put in my mouth."

A bolt of lust zings between my legs. There hasn't been any mouth on my peaches in a few weeks, courtesy of injuries and play-offs focus.

"Do you *love* your peaches?" I take the melted ice pack off his knee and rearrange the heating pad there. Mindless activities to go with a mindless question.

"I do." He reaches up to caress my cheek with a single finger. "I love my Tori."

I mentally kick myself. He hasn't said that out loud to me yet, and this was a horrible occasion to hear words that might come back to bite him in the rear. His sweatpants emphasize the definition of his erection, so it only seems fair to use what he's giving me to work with. It buys me a few more minutes anyway.

"What do you want to do with the peaches you love so much?"

He squints one of his eyes at me like he's trying to think really hard. "Do you want the short list or the long list?"

More stalling? Yes, please.

Maybe he'll give me some direction for planning without his usual filter in the way.

"The long list."

"Okay." He blows out a harsh breath. "Anal. Maybe some light bondage—I'm not into whipping or anything, but some handcuffs might be nice. For you, not me. I could probably be persuaded to wear the shoe on the other foot if the moment's right. I've overheard some of my teammates talking about prostate massages. The idea kind of freaks me out, but I'm also curious. Who wouldn't want to experience the best orgasm ever? Hard pass on any threesomes or sharing, but toys might be okay. How do you feel about nipple clamps? I'm not into pain—for obvious reasons—but some of these guys are members of actual sex clubs. You wouldn't believe the stories I've heard."

My eyebrows might never come back down, and my mind might never stop imagining new, unexplored possibilities. "Wow, um. That wasn't what I meant at all, but okay. What does the short list look like?"

He sort of shrugs from his prone position. "Oh, easy. Get married. Have some babies. But later. Way, way later. I'm honestly a little terrified of being a father. What if I turn out like mine?"

How can I tell him what I need to after such a heartfelt admission?

"Is there anything I can do for you?" My conscience is eating me alive.

He nods. "I would like a massage."

"What?" I replay his words, but that's definitely what he said. "You told me massages are bad, and I should never, ever try to give you one."

"Between my legs," he clarifies, his words slurring a little. The pain pill is definitely kicking in now.

Anxious laughter pours out of me. Mike usually insists sex be all about me—not that I'm complaining at all. A generous lover is never something to whine about. It's just that I can't ever shake off the feeling it's because my big mouth blabbed I was missing out on searching for my unicorn by pretending to be with him. So, he does what he always does. Solves the problem in front of him.

This...this would be different. Giving without receiving. Giving because he wants it, and I want to.

I *so* want to.

I slip him out of his sweatpants. He's firm, thick, and clearly wanting in my grasp. I give him a good squeeze to test the waters.

He throws his head back against the arm of the couch and moans, his eyes drifting closed. "Peaches, yes. *Please.*"

"What do you want?" I coax, my mouth brushing over the velvety soft skin of his crown. My dirty mind runs rampant with images of me on my knees, Mike taking my mouth in the way that pleases him most. Rationally, I know he's not capable of that right now, but he's never let me do this to him before.

His voice is a guttural plea. "Suck me dry."

The sensitive flesh between my legs swells and aches for attention. No-filter Mike Mitchell is a dirty, dirty man, and it's turning me on. Which is saying a lot because this guy is a professional football player who's stacked with muscle and well-endowed with a package he definitely knows how to use for my pleasure. He keeps my fire burning on low heat at all times.

He's taking it to the next level, and I'm not even sure he knows what he's doing to me.

I lick him, tasting his soap and an indescribable flavor that can only be labeled as...Mike. Clean, yet earthy. Smooth but with a spicy afternote.

He's delicious. My mouth waters for *more*.

He groans and threads his hands through my hair like he's going to give *me* a massage. Even doped up, his touch is loving and gentle.

"Nuh-uh, buddy." I disentangle the hand from his bad arm and replace it against his chest. "If you want this, then you have to behave. No doing anything that will only hurt you more later."

His eyes are glazed over. He swallows thickly. "Okay. I'll be good. Promise."

I take him fully into my mouth and swirl my tongue around his head, all while meeting his gaze directly. Playing the part of the sexy vixen. Just to see if he'll really follow orders.

He does. His good hand fists tighter in my hair, but he leaves his other arm flat against his chest.

I've wanted to do this for so long. Now, I have free rein. I trace every veiny ridge with my tongue, laving his skin with the sort of adoration he's always shown me. He's so firm, I'm tempted to bite. Instead, I graze my teeth—just the barest pressure—up his length.

A stuttered groan rattles his chest. His skin breaks out in goosebumps.

"Do that again," he begs.

"Mike Mitchell..." I breathe against his head. Surprise coils my muscles with anticipation. I'm way too eager to see who he might be when he's not being so careful. "You do like a little pleasure spiked with pain."

"I didn't know it until just now," he slurs.

Oh, crap. It's probably the meds. He might not be able to tell me if I'm actually hurting him. Better not to risk it.

I seal my lips over his crown, sucking until his hips tip up like he can't control himself.

He hums—a deep, low sound that emanates from his throat. His eyes slide closed again.

Satisfied he's enjoying himself, I slide further down his length.

He shudders. "Deeper. I wanna feel the back of your throat with my cock."

I'm not sure I can go much deeper, but I'm absolutely going to try. A burning need to please him overrides my anxiety. I can't tell him I love him, but I can give him this.

I fold my lips over my teeth and relax my tongue, inhaling through my nose.

Mike's fingers squeeze my scalp. "Suck. Hard."

There's something so deliciously sexy about him telling me exactly what he wants and the way he wants it. This isn't hard and fast until he gets off. Rather, savoring slowly so that the journey is as good as the destination.

I don't think I've ever been more turned on in my life, and I'm not even the one receiving any of the pleasure I'm obviously giving him. Could he possibly know how much empowerment he's giving me?

I might never again rush through the act to reach the goal line or hesitate to tell him exactly what I want.

His fingers twitch in my hair then he pulls firmly until I follow his direction. He guides my head up and down his shaft—slow, steady, purposeful. The entire time I hollow my cheeks and suck hard as he commanded. Being at his mercy strangely makes me feel free.

Desire pools between my legs. A steady thrum of insistence keeps rhythm with the motion of his hand pushing and pulling. The bite of my scalp wars against the building pressure between my legs. I'm going to come. Another myth I would never have believed possible until this moment.

He really might be my unicorn. Life is so unfair.

Suddenly, he shoves my head down until my lips seal around the base of his cock. My gag reflex kicks in, but I swallow it down. Hard.

On a long, low moan he releases, wave after wave spilling down my throat.

That's all it takes for me to break even as tears roll down my cheeks.

Ecstasy seizes my muscles. I cry out my own release through swallows, my throat working double time to take and give.

"Fuck. Peaches," he grunts. He holds my head in place as he thrusts once, twice into my mouth, deeper than I ever thought possible.

My body trembles as the waves crash and break, ebbing slowly away but leaving a decidedly hollow sensation in their place.

I suddenly realize why Mike has never let me do this before. The last time someone put their mouth on him, it wasn't his choice. He was drugged then, too. For an entirely different reason.

Warmth unfurls through my chest as the implications of his request sink into my bones.

He trusts me. He loves me.

There's nothing fake about it.

His hand is limp in my hair. He disentangles his fingers then pets me as I rest my cheek against his stomach, my tears spilling onto his skin.

If he notices, he doesn't say anything. His eyes are half-lidded, and he releases a long rush of air. "Thank you, babe. Now, come sit on my face."

I hide *my* face against his stomach as laughter loosens my tight muscles. "Number one, that would likely hurt you. Number two, not necessary."

He barely raises an eyebrow. "Oh, really?"

I nod, still hiding as I fight to pull myself together. "I should be thanking you. That was one of the most erotic moments of my life."

After several beats of silence, I peek up at him. He might be confused, but it's hard to tell with the muscles in his face so relaxed.

"Can I come lay with you?" A need I can't squash begs for our hearts to beat together as closely as possible. Maybe for me. Maybe so he can feel this wasn't fake on my part either.

If only I didn't have to say the words I have to say.

He opens his arms, his movement sluggish.

I crawl up his body, careful not to jostle his bad knee or elbow. When I'm comfortably cradled against his chest, I press my nose into the soft, masculine scented skin at his neck. My tongue darts out for a tiny taste. Just a sliver.

He hums, a satisfied, sleepy sound.

I smile. "You're dirty, Mitchell, but you're still my teddy bear."

There's a smile in his voice, too. Even though his words are more slurred than ever. "You can't call me that in public. I'll never live it down. It'll be so much worse than Monk."

"Speaking of in public…" Great. Now, I'm crying again. "We have to break up."

# Chapter 32
Marry You

## Mike

I AM SO EXHAUSTED. It has nothing to do with the training camp I just co-hosted at my old high school. It doesn't even have anything to do with helping my buddy pull off another marriage proposal in a place that still gives me the absolute creeps. The past ten weeks have felt like a goddamn eternity, and there's only a small break in sight. I slam the door to the hotel room behind me like it's responsible for this bullshit.

Then, do a double-take at the bed.

Where a red-headed goddess is splayed out in peach-colored lace lingerie.

Her smile is shy. "I figured the least I can do is make all this sneaking around worth your time."

"Oh, you're worth my time and then some," I breathe. My tongue lolls out of my mouth, probably like a damn cartoon character.

She looks like something out of my best dreams. No makeup, hair a wild mess fanning all over the pillows, smooth, pale skin spread out across the mattress. The lace teddy stretches across her full breasts, barely enough to cover them completely. My gaze sinks lower, taking in all the crisscrossed ribbon that's wound around her waist like a goddamn gift. And then my eyes zero in on what's missing. There's no way to tell she's a natural red head now. Because she is completely bare.

My mouth feels drier than desert sand. There's only one thing that's going to quench me.

My exhaustion forgotten, I practically jump on the bed and dive between her legs, giving her a firm lick right through the lace. Her taste is pure heaven, and I have been in serious withdrawal.

She squeals then moans then threads her fingers through my hair.

"How did it go?" she pants, spreading her legs wider for me.

I peek up at her. "Seriously? You seriously want to have a conversation about my day right now?"

"I haven't seen you for months!"

No, she hasn't. She also hasn't abandoned me just because our puppet masters demanded it. She's walking a very thin line of losing her scholarship if our little secret is discovered.

So, if she wants to talk all night, then that's what we'll do.

Still, she can take a little payback for torturing me this way. I latch onto her bud and give a good solid suck before disengaging.

She whimpers when I crawl up her body.

"Hey, you asked for this," I remind her.

"Mmm." She wraps her arms and legs around me. Even though she still hasn't said the words, I feel like the most loved man in the entire world. No number of fans cheering my name could ever be this good. "I know, and I'm sorry, but I miss you so much. I got so used to being together nearly every day."

Music to my ears. I pull away to grin at her. "I miss you, too, Peaches." I wink at her. "But not in public."

She tilts her head to the side and squints her eyes a bit. "I don't know. Shouldn't you actually miss me in public? How are you supposed to gain fan sympathy if you don't seem miserable because I dumped you to pursue my master's degree?"

"Okay, fine. I'm fucking miserable, and I hate this shit." I'm not pouting for pretend. This is completely real.

"I know. Me, too." She soothes me with her mouth.

I haven't kissed this woman in forever, so I pour everything into it. Her lips are pillow soft; her tongue molds to mine like she's part of me. Her taste bursts in my mouth like my favorite flavor that I never want to share with anyone else.

How did I ever live without this? It doesn't matter that I didn't know what I was missing for most of my life.

I don't break away until we both desperately need to breathe.

"I'm not sure how long I can keep this up," I confess, burying my face against her neck. Maybe if I can just inhale enough of her, it'll last me for the next few weeks until we can sneak away again. "I thought I was signing up to play professional football. How was I supposed to know I'm actually a walk-on in a soap opera?"

She runs her fingers through my hair and nuzzles me. Yeah, she won't say it out loud, but she can't hide her feelings anymore. "I've actually been researching that. I might not be a lifelong football fan, and I was only an intern with the Wolves, but...This seems extreme, even to me. Not normal, you know? Anyway, from what I can tell without insider information, it seems to be dependent on the team. Not every franchise in the league operates this way."

I smother my grin against her neck. I don't want to be too smug about more proof that she's thinking of me even when she doesn't have to be. I know damn well how busy she is with her classes. "I could've told you that. Even Rob's team doesn't play games this way. After he tanked his debut season, they didn't jerk him around like a trick pony. Alex loves the celebrity part of the job, but that doesn't come from his team's front office."

She sighs, her body moving against mine in ways that aren't going to let me hold back much longer. "I hate to say this, but maybe you should have a discussion with your agent about getting you out of Albany. Who knows what they're going to make you do next?"

That's a chilling prospect. Enough to make shivers race down my spine for a not so pleasant reason. "I'm locked into a four-year contract. I still have two seasons left. The only way I can get out of it is if the Wolves release me."

I can't fail my family like that.

Who will make my sisters' tuition payments? Who will pay off my mom's mortgage if I go a year or two between steady paychecks? Hell, what if Chelsie's situation gets worse, and she decides to call in my offer for help?

If I get released from the team that drafted me, there's no guarantee another will even be willing to pick me up.

Then, I'll be useless to everyone.

"Mike…" Tori kisses my cheek and sighs again. "I'm not there to mitigate threats to you anymore. I know how much you love football, but what if they assign Kaylie to be your fake girlfriend after enough time has passed? Are you just going to go through with it? What if they want you two to fake an engagement? Then, what?"

A hint of anger simmers in my stomach, but the excitement in my chest tap dances all over it. I push myself up to gaze at Tori's beautiful face. "Are you saying you want to get engaged?"

She bites her lip and glances away. "We can't. I already floated that idea instead of the breakup. They didn't want to hear it. David said fans wouldn't respond well to you having something to celebrate when they were still licking their wounds from a playoff loss."

The stupid smile splitting my face might never go away. Ever. "You…fought against their idea? You suggested we get engaged instead of breaking up?" I jump off the bed almost as fast as I jumped onto it. "That's it. Get dressed."

"I knew you'd be mad," she mumbles, slowly rising from the bed then fumbling through a duffel bag for clothes. "I didn't think you'd kick me out if I told you the truth though."

"Mad?" My laughter actually sounds a little mad. As in the insane variety. There's a part of me that will never stop believing some things in life are too good to be true. "I'm not mad. I'm not kicking you out. I'm taking you ring shopping."

She's trying so hard to fight the grin that wants to stretch her sweet lips that she actually bites down on the bottom one to keep her expression somewhat serious. She can't hide the gleam of excitement in her eyes though. "We can't do that, and you know it."

"The hell we can't! You're right. I'm not going to wait around for them to order me to date Kaylie when this stupid media ploy tanks." I fish my keys out of my pocket and latch onto the doorknob. "Come on. I know a great place in town. It's a small family business."

She shakes her head. A hint of that smile breaks free. "And the owners will know you. Just like everyone else in town who will be all over this in a heartbeat."

She is *not* saying no.

She's just saying we can't do it publicly.

I scrub my hands over my face. "Good point. We have to be smart about this. I don't want to risk your scholarship or my playing time. We'll look online instead."

The happiness slips off her face as she sinks to the bed. "We can't do that either. Just like we lied to our families in the beginning to prevent the truth from getting out, we'd have to hide this from them, too. This is a big life decision, Mike. My dad would lose his mind if you didn't ask him permission to marry me. We can't risk it."

Okay, she's still not saying no. She's just saying not right now.

I walk back to where she's seated at the edge of the mattress and drop to my knees in front of her. It's not the kind of proposal my sisters squeal about in movies, but I never planned for this to happen. I fold her hands in mine. "I understand all that. I do. I will ask him when the time is right, but it would be stupid not to ask you first."

She pulls one of her hands free to plaster it over my mouth. Tears shine in her eyes. "Don't. Like you said, you have two years left on your contract. We have to lie to the whole world for the next *two years*. They might force you to publicly date Kaylie. Or anyone. You might not like it, but you'll do it because you love your job. Just like you didn't want a fake relationship with me, but you gave in anyway." The barest hiccup of a cry slips past her lips. "You can't ask me to marry you now, then give in to the next woman to warm your bed. I love you, Mike, but…I can't live like that."

"Babe…" I push her body flat against the bed with my own and cover every goddamn inch of her skin with my mouth. I kiss her, already dizzy from stupid words that she's shown me for so long. It's a fucking miracle she's held onto them as stubbornly as she did.

I rest my forehead against hers and just…breathe her in.

Another sob pushes her chest harder against mine. "I love you too much to ask you to choose between your career and me. Someone already sacrificed everything for me, and I can't ever let anyone else do that."

Her mom.

I pull my head away to gaze down at her. "Is that why you've been fighting this? Not giving in all the way? Because you don't want me to have to choose either?"

She nods, biting her lips like she's trying to stuff all her love back inside.

"Peaches…" I trail my mouth over her face, savoring every smooth dip and curve and memorized feature that I see even in my sleep. "Because I love you—because *she* loved you—it's not a choice at all. That's what love is. Being willing to give up everything for someone else. Being selfless. Not selfish."

She squeezes her eyes tightly shut and cries harder.

I kiss her tears. "Just like you did for me. You've already nearly been fired and lost your scholarship, right? You were willing to lose all that because you thought that's what I wanted, weren't you?"

Her eyes pop open. "That's not nearly the same thing! I would have just been a year behind on my plan, that's all! It wouldn't have ruined my whole career!"

"This is the same. We'll be behind two years on our plan, that's all. I won't do anything to jeopardize my job or your scholarship." I kiss her again. Because she loves it when I kiss her and because I'll never get enough. "We can make it two years, babe. I believe in us."

"Two years…" She whimpers. "I live in Virginia again. You still live in Albany. We won't have time for secret rendezvous during the season."

I fight back the laugh building in my chest and plan to buy her a very special delivery to help get her through the drought that's coming. I roll off her and pull her body against mine on the mattress. "Ask me how my day went again."

She blinks at me. "Uh, how did your day go?"

I kiss the tip of her nose and try not to smile too hard. "The proposal was a success, and the wedding will be here in Ironville. In two months."

The corner of her mouth tips up. "That's wonderful. I'm so happy for them."

I chuckle because she's definitely not following me. "After tonight, you only have to make it two months. That's how I reach tough goals. I break it up into baby steps. So, that's what we'll do."

Her bottom lip puffs out. "Two months is so far away though!"

"Maybe it'll be enough time for you to work on your alcohol tolerance, so you won't pee in front of me after the next wedding reception."

She punches me square in the chest. Then, she makes love to me.

# Chapter 33
Friends

## Tori

EVERYTHING IS IN PLACE, right down to the last rose petal. All I need now is the guy.

And some way to pass the next ten or so hours.

I glance at the bed, where every toy he's sent me for the past two months is displayed for his choosing. A shiver of anticipation runs up my spine. The real thing is going to feel so much better than the silicone mold.

A knock on the hotel room door startles me. I didn't order room service, but maybe Mike snuck away before the ceremony. The big surprise for later will be ruined. A quickie would make up for that.

I fling the door open with a wide smile only to find a familiar woman in a white wedding dress grinning back at me.

"Hurry up! Grab your stuff! I have a dress waiting for you! We're going to sneak you in!" She barrels past me in a flurry of words and silk. Then, stops dead in her tracks, her mouth hanging wide open as she stares at the bed.

"Nuh-uh. Nope. Did not need that much information about my brother." She turns around to face me again, her back to the damning evidence that can in no way be denied.

My face must be brighter than the surface of the sun. It certainly feels as hot. "I, um, I can explain. It's a joke!"

"Haha, yeah." She chuckles dryly. "And it's on me. That's what I get for inviting myself in."

"Come on! If we're gonna pull this off, we don't have much time!" A voice at my back calls from the hallway, footsteps approaching.

Evie holds up a hand and opens her mouth, probably to stop whoever it is from walking through the door.

It's too late.

A low whistle makes me cringe.

"Damn. It's always the ones who seem the most straight-laced that are the kinkiest behind closed doors."

Is death from embarrassment a thing? Because I feel like it's a thing. I can barely breathe. Evie will have to apologize to Mike for me not making it two years. Because I'm dying.

She nods once—a curt, resolute movement that makes her curls bounce. "Right. So, Tori Russo, meet Alyssa Quentin. Alyssa, this is Mike's girlfriend, Tori. I'm invoking the circle of trust. Aside from introductions, nothing seen in this room will ever be spoken of again."

"Speak for yourself," the woman—Alyssa—mutters. "I'm going to give him so much shit about this."

Evie points a finger at her. "No, you will not. For the same reason you kept your mouth shut about me moving to Sacramento."

Alyssa scoffs. "That was to protect you from the media and your psycho stalker. I'm not going to post a picture of this on Twitter. I'm just maybe going to tell Alex all about it, so we can have fun at the reception."

That snaps me out of my embarrassed haze. "No! Not Alex!"

Alyssa narrows her eyes at me. "So, you're clearly familiar with Alex." She turns her gaze to Evie. "Why did Alex get to meet her first? At least I live in the same state as Mike!"

Evie rolls her eyes then tears into the adjoining bathroom, calling over her shoulder as she goes, "If it wasn't for Alex, they wouldn't even be together! And you're going to keep your trap shut because the media isn't supposed to know they're still together!"

Alyssa sighs. "I don't know how you people live like this. I thought artists were dramatic. Football is a whole other level."

Evie reemerges from the bathroom with my makeup bag. Her

expression is an odd combination of severe and sympathetic. It's obvious her response is meant for me. "It's a hard life in many ways, but it's worth it. I'm so sorry for what you're being put through." She steps toward me and opens her arms then freezes. "Nope. Can't do it. Still too awkward with what I'm trying to ignore on the bed behind me. Come on. I'll hug you later."

The spin cycle going on in my brain intensifies when I'm pushed into a different hotel room on the same floor. A bustle of activity flurries around the room in various shades of taffeta.

"The ball is in play," Alyssa announces to the other women. "It's game time!"

They descend on me like rabid hyenas. I'm shoved into a chair in front of a mirror. A woman I don't know starts combing my hair while reaching for a curling wand. Another kneels in front of me and accepts my makeup bag that Evie hands over.

The idea of anyone other than Mike doing my makeup kind of freaks me out.

All motion stops when Evie slaps a hand over her mouth. She holds up a finger then rushes into the bathroom.

Seconds later, the distinct sounds of retching fill the space.

Oh, no. Is she getting cold feet?

The woman on the floor in front of me yells, "You better not ruin your makeup! That took me an hour!"

Wow. That's not very supportive.

"Jesus, Tini," the woman who's already resumed curling my hair responds. "We can re-do her makeup. It's the dress you should be worried about."

"Shut up, Jess," Tini snaps while dabbing foundation on my face with a sponge. "You're the one who insisted she wear her hair down because Rob loves it. There's probably puke in it now."

That's it. I can't take anymore. "Who are you people? What's wrong with you? The bride is so nervous, she's throwing up, and none of you are even in there helping her!"

Alyssa leans against a nearby dresser, a smirk on her face. "She's not nervous. She's knocked up."

"Alyssa," Tini hisses, her eyes wide as her gaze bounces between me and the bridesmaid who's still probably going to give Mike crap at the reception. "Shut. Up! No one's supposed to know!"

Alyssa shrugs. "She's in the circle of trust. Evie said so herself."

The woman of the day reappears, only a little pale. Thankfully, there's not a drop of vomit anywhere. Not that an errant puke splatter could be more embarrassing than what she saw in my hotel room.

"Ugh, I can't wait to tell Rob. This morning sickness isn't going away, and it's getting harder and harder to hide."

For a supposed circle of trust, there seem to be a whole lot of secrets going around—me included.

Tini's expression softens. Her hand freezes mid-air, still clutching a blush brush. "You're five months along, sis. I think this one is going to stick. You're lucky you're not showing more at this point. Tell him during your first dance like you planned. It's going to be his favorite wedding present."

Ohhhh, the lady doing my makeup is Evie's sister. That explains her role in the circle of trust.

A pang of jealousy streaks through my chest. Not only did I grow up with brothers who I could never talk with like this, but I haven't had a circle of girlfriends in so long, I almost forgot what it feels like to have other women I can count on.

A peach-colored gown is thrust into my field of view. Evie's voice carries around the fabric she's holding up. "We guessed your size from pictures. I hope it fits okay."

My gaze bounces around at the women surrounding me. All the women wearing the exact same style of dress except the bride.

Tears threaten to choke off my words. I didn't think I'd ever get this chance. "You...you want me to be one of your bridesmaids?"

Evie's head pops up from behind the gown. A frown creases her forehead, and she bites her lip. "You absolutely don't have to if it makes you uncomfortable!"

"I'd be honored." What else can I say? Why doesn't this make *her* uncomfortable? We barely know each other. The first time we met in person, I was kind of a jerk to her.

She smiles, but it's soft and tentative like she's about to break some bad news to me. "You don't have to worry about pictures being leaked online. It's going to be a very small wedding with only close friends and family. Everyone attending is aware that Rob and I like to keep our personal life out of the limelight. We'll choose pictures to release to the media very carefully."

"Oh." Sadly, that wasn't even my first concern. A few months of being nothing more than a grad student, and my focus is already slipping. "Thank you. That's good to know."

She sits on the bed like her legs give out beneath her.

Alyssa hands her a bottle of ginger ale.

After a few sips, Evie continues, "I realize we don't know each other very well...yet." She cracks a more genuine smile. "Mike has been like my brother for so long, I forget that we're not actually related sometimes. He's walking me down the aisle today, and I wanted to give him a meaningful thank you gift." She tips the bottle toward me. "That's you."

I try not to let my shoulders visibly fall. "Oh, okay. That's really sweet of you."

Her expression makes it obvious I haven't hidden my disappointment very well. "I know things seem...hard right now, but it won't last forever. Being with a pro football player isn't easy. I won't lie to you." She nods—that same decisive motion as before. "So much of what the media portrays, what the fans believe, is fake, but when you have something real? That's worth fighting for. Mike trusts you, and believe me, he doesn't give that out to just anyone."

Everyone around me laughs. They obviously know it's true.

Evie is the first to regain her composure. "If you want to make it in this world, you have to hang onto the good and let go of the bad. My brother loves you, so I love you, too. Anything you need? I will move heaven and earth to keep a smile on that man's face. And on yours. Whenever you feel like it's you against the world, I want you to know you have people in your corner. You can call any time of day or night, and we'll always pick up the phone."

A tissue dabbing at my cheek startles me.

I glance down at Evie's sister, who's wearing a small smile of her own. "We haven't seen him this happy in years, but that doesn't mean you can ruin your makeup either!"

I don't know if it's hearing from people who've known him far longer than I have that Mike's truly happy with me, or if it's the offer of friendship, but all the pent-up stress I've been clinging to bursts out of me like a levee being overpowered by a hurricane's storm surge.

"Are you planning to break up with him?" Tini stares at me with wide eyes.

"No!" I try to defend myself while blubbering like an idiot. "It's just that I grew up with five brothers, and I've always wanted to know what it would be like to have sisters!"

Alyssa snickers. "After what I just saw in their hotel room? There's no way she's planning to break up with him."

My cheeks flame, but I laugh anyway. The circle of trust feels safe enough to explain, "We don't get to see each other that often anymore, so he sends me...presents."

Evie crinkles her nose in obvious disgust, but she heaves herself off the bed anyway. "Still TMI, but you're getting that hug now."

"No!" I yelp again, placing my hand on the stomach that's causing her so much illness to keep her at bay. "Tini didn't put on the setting powder yet! I'll ruin your white dress!"

Evie folds her hands over mine. It's an entirely different feeling than our first meeting where we sized each other up. "Then, let's finish getting you ready to surprise him."

Alyssa snickers. "I think the surprise is actually going to happen later."

# Chapter 34
## The Great Escape

### Mike

I KISS her on the cheek and fold my hand over hers that's resting in the crook of my elbow. "You look beautiful."

She smiles then rolls her eyes, sniffling to keep obvious tears at bay before focusing on the closed double doors leading to the church sanctuary in front of us. "Is this where you threaten to castrate him if he isn't the picture-perfect husband for the rest of our lives?"

"No," I say, trying to soothe her palpable anxiety with a soft tone of voice. "He's proven his worth. I know he'll be good to you."

"Really? Okay. Wow. Then, let me step into your shoes for a minute." She turns a determined gaze to me. It's the kind I'm all too familiar with after so many years of watching this woman dig her heels in to whatever problem faces her. "If she ever so much as makes you shed a single tear, I will rip her hair out, tear off her eyelashes, then maybe pull off her fingernails for good measure."

"Jesus Christ," I mutter then cringe—because we're in a church and all. "You missed your calling as a CIA operative."

Evie shrugs beside me. "Not really. I'm just not giving up my calling as your sister because I'm married."

"Getting married," I correct her.

A smile spreads across her face. The tension in her muscles bleeds away until she's relaxed and poised beside me. "I'm already married. I have been for a long time. This is just a big party we're throwing for everyone who missed the announcement."

"If anything happens, we'll pick up the pieces," I promise,

squeezing her hand and choking back tears of my own. It's hard to imagine a world without her in it, but I respect the way she's choosing her own risk this time. "Alex and I will be there even if you can't be. We won't let him face the road alone."

"I know."

That's all she says before the doors open and the chords of a familiar piano tune fill the air.

The small church is full. All the guests rise as we take our first step into the center aisle.

"Remember when most of these people thought we would be getting married?" I whisper.

Her family watches us with sharp eyes and wide smiles. The time of mistaking me for her boyfriend instead of her adopted brother feels like forever ago.

"No," she murmurs, her gaze locked on the man who's waiting at the other end of our approach. "I don't remember anything before Rob."

Her sarcastic words make me laugh. There was a time she didn't remember him either. Some circles can never be unbroken though.

I have never empathized with that idea as much as I do now. My eyes land on an extra bridesmaid. One who wasn't supposed to be here. A woman who takes my breath away with a single glance.

This is Evie and Rob's day, so I don't want to question how or why Tori is standing at the front of the church with all our other friends.

I get an answer anyway when I place Evie's hand in Rob's.

He leans forward and wraps me in a bone-crushing hug. His words are a whisper in my ear, "Selfless, not selfish. Now, go get your own happily ever after and stay the hell out of mine."

I laugh and tamp down the urge to cross to the wrong side of the aisle and kiss Tori senseless. There will be plenty of time for that later. Instead, I take my place beside Alex. "No hard feelings about who got to walk her down the aisle. I was here before you, buddy."

His deep chuckle is drowned out by the priest chanting in Greek. "I get it. I know my place." He glances at me for a split-second, but a world of promises drift between us. "We're a team, Mitchell. For better or worse."

He gets to hand over the ring. I get to walk back down the aisle with the most beautiful woman on my arm.

We make a big deal of double-teaming the best man's speech. One woman's laughter rings louder in my ears than anyone else at the packed reception hall.

She's perched on my lap while we all watch Rob and Evie have their first dance as husband and wife.

"Oh!" she gasps as Rob pulls back, an expression of absolute shock crossing his face. "She told him! Yay!"

I glance down at Tori. Her eyes are filled with the kind of hearts the emoji was created to represent. "She told *you*?"

"I found out when we were getting ready." Tori smiles. It's one of the most perfect expressions of pride she's ever shown. "I'm in the circle of trust now."

Alex cackles beside us. "I claim best man at your wedding!"

He doesn't even question it.

Maybe it's growing up with sisters who swooned over everything to do with weddings, or maybe it's the mood in the air, but I'm falling for it. Head over heels.

It's not a potential disaster I'm fighting against anymore. It's real. It's tangible. It's going to happen.

I smile at Tori. "We have two years to come up with a scavenger hunt and tests of worth to award best man honors. Get your genius ideas ready, Peaches."

She glances between me and Alex with obvious confusion. "What are you talking about?"

Alex downs the rest of his champagne then rolls his eyes. "Rob made us do this stupid scavenger hunt for best man honors way back in college. We really thought we were running all over campus to win. He never told us it was always going to be a tie."

"I think he just wanted us out of their hair for Valentine's Day," I admit.

Tori raises an eyebrow. "Do you all usually spend Valentine's Day together?"

In hindsight, I feel a little guilty. I can't imagine Rob and Alex crashing my romantic plans. "Uh...yeah. Well, we used to. Before we lived in three different parts of the country."

A slow smile spreads across Tori's face. She stares at Alex. "I can see so many ways of making this work in my favor."

He barks out a laugh. "You're gonna fit right in, Tori."

She already does. In the most important place that matters.

I tighten my arms around her waist. "No wife swapping. Don't get any ideas."

He grins, licks his lips, then winks at her.

Tori blushes then just as quickly smiles. It's not her cute one. "You couldn't handle me, Fossoway."

I nearly choke on air.

He opens his mouth, probably to list in graphic detail all the ways he would handle her.

"Make a hole!"

All of us turn our attention to the dance floor, where Evie's suddenly—literally—in Rob's arms, holding her hand over her mouth. He races through tables and bodies, then they disappear through the doorway.

Alex cocks an eyebrow. "Is the reception over already?"

Tori digs beneath the table then comes up with a pack of crackers and a bottle of ginger ale. "I thought you two knew she was pregnant? She has morning sickness!"

Alex looks zero percent less confused. "It's seven o'clock at night!"

Tori rolls her eyes then abandons my lap and follows the same path Rob and Evie took.

I stand, too.

"Where are you going?" Alex hasn't moved a muscle.

"To see if they need anything. To help?"

His lip curls. "I'm pretty sure they've got it covered. Why would you want to see Evie barfing?"

I roll my eyes, too. Alex has never been the touchy-feely type. Some things haven't changed.

There's an awkward moment of hesitation just outside the Ladies' Room door. Then, I shrug it off and push inside, half expecting to see Tori peeing again.

Instead, there's a ball of white fluff practically swallowing Rob on the floor. He's leaned back against the wall, and Evie's leaning against him.

It's already a party in here. Tini's wetting some paper towels at the sink; Alyssa and Jess are yapping about baby shower plans; Tori's crouched beside the happy couple, offering crackers.

Even Alyssa's husband, Jeremy, pokes his head through the door behind me. "We good?"

"We're great!" Rob smiles. There are still visible tear tracks on his face. Even the toughest football player in the league wouldn't blame him if he knew the full story of the road they've traveled to get here.

I stuff my hands in my pockets. Alex is right. Everything is covered.

I'm not needed anymore, but judging by the way they both smile at me, I'm still wanted. "Is this going to be a ladies-only shower?"

Jess and Alyssa stare at me like they can't tell if I'm seriously angling for an invite.

"No," Jess drags out. "It doesn't have to be. How are you going to get away during the season though?"

"I can make time for important things." I mean it as just another way to let Tori know we can make it through whatever the next two years throw at us, but somehow my words shift the mood in the room. Snickers of awkward laughter bounce off the tile walls.

"I bet you can, stud." Alyssa winks at me. Which is weird. The whole look on her face is weird. "How long did it take to get that custom-molded dildo made?"

No one in the room even breathes.

I only have one question. "Peaches? How does she know about that?"

Suddenly, voices shout over each other like some higher power pressed the play button.

Tori. "It was an accident!"

Evie. "It was my fault!"

Alyssa. "So naughty, Mitchell."

Tini. "Circle of trust!"

Rob. Coughing and sputtering like he's going to puke next.

Me, too.

Jeremy steps up beside me. "How expensive was that? Did it take long? Did the wax burn your dick?"

Just when I think things can't get any worse, I turn around.

To find Alex grinning at me.

Oh, sure. *Now,* he cares enough to see if anyone needs help. He's about to offer it. I can practically see the shit building up behind his mouth.

I point at him. "Not a word."

He mimes zipping his lips, but the look in his eyes tells a different story.

I'm never going to hear the end of this.

Maybe Peaches fitting in with my friends isn't as perfect as it seems.

# Chapter 35
## Secrets

### Tori

THE WAIT IS KILLING ME. It's bad enough that I haven't seen his face in person or touched his warm skin in three months. The only time I hear his voice is over the phone late at night.

I can make up an excuse to miss classes for the next few days, sneak through Albany airport undetected, take an Uber to Mike's house with relatively little notice, and even let myself inside without well-meaning neighbors calling the cops, but there's no way I can maintain my cover by showing up at the stadium. I'm not sure anyone would give me access even if I'm a former Wolves employee.

My cell rings. One glance at the caller ID has me clutching the phone like a physical lifeline of potential information that I don't have access to.

She doesn't waste time with meaningless greetings. This isn't our first exchange of the day anyway. "Shawn finally got through to Mike's agent. He doesn't know anything yet."

The first sob slips past my frozen façade. I'm not sure who I'm trying to keep it together for at this point, since I've been in this big house all alone for hours. The game is over. Mike's agent knows *something* by now. He's just not willing to share. Not even with Rob's agent.

"Calm down," Evie advises, her voice low and steady. "I know the hit looked bad on TV, but the announcers love to play up that sort of thing for drama."

"He was in the locker room for the rest of the game," I hiss.

That was what triggered my call in the first place. There's no way

Mike would willingly not play if there wasn't something seriously wrong. Evie said I could reach out to her for anything at any time. So, I did.

"That's a good thing," she reminds me. "Remember what we discussed about concussion protocol? The trainers decided to play it safe. I would be more worried if they had forced him to play since it was such a close game."

Judging by the background noise, she's at a different game on the other side of the country. True to her word though, she's making time to talk me down off the ledge.

"How have you been doing this for *years*? I want to crawl out of my skin right now."

She chuckles. "Did you think I was joking when I warned you that loving a professional football player isn't easy? Every time Rob takes a hit on the field, I can feel it in my own body."

"That doesn't make me feel any better," I admit.

"You'll feel better when you can see and touch him for yourself," she responds without any offense. "That's why I suggested you fly up there. Otherwise, you'll just spend the next however many weeks until you can see him again picking apart that one single play and questioning every picture you see of him online."

"Thank you for the flight," I murmur, embarrassment heating my cheeks. "I'll pay you back."

Not sure how since I no longer have even an intern salary. We're not actually sisters though, so it seems obligatory to offer.

"You can pay me back by calling and telling me how he really is once he gets there," she says. "There's no way I can make a cross-country flight right now. Even the private pilot Rob has on retainer won't clear me at this stage of pregnancy. Probably *because* Rob has him on the payroll," Evie mutters.

"I wish we weren't all so spread apart," I confess, knowing I should let her go watch her husband play but unable to sever this connection until Mike walks through the door. "I feel guilty for not even checking on Alex's game today."

Evie sighs. "I wish that, too. Now more than ever. Sadly, that's not how any of this works at the pro level. It would take a miracle for them all to play on the same team again."

"Miracles aren't impossible," I hedge. "The reason you can't fly across the country to check on Mike is proof, right?"

"I'm afraid I've used up all my miracles in this lifetime," she says. "I'll be grateful if I can pull off one more."

I don't quite know how to respond. I'm not sure how far this circle of trust extends yet.

Mike explained to me in bed after the wedding reception that Evie's pregnancy is extremely high risk. He and Alex promised her to be there for Rob should the worst happen. He wanted to give me a heads-up that he might have to drop everything to fly to Sacramento in the middle of the season.

I was just happy to hear he wouldn't put football above the most important thing of all—family.

"I will FaceTime you as soon as I can," I promise, hoping it's a small part I can play for her not to have anything else to worry about. My words sound way more convincing than I feel. Maybe it's the marketing professional in me. "I'm sure you're right, and he's fine. You can see for yourself in a few hours."

"Thank you," she breathes. "I'll call you if I hear anything else from the agents."

The distinct sound of a key turning in the lock to the front door catches my attention. My muscles tremble with anxiety but also with the promise of relief. "Not necessary. He's here. I'll call you back."

She disconnects immediately.

I hop up from the couch and smooth the wrinkles in my shirt. If I don't do something with all this nervous energy, I'm likely to pounce on him. He's probably way too sore for that. I'll be content just to look at him with my own eyes. I hope.

"I'm fine," Mike grumbles as the door swings open. "I don't need a babysitter."

Oh, shit. He's not alone.

Thankfully, it's Templeman who steps in behind Mike. If anyone on the team is trustworthy, it's him. "Stop your bitching. You shouldn't be alone after a concussion, and you know it."

Mike's gaze lands on me. A slow smile spreads across his gorgeous face. "I won't be."

"I'm not here," I explain to Templeman in only a slight panic. "You didn't see anything."

He raises his eyebrows. "I knew that breakup wasn't real."

"Mike told you?" I can't keep the shock out of my voice.

"Hell, no! This motherfucker lied right to my face!" Templeman smirks. "He wasn't near grumpy enough for his unicorn supposedly dropping him and tucking tail to Virginia, so I knew better."

I'm his unicorn. Me.

So, I prance right over to where they're standing in the kitchen and oh-so-carefully run my fingertips over his face that doesn't look injured at all. It's just a little touching. Feather light.

He kisses my fingers when they roam over his mouth. "Are you here because you're worried, or because you're needy since Alex snuck into our hotel room and stole your special present?"

My eyes bug out of my head, and my cheeks flame. It's not like Mike to say something so personal out loud in front of anyone else. He was so embarrassed about it with his friends who he trusts implicitly.

I cut a quick glance to Templeman, who's watching us very carefully. "Worried. Are you okay?"

Mike tries to roll his eyes, but he literally stops mid-motion and winces instead. "I'm *fine*."

Templeman doesn't roll his eyes at all. "You have strict orders to rest."

"I passed all the concussion protocols," Mike boasts then winces again when his phone rings. "Goddamn, that's loud." He taps the speaker instead of holding the phone to his ear. "What?"

"Hello to you, too, Sunshine." It's Alex. "Are you okay?"

"Why is everyone asking me that? I'm fine!"

"Great," Alex chirps. "Then, I guess I should thank you for the new pre-game ritual we have in the locker room. We kicked ass today!"

"Good for you," Mike grumbles.

The Wolves lost by a field goal.

"Yeah," Alex continues, barely pausing. "We passed around your dildo mold. Everyone jacked your manhood for luck. It worked! Your rubber dick is magic!"

Mike sighs, closes his eyes, and rubs his forehead. "Why are you the way that you are?"

Alex's tone changes. He goes from playful to dead serious so fast, it makes *my* head spin. "I'm boarding a flight right now. I'll be there in three hours. Is Tori there? Put her on the phone."

Mike shoves his cell at me. "Just...deal with him. I can't."

His admission makes me nervous. Not only does Mike never ask me to handle something that isn't business-related, but he also never openly admits that he's not capable. Of anything.

Templeman's eyes are darting around so quickly that he's going to give himself a concussion, too. Mike lumbers over to the couch and practically collapses on it.

"Alex?" I leave the phone on speaker for Templeman's benefit. "I'm here. Why are you flying up?"

There's a bunch of staticky background noise before Alex's voice filters through again. "Because that was a test, and he failed miserably. If he was *fine*, he would've been pissed as hell and told me off like he usually does. Listen, I need you to hunker down somewhere safe, all right? Mike's never taken a hit that violent. I don't know how he'll react. Some guys get really belligerent when they can't think straight, and their playing time is on the line."

"Mike would never hurt me," I insist, offended on his behalf.

Even if that was a remote possibility, Evie would have warned me. She knows what he's capable of. According to Mike, she's the only other person in his circle of friends who knows the truth about his past.

"Fossoway?" Templeman interjects. "Elliot Templeman. I'm here, too. I won't leave her alone with him. If you don't wanna waste your Monday off by flying up here, you don't have to. I got this."

Alex laughs. Outright laughs. "What's his favorite food?"

Templeman glances at me with questions dancing in his sharp eyes. "I have no idea. What does that have to do with anything? You want me to cook his mama's favorite meatloaf for him?"

"You have no idea," Alex repeats with emphasis. "You've been playing together for a little over two seasons. I could ask you a fucking list of questions, and your answer would be the same—no idea."

"It ain't my fault ya boy's a salty motherfucker who won't open up to no one!"

"No, it's not your fault, and no, he doesn't." Alex laughs again, but this one is dark and chilling. "I'm not gonna bullshit you, Templeman. I like your style. On the field. I have no idea who the fuck you are off of it."

Templeman glares at me like I'm the one insulting him. He doesn't understand what Mike and his friends went through at the hands of their teammates in college though. It's not my place to tell him why three of the top players in the league harbor a whole host of trust issues to this day in their new, separate locker rooms. I'm not even sure if Alex really knows all of it. I don't know if anyone has told him about the night they were all drugged.

All I know is that in spite of the secrets they keep to protect each other, when one of them is down, this circle of trust closes ranks. Alex isn't just flying up here for Mike. He's flying up here for me, too.

"Templeman is a good guy," I explain to Alex if for no other reason than to give him one less thing to worry about while he's in the air. "He's one of the only people on the team Mike's friends with. And *he* would never pass around a mold of Mike's penis in the locker room."

Templeman snickers. "Yes, I would."

"Shut up," I hiss at him, my cheeks an inferno. "You're not helping!"

"On second thought, I like you already, Templeman." Alex chuckles. "Okay. You can stay."

Templeman rolls his eyes. "Boy, you ain't even here. How you gonna keep me away?"

"I won't have to do a thing." There's a sinister smile in Alex's voice that makes me nervous. "The cavalry should be arriving any minute. If they don't like you, you'll be gone."

My gaze flits between Mike—already asleep on the couch—and the closed front door. There's no way Evie will be walking through it any second.

"Who's coming?"

"Jeremy and Alyssa live in New York City," Alex explains, his voice irritatingly patronizing. "They're closest, so they were already on their way by the time I made the call. Let Evie handle Mike's mom and sisters. He doesn't like them to worry about him. We'll make that decision if it needs to be made later."

"I already know that," I snap, my anxiety bubbling over. All I wanted was to see Mike. To make sure he's really okay with my own eyes. This is turning into a five-alarm fire in spite of Evie trying to convince me it was just a faulty smoke detector. "That's why he let his mom and sisters believe we really broke up. So, they won't worry about all the stupid hoops he has to jump through just to keep his job."

Templeman's eyes widen. He puts his hand on my shoulder then gives me a comforting squeeze. "Shit, Tori. I'm sorry. That ain't no way to treat a unicorn."

"I'm sorry, too," Alex murmurs over the phone. "I gotta drop. We're taking off."

I grit my teeth when a soft knock sounds at the door.

Sure enough, Alyssa and Jeremy are standing on the other side.

"Come on in, but be quiet," I warn. "He's asleep on the couch."

"How is he?" Alyssa wraps me in a warm hug.

"I don't know," I admit. I haven't had enough time alone with him to find out.

I'm grateful Mike has so many people in his life who care so deeply—especially after getting the sense he was such a loner when we first met. I just can't help but feel that they don't think I can handle being his girlfriend. I've traded in the team expecting me to fail at representing him for his friends believing I can't support him on my own.

Maybe they're right. Because when Alyssa asks if there's anything she can do, I have no idea how to answer.

# Chapter 36
Mess Is Mine

## Mike

I CRACK OPEN MY EYES. There's a party going on in my kitchen that's way quieter than the one in my skull. Hushed whispers roll over my sore muscles. It even hurts to smile, but I can't help it.

Tori's here. She's bent over—giving me a nice view of her ass while she pulls a tray out of the oven. Alyssa and Jeremy thank her when she puts something on their plates. Templeman offers her a smile of gratitude after she places a fresh drink in front of him.

My happy dream turns into a nightmare when my gaze lands on the next face.

No. No, no, no, no, no.

"You two can't be in the same room together!" I blurt.

All eyes point my direction when I roll off the couch and stumble toward what promises to be an absolute disaster.

"You!" I point at Templeman. "I said I don't need a babysitter! Peaches is here! And you!" I point at Alex then lose steam when the floor tilts beneath me. "When the hell did you get here?"

He's not a star wide receiver for nothing. Alex is beside me in less than the blink of an eye. I'd be lying if I said I'm not grateful for him practically holding me up.

I don't think Tori's strong enough to support my weight.

And I don't think I've ever heard Alex's voice be this quiet. "Hey. Take it easy. No fast movements for a while. Do you feel sick, or do you wanna try to eat something?"

I really did get my brain sloshed earlier. I stare at him. This has to be a trap. Either that, or I'm hallucinating because of brain sloshing. "Is this a trap?"

He squints at me. "Mike? Do you know who I am?"

"Yeah. That's why I'm asking if this is a trap."

Alex opens his mouth. Blinks a few times. Closes his mouth again.

Entirely different sensations from a different set of hands divert my attention.

Peaches.

"Why don't we sit down? I don't want you to fall."

I'm already down for the count, and I never want to get back up.

I wrap her in my arms even though it hurts like hell. "You came. You're here. Can we get married now?"

"Of course, I came," she whispers then kisses me everywhere she can reach.

"She ain't coming at all!" Templeman yells. "Not while she's your secret side piece!"

"This is why you and Alex can't be in the same room together!" I yell back then immediately regret my choices. "Babe, I'm gonna throw up."

She snaps her fingers. A trash bin appears in front of my face, and I use it for all I'm worth.

"Thank you," I tell Alex. I need to remember to thank him for so many things. Holding the puke bucket when I know he hates puke seems like a good place to start. The rest of the crew doesn't need to hear this next part, so I whisper in Tori's ear, "It's your turn to see me pee now."

She chuckles. My brain feels like mashed potatoes, but I know this is it. She's here for the hard parts, so she'll stay for the rest.

She wraps her arm around my waist. Not that she could possibly hold me up, but she's trying. That's all that matters.

Alex flanks my other side.

"No," I try to shove him away, but I can't. "You don't get to see my dick anymore. Just Tori."

"You really wanna spray her with piss? Or do you want to douse me?" Alex smirks. He knows he's got me.

"Fine," I sigh. Even that hurts.

Tori reaches up to plant a gentle kiss on my cheek. "I'm not going anywhere. I'll be here when you're done."

I can't believe my life has been reduced to this, but Alex keeps his word. He helps me to the bathroom then insists I sit instead of stand to take care of business.

"Wouldn't want you to actually crack that pretty head open." He crouches in front of me, meeting my gaze directly.

"I knew this was a trap," I mutter, closing my legs.

He rolls his eyes. "Just because I'm the proud owner of your plastic dick doesn't mean I'm going to grab your junk to compare texture. I need you to listen to me, Mitchell. Your head hurts, and your brain isn't working, so you have to really concentrate, all right?"

Oh, shit. This sounds bad. "What's wrong?"

"Nothing yet." Alex blows out a breath. Whenever he gets serious, the rest of us pay attention. It's a rare event. "I know you want Tori to help you. I get it. What I also get is that you love this woman, so I'm not gonna let you fuck it up when you might not be able to control yourself."

"What is that supposed to mean?" I don't dare yell the way I want to. My head throbs even when I'm sitting still. The pressure building in my chest isn't helping.

Alex swallows. His gaze studies me a little too harshly. "You have never taken a hit like that before. We don't know yet how you're going to react. Do you really want to risk getting violent with her when there's no one else around to stop you from doing something you can't take back?"

A shivering sensation spreads over my skin. All the blood in my body pools at my feet. Alex doesn't even know the kind of violence I'm capable of. If he's worried now, how much worse would it be if I told him everything he doesn't know about me?

"Have you seen that before?" I swallow the dread in my throat, already knowing the answer. We've all seen some version of it for as long as we've been playing. We know the risks. We stay on the field anyway.

Alex nods. "Remember last year when Brown took that illegal hit? He beat the fucking shit out of his wife later that night. She was the one who ended up in the hospital when he never should have been released from it."

Brown was one of the most promising tight ends on Alex's team in Orlando. He's been in the media ever since that hit for all the wrong reasons. There's no end in sight to the guy's downward spiral. Those of us who play the game know exactly why. We also know how it will end.

"How long?"

Alex's eyes crinkle at the corners. "How long, what?"

"How long should I keep her away?"

He shakes his head and drops his gaze to the floor. "I don't know, man. However long it takes until you feel like yourself again."

That's the other thing we all know. It could be days, months, or years. If ever.

The thought of being without Tori makes me want to throw up again. It was easy enough to muscle through going weeks apart when there was a finite end-date to this torture. Now? I have to let her go for her own good for who knows how long.

"Alex?"

"Yeah?"

"What if I never play again?" It's been in the back of my jarred mind since I came to on the field. If I lose my job, how can I ever get Tori back? I'll be useless. To everyone.

Alex plants his hand on my shoulder and gives a firm squeeze then recoils when he remembers I'm still sitting on the toilet, and we're having a heart-to-heart in my bathroom. "Let's just take it one day at a time for now. We'll call audibles as we go along."

"Alex?"

"What?"

I've never felt like such an asshole for judging Rob so harshly when he walked away from Evie. "I think we need our QB to call plays this big."

Alex rises from his crouched position and shakes his head. "He's got a pregnant wife to worry about, and the game of his life on the line even if he doesn't know it yet. Besides, you know he'd tell you the same thing I'm telling you. It sucks, but you've gotta put her first. You might not have very much faith in me, but I've got your back, bro. We'll get through this."

"Alex?"

"What?" His tone proves he's losing patience with my stupid questions, which actually does make me have a little less faith in him.

"I'm gonna puke again."

∽

I PLAY WITH HER HAIR—TRYING to memorize the way it feels between my fingers, how brightly it shines on the dull gray pillow. I'm afraid to touch her silky soft skin. One touch might not be enough. One touch might be too rough.

Alex is on the other side of my closed bedroom door. He agreed to give me this time alone with her to break the news, but he refused to leave us completely alone in case things get too out of control.

Just another thing I need to thank him for.

"Mike?" The uncertainty in her voice grates my ears. She knows something's off. Something more than just my brain.

I see my future staring back at me in her deep brown eyes. I also see the potential for a million more failures if I selfishly keep her.

With a deep breath that feels like razor blades, I rip off the bandage. "I think we need to take a break."

She chuckles. Sobs. I can't tell the difference.

"That's just your concussion talking. I know you're scared, and things are rough right now, but I already made arrangements to shift my classes online, so I can stay here with you for as long as—"

"No!" I cut her off and bolt upright in bed. That single word hurts far worse than my abrupt movement.

I squeeze my eyes shut as nausea builds in the pit of my gut.

*Selfless, not selfish. Selfless, not selfish.*

Rob's words are the only thing I'm capable of holding onto in my abused mind. It's the root of all the branches I'm breaking. On purpose.

"You need to go," I grind out. "Alex booked your flight. He's taking you to the airport with him in the morning."

She sits up beside me and reaches for me.

I barely have the energy and balance to evade her outstretched hand.

"I don't understand," she whispers. "You want me to leave?"

"Yeah," I say.

"So, I'm your toy after all," she murmurs. "You're done with me, then? You've had your fill?"

*You're not a toy. I'll never be done.*

"I need you to trust me," I bite out, trying so fucking hard not to dry heave all over the bed.

She stares at me blankly like I haven't said a word.

Maybe I haven't. I can't tell anymore. My tongue is so heavy in my mouth, it feels like I'm trying to swallow a tennis ball.

An image of everything I never knew I wanted swims in front of my eyes. She's blurry around the edges, like she's going to disappear if I breathe too deeply.

Maybe this has all been a dream.

She snaps her fingers in front of my face.

I jerk back to attention. Fuck, that hurts.

"What?"

Tori blinks at me. "You were in the middle of saying you need to focus on your recovery."

I was? Did I say those words? I don't remember that.

Fuck. Alex is right. She can't be here.

# Chapter 37
Open

## Tori

I shouldn't be here. I don't belong. Not when everyone is happy, celebrating a joyous life event, and laughing when all I want to do is cry. There are limits to these new friendships, even in a circle of trust.

Evie cackles as she opens another gift. The box slides off her practically non-existent lap. "He can't wear this!"

"Why not?" Alyssa winks. "That's a custom creation!"

Evie holds the onesie up for everyone to see. It reads *Daddy plays football, but he has strong swimmers.*

Rob's smile is so blinding, it hurts my eyes to look at it directly. "It could be worse. I was kind of expecting a drum set."

Jeremy waves off that suggestion. "We're saving that for his first Christmas."

Alex grins then gestures toward the rather large box he brought. "That's okay. I've got the noisiest toy covered already."

Evie arches an eyebrow. "Do you all have a different sort of baby bet going for this one?"

The guys in the room exchange guilty glances, which only makes it more apparent there's one guy missing from the group. A guy I haven't seen since he all but kicked me out of his house.

I need a break from keeping my game face firmly in place. The empty tray of appetizers is a perfect excuse. The kitchen is a lonely refuge, but I let out a breath of relief anyway.

"Peaches."

The single word is whispered with such an undercurrent of pain,

I might be imagining things. The image of Mike standing in the doorway could absolutely be a mirage.

He looks so handsome, so perfect, so…here.

The air between us crackles with potent electricity that even my imagination could never come close to replicating. It's the same sizzle we tried to ignore for so long, and now we're apparently back where we started. I feel so stupid for giving in.

"I thought you needed to focus on your recovery and didn't want any distractions?"

"I got a little time off for good behavior. Things are going well." He shrugs.

Oh, I know they are. He's played the last two games, but he still won't return my calls. That's what hurts the most. If he wanted to break things off permanently, he could at least have had the balls to tell me to my face. Even Ben gave me that simple courtesy before he changed his mind.

Fire sweeps across my cheeks. I put the stuffed mushrooms on the tray a little too harshly, crushing a few.

Mike pulls a mangled morsel from my grasp. "Here. Let me."

"Right." I nod, my temper flaring. He'll arrange appetizers on a tray with the gentlest touch possible, but I don't get so much as a swipe of his finger down my cheek the way I'm craving. "Thanks. I've barely been able to function without you around to solve all my problems for me."

His tone is equally biting. "Your sarcasm is noted. Nice to know you miss me at all. Are you back with Ben already to fulfill your needs?"

I choke down the sob threatening to erupt from my tight throat. This is not the time or the place to break down.

"You know what? Fuck you, Mitchell," I hiss. "I don't deserve this. When have I ever distracted you from doing your job? I know what it means to you. I've done nothing but support you from beginning to end. If this is how you want to repay me, then I'm sorry I ever wasted a second of my life with you."

"I know," he murmurs, his fingers twitching on the countertop like he wants to reach for me but won't let himself. "That's why I won't risk hurting you any more than I already am."

"Well, guess what? You're doing a great job. *You* are."

He at least has the decency to face me and meet my gaze. "Better emotionally than physically."

"*What?*"

His face crinkles like he can't understand why I'm confused. "I get that you're pissed, but we discussed this. I don't want to hurt you if my symptoms get out of control. You know better than most what I'm capable of. It's too much of a risk."

I blink at him. Did I get a concussion? Because at no time did we ever have a conversation about what he's implying. "Mike. We absolutely did not discuss that."

He squints. His eyes move back and forth like he's replaying the events of the past month in his mind. "Yes, we did. You agreed you should keep your distance for your own safety."

I study him. Really look past his devastatingly handsome features that distract me with lust. His eyes aren't quite as sharp as usual, and he's not nearly as relaxed and calm as his words sound. His muscles bunch and flex with visible tension from an invisible source.

More anxiety presses against my chest. I keep my words hushed and slow. "We never discussed any of that. You basically kicked me out of your house a month ago. You told me to leave with Alex because you didn't want me around while you focused on your recovery, so you could get back on the field sooner."

"Yeah," he nods a little too quickly. "And to protect you from me. In case my brain's too messed up, and I lose my temper." Finally, finally he drags his fingertip down my cheek. "I don't want to hurt you, Peaches."

I step closer and glance into the living room, but everyone else is occupied with more gifts than I've ever seen in my lifetime for one person who hasn't even been born yet. "Are you telling me you've played the last two games while you're still experiencing concussion symptoms?"

"My balance is back to normal, and I've passed all the protocols," he defends, his voice a grating hiss that sizzles against my skin. "I've already been reactivated from the IR list."

I nod, trying to absorb what my ears can't believe I'm hearing. "And yet I'm still not allowed in your house. You won't even talk to me on the phone. Care to explain that?"

"I already explained it," he grinds out, stepping away from me. "You know I have a violent history. Until I'm one hundred percent back to normal, I'm not willing to risk hurting you."

"Then, why are you willing to risk hurting yourself? You shouldn't be playing like this!" I gesture to the people who know him so well who are sitting mere feet away. "Do they know? Do they know what you're risking just to play a fucking game? Does your *mother* even know?"

His hand curls around the edge of the countertop until his knuckles turn white even as his face turns red. "Leave my mother out of this. She's been through enough, so you know why I need to keep playing as long as my body holds out."

"I know she wouldn't want you to! No amount of money is worth your life!"

He shrugs. Again. His voice is eerily calm, which doesn't match the fire in his eyes. "A life for a life."

"That's not how any of this works!"

He opens his mouth to respond then snaps it closed when Evie waddles into the room.

"Ugh. I have to pee. Again." She glances between us at our obviously stiff postures but says nothing about the tension still rippling in the room. A wide smile spreads across her face. She throws open her arms instead. "You made it!"

He strides quickly to her and wraps her in the hug he denied me. Apparently, he's not afraid of losing his temper with her.

I never thought I'd be the jealous type, but here I am.

His gaze meets mine over the top of Evie's curls. He shakes his head subtly, a silent plea to keep his secret.

I nod. I won't be silent for selfish reasons, but I'm not going to ruin her big day by blabbing what I know either.

Mike kisses Evie on the cheek then grabs the refilled tray from the kitchen island. "Did you open the gift I sent yet?"

"Uh..." She blows out a breath. "No. I saved it until last to see if you'd get here. Go make yourself comfortable and eat. I'll be back in a minute."

He escapes into the living room, probably grateful not to have to lie to her face for too long.

I'm not so lucky.

She stares at me until sweat breaks out on my upper lip. "Is he mad that you accepted the PR position with the Sing Out Foundation?"

"Yep," I lie through my teeth. "You were right. He doesn't like the idea of me switching to online classes and working full time while I finish my master's. He thinks I should wait until after graduation."

She rolls her eyes. "He'll get over it. What he really doesn't like is the idea that he doesn't have to support you because you're a badass woman all on your own. These guys might be modern gladiators, but in some ways, they're still total cavemen."

I couldn't agree more. I exhale both frustration and relief when she waddles past me to the bathroom.

Evie has enough to worry about right now, but this is one secret of Mike's that I have no intention of keeping.

I love him too much to stay silent.

# Chapter 38
## By Now

### Mike

SHE PICKS up on the first ring like she's been waiting for my call. She probably has.

"I can't fucking believe you! You had no goddamn right!"

"I'm sorry," she whispers, tears choking her voice.

"Sorry doesn't fucking cut it!" My big-screen TV makes a horrible, satisfying shattering noise when the remote hits it with all the force I can muster. "Do you have any idea what you've done? I'm out for the season, Tori! The rest of the fucking season! This puts my contract in jeopardy!"

"They didn't cut you! You're on injured reserve again, but your contract is guaranteed against injury! You'll still receive your full salary!"

Oh, well. At least she read the fine print on my contract before pulling this little stunt. That makes it all better. Not.

"I *trusted* you," I bite out, my heart thrashing in my chest. "You sold me out the first chance you got."

"Why do you even care if you don't finish out your contract with the Wolves?" she argues through sobs that cut me like a backstabbing knife. "Any other team in the league would treat you better than they have! You wouldn't even have to fake a relationship for some stupid media stunt!"

So, that's her agenda. She doesn't want Kaylie to sink her claws into me for the rest of the season if the front office decides to try a new marketing play. She fucked me over because she's jealous.

I take a deep breath and stuff down my rage. Trashing my house isn't going to solve a damn thing. "My base pay is guaranteed. My bonuses are performance-based. Do you have any idea how much college tuition costs these days? Without those bonuses, I have to choose which sister to help! Or decide to quit making payments on all my mom's debt!"

"Who helped you, Mike? Huh?" The tears are gone. Her voice is angry now.

"I got a full ride! Because I play fucking football!" I explode.

"Yeah, well..." She chuckles, but it's the least happy sound I've ever heard. "I love you, but I can't sit on the sidelines and watch you kill yourself."

"Peaches, wait..." Damn it. I'm mad, but this isn't what I want either. She just doesn't understand where I'm coming from. That's on me. I have to make her see reason.

"Don't," she cuts me off before I can even start explaining myself. "Whatever you're going to say, don't. I didn't have any say in the matter when my mom chose me over her own life. My brothers resent me to this day because of a choice I didn't make. I don't want to resent you because of another decision that isn't mine to make. But I will be *damned* if you add me to your list of reasons for valuing money over your life. I refuse. Do you hear me?"

"Babe, no..." All my anger rushes out with a tackle I never saw coming.

"Goodbye." She sniffles. "Take care of *yourself*, Teddy Bear."

She hangs up then another call immediately comes through.

If it was anyone else, I wouldn't answer.

"It's time. We're on our way to the hospital," Evie pants, her teeth obviously gritted in pain. "I need you here. Just in case..."

It's a month early, but she doesn't need me to point out the obvious. "I'm on my way."

I have no control over this outcome, but *I'll* be damned if I don't keep my promises.

# Chapter 39
## The One That Got Away

### Tori

"Do I make myself perfectly clear?"

Wide-eyed faces stare back at me from around the conference table. The guy who spent the past hour arguing every point I made actually has his mouth hanging open.

"Is that a yes or a no? Because if no, then we can go over the entire slide deck again. I'll even order dinner for everyone, so we can stay until the plan is crystal."

Mr. Mansplain snaps out of it. "Miss Russo, with all due respect, we're not going to earn any brownie points with the universities we want to land contracts with by blitzing them this way. I'm telling you, we need to start small."

"And I'm telling *you*, Sing Out squandered too much momentum during the re-org last year. We're out of time to save this foundation. It's now or never. You're either in or you're out. Your choice."

"You're not giving us much of a choice," he mutters.

"What was that?"

"Nothing," he says, straightening in his seat and gathering his papers.

"That's what I thought."

No one is ever going to ignore what I have to say ever again. If I have to be a bitch to make that happen, then so be it. I'm just grateful Mike's coaches opened their eyes and paid enough attention to his symptoms so that my unanswered pleas to Mr. Gallo didn't matter.

A high-pitched wail fills the room. Even over a speaker, the sound is enough to make my ears bleed. It's the best birth control I've never heard of. I don't even miss sex anymore.

"Sorry, everyone. It's almost feeding time." Evie's voice crackles over the com in between shushing her little bundle of joy. "Paul, we're going to go with Tori's plan. She's right. If we don't hit the ground running this year, it could mean lights out for the foundation. We've all worked too hard not to give it our all in the fourth quarter."

Ugh. More football analogies. I hate those. I hate everything about football.

Thank God I don't work in that sector anymore.

I don't even watch the games on TV.

The cries turn to gurgling coos, and everyone around the table takes turns babbling in adult baby-talk. I tune it out and save my slides, disconnect from the projector screen, then gather the extra papers from around the room. I still have to draft emails to twenty universities, make copies of multiple check-lists for next week's preparation meeting, and lock up the office. At least there's a nice package of Ramen waiting for me at home. I even sprung for the pricier roast chicken flavor instead of just plain chicken.

By the time it's just me in an empty conference room with the sound of happy suckling in the background, I'm exhausted from my own mental to-do list. So, I collapse into the nearest chair, toe off my heels, and prop my feet on the table. Being a badass woman is hard work, but I'd rather be in the office at Sing Out's East Coast headquarters than in my two-bedroom apartment anyway. My roommate drives me a little crazy.

"You know you want to ask." Evie chuckles. "I might not be in the same room with you, but I can feel it."

If I can't admit it to myself, I'm certainly not about to confess it to her. "I have no idea what you're talking about. Is Robbie finally latching on properly?"

"The gala is next weekend," she murmurs. "You really don't want to know if he's going to be there?"

She doesn't even take the baby bait, darn her. It's always worked until now for a sure-fire distraction from this topic. It's not like I can tell my boss to mind her own freaking business even though I really, really want to sometimes.

"I'm prepared for that contingency, but I'm sure it won't be an issue. He's probably too busy with gearing up for the playoffs now that he's off the IR."

I can practically hear the grin in her voice because of my utterly stupid slip-up. "I thought you don't watch football anymore?"

"I don't." It's the truth. However, as head of the PR department for a non-profit foundation that relies on football players for social media proof, it's part of my job description to pore over every last bit of the internet until my eyeballs feel like they're bleeding in the late, late night hours. She doesn't need to know that. It's my job to captain this ship until she's back full-time from maternity leave. "Have you confirmed with the caterer that there won't be any seafood served at the event?"

"I have." Thankfully, this is a serious enough topic to divert her attention. "They're relatively new in the Sacramento area, but they come highly recommended, and they seem very eager to please. No seafood and no coconut. We're good to go."

"Awesome. Because the slinky cocktail dress I picked out does not go well with my giant handbag full of allergy supplies."

Evie chuckles. "Oh, I see how it is. You're *hoping* he'll be there."

So much for distraction. That's my fault.

"You know what? Maybe I should just book a hotel room. I don't want to impose by staying with you while I'm in town. Just because you're going to get a few hours' reprieve at the gala doesn't mean you won't have a baby to nurse all night when you get home. I don't want to be in the way, making you uncomfortable at all."

"I don't pay you enough to afford a hotel room *and* slinky cocktail dresses while living in New York City. Hopefully, this kick-off fundraiser will change that. You're doing an amazing job, Tori. I can't thank you enough for taking a chance on our little start-up. Pretty soon, you're going to have an MBA under your belt, and I'll have to pull out all the stops to keep you."

"Yeah, well, you could start by not bringing up Mike every chance you get," I mutter under my breath. I love this job. This is exactly what I envisioned doing when I first decided to go into marketing. It's also a cause I fully support unlike a game that glorifies bashing people's brains in.

"He's the only brother I've ever had. I just want what's best for him." Evie sighs. "You have my word though. Whatever happens between you two is exactly that—between you two. I won't bring him up anymore if that's what you really want."

"It is." My mind is made up. Now, if I could only convince my heart.

THE FIRST SOUND I hear when I open the door to my apartment is the blaring noise of SportsCenter on the television.

Darn it.

The second sound that floats to my ears is the distinct moan of a female.

Actually, I'm kind of excited about that.

I peek my head into the living room. Not that I'm a secret voyeur or anything. I just need to confirm we have a guest instead of assuming Ben is multitasking by watching porn on his phone before I yell at him to take happy, fun time to his own freaking bedroom.

He is definitely not alone.

A woman is on his lap, writhing and moaning, her head thrown back in ecstasy even though he has a hand fisted in her thick, brown hair. His face is buried in her neck, and he's moaning, too.

At least they still have clothes on. If I arrived even five minutes later, this might look a lot more like a champagne room than my living room.

I clear my throat.

She leaps off him like he's given her an electrical shock, her eyes wide as she tries to smooth her wild hair down.

"Oh. Hey, Bethany." It's a small miracle that I manage to keep the glee out of my voice.

These two have been circling around each other for over a month now, and I'm happy for them. It's also exhausting listening to Ben dissect every nuance of their phone calls and coffee dates, hoping against hope that she'll give him a second chance.

It looks like she has.

"Tori!" Her cheeks are brighter than mine usually are, and she's not even a redhead. "I'm so sorry! Ben said you usually get home much later than this…"

He chuckles with an embarrassed undertone, but his eyes are bright. He's not sorry at all.

I'm not either. Hopefully, he won't need me to be his unpaid relationship coach anymore.

"He's absolutely right, but I'm starving. Don't mind me. I'm just going to make myself dinner real quick then retreat to my bedroom. Give me five minutes, and I'll be out of your hair."

Ben smiles in gratitude, but Bethany can't quite meet my eyes.

I let her off the hook. If I put myself in her shoes, I'd be embarrassed, too.

I've just dropped my block of noodles into the boiling water when footsteps approach at my back. Strained silence stretches out between us.

"It's awkward, isn't it?"

I spin to face Bethany then lean against the counter. "It doesn't have to be."

She blinks at me.

"When we first met, I immediately thought we could be friends," I offer.

Her smile slowly spreads, but it's genuine. "I thought so, too."

"I want to apologize." I've been hoping for this reconciliation for somewhat selfish reasons. "It was never my intention that day to make you question your relationship with Ben. It's been eating away at me to think I played a part in your breakup."

She pulls out a chair at the kitchen table and takes a seat. "I hate to think you've been living with that guilt for over a year. It wasn't you, I swear. It was a domino effect of doubt that I gave in to."

"Because you felt like it all happened so fast?"

She admitted as much at the time.

"Yeah." She nods, but there's an element of shame in her voice that I hate to hear. If she's still having doubts, then what is she even doing here?

I sigh and spin around again to stir my noodles. "Yeah, well...My last relationship took years to build, and it crashed and burned anyway. Fast isn't necessarily a harbinger of doom."

"I'm sorry," she murmurs. "Please don't be mad, but Ben told me a little about it. Woman to woman, I want you to know that you didn't deserve to be a fake girlfriend, then a secret girlfriend, all for him to choose football over you anyway."

"He didn't." I would never put someone in the position my mother was forced into. "I didn't ask him to choose."

"Oh. I must've misunderstood. I thought that was why you broke up."

"No. We just have...different priorities in life." No matter how much I wish that wasn't true.

"Did Ben ever tell you I'm a law student?"

Ben has told me things she'd likely blush about. "Yes. NYU Law, no less. Good for you. I'm sure you'll pass the bar with flying colors."

"My focus is actually family law and arbitration. Having different priorities in life can be a deal breaker, yes, but it doesn't have to be if both parties come to a reasonable compromise."

I chuckle and sneak a glance at her completely serious expression. "Are you...are you trying to give *me* relationship advice?"

She shrugs. "It seems like you really love him if you're adamant about not asking him to choose you over anything in life. I hate to see you throw a love like that away like I almost did."

I have no idea how to respond to that. I have no intention of telling her Ben begged *me* for a second chance. All because he couldn't get over *her*, and just didn't know how to be single for a while.

"You know what?" She waves her hand through the air. "Forget I said anything. God knows I don't want to make things more awkward between us than they already are. I really would like it if we could be friends."

"Seriously, stop overthinking it. I'm still friends with all of Mike's friends." My phone rings on the countertop. I mutter, "Speak of the devil."

Bethany jumps up from her seat, way too excited. "Is it Mike?"

I arch an eyebrow as suspicion stacks up in my brain. "If you're only so gun-ho about me patching things up with Mike because you still secretly believe I'm competition for Ben, I'd like to assure you that you're entirely wrong. Sharing an apartment is nothing more than a business decision. New York City is expensive, and we're both grad students. Even Ben is better than sharing rent with a stranger."

Her cheeks pink, so I know I'm right. My phone stops ringing only to start again.

"You've gotta give him points for persistence at least." Her smile is full of guilt. And hope.

"I wouldn't, actually. That's called being a stalker and not respecting boundaries. For a modern woman, I'd think you would recognize that's not healthy behavior. Mike knows better. It's Fossoway being a pain in my ass tonight." I completely understand the love/hate relationship Mike has with him now. For the past few months, he's either making me want to strangle him or making me want to hug him. There's almost no in-between.

Bethany's eyes widen. "*The* Alex Fossoway? As in the star wide receiver for the Orlando Sharks?"

Oh, great. "You're a football fan, I take it?"

"Um, yeah," she breathes. "That's how Ben and I met. I kicked his ass in our shared fantasy football league."

The promise of fancy Ramen fades away, replaced by nausea. "On second thought, Bethany, this isn't going to work out between us after all."

Ben strolls into the room, a grin stretched across his face. "You can't break up with my girlfriend!"

"I'm pretty sure I just did."

My phone rings. Again.

Ben shakes his head, but that smile just won't fade from his face. It's almost as annoying as the incessant phone calls. "He's not taking no for an answer tonight, huh? Want me to deal with him?"

"Please," I beg. This isn't the first time Ben has fielded Alex's calls. It's the least he can do to repay me for all the free therapy.

Ben picks up the phone. "Fossoway, my man! What's up?"

Alex's annoyed voice fills the kitchen. He's on speaker. "I'm not your man and stop answering Tori's phone."

"Traitor," I hiss to Ben.

He grins. "Sorry, buddy. She makes me do her dirty work when she doesn't feel like dealing with you."

I punch him in the shoulder for ratting me out. He just keeps smiling like a loon.

"Are you two back together? Because if she doesn't have the heart to tell me, you can. I'll let Mike down gently, but he deserves to know either way."

"Oh my God," Bethany gushes. "Are you playing matchmaker? You're talented and have a big heart!"

"Who the hell is that? Am I on speaker?" Alex sounds ten seconds away from losing it. "Whoever you are, you can't tell anyone about this. You'll ruin my reputation!"

"That's my *girlfriend*, Bethany," Ben announces with an even bigger shit-eating grin. "Tori's heart belongs to Mike. We're never, ever getting back together."

"I'm going to kill you," I mouth to him.

He rolls his eyes, obviously not taking my threat seriously.

"Did you just quote a pop song to me?" Alex questions.

"Do you listen to pop songs enough to recognize that as a quote?" Ben fires back.

"Touché." There's a hint of respect in Alex's voice. "I'm going to mail you people NDAs, I swear. Anyway, relay a message to Tori for me since she doesn't want to *deal* with me tonight."

A hint of guilt tightens my shoulders.

Ben's smile finally fades as he glances at me. "Sure. What do you need me to tell her?"

"Let her know Mike can't make it to the Sing Out gala in Sacramento next weekend. She doesn't have to worry about running into him, so she can have a good time and do her job."

"Will do." Ben ends the call.

"Well." I dump the pot of noodles into the garbage disposal. "I guess I could have answered after all. Sorry for making you my go-between and interrupting your evening. I'm going to head to bed."

Bethany places a hand on my shoulder. "Don't apologize. If anything, *I'm* sorry."

My smile is half-hearted at best. "I'm just glad you still had clothes on when I walked in."

She laughs. "Oh, I'm not apologizing for that. I meant I'm sorry things aren't working out the way you hoped."

That doesn't make any sense. "Things are going exactly as I hoped for. I've been stressing out about how to keep the peace between everyone while I'm in town. I don't want to force his friends to choose between him or me any more than I want Mike to choose between me or football. I'm glad he won't be there."

Bethany smiles, but it's full of pity. "Then, why do you look so disappointed?"

Why, indeed.

# Chapter 40
It's Time

## Mike

"I never thought I'd live to see the day where I admit I'm grateful to Ben for calling me."

Rob's brow furrows. "Who's Ben?"

"Tori's ex."

He places his glass of water down on the bar and faces me fully. "Work with me here, Mitchell. I don't get a lot of sleep these days. Why did Tori's ex call you, and why are you grateful about it?"

A rough slap to my back nearly makes me choke on my drink.

Alex steps up between us with a stupid grin on his face. "Because Ben's a total douche nozzle who played right into my very capable hands."

Rob sighs and rubs his forehead. "What do you people not understand about new parents getting less than zero sleep? Nothing you're saying makes any sense!"

Alex rolls his eyes. "Stop whining. You love it, and you know it."

Rob straightens. "The baby? No question. You two? Losing my patience."

Alex flags down the bartender to order a drink. "Still don't see why you're whining. This just proves that as much as things change, they stay the same."

"I dunno. I get the feeling you two have teamed up without me, and that's part of why I have no idea what's going on." Rob waves a hand in front of my face. "Are you still experiencing concussion symptoms? I thought you decided to be honest with everyone for a change?"

Alex takes a swig of his drink. "Calm down. He's fine. He's searching the room for his favorite fruit."

He's got my number. This ballroom is packed with bodies, but I wouldn't miss that head of red hair even in a mob. She's not here.

"Are you sure she's coming?" My nerves are flayed raw at this point. I've been on edge ever since Ben's phone call when I made a snap decision to do this thing.

"Relax," Alex advises. "She's one of the keynote speakers. Of course, she's coming."

"Actually," Rob winces, which makes me brace for bad news. "She might be giving two speeches tonight. Evie's running a fever, so I don't know how long we'll be able to stay."

It's kind of alarming how much effort I have to put into focusing on something other than the promise of seeing Peaches. "Why is Evie running a fever? What's wrong?"

"Don't panic. It's nothing horrible; she's just really uncomfortable right now. We've already been to the doctor."

Alex and I exchange a suspicious glance. We know a screen play when we hear one.

"What's wrong?" Alex repeats very slowly.

Rob squints exactly one eye. "Mastitis."

"Which is?" I lead. Now, I'm the one losing patience.

"It's basically a blocked milk duct in her breast…"

Alex spits his drink out everywhere.

"Yeah, see, this is why I didn't want to tell you," Rob says, deadpan.

I grab a napkin from the bar and dab at my tuxedo jacket. "Watch it. This is a rental."

Rob and Alex exchange a confused glance.

"Why are you wearing a rental tux?" Alex asks.

"Why would I buy one? These things cost thousands of dollars."

Alex shakes his head and laughs. "You really do not understand that we're millionaires now, do you?"

I roll my eyes. Just because he grew up rich doesn't mean all of us have the same burn-through-money mentality. I gesture toward Rob. "He probably didn't waste a couple grand on a penguin suit either."

"I did not." Rob looks way too pleased with himself.

Alex eyes him carefully. Sometimes, it's scary how much he notices. "Liar. That's a custom tailor job. You own that."

"I didn't buy it," Rob specifies. "My wife did."

Alex shakes his head. "Right. And the fairies magically tailored it to your abnormal giant size. Dude. Why are you lying about something so stupid?"

"I'm not lying," Rob swears. "She had it delivered to my condo before Jeremy and Alyssa's wedding." A slightly evil smile spreads across his face. "Evie knows *all* my measurements. Exactly."

The woman in question sidles up to her abnormal giant. He throws his arm around her shoulders and plants a kiss on top of her head. "Hey, baby. How are you feeling? Do you need help with anything?"

I rub the aching spot in my chest that hasn't gone away since Peaches called it quits. Fuck. I want what they have. I want all of it, right down to someone knowing all my measurements that she claims are very marketable.

I'm dying to ask Evie if she's seen Tori anywhere, but I have to slap Alex on the back of the head first.

"Stop staring," I hiss.

Evie glances down at her own chest with a frown. "It's really noticeable, isn't it? I pumped and pumped, but it's still blocked, and oh my God, Rob, I can't get up in front of all these people and speak with one of my boobs grossly larger than the other! Even I can't stop staring at it!"

He keeps her chest at a very distinct distance while he hugs her on the side. "It's not that bad. You're short. The podium will probably give you some cover."

Alex chokes on his drink. At least he doesn't spray it everywhere again. "Does being a new parent also make you a pathological liar?

How can you say it's not that bad? Her chest looks like a grapefruit next to a cantaloupe!"

Evie whimpers. So, do I. All this fruit talk is ruining things for me. My mouth is still watering for a glimpse of peaches though.

Rob points at us. "If you don't want to die today, then cover."

We're such well-trained receivers that we immediately obey our QB's one-word command. Luckily, we have broad enough bodies to make this work in a room full of people.

"You're stuffing her bra with bar napkins, aren't you?" Alex mutters beside me. "It'll never work. You're just going to make one side look lumpy."

"Shut up and let me do my magic," Rob grumbles.

Evie chuckles. "I actually did stuff my bra once in ninth grade, trying to get you to notice me."

"Oh, I noticed," Rob admits. "What was I supposed to say though? Hey, Evie. I noticed your boobs look weirdly bigger today, and would you like to go on a date with me even though I'm a total pervert with a raging hard-on that I can barely hide?"

What am I supposed to say? *Hey, Tori. I've missed your peaches so much that I've changed my ways. Can we get married now?*

"Jesus," Alex mutters. "You two are perfect for each other. Neither of you have any game."

My mouth runs dry. I elbow Alex. He doesn't respond. I elbow him again. Harder.

"What?" he hisses.

"Alex, I need help. I have no game."

My brain and all my carefully laid plans have completely fled the building. Because the exact same ill-fitting suit that I thought was a hooker trying to pull off a hot librarian look has just entered the room. Her mop of red hair shines like a beacon of hope that I'm too terrified to put any real stock in.

I swallow, but my tongue still hangs heavy in my mouth. "You guys can't let me fuck this up again. Seriously. I need help. What do I say? How do I act? I can't lose her."

A strong hand spins me around. Rob's expression is way too smug. "Remember what I said. Be selfless, not selfish."

Evie places her hand over my racing heart. "She's hurt, Mike. She's trying to protect herself. Don't seek her out. Let her come to you. If it's meant to be, she will. It has to be her choice though."

I glance at Alex, but he's staring at Evie's chest. "You're an idiot, Falls. That looks worse!"

"Don't call me an idiot!" Evie yelps. "Focus, Fossoway! What's the game plan?"

"Stop trying to fake it and tell the truth," he mutters, pulling napkins out from beneath the neckline of Evie's dress.

Rob swats Alex's hands away.

"You assholes are going to ruin this for me!" I hiss. "She's never going to sign on for this shit show, no matter how much I grovel!"

Rob has the nerve to look offended even though he was the one pulling Alex away from his wife's chest. "We're a package deal. If she can't understand that, then she's not the woman for you anyway."

"She absolutely fucking is, and you three will be left in the dust if she demands it," I tell them in no uncertain terms.

"We'll behave." Alex is surprisingly first to fall in line.

Evie winces as she hugs me. "You don't need us for anything. You're ready to do whatever it takes."

Rob claps a hand on my shoulder. "Seal this deal, then we'll make a pact to find Alex a woman to get him out of our business."

Alex suspiciously glances away.

I'll come back to that later.

First, I just need to…

"Hey, guys." Her voice sounds like angels singing from the heavens. I nearly weep with joy.

"Oh my gosh, Evie!" she squeals as she gapes at Evie's uneven, lumpy chest. She still sounds angelic. "What did they do to you?"

"Oh, this?" Evie glances down then up, her eyes wide and her expression guilty as hell. "Nothing. I did it to myself. Bad choice. They're going to come help me fix it somewhere a little more private."

Rob yelps, "What?"

Alex nods. "Yeah, we will."

Fucking liar. I knew he wouldn't behave.

My sister from a similar mister is stronger than I ever gave her credit for because she manages to physically drag two professional football players away until Tori and I are left by the bar, staring at the odd trio as they weave their way toward the ballroom doors.

"Should I intervene on her behalf with Alex?" Tori asks.

My knees buckle with relief, so I grab onto the bar for support. I didn't think we'd dive back into natural conversation so easily after so many months apart. "Nah. He's annoying as shit, but he means well."

Her luscious lips tilt into a smirk. "He really can be annoying, but I agree. He has a good heart."

Weird silence punctuates the widening space between us. So much for natural.

"So..." Tori chuckles then flags down the bartender.

"You don't have to get drunk tonight to distract me," I blurt.

She raises an eyebrow. "I was going to order a glass of wine. I'd like very much not to sound like a robot if I end up having to read Evie's prepared speech."

Shit. Evie's been holding out on me.

"So, you know about the mastitis?" *Damn it, Mitchell. That's all you've got? Really?*

Tori nods then orders a chardonnay. "Yes. I've been staying with them for the past few days while we put the finishing touches on the plans for tonight." She shudders. "I'm not sure I ever want to have babies after hearing Evie's howls of pain in the middle of the night. And that's not even labor!"

Okay. So, it's not just me. We're really doing this. I guess finding a neutral middle ground of commiseration isn't the worst thing in the world. Definitely better than the disjointed way we left things between us.

"Rob is barely functional even though he's completely sober. I've read studies that sleep deprivation can cause the same symptoms as intoxication, but I've never seen it for myself before. I really like sleep. I don't want to give it up anytime soon."

She nods, her eyes wide. "I haven't slept in three days. Three days! That kid is up screaming at all hours of the night! I had to do my own concealer this morning, and you know how bad I am at that!"

She's just given me the perfect excuse to lean in close and study her makeup. If I happen to deeply inhale her peachy sweet scent like a total addict going through withdrawal, that's just an accidental bonus. Somehow, I manage to fight the urge to pull her shirt a little tighter. Those buttons still look ready to pop.

"You forgot the setting power again, didn't you?"

She gazes at my chest in horror like she might have left a yellow mark behind even though she hasn't so much as touched me. "How did you know?"

I hate to be the bearer of bad news, but I'd hate for her to embarrass herself even more. "You've got some, uh, creasing going on."

"What?" She covers her cheeks with her hands, but it doesn't do anything to hide the furious blush that bleeds through the makeup.

"It's okay. I can fix it." I pull her hands away and gently smudge the sensitive skin beneath her eyes as she watches me intently.

"We're in public, Mike. People are watching you fix my makeup right now."

Shit, she's right. My greedy hands took the first opportunity she offered without thinking this would embarrass her just as much. I cup her cheeks to hide what I'm really doing. "No, they're seeing two people share an intimate moment after being apart for so long."

"You might have a future in marketing." She chuckles then sighs. Most importantly, she does not deny we're sharing something here. "The makeup doesn't matter. I'm horribly underdressed. I already look like an idiot."

"You look beautiful as always," I insist. "Did Robbie spit up on your nice dress or something? Was this a back-up?"

"No." Her cheeks flame again. It's all I can do not to kiss her. "I packed the wrong stuff in my rush to make my flight."

I'm not sure what else to say. Already, her makeup looks fine, but I can't bring myself to let her go. "I'd offer you my jacket, but you have one of your own."

Her smile is just a shade self-deprecating. "I'm not sure yours would fit any better than mine either. At least no one has mistaken me for a prostitute yet."

We laugh together. God, I miss laughing with her. I miss everything with her.

Her brown sugar eyes bore into mine. A second longer, and I won't be able to play it cool anymore.

"Miss Russo," a panted voice interrupts our staring match. "We can't find the laptop with the slide projections on it."

Tori breaks her hypnotizing gaze. "I'll be right there, Paul. I'm sorry," she tells me. "I have to go."

I can't take it anymore. I lean down and kiss her cheek. "Don't apologize. It's your job. You're doing amazing work for Sing Out. You're going to be the one to finally turn this foundation around. I know it."

"Thank you," she breathes. Then, she's gone.

New faces come and go. I shake hands, smile for cameras, and play nice. Not just because Tori taught me how to work a room, but because I really do want to see this foundation take off. It's something we all believe in.

"Well?" Alex questions when he finds me in the crowd again. "How'd it go? Did you win back the girl?"

"Nah." I snatch an appetizer off a passing tray. Dinner isn't for another hour, and I'm starving after all this schmoozing. "I just wanted to see her."

"What?" he whines while grabbing a bite for himself. "After all that recon I did? What happened to your grand groveling plan? Did you at least tell her you know it wasn't her who got you benched all season?"

"No. She's busy and nervous tonight. This is her first gala. I wasn't going to be selfish by unloading all that shit on her when she's trying to do her job. Besides, just because she's my unicorn doesn't mean I'm hers," I answer calmly with my mouth full. The more I chew, the less calm I feel. "Alex? Does this taste fishy to you?"

"It's not the best I've ever had," he admits after swallowing.

"No. I mean, does it taste like seafood?"

"I guess." He shrugs. "Hard to tell what's in the weird paste they plop on a cracker and have the nerve to call food."

Oh, shit. Peaches.

# Chapter 41
## Little Do You Know

### Tori

"Mmm. These canapés are delicious," I mumble to Evie, covering my mouth with my hand. "I can't get enough."

"I'm kind of disappointed." She squints at the petite cracker clutched in her fingers. "When I ordered hors d'oeuvres service, I thought there'd be...more."

"Huh." Rob rocks back and forth on his heels, his hands stuffed in his pockets and a weird smile on his face. "I'm already full. I don't even care about dinner."

"Shut up," she hisses. "You said you wanted to help, and I was desperate."

His grin spreads. "I did a great job. You should ask me for help more often."

She rubs her forehead. "I've created a monster. I really should've known better."

"You really should have," he laughs.

My gaze flits back and forth between them, questions perched on the tip of my tongue.

My tongue that's tingling.

Suddenly, I know why I can't get enough of the tasty bites. I drop the rest of them along with the napkin onto the floor.

"Oh, fuck."

Evie and Rob snap their attention to me.

She wraps her hand around my elbow. "What's wrong?"

"Crab." My throat itches. "There's crabmeat in them."

"What?" she squeals. "Rob, call 911."

"Need Mike." Already, a burning sensation spreads across my skin. I don't have much time. I spin around and only make it a few steps before strong arms catch me on the way down. "I don't...have... my EpiPen," I wheeze.

"I've got you, babe." He reaches into the pocket of his pants and pulls out my lifeline, popping the cap off with his teeth before stabbing me in the thigh.

Just like I taught him.

My limbs are too heavy to touch his handsome face with the worried eyes.

He caresses my cheek instead. "Hey, you don't need to die just to avoid me."

"Happy...you're...last...thing...I...see," I lisp, my tongue too big for my mouth.

"Then, stay. Stay with me." He kisses my forehead then glances away.

Sounds are fuzzy, but someone says, "ETA, two minutes."

"Does anyone have an EpiPen?" Mike yells.

Another appears. Mike injects me again.

I barely feel it.

"I love you, Peaches," he whispers against my swollen lips.

The world goes dark.

∽

I CRACK my eyes open to a dimly lit hospital room. The starched sheets scratch against my hypersensitive skin. Legions of ants are crawling around inside me. My muscles tremble, but my body is too heavy to move to relieve the tension.

"You sure do love your crab," a low voice chuckles beside me. "Evie said you popped down at least ten of those things. It's no wonder we had to do two injections."

I inhale deeply—a lungful of glorious, sweet air. "The food was supposed to be safe. I didn't realize until it was way too late."

"Accidents happen." His face comes into view when he rests his chin on the edge of the bed. He looks exhausted, but he's still smiling. "I'm just glad someone else had an EpiPen they didn't hesitate to hand over."

I'm just glad he's still here with me. "Why did you have one?"

He finds my hand beneath the blankets and squeezes. "Ever since you showed me how to work yours, I've always carried one with me in case you need it."

Tears blur my vision, but I blink them back. The memory of the last time my vision went fuzzy is still too fresh. "We haven't even lived in the same city for almost a year."

"I know, but it seemed stupid not to still carry it if it could save someone else's life in an emergency."

"You are one of the best men I have ever met," I breathe then breathe again. Just because I can.

He pulls my hand up to his lips. "I wasn't the best man when I screamed at you for doing what you had to do to save my dumb skull. I blamed you for losing my spot on the starting roster, and you weren't even the reason I got benched. I wanted to apologize at the gala, but I didn't want to interrupt your work either."

I'm still weirdly jittery yet foggy from all the medications coursing through my system. I'm absolutely incapable of filtering my thoughts. "I tried though. I tried to get you benched. I went straight to Mr. Gallo. He didn't believe me. He said I was only pulling a stupid stunt because I was your jilted ex-lover."

Mike shakes his head, a smile spreading across his face. "I'm a sack of potatoes; you're a jilted ex-lover. That guy has a very vivid imagination but a terrible way with words."

"How can you be so calm about all this?"

He frowns. "Because I learned a really hard lesson. I'm ashamed of the way I lost my temper with you. Violence never solves anything. I would know."

"I would argue intentional violence actually saved your mother's life."

He smirks then taps my nose that thankfully doesn't itch at all.

"I know what I'm capable of, Peaches. Not a day goes by that I forget. That's why I needed to keep you away for a while. I stand by that decision. I'm fucking grateful you weren't there that day to see me break my TV. That's still no excuse for the way I screamed at you."

I swallow, my throat blissfully free of hot razor blades. "You were understandably upset about being blindsided. I should have talked to you more about it. What kind of PR rep can't even mount a convincing argument for why sitting out is the best course of action? To her own boyfriend?"

He squints a little. "The kind that knows how thick-headed I am?"

We laugh. Tiny pinpricks of happiness spread across my skin where hives used to be.

"How did you do it?" I whisper, those stupid tears building up again.

"Become this stubborn?" He straightens and shrugs. "Persevering through adversity, I guess."

"No. How did you stay so calm while I was basically dying in your arms?" A shudder rolls through me. That was a close call. Too close.

"You needed me to be calm," he says simply. "If I had panicked, you might not have made it until the ambulance arrived."

"I panicked," I admit. "From the split-second I saw you take that hit on TV. I'm still panicking. I can't stay calm. I can't even watch anymore."

"I know." He stands up and stuffs his hands in his pockets. He's still wearing a tux. He's a thousand times more devastating with the top buttons of his shirt undone and the bow tie hanging loose around his neck. "I'm happy as hell you put your foot down with me. You shouldn't have to be panicked for the rest of your life—either because you're worried about what's going to happen on the field or because you have to worry about how I might take it out on you." He nods. "I've always respected you, Tori, but that was some next-level shit you stood up to that day." He chuckles. "I'm so fucking proud to know you."

I'm in marketing. I know a shit sandwich when I hear one. "You didn't come to the gala to pull off some grand gesture to win me back, did you? You came to say goodbye."

He sort of laughs and blows out a breath at the same time. His smile is wide, but he stares at the floor. "I'm not the grand gesture kind of guy. Alex sure as hell was hoping, but no. You laid out your terms, and I have to respect them." He raises his gaze to mine. "I'm not going to quit playing ball, but you deserve more than an apology over the phone."

A sob builds in my chest, but I laugh away the pressure. "You went above and beyond, Mitchell. Saving my life is a damn good apology."

He winks. "I've always been a hard worker when I put my mind to something."

We laugh a little more, but it's strained now.

His hand is on the doorknob. "The doctors said you'd be groggy for a while. They want to keep you overnight to make sure you don't have any delayed reactions. I'm gonna crash at Rob and Evie's place. If you need anything, call or text. I'll answer."

"When is your flight back to Albany?" I croak out, my throat feeling tight again.

"Tomorrow afternoon. I only got approved time off because this is a really good charity to publicize for the team."

"Right." I nod. "You have to get back to work to be ready for the playoffs now that you're off the IR."

He raises an eyebrow. "Thought you couldn't watch anymore?"

"I can still read," I mumble, my cheeks flaming.

Mike chuckles as he opens the door. "Get some rest, Peaches. I love you."

"I love you, too," I whisper to an empty room.

I can't fight it anymore. I didn't want to give in. Not because I was afraid he wouldn't choose me. Because I was afraid he would, and neither of us would be able to live with the kind of consequences I've had to live with my whole life. Ever since my mom chose me.

If he's willing to respect my terms, then I have to respect his, too.

# Chapter 42
Let Her Go

## Mike

"What?" I yell. Then, immediately remember the sleeping woman upstairs who hears people sneeze in China. "What the fuck, Alex?" I whisper.

"Watch your language, Michael," Evie's mom admonishes from the living room. "There are young ears present."

"Honestly, you three," Rob's mom joins in. "If you're going to act like you did in high school, at least take it outside by the pool."

I'm surprised they're even paying attention to anything other than the babbling baby on the playmat between them.

Rob rolls his eyes and mutters, "This is *my* house."

"We had sex ed in ninth grade, Mitchell." Alex props his arms in a wide stance on the kitchen counter with a grin like he just knows he's inviting mayhem. "Do you really need me to explain to you how a sperm and egg fuse together to make a baby?"

"Alex!" Rob's mom snaps.

He laughs.

"No," I drag out, much more quietly. "I need you to explain to me how you didn't learn the part about condoms and birth control."

"No method is one-hundred percent effective." Alex grins. "Accidents happen."

"Those chances are reduced when you use *multiple* methods," I argue.

He shrugs. "It was a passionate moment. We were careless. It was only one time."

"One time is all it takes." I blow out a breath. I'm nervous on his behalf. "What are you gonna do?"

"She's staying with me through the rest of the pregnancy, but she doesn't want to get married. She knows how I am."

I blink. "Do *you* want to get married? Who is she anyway?"

He grins. "Remember my hot tutor from college? Amira?"

I glance at Rob, but he's staring into space. "I remember she didn't want anything to do with your ass, no matter how many stops you pulled out. How is she pregnant with your baby now?"

His smile is reaching blindingly annoying levels. "I'm too charming to resist forever."

Yeah. Something's not adding up here. "What are the odds of her living in Orlando now, too?"

"Pretty good. She's the team therapist."

Oh, this just gets better and better. Or worse and worse. Jury's still out.

Rob's still being suspiciously quiet.

I wave at him. "Is this part of that whole sleep-deprived, fuzzy-brained new parent thing? You're really not going to react to this news at all?"

He shrugs and leans against the counter like it's literally holding him up. "I already knew."

"What?" I glance between the dynamic duo, side by side like always. A sense of betrayal pricks my chest. I stare Alex down. "You've been riding my ass for months about how to win Tori back, and you couldn't even mention this to me?"

He shrugs. "Dude, you had bigger problems to deal with."

I point at Falls. "He just had a baby and never gets any sleep!"

"Exactly." Alex nods. "He just had a baby, so he's obviously got more experience than either of us."

I can't argue that, actually. My phone dings with an incoming text. It's Tori.

Peaches: They're keeping me an extra night. I had another slight reaction a few hours ago. I'm sorry I won't get to see you again before your flight.

I RISE from my chair and head toward the patio. It's way too loud in here. "I'll be right back. This conversation isn't over."

The second I close the French doors behind me, I'm pressing her name.

She picks up on the first ring. "Hey. You must be heading to the airport. I just didn't want you to worry since I hadn't sent any updates all morning."

I have been worried, but I've been fighting not to be. "Thank you for the update. I don't have to leave for another few hours. Do you want me to come visit since you're stuck there another night?"

"No, that's okay," she murmurs. "I'm sleeping most of the time anyway. I've never had a reaction that severe before, and it really took it out of me. Besides, you didn't want to interfere in my job last night. I'm not about to interfere in yours."

What she doesn't know is that I'd cancel my flight if she asked me to. She's not. So, I have to do the right thing and let her go. "Do you want to hear something that will pick up your spirits a little at least?"

She chuckles. The sound washes over my tense shoulders like an invisible massage. "Sure."

"Alex is going to be a father."

She hums. That sound doesn't relax me at all. My dick twitches in my pants.

"Most men on the planet are going to be fathers someday. I'm sure you will, too."

"No." I ignore that last part. "I mean, he's going to be a father in a few months. He knocked up his team therapist, and they're keeping the baby."

"Oh my God," she breathes. "The media will have a field day with this! The playboy player finally tied down and settling down! With someone from his team, too! It's so romantic!"

I chuckle. We could have been that romantic story. "Of course, you'd think of that angle."

"I'm a marketing specialist." She makes no apologies. I love that about her. "It's too bad the media doesn't realize he hasn't been a player all this time."

I couldn't breathe a word of this to anyone inside, but Tori's fair game. "Is it weird that I'm relieved? If he's sleeping with other women again, that means he's finally over Evie. I've honestly been waiting for him to do something stupid, even after the wedding."

"The fact that he gave up so easily without even fighting for her says a lot. To me, that means he didn't really love her, so much as he wanted what she and Rob have together."

"Or, he loved her enough to let her go. He gave up without a fight because he knows deep down that's what's best for her," I counter. I rub the aching spot in my chest again. My head might be back to normal, but I don't think my heart ever will be.

"Do you really believe that?" she whispers.

"Yes." I'm not talking about Alex. "Men fighting for women is sexist bullshit as Evie would say. It's a little stalkerish, honestly. You work for Sing Out now. No means no. If two people are supposed to be together, then they fight for *each other*. It can't be one-sided."

She hums again.

I have to pinch my thigh to keep from getting to full mast. There's a baby in the house. I can't walk in with a hard-on. That's way worse than dropping an F-bomb.

"The nurse just came in for my vitals check," she says. "Good luck in the playoffs."

"Thanks. I'll see you around at Sing Out fundraisers." It's the best we can do for each other. "You might not be my PR person anymore, but if you need me to do anything to help for the foundation…appear anywhere, share anything on social media…you let me know."

"I'll let you know exactly what I need from you, Mike."

I know she will. She already has.

The next few hours are a mix of mayhem, taking way too easy jabs at Alex, and a new family fighting over a baby.

It almost makes me miss the way mine and Tori's family got at each other's throats at Christmas. Mostly, it just makes me miss Peaches.

Rob's staring into space again, so I clap him on the shoulder.

"I better get going, too. I'll see you next week at the game."

"You bet," he says. The smile on his face only makes the dark circles under his eyes more obvious.

"No." I laugh, happy for this happy ending. It helps me cling to a thread of hope for the distant future. I made it to the NFL, so anything's possible. "No more bets. Next thing you know, I'll be expecting a kid."

"You'd make a good dad, Mike."

"I never said I wouldn't. But you know me. I'd rather have a plan." And a few more years of sleep. Maybe when I retire from the game, Peaches will be willing to give us a shot.

"Plans are overrated," Rob fires back.

"Tell me that when you're expecting an Irish twin in nine months." With Alex expecting a baby, too, there are all sorts of new competitions in the future.

Just not for me.

I'm settling into this new reality and my seat in first class on the plane when a blonde bombshell takes the seat beside me. She's not subtle about showing off her cleavage as she stows her purse beneath her chair.

Her smile is an open invitation. "You're Mike Mitchell. Glad to see you're looking completely healthy after that awful hit earlier this season. What's a Wolf doing in Gold Rushers territory?"

I don't think I'm actually the wolf here. "Visiting some friends. Thanks for your support."

Peaches would be so proud.

The she-wolf licks her lips. "I could be persuaded to join the mile-high club if you'd like to find out just how supportive I can be."

Nope. Not subtle at all.

"I'm flattered, but I've already found my unicorn, so no thanks."

Her flawless makeup cracks a little when she scrunches her face in confusion. She obviously doesn't know the wonders of setting powder either. "Excuse me?"

"Just because I'm a free agent on the market doesn't mean I'm not in love with a woman. I'm not going to have sex with you."

Okay, Tori wouldn't like that response as much. I might have been a little too blunt, judging by the lady's obvious pout.

"So, you're back to being Monk again, huh?"

I laugh. I'm okay with that.

# Chapter 43
I Run to You

## Tori

"I HOPE your husband suffers a horrific loss but thank you so much for the last-minute ticket."

Evie laughs. "Almost, but not quite. If you really want to distract your anxiety with smack talk, then you have to fully lean into it. You can't serve shit sandwiches and expect results."

Through the plexiglass of the luxurious box Evie so graciously allowed me into, I watch the players run through their warm-ups on the field. "That was just a test run. My anxiety isn't that bad yet."

She chuckles, low and steady. "Oh, it will be. Just you wait."

"You're not helping," I mutter.

"Do you want Robbie?" She offers her kid, holding him out between us.

He stares at me with his big, blue eyes, practically promising to dirty his diaper the second he's in my lap. A string of drool drips from his mouth onto his Gold Rushers onesie. He smiles a toothless grin that pops the dimple in his cheek that matches his father's.

"I don't want to accidentally crush your baby," sounds much better than *Eew, no.*

Like he's personally offended, he lets out a wail.

Evie pulls him close and tucks him beneath her jersey without batting an eyelash.

An audible scoff from another woman floats to my ears.

I lean closer to Evie and whisper, "Are you sure it's a good idea for you two to be here?"

"It's the playoffs," Evie says as if that's all the reason in the world not to watch the game from the comfort of her home with a 3-month old baby. "At least I'm not in my usual seat near the field."

"People are staring," I whisper again. "Maybe you should nurse him somewhere a little more private."

She barks out a short laugh. "Number one, most of these people have seen my actual breasts at this point. I'm not feeding my baby in the bathroom when I literally have nothing left to hide."

A hot blush steals across my cheeks because I've seen that photoshoot, too.

"Number two..." She aims an evil smile my way. "They're probably staring at your Wolves jersey and wondering why the hell you're in the Rushers box."

"I'm trying to be supportive," I hiss, glancing around to see if she's right. She is. Several glares are directed solely at me. "Maybe I should take it off...I have a regular shirt underneath."

Evie snaps her fingers in front of my wandering eyes. "Hey. Why are you here?"

"To show Mike I love him, and that I'm willing to take the bad with the good."

"That's right." She nods once—that same decisive movement as the first time we met. "So, you focus on that. Your purpose here today is to support your player. If you're constantly worried about what everyone else in the league thinks of you, then you're not doing your job. Got it?"

"Um..." I hate to point out the obvious, but that's also part of my job. "Creating bad blood with other people in the league isn't exactly doing Mike any favors either."

"The bad blood is there, regardless of what you do or don't do." Evie leans a little closer and lowers her voice. "These women are all pros. They know the score. They're jealous because we're going to get a hell of a lot more screen time and commentary than they will today."

I already know that because of my job. Mike and Rob played together in college. This is the first time their pro teams are meeting on the field during the playoffs. Fans are going to love seeing their SOs sitting together in a box, wearing opposing team colors. Not to mention this will be their first glimpse of baby Falls. I'm just thankful Mike won't see any of that footage during the game. I still don't know how he's going to react to my grand gesture.

He's not a grand gesture kind of a guy. He said so himself.

"Am I making a mistake?" I worry aloud. My nerves skyrocket as the pre-game clock reaches zero. "Maybe this is a mistake. I should go."

Evie wraps her hand around mine then intertwines our fingers. Her blue gaze is strong enough to make me shiver. "Do you love him? Don't bullshit me, Tori. More importantly, don't bullshit *yourself*."

"I do." I nod and breathe deeply. I don't care if she's my boss or his adopted sister or the wife of the quarterback of the opposing team. I have no shame, and no reason to lie. "I love him. I'm not bullshitting anyone anymore."

She squeezes my hand. "Then, you are exactly where you're supposed to be. If you need to excuse yourself to the restroom when he's on the field, then do it. If you need to get drunk to tamp down your anxiety, then you'll have a ride home and a safe bed to sleep in tonight. But you will be on that sideline when the clock winds down —either to celebrate with him or to dry his tears. No excuses."

"Yes, Mrs. Falls." Okay, so I still automatically react like she's my boss when she takes that no-nonsense tone. It's years of conditioning from being raised by a Navy captain.

She gives me a look of exasperation before turning her attention to the field. "Oh, yes! It's game time!" She plants a kiss on her baby's head and whispers, "Go, Daddy."

"You're going down, Falls," I mutter as I watch Mike and Rob meet in the middle of the field along with the other team captains for the coin toss. They bump fists before parting to opposite sidelines.

"Bring it on, future Mrs. Mitchell," she retorts. "You've got this."

I don't got this.

I grind my molars into powder; I sit on my hands; I bounce my knees incessantly. I shriek whenever he gets tackled. Which is a lot. I even hold Robbie because I would never actually crush a baby to death, no matter how panicked I am.

Every time I'm tempted to close my eyes, I remember the feeling of his strong arms around me as I fought for air. I picture his calm, sure actions in the face of disaster. I imagine how panicked he must have been when the doctors whisked me away into the ER, where he wasn't allowed to follow. I think of how exhausted he looked when I woke up in a hospital bed with him beside me again.

He's already made a grand gesture, and he doesn't even realize it.

He stayed after the threat was over.

Then, he came back for more.

It's his choice to love me. For better or worse.

The clock winds down on a Wolves loss. By a field goal in the last minute of play.

The mood in the private box is celebratory, except for me and Evie.

For her, because there's a sleeping baby snuggled against her chest.

Me? Because I don't know if this Hail Mary will be enough to sway the thick-skulled man who's currently shaking hands with his opponents.

"Go get him." Evie actually pats my butt like the guys on the field have been doing the whole game.

My muscles tremble with anxiety. "You're not coming down to the field?"

"No. There are way too many germs floating around down there, and Robbie's little ears can't handle that level of deafening noise." She smirks. "Although, I've ordered a special pair of infant headphones just in case we make it to the Super Bowl."

"No need to gloat," I grumble.

She flags down a security guard with a chuckle. "Please escort Miss Russo to the Wolves' sideline."

"Sure thing, Mrs. Falls. This way please, Miss Russo."

I follow the imposing man who's big enough to suit up in a football uniform of his own. He leads me through crowds exiting the stadium, past other guards who nod as we enter doorways marked Staff Only, until finally, my eyes blink from the stark contrast between the darkness of a hallway and the bright lights of the field.

"Oh! We're on the Wolves sideline already!"

He chuckles. "I thought that's where we were supposed to go? Did you want me to take you to the Rushers sideline?"

"No, no," I wave off that suggestion. I'm just not prepared yet. I've never made a grand gesture in my whole life. Suddenly, playing this off the cuff seems like a horribly rash idea. "This is perfect. Thank you."

He pulls a badge out of his pocket. "Put this on, and you'll be all set."

"Right. I almost forgot teams don't just let any random weirdo on the field after a game." I pull the lanyard over my head without even glancing at it. I'm too busy looking for Mike amid the throng of bodies.

The security guard laughs at me and raises his eyebrows. "Good luck, Miss Russo."

I don't need luck. I already have it. I've found my unicorn.

Only one thing propels my feet forward—need.

The moment I'm close enough, I launch myself at him and climb him like a tree, planting kisses all over his face and not giving a damn that he's probably so sore.

Thank God he doesn't mistake me for a jersey chaser. He just holds me tight and squeezes my ass a little too indecently for public. Not that my behavior isn't completely indecent.

"Babe," he laughs between my assaults. "Babe. What are you doing here?"

I cup his sweaty cheeks in my hands and make sure he's meeting my eyes. "You were the first person I wanted to run to."

# Chapter 44
## Believer

### Mike

I'M NOT SUPPOSED to be the happiest man in the world after such a tough loss, but with my hands full of Peaches, I can't help it.

"I hope I'm the first person you kissed on this field."

She's still holding onto my face like she's never going to let go, and goddamn, am I okay with that.

"No. I mean, yes. What I really mean is when I had my reaction to the crab. It was you. I knew I didn't have much time, and you were the first person I thought to find."

"Okay..." My ears are still ringing from a tough game; my skin tingles everywhere she's touching me, and I really don't need to know the reason why she's here.

She huffs out a little growl of frustration that makes me wish we weren't standing in the middle of an open field. "My dad said that's how I would know if it was real. If the first person I wanted to run to for anything was you. It happened when I wasn't even thinking about it, and you were so calm, and you still love me even though I'm a walking potential for death, and damn it! You're my unicorn, so I'll deal with the football panic!"

I blink and rewind her rushed words, trying to make sense of something that's never made sense since the very beginning.

It doesn't matter because she crushes her lips to mine. There's no way to mistake what she's telling me without words.

Her tongue tastes like her nickname. She's sweet and soft all around me. I want to bury myself in her and not come up for air for days.

*Damn it, why did this have to happen on the field?*

"I wish we were alone," I whimper against her lips. "I'm not gonna get to see you again until tomorrow."

"I'll let this go another day," she wraps her arms around my neck and squeezes tight. "I wanted to give you a grand gesture by being at your game and proving to you I can handle it, but I didn't think this through all the way. I love you. I can wait until tomorrow to kiss you again."

"Babe," I choke out. "Can't breathe."

She loosens her strangle hold. Slightly. "I know you're sore after a game, but I need to touch you. I need to love you. You're part of me, and I have the bruises on my thigh still to prove it."

Holy shit. I left bruises on her? "You told me I had to stab the injector!"

She laughs, a deep husky sound in my ear that shoots straight to my dick. "I know. And you told me not to touch you after a tough loss, but I'm sorry not sorry right now."

"I'm not sorry either, Peaches." My teammates are reeling from getting knocked out of the playoffs, but I'm kissing my unicorn in the middle of the field again.

A wolf whistle comes from somewhere over my shoulder. "Damn! I wanna get consoled like that!"

Tori pulls away, a deep blush staining her cheeks like stupid Templeman just made her very aware of the position we've been in all this time.

I squeeze her luscious ass in my hands and laugh. I don't fucking care who sees this or what spin the media put on it.

Tori frowns then pulls a badge out from her cleavage that was digging in enough to leave an angry red mark behind. Her cheeks get impossibly brighter. "Um, I think this message is for you."

I glance down.

> HERE'S YOUR CONSOLATION PRIZE.
> LEFTMOST CORRIDOR. TWO DOORS ON THE RIGHT.
> —ROB

"WHAT THE HELL?" I mutter before turning over the badge where—sure enough—a key is taped to the surface.

Tori's cheeks are still redder than a tomato, but her eyes are burning bright. She whispers, "Do we have time?"

"Fuck that. I'll *make* time." Still, I don't want to draw undue attention. If we're gonna make this work, we've gotta play it smart. I set her down on the turf. "Go first. I'll follow. Don't open the door unless you hear four knocks."

"For being so risk averse my whole life, I'm really excited about this."

I laugh and send her on her way with a quick pat on the ass. There are still plenty of Wolves on the field being interviewed by reporters, talking with Rushers players, and hesitant to step off any field for the last time this season. The coaches and staff are busy tearing down our equipment on the sideline. It's the usual controlled chaos. Just enough distraction for me to slip away unnoticed.

Tori swings open the door while I'm still on the fourth knock. She's already down to her bra and panties and wearing a wide smile.

I flip the lock behind me then get to work unlacing my pants. I don't have time to peel off my shoulder pads. "Beggars shouldn't be choosers, but, uh…could you put the jersey back on?"

She raises an eyebrow. "I have some conditions first."

I'm calling her bluff and getting increasingly frustrated with these laces. "You're already half naked, and now you want to negotiate?"

She smiles and holds the jersey with my name on the back on a single finger. "How much do you want this fantasy, Mitchell?"

"The clock's ticking, Peaches. How much do you want this?"

Finally, finally I get my dick free of these fucking tight-ass pants. I am ready to go when she is.

"I can multitask." Her voice comes out mumbled as she pulls the jersey over her head.

I hoist her up around my waist and pin her to the wall. "Fine. Name your terms."

Since she needs her mouth, I suck on her neck. We don't have much time, but I don't want to impale her after a few months without at least a little foreplay. I'm horny, not an asshole.

"Uh," she moans. "No more lying about injuries. If you're hurt, you're not playing until you should be."

"Deal," I mumble through nipping at her soft skin.

She whimpers and whines and grinds her hot center against me. I slide the head of my shaft through her slick folds, lining us up while waiting for the rest of her terms before we seal the deal.

"What else?" I pant. I can't hold back much longer. I need to be inside her more than I need my next breath.

She kisses me long, deep, and enough to steal my next breath. "If anything happens to me, find another unicorn. I don't want you to live a long, lonely life like my dad."

"Okay," I lie then push into her as deep as I can.

Her head falls back against the wall even as her nails dig into the skin at the back of my neck. She lets out a long, low moan of satisfaction and presses her hips more firmly against mine.

I hold perfectly still and breathe through the urge to make this the fastest dash I've ever run. "Now, my terms."

She blinks glassy eyes at me. "I'll agree to anything if you'll just move already."

I file that information away for later as I drag myself out then back in slow enough to drive me insane. "Never mention your dad while doing this ever again."

She chuckles. Her pussy grips my cock tighter. She's so tight and hot and wet, I have to fuck her harder to distract myself from coming too fast.

My words come out stunted in between thrusts. "No living apart just for our jobs. We'll split the difference between Albany and New York and buy a new house."

"Deal," she moans. "Harder, Mike. Please."

I love it when she tells me exactly what she wants. I grip her ass tight and use the wall as leverage to pound her until her pussy spasms around me. She cries out, so I swallow down her ecstasy with my mouth. The blush would never leave her face if anyone overhears us.

A few more thrusts, and I follow her over the edge, emptying myself inside her as deep as possible.

Our foreheads rest against each other as we catch our breath. I want nothing more than to wrap her in my arms in bed tonight and smell her sweet hair beside me, but this will tide me over for now.

"I love you," she whispers, kissing me tenderly.

I take what she offers. Gratefully. "I love you, Peaches."

"Teddy Bear." She smiles.

Slipping out of her is the last thing I want to do, but it's time. I place her gently on the floor again and wait to make sure she's steady before letting go. "You still can't call me that in public. Templeman will never let me live it down."

"Your balls are already drained, and now you want to add terms to the list?" She chuckles as she straightens her panties that she never even took off.

Damn, that's sexy as hell.

"I'll probably think of a few more."

"I look forward to doing business with you, Mr. Mitchell. I think this is going to be a beautiful partnership." She grins.

"I might be okay with you calling me Mr. Mitchell in bed every once in a while," I admit as I redo all these damn laces. Why can't football pants be simpler?

"Ooh. Kinky." She tsks. "It's always the quiet ones."

"Keep it up, and I'm not going to replace your favorite toy that Alex stole."

She opens her mouth, but a knock on the door makes her snap it shut again. Red spreads all the way down her chest. She's probably blushing beneath the jersey, too.

"Psst. Hurry up." Rob's voice comes through the door. "You're out of time."

Tori's mouth drops open. She hisses, "Has he been standing out there all along? Did he *hear* us?"

"He would've heard a lot more if I wasn't strategically kissing you," I mutter.

"You weren't exactly silent," she fires back.

As soon as she slips her shoes on, I swing open the door. We don't have time to be embarrassed, and I'm still grateful for this opportunity.

Rob pushes off the opposite wall and holds his hand out for the key. If he really was standing out here all this time, he doesn't seem fazed in the slightest. He tips his head to the tall guy in a suit standing at the end of the hallway. "Byers will take you back to Evie in the box. I'll see you at the house in a few hours." He turns his attention to me. "Most of your team is in the locker room already. A few of the reporters wanted shots of us together and to get a quick blurb. Come on."

Tori turns to leave, her cheeks still bright.

I catch her around the waist and pull her to me, not caring who's watching. "Hey. I'll see you tomorrow. Maybe we can grab a *safe* dinner in the Big Apple and get some of those shots you wanted."

She reaches up to kiss me. "Deal."

"Love you, Peaches," I whisper against her lips.

"Love you, Teddy Bear," she whispers back.

Rob cracks up laughing. "Holy shit, wait until I tell Alex!"

Tori laughs as she saunters down the hall.

"What the fuck? You promised!" I call after her.

Rob's laughter echoes in the corridor. The asshole already has his phone. His thumbs are flying over the screen.

"I didn't break my promise," she yells over her shoulder. "This isn't public! It's the circle of trust!"

"Gimme that!" I dive for Rob's phone as soon as Tori and the security guard are out of sight.

He holds it up over my head like we're kids, and he still loves to push me around because he's taller. "No way! Get your own phone!"

"I can't believe you told Alex about this!"

He cackles as we walk toward the stadium lights. "Oh, I didn't... yet. I wanted to tell Evie first."

Suddenly, I understand perfectly what Peaches meant about wanting to run to me first.

# Epilogue
## Thinking Out Loud

### Rob

"She's pregnant," I mumble to my wife under my breath while my son does his best to gnaw my finger off. It's too bad I forgot to pack the teething rings, but at least my finger is a better option than Evie's poor nipples.

She's handling the inevitable biting way better than I am.

"Yes, dear. That's why we're at a baby shower." Evie's not paying attention to anything other than the mother-to-be, who's seated in the center of the open-concept living room, unwrapping gift number ninety thousand.

I lost interest a long time ago. I can only fake excitement about onesies for so long. I've had to occupy myself for the past forever hours in other ways. "No, not Amira. Well, yes, Amira. That's not who I'm talking about though."

"Who are you talking about?" Evie sighs. She's probably tired of trying to entertain two Robs. I'm tired of needing to be entertained in ways that I don't find remotely entertaining. I swear, becoming a father has shrunk my attention span to the level of my son's.

"Tori," I whisper, forcing myself to focus.

"What?" Evie finally snaps her attention to me, even though she manages to keep her voice low. "What makes you think that?"

"Just *look* at them!" I gesture toward Mike and Tori nearby.

He's fawning over her in ways that are completely obvious to my highly observant eyes. Keeping her plate full of food, refilling her drink before it's even completely empty, constantly watching her instead of even trying to pretend to be interested in baby games and baby gear and...someone else's baby mama.

"She's not pregnant," Evie decides after only a few milliseconds of watching them. "They would have told us."

"Baby." I give her my best disappointed look. "Bet me."

"Okay, fine." Evie crosses her arms. That determined glitter in her ocean eyes proves she's about to dig in her heels. "What's the wager?"

"A weekend away. Just the two of us." I'm not going to lose, so I pull out the big guns. I love my son more than life itself, but I miss my wife dearly. We're constantly pulled in so many directions that our schedules are increasingly like ships passing through the night.

"All right," she agrees. "We'll ask when we break for dinner."

I wince. "Can we do that? If they wanted us to know, wouldn't they have told us?"

She flattens her brow. "Exactly. So, you see how you're going to lose this bet."

"Just because they don't want to tell us, doesn't mean I'm wrong," I insist.

Robbie bites my finger particularly hard then has the audacity to laugh about it.

"See?" Evie grins. "Even our son agrees with me."

"Traitor," I whisper to him.

He laughs again and bats at my face. I kiss his chubby hands.

Evie leans closer toward me. "I think we have a bigger problem, Rob."

"You're right." I move my tongue around in my mouth. "His hands taste funny. Where did you let him crawl?" Something crunches between my teeth. "Jesus Christ, Evie, was he in the litter box?"

Alex has never been a cat person, but apparently, Amira is. Now that she lives here, Alex has cats for the first time in his life. He whines constantly about having to be the one to clean the litter box because pregnant women aren't supposed to.

Evie snatches Robbie off my lap and inspects his hands. Her expression turns guilty, guilty, guilty. "I thought I cleaned it all off of him!"

I gag.

She hands me her drink. "Seriously, honey. Something's really wrong here."

"I know." I drain her cup and still can't get the crunch out of my mouth. "This is like a war zone, complete with trenches."

We glance back and forth at the obvious division. Alex's family and friends are on this side of the room, clapping with glee and enjoying all things baby. His mom is showing off a diaper tower she made. Amira's family sits on the other side. They look like they're at a wake instead of a baby shower.

"Maybe they're really traditional. Didn't YiaYia pitch a fit about our baby shower because it's bad luck to celebrate the baby before it's born?"

"Amira's family is Lebanese, not Greek. The traditions are probably similar, but it's more than that. Alex looks like he could care less."

Alex has been on the periphery of the room the entire time. He's leaning against the doorway to the kitchen, a blank expression on his face.

"He has a really strained relationship with his mom. I'm actually surprised he invited his family at all."

Evie pins me with a look that screams *You don't think I know that by now?* "He would never exclude his brothers from something this important."

That's true. Alex loves his younger brothers dearly. Now that he lives in Florida, he doesn't get to see them nearly as often as he'd like.

Evie squeezes my knee. "Baby, what I'm worried about has nothing to do with either of their families. When you told me to look at Mike and Tori, what did you notice about their behavior that makes you think she's pregnant?"

I describe exactly what I'm seeing even now. Mike is not letting up, and Tori looks increasingly green around the edges when she's normally red.

"Okay," Evie concedes like she's finally admitting I might be right.

"Now, do you see any of that same behavior from Alex toward Amira?"

"No, but why would he have to cater to her? Her entire family is here."

"Rob." Evie's voice is losing patience. "My mother and grandmother moved in with us when I was six months pregnant. You still fawned over me every second that you weren't at work."

"Well, yeah," I say, a little offended that she seems offended. "Because I lo...Oh. Ohhhh, shit. He's been lying to us."

She nods, her lips pursed. "He said he was going to fight for her to stay with him. To make her realize he's in it for the long haul, that he's never been happier. He told us he's excited to be a father. What about any of that..." She gestures subtly in his direction. "...seems excited to you?"

None of it. None of it at all. If anything, Alex looks bored out of his mind. Even if he doesn't love Amira—and she really is just a baby mama to him—the Alex I know would be out of his mind if a woman was having *his* baby.

The answer slaps me in the face.

"Oh my God, Evie," I whisper. "It's not his."

# ALSO BY KATA

Moving the Chains series

First and Goal

Second Down

Third and Long

Fourth and Inches

Standalone Novels

Revenge Love

Keep the Beat

Homebound

A Bird in the Oven

# ABOUT THE AUTHOR

Kata Čuić lives in Pittsburgh, PA with her husband and three teens. No one told her life was gonna be this way. She holds a degree in Linguistics with a minor in Religious Studies from the University of Pittsburgh. Her plans of becoming a pediatric neurosurgeon were foiled by OChem 1. Fortunately, she'd been making up stories in her head since the days of her imaginary friend, Choosy. Putting pen to paper, er—fingers to the keyboard—came surprisingly naturally after her aforementioned teens decided it was time for them to cut their respective cords.

Kata writes everything from angst-filled series to standalone rom-coms and has been known to dabble in a bit of paranormal on the free stories section of her website. She believes nice guys shouldn't have to finish last (except in the bedroom where she prefers an alpha between the sheets but a gentleman in the streets), and that the surest way to a woman's heart is through laughter and food.

You can judge her standards to your heart's content in the following places:

Facebook Reader Group
Website
Newsletter

facebook.com/katacuicbooks
twitter.com/authorkatacuic
instagram.com/authorkatacuic
pinterest.com/authorkatacuic
bookbub.com/authors/kata-cuic

# ACKNOWLEDGMENTS

I was genuinely unsure if this book would ever happen, but here we are. I think that about every book I write. It's simultaneously my favorite yet also perhaps the last I'll ever create. Maybe one of these days the muse will work for me instead of the other way around. In the meantime, it's good to have people in my corner who understand the perils and pitfalls of authoring and who are willing—sort of—to listen to me bitch about my fickle willpower.

Karin Enders and Ryan Ringbloom, author buddies extraordinaire—I'm glad we're not neighbors on one-way streets.

My family—Please, stop leaving lights on in empty rooms and every door in the house open. You know I can't concentrate when random things are out of place. It's like you're training me to work no matter what. Oh. Wait...

Sarah Kil, Lisa Salvucci, and Alison Evans-Maxwell—my team without which I could not produce such beautiful finished products. I swear, I'll get better at scheduling. As soon as I can master the muse...

Danielle, Jo, Kylie, and Alyssa—thank you for rolling with my hectic schedule and always so graciously, too. You make the world a better place with your joyfulness (and Star Trek memes)!

Bloggers and readers—literally no author would exist in a vacuum. Thank you for your voracious appetites for the written word. I'll happily share imaginary people with you for as long as they continue to whisper to me. I also fully recognize that outside of reading circles, that statement would sound like a verbal acid trip.

Onto the next wild ride!

# HOLDING PLAYLIST

Holding Playlist
Lean on Me | Bill Withers
Over My Head (Cable Car) | The Fray
Thnks fr th Mmrs | Fall Out Boy
Bite My Tongue | Relient K
Natural | Imagine Dragons
Tightrope | Janelle Monáe
Crush | David Archuleta
I Knew You Were Trouble. | Taylor Swift
Wicked Game | Theory of a Deadman
Don't Hurt Like It Used To | Grace Carter
Bad Day | Daniel Powter
Lie To Me | 5 Seconds of Summer
Beautiful Distraction | Josh Hoge
In the End | Linkin Park
Whatever It Takes | Imagine Dragons
Faking It | Sasha Sloan
Smile Like You Mean It | The Killers
Close | Nick Jonas, Tove Lo
Only the Lonely Survive | Marianas Trench

# Holding Playlist

Pressure | Koffee
Not a Bad Thing | Justin Timberlake
Fix You | Coldplay
All These Things That I've Done | The Killers
Truth or Dare | Marianas Trench
Crash into Me | Dave Matthews Band
We Are Never Ever Getting Back Together | Taylor Swift
Honest | Kodaline
If I Lose Myself | One Republic
Glimmer | Marianas Trench
You and I | Ingrid Michaelson
I Knew You When | Marianas Trench
Love Me Now | John Legend
Marry You | Bruno Mars
Friends | Meghan Trainor
The Great Escape | Boys Like Girls
Secrets | One Republic
Mess Is Mine | Vance Joy
Open | Rhye
By Now | Marianas Trench
The One That Got Away | Katy Perry
It's Time | Imagine Dragons
Little Do You Know | Alex & Sierra
Let Her Go | Passenger
I Run To You | Lady A
Believer | Imagine Dragons
Thinking out Loud | Ed Sheeran
You can listen to the playlist here:
Spotify